the **venetian** judgment

the **venetian** judgment

david stone

G. P. PUTNAM'S SONS • NEW YORK

PUTNAM

G. P. PUTNAM'S SONS
Publishers Since 1838
Published by the Penguin Group
Penguin Group (USA) Inc., 375 Hudson Street, New York, New York 10014, USA • Penguin Group
(Canada), 90 Eglinton Avenue East, Suite 700, Toronto, Ontario M4P 2Y3, Canada (a division of
Pearson Canada Inc.) • Penguin Books Ltd, 80 Strand, London WC2R 0RL, England • Penguin
Ireland, 25 St Stephen's Green, Dublin 2, Ireland (a division of Penguin Books Ltd) • Penguin Group
(Australia), 250 Camberwell Road, Camberwell, Victoria 3124, Australia (a division of Pearson
Australia Group Pty Ltd) • Penguin Books India Pvt Ltd, 11 Community Centre, Panchsheel Park,
New Delhi–110 017, India • Penguin Group (NZ), 67 Apollo Drive, Rosedale, North Shore 0632,
New Zealand (a division of Pearson New Zealand Ltd) • Penguin Books (South Africa) (Pty) Ltd,
24 Sturdee Avenue, Rosebank, Johannesburg 2196, South Africa

Penguin Books Ltd, Registered Offices: 80 Strand, London WC2R 0RL, England

Library of Congress Cataloging-in-Publication Data

Stone, David, date.
The Venetian judgment / David Stone.
p.   cm.
ISBN 978-0-399-15573-4
1. Dalton, Micah (Fictitious character)—Fiction.   2. Intelligence officers—Fiction.   I. Title.
PR9199.3.S833V46   2009   2009002506
813'.54—dc22

Printed in the United States of America
10 9 8 7 6 5 4 3 2 1

BOOK DESIGN BY MEIGHAN CAVANAUGH

This is a work of fiction. Names, characters, places, and incidents either are the product of the author's
imagination or are used fictitiously, and any resemblance to actual persons, living or dead, businesses,
companies, events, or locales is entirely coincidental.

While the author has made every effort to provide accurate telephone numbers and Internet addresses
at the time of publication, neither the publisher nor the author assumes any responsibility for errors, or
for changes that occur after publication. Further, the publisher does not have any control over and does
not assume any responsibility for author or third-party websites or their content.

for **catherine stone**

the **venetian** judgment

JANUARY 27, 1973:

Linebacker I and II B-52 Air Operations over North Vietnam leave the NVA war-fighting machine in ruins. Cut off from the North, despised as murderous butchers by the people of South Vietnam, the Viet Cong insurgency collapses. Demoralized, with forty thousand NVA killed that year alone in their failed Easter Offensive, North Vietnamese leaders remove General Giap from command and sign the Paris Peace Accords. The Vietnam War ends in a de facto USA/RSVN victory.

APRIL 20, 1973:

Nixon and President Thieu of South Vietnam meet at San Clemente. President Nixon reaffirms an earlier promise, backed by the U.S. Congress, that the U.S. would recommence Linebacker Air Operations over Hanoi if the NVA violated any elements of the Paris Peace Accords.

JUNE 19, 1973:

Intimidated by antidraft student riots, and sensing Watergate blood in the water, a Democratic Congress passes the Case Church Amendment, forbidding *any* U.S. involvement with Southeast Asia as of August 15, breaking solemn American covenants made only nine weeks earlier. Freed from the Linebacker threat and given massive material support by the USSR, the NVA immediately and aggressively violates the Paris Accords. Abandoned by the U.S., fighting not only the NVA but a proxy war with the USSR, Saigon falls in April of 1975. That same month, Pol Pot and his Khmer Rouge army of psychopathic fifteen-year-olds arrives in Phnom Penh and the killing begins. Over the next ten years more than three million Laotians, Cambodians, and South Vietnamese die in "reeducation" camps, at the hands of roving murder squads, or in suicidal attempts to flee.

part **one**

KROKODIL

Dalton shot the bodyguard first, because that's how these things are done, taking him as he came out of the west gate of the Piazza San Marco, right where it opens into the Calle de L'Ascensione. The guard was a bullnecked, buzz-cut Albanian kid, likely some hapless third-rater drummed out of the Kosovo Liberation Army, judging from the way he pixie-pranced right out into the calle, looking this way and that in the dark, with his war face on and his brows all beetled up, as if he actually knew what he was doing. He had a Tokarev in his left hand, a deeply useless piece of scrap iron, and he never even got it into play before Dalton stepped out of the alcove on his left and punched a soft-nosed, subsonic .22 caliber round into his temple. That was pretty much that, as the slug pinballed around inside the kid's skull for a few seconds, making a lumpy gray soup out of his life so far. The boy went down—straight down, like a sack of meat falling off a flatbed.

Mirko Belajic, the kid's boss, had been hanging back under the arch, waiting for the all clear, so when Dalton took out the bodyguard the wily old Serb flinched a half step back and reached into his Briony topcoat. But by then Dalton had the muzzle of his Ruger up against the man's barrel chest.

"*Dah, Krokodil!*" he grunted, as if his most depressing expectations for the evening had just been grimly confirmed. Dalton stepped out into the faint glow from the lights of the piazza, his face stony and a green spark in his pale blue eyes, his long blond hair pulled back from his hard-planed face. He was wearing a blue Zegna topcoat, black leather gloves, and a navy blue turtleneck, so in the dim light from the piazza he looked like a skull floating in the shadows. The snow was sifting down, a curtain of powdered glass, diamond-lit by a sickle moon. Their frozen breath hung in the still air between them, a pale glowing mist, slowly rising up.

"*Krokodil,* you . . . you *wait* now, just a bit," the old man said, in a flat, steady voice, no quaver, not begging, just making a suggestion, as if they were arranging to meet for drinks. "Not too late for you. We talk—"

"No. We don't," said Dalton softly, squeezing the trigger once, popping a round into the old man's chest about an inch below his left nipple. The old man staggered back, his roast-beef face losing color and his mouth gaping open. He plunged his hand into his coat and brought out a small stainless-steel revolver, which Dalton easily plucked from the man's gnarled, arthritic hand. He threw it into the alley behind him. It struck and skittered across the frozen cobbles with a dull metallic clatter.

Belajic stared at Dalton for a time, blinking slowly, then pulled his suit jacket to the side and looked down at his shirt, where a black stain around a tiny frayed hole was starting to spread open like a black poppy. He put a meaty palm over it, winced, looked back at Dalton, his breathing now coming in short, sharp puffs as his lung slowly collapsed. The expression on his face wasn't fear, or even anger.

He looked . . . *offended.*

"I am . . . stabbed? Mirko Belajic is . . . *dying?*"

"Cora Vasari," said Dalton, and had his suspicions confirmed by the flicker of recognition in Belajic's face, a fleeting muscular contraction around the old man's left eye, a blue vein flaring in his neck, gone in an instant.

"I was . . . *nothing* with . . . that. That was Gospic—"

Dalton reached out and plucked a small Razr cell phone out of Belajic's breast pocket, beeped it on, and handed it back to Belajic, who looked confused.

"Make a call."

Belajic blinked at Dalton, his wrinkled face closing up.

"Call? Call who?"

"You've just been *shot*, Mirko. Call out your people."

Belajic blinked at Dalton for a while longer, trying to make sense of the words, then looked down and pressed in a number using both fat thumbs and lifted the phone to his ear. Glaring into Dalton's eyes, he spoke rapidly into the handset, a low growl in gutter Serbian, ending with a harsh, coughing curse that included the name *Krokodil* more than a couple of times.

He snapped the phone shut, still locked on Dalton, a killing stare. Twelve years ago, over a disagreement with an obscenely overweight son-in-law regarding the distribution of the proceeds from an opium-paste-for-SAMs deal with the Chechens, Belajic had made a point about greed, gluttony, gratitude by throwing the man, naked and bound hand and foot, into a small feed pen filled with hungry boars. As the story goes, in spite of their best efforts, the animals took several days to rip away everything considered tasty to a boar. In the process, the fat man's shrieks grew so pitiful that Mirko himself got up from a large family dinner with his steak knife in hand and went out back to the barn to slice the man's voice box so his screams wouldn't upset the grandkids, one of whom was the victim's only son, a ten-year-old lad named Zakary.

Belajic doted on the boy, and, as an act of mercy, suspended the ancient law of Serbian vendetta that required that all sons must die with their fathers. Zakary lived a privileged life in the bosom of Mirko's family in their sprawling mansion in Budva. At an engagement party for the popular young man, laid out on a broad terrace overlooking the sparkling sapphire plains of the Adriatic Sea, with Zakary's gazellelike Danish fiancée at his side and all the family present, Belajic's wife, Anna, rose to propose a toast to Zakary on the occasion of his twenty-first birthday, pointing out that, according to Serbian custom, he was now an adult, with all the related privileges.

Mirko raised his glass along with all the company, and then they sang happy birthday to Zakary. At the end of the evening Mirko took the boy aside and walked him out to the garage, where, with some ceremony, he opened the double doors to show his favorite grandson a special birthday present, an emerald green Maserati. Zakary, deeply touched and genuinely surprised, bear-hugged his beloved *poppi*, pronounced this "the happiest day of his life," and stepped forward to touch the splendid machine, running a hand gently over it, his face glowing. Belajic shot him in the back of the head.

It is said that Mirko had tears in his eyes as he wiped a spray of bright red blood off the hood of the Maserati. Simple prudence dictated that once Zakary reached full manhood he had to die, but Mirko was greatly comforted by the knowledge that Zakary had died on "the happiest day of his life."

So Mirko Belajic's killing stare was a pretty good one.

Dalton, ignoring the stare, took the cell from his hand, thumbed up LAST CALL, read the number, and gave Belajic a look with some sympathy in it.

He didn't have anything personal against Belajic, whose role in the attempted assassination of a woman who, in a better world, he might have loved was peripheral, but if you're going to start revenge-killing Serbian mafiosi, it's best to be thorough.

"Mirko, you'd have been better off with the Carabinieri."

Belajic showed his ragged teeth, his bloodred gums.

"Ha! For why? Brancati runs them, and he is your *cinci băiat*."

Dalton shut the phone off and tossed it out into the dark. It hit a wall with a crack, clattered onto the cobblestones, and bounced with a wet plonk into an open drain. Then the silence came back.

"So," said Belajic, his chest heaving and his face wet, his expression defiant, "now the *Krokodil* will shoot me again?"

"No. I just wanted to stick a *banderilla* in you."

Belajic had no idea what Dalton was talking about, but he sensed a reprieve. "So, now . . . ?"

Dalton, smiled, stepped aside, clearing the way into the Calle de L'Ascensione, waving Belajic through the ancient gate with a slight bow.

"Now? Now you . . . go."

Belajic stared at Dalton.

"Go? I . . . go?"

Dalton nodded.

Belajic held Dalton's eyes a second longer and then lunged forward, shoulder-butting Dalton aside and plunging out into the street, his thin Ferragamo slippers slithering on the icy cobbles, his topcoat flaring out like bat wings as he lumbered heavily across the shadows of the narrow lane and into the Calle Moisè, heading for the brighter lights at the far end, the Calle Larga 22 Marzo, a wide, open mall of exclusive shops behind the Gritti.

Dalton held back for a full minute, waiting until the old man reached the set of steps where Calle 22 began, watching as the man broke out of the shadow and into the hard halogen downlight of the mall's security lamps. Belajic ran pretty well, thought Dalton, for a syphilitic old rhino with a soft-nosed bullet in his left lung. Dalton slipped the Ruger in the pocket of his coat, sighed, and stepped out into the street. Fifty yards away, Mirko Belajic was pounding on the

steel security plates of Cartier, calling hoarsely for help. Dalton, coming on now, playing by the rules of the *corrida,* his hands in his
pockets, his collar turned up against the bitter burn of the snow drifting down, smiled to himself.

Help?

This was Venice in December, and in December, after midnight,
the San Marco district was basically a stone-walled cattle chute lined
with barricaded villas and shuttered stores. Even if someone had
heard the man calling, no sensible Venetian would leave his warm
bed to help some frightened old Serb. The Venetians hated the Serbs
almost as much as they hated the Bosnians and the Montenegrins
and the Croats and the Albanians and all the rest of those murderous
Slav pigs from across the Adriatic.

Belajic, his breath chuffing out in a white plume, turned under the
glow of the light. His face was in shadow, his bald head slick with
sweat, staring back into the Calle de L'Ascensione at Dalton's silhouette. Belajic slammed the steel shutter of the Cartier store once more,
making it ring like a temple gong, leaving a bloody smear on the
ice-cold metal.

"I am not . . . to die . . . like old . . . bull in . . . *abattoir?*"

"They shot her in the head, Belajic."

"Fah," said Mirko, backing away up the calle, still facing Dalton.
"They? Who . . . the fuck . . . is *they?* It is only business."

"They?" replied Dalton in a tone of sweet reason, as if he were
taking Belajic's question seriously. "*They* were Branco Gospic's people. Radko Borins. Emil Tarc and Vigo Majiic. Stefan Groz. Gavrilo
Princip. Milan somebody, never got his last name—"

Belajic flared up at that.

"Milan *Somebody-never-got-his-fucking-name?* His name was Milan
Kuchko! He was my . . . *cousin!*" said Belajic in a wet, wheezing
growl, fighting for every breath. "And *you, Krokodil!* For . . . *noth-*

ing, to amuse, you . . . kick him . . . half to death . . . in the cloisters by the Palazzo Ducale . . . while you sing a song. Now he is all day . . . in a shabby room . . . over a sheep-stinking wool shop in Budva . . . where he moans like a calf and . . . stares and . . . fouls himself . . . and . . . his tongue sticks out—"

"Better keep it moving," said Dalton, lifting the weapon and punching a round into the cobblestones at Belajic's feet. Chips of cobble spattered Belajic's coat, and the round sizzled off into the gloom beyond the storefront lights.

Belajic cursed him again and turned to stumble away, his head down and his arms slack at his sides, chest heaving, blood on his thick blue lips, his chubby legs working as the final minutes of his life flowed past him, his breath pluming out over his shoulder as he made his slow way down the Calle Largo, past the darkened hulk of the Santa Maria del Giglio, down the steps over a small canal and on into the narrow Calle Zaguri. There he came out into the cold blue moonlight again as he crossed the open campo near the Bellavite, his light Italian slippers leaving black sickle-shaped ribbons in the powdery snow. Dalton let him gain some distance, let him think he was going to—

Dalton froze in midstep, lifted his haggard face to the knife-edged moon, his head cocked to one side, thin lips tight, looking much like a raptor as he did so. There was a muted rumble in the air, a soft, churning mutter: a boat, some kind of launch, in one of the canals, and it was *close.* He looked back across the open square of the Campo Bellavite and saw Belajic stumble into the darkened archway that hid the doors of the chapel of San Maurizio.

And stay there.

Going to ground, thought Dalton.

He was expecting this boat.

Dalton listened intently to the sound of the cruiser's engines, deciding that it was too deep and steady for one of the Venice police boats, and not *pockety-pockety* enough for one of those late-night water gypsies. It had to be private. He was trying to guess which canal it was running in—there were three small canals running off the Grand Canal at this point, just across from the domes of Santa Maria della Salute. He lifted his mind up, tried to see Venice as if from the air, picturing the way the narrow waterways threaded through the tightly packed maze of hotels and villas and overhanging archways of the San Marco district.

Belajic had stopped running when he reached the chapel gates. The last bridge he had crossed was a narrow walkway over the Albero canal. They were now in the tangled medieval warrens just behind the Gritti . . . and the sound of the boat's engine was getting louder. Dalton stood still, holding his breath, listening so hard it was making his neck hurt.

After a moment, he got a fix: the engine sound was coming from the direction of Teatro La Fenice. Dalton slipped into a lane on his right and ran softly up the alley behind San Giglio chapel. The dark bulk of the ancient theater loomed up on his right. The sound of the boat's engine was growing louder, coming, he was pretty certain, from the wide canal that ran east to west beside the theater.

Dalton reached the small square by the Calligari, where the Rio Fenice opened up into a kind of broad, shallow pool that, in the high season, would reflect the illuminated façade of the theater. Now, in late December, it was a quadrangle of still black water with a thin dusting of melting snowfall.

The vibrato burble of the boat engine was carrying clear across the lagoon, but there was no light nor movement. Dalton stepped back into a recessed doorway and waited. The snow sifted silently down in the moonlight. He could feel his heart working steadily in his chest, see his breath in a cold blue cloud in the chilly air in front of him. He went inward for a time, as he always did just before a fight.

He may have been afraid, or bitter, or sad, or a combination of all three: he wasn't sure he gave a damn either way. In the main, what he was feeling was a kind of dark anticipation, an early tremor of that corrosive joy that violent action always delivered: the formal strike-counterstrike of hand-to-hand killing, the aesthetic fulfillment in a well-placed skull shot, the my-work-here-is-through feeling of professional satisfaction when you stood over a dead man who, a few seconds ago, had been trying his hardest to kill you.

Dalton had killed many men back in the Fifth Special Forces, and later on for the Company, and most of them had deserved it, some less so, which he had often tried to regret.

On the subject of regrets, with some luck tonight, if these guys were any good at all, from some unexpected angle there'd come a bright muzzle flash, he'd feel a numbing impact, then the sound of a gunshot and that nauseating flood of vertigo, pain too, of course, he'd been shot before—"a pang, soon passing," some optimistic fool of an unshot poet had once said—and then the cobblestones coming up at his face like the pitted surface of an onrushing moon: in brief, a nice, quick death, in the heat of a lively gunfight, and a blessed end to regret and remorse and all the self-inflicted grief of his short and brutal life. Then, if Porter Naumann's ghost was a credible source, a chilled magnum of Bollinger in the eternal twilight of the Piazza Garibaldi in Cortona, watching the light change far below them in the broad checkerboard valley of Lake Trasimeno, surrounded by the shades of all his long-dead friends and a select few sometime lovers.

Somewhere in the farther recesses of his disordered mind a woman's voice—possibly Cora's, more likely Mandy Pownall's—was asking him why he was doing this mad, bad thing, arranging to die in a suicidal vendetta with the ragtag remnants of a Serbian gang he and the Carabinieri had already decimated, crushed, and scattered across the eastern Med from Venice to Kotor to Split. Dalton had no good answer other than that eventually everyone dies and wasn't this a lovely evening for it, and if Venice wasn't a good place to die, it was still echelons above all the competition.

Something low and shadowy developed slowly out of the thicker gloom of the canal across the lagoon, a crocodile shape that slid quietly out into the open water, its sharp destroyer bow slicing through the half-frozen water with a reptilian hiss.

In the moonlight, Dalton could make out the vague shapes of three men huddled in the launch and the pale red glow from the control panel on the face of the driver. A tinny crackle from a walkie-talkie, quickly squelched, someone cursing someone else, a guttural snarling sound with plodding Slavic cadences; Mirko Belajic's people, racing to the rescue of the Big Boss, just as Dalton had hoped they would. The sound of a radio handset let Dalton know that there was at least one other man to deal with, probably in the streets already, shadowing the launch, looking for Dalton, knowing that the sound of a boat at this hour would certainly draw him in. The murmur of the boat's engine reverberated around the deserted lagoon, bouncing off the shuttered windows and barred doors of the empty summer houses that faced Teatro La Fenice.

If the driver of that cutter wanted to thread a launch through the local canals, he had a problem: the Adriatic had risen to record flood levels this winter, the Piazza San Marco half flooded once more, and most of the canals of the city had risen too high for a boat to pass under the bridges that crossed them. In order to reach a canal that led to the chapel of San Maurizio, or even to the quay beside the Campo San Stefano, he'd have no choice but to go under the stone arch that spanned the Rio Fenice. And Dalton was already there, waiting.

He saw the long black shape come fully out of the shadow and into the half-light of the moon. It was one of those exquisite hand-built Rivas, twenty-five feet long, slender as a rapier, a thirties-era Art Deco masterpiece, its mahogany deck gleaming in the moonlight like the hide of a horse, the low, curving stern trailing a fan of lacy diamond sparkles in the black water.

Dalton slipped the Ruger out of his pocket, pressed the slide back far enough to see the pale, brassy glitter of a round in the chamber, eased it forward again. There was a sudden flicker of motion at the side of the doorway. He brought his right hand up, still holding the Ruger, saw a flash of bright steel. A large black shape filled the archway and lunged at him. He caught the edge of the blade on the Ruger's slide, heard the slither of steel on steel, and drove the man's blade hand into the stones beside him. Sparks flew as the blade edge grated along the wall—the man twisted, a violent muscular surge, he was *incredibly* strong—a hulking figure in the dark. Dalton could smell the man's last drink on his breath, possibly grappa. He drove into Dalton hard, slamming him into the door, all this in total silence, just the grunt and heave and hiss of desperate muscular exertion.

Dalton sensed the rising knee, twisted to his right, and felt the thudding impact of it striking his left hip. The man struck Dalton's right wrist and the Ruger went flying. Now the knife came punching back again, a wicked streak of silver glinting in the shadow. Dalton felt the blade drive through the folds of his topcoat along his left side, a slicing, burning fire. The man was fully extended, totally committed to the power of the thrust and the necessary follow-through.

Dalton shifted to the right, caught the man's wrist in his left hand and kicked him behind the right knee. The man went down, striking the door. The knife bounced out of his hands, a muted, tinny clang sounding as it hit the cobblestones.

Behind him now, Dalton got his left forearm under the man's chin, jammed his foot down on the back of the man's calf to keep him down, set himself, braced the other hand on the man's left temple, and jerked the man's head to the right *viciously* hard, meaning to tear his head right off his neck—*Christ*, the guy was a gorilla—it was like trying to rip a fire hydrant out of a sidewalk.

The man now knew his own death was in immediate play, one hand gouging at Dalton's eyes, the nails of his other hand raking the skin on Dalton's left forearm as he tried frantically to buck Dalton off his back. Dalton used all his weight and power to ride this monster backward and down, to lock him in place. If the man got his legs under him, Dalton was a dead man.

Dalton wrenched the man's cannonball skull as hard as he was able to, his left forearm an iron bar across the man's windpipe, his face a killer's ugly mask. He could feel the powerful sinews and steel-cable tendons in the man's neck straining, stretching.

Dalton put everything he had into it, and something deep inside the man's bull neck slowly began to give way. In the muscles of his forearm, Dalton could feel the bony cartilage of the man's voice box start to crumple. A high, keening wail, full of mortal fear and agony, came like a needle-sharp jet of high-pressure steam from the man's gaping mouth: he was trying to speak. *"Aspetta, Krokodil . . . per Dio . . . Aspetta . . ."*

Dalton jerked the man's skull around in one final surge, his powerful shoulders flexing hard, his lean, ropy muscles burning with the strain. A low, grinding creak way down deep—a sudden, meaty snap—and now the head was flopping heavy in his hands, a fat gourd on a broken stalk. The alcove filled with the sudden stink of sewage.

This was the "outside man" they were talking to on the radio, or one of them. A nice tactical move. He would have done the same, if he had anyone to deploy. Were there others? He would have to assume there were.

Dalton let the body drop, plucked the Ruger up off the ground with his left hand, the stiletto with his right, the breath burning in his lungs, his shoulders on fire with the ferocious effort it took to break a strong man's neck.

He moved silently across to the opening of the alcove, looked out at the lagoon. The launch was still slowly crossing the open water. What had seemed like an hour of silent murder had really lasted less than ten seconds. One of the dark shadows on the launch lifted something to his lips. There was a crackle of static close by, then a hoarse whisper in Serbo-Croatian:

"Zorin? Jeste li tu? Zorin?"

Dalton bent over, ripped through the dead man's pockets, tugged out the radio, put the mike to his lips, spoke in the same croaking whisper:

"Dah. Ja sam ovdje—"

"Krokodil?"

"Dah. Sam ubio ga. On je mrtav."

Yes. I killed him. He's dead.

A quick aside, something Dalton could not catch, and then an order:

"Dobar! Prižekatje ovdje. Dobiti Mirko. Prižekatje!"

Good! Wait there. We will get Mirko. Wait!

Dalton watched from the darkness of the doorway as the launch picked up some speed, heading for the stone bridge that led into the next canal, its stern digging in and white wings now curling from its prow. They made no other radio call, which meant there was prob-ably no backup man out there.

Time to move.

He ran lightly, keeping close to the shadows by the walls, until he was almost at the bridge. The launch was nearly there as well. He could hear the men talking, cheerful, an after-action tone in their voices: *Of course Zorin had killed the Krokodil . . . Zorin was the Bull of Srebrenica . . . Zorin was the man.* Dalton bent down, keeping himself below the edge of the stone railing that ran along the side of the bridge. Now the launch was directly under him, passing slowly through the narrow opening, filling the tunnel with the mutter of its engine and the smoke of its exhaust, gliding carefully along. Dalton waited, in a low crouch, timing his move, trying to catch his breath without making a sound, his pulse pounding in his throat.

He slipped across to the other side, stood poised at the railing, watching the prow of the launch as it began to emerge from the tunnel.

The bow was fully out, then the curve of the windshield, then the faint red glow of the instrument panel, the silhouette of the driver at the wheel on the right, another silhouette standing beside him, peering over the windshield as the canal opened up, and a third silhouette in the stern, crouching as the bridge loomed over him, straightening now as the launch came clear.

Dalton reached down from the railing, caught the last man by the collar of his coat and plucked him off the deck. There was a strangled grunt from the man as he felt himself jerked upward.

Dalton sliced the man's throat wide open, feeling the edge grate along the vertebrae as he jerked the blade through gristle and tendon. A black spout of blood shot out onto the backs of the two men in the front seat. The man in the passenger seat had already turned. Dalton let his dead man drop into the canal. The man who turned around had his pistol aimed. There was a bright blue flash and a deafening blast, and Dalton felt a slug pluck at his cheek.

He brought the Ruger up and put two rounds into the pale oval of the man's face, pushing him backward onto the windshield. The driver hit the accelerator and the props roared up.

Dalton saw the driver's silhouette backlit by the red glow of the dash. His lungs heaving, he steadied the Ruger. Even with the luminous tritium dots, the sight picture was jumping around like a compass needle, the roar of the engine echoing off the buildings lining the canal. The launch was twenty yards away when Dalton fired off two careful shots.

The launch swerved to the right, scraping along the pier. Dalton put out three more rounds, heard a cry of pain. The driver reached out to clutch at the pier, missed, and tumbled into the canal, taking with him the safety switch that was tethered to his wrist.

The engine cut off in a second, and then there was nothing but the slow surging of the boat wake against the walls of the canal, the graveyard reek of churned-up water, and Dalton's ragged breath rasping in his throat.

THE GATES of the San Maurizio chapel stood open, and a soft amber light was pouring out through the open doors, pooling on the snow-covered steps that led up to the entrance. Dalton climbed the stairs slowly, blood running freely down his thigh from the knife wound that had opened up the flesh over his ribs. The left side of his face was swollen and numb from the glancing strike of whatever it was the man had fired at him.

He thought perhaps his cheekbone was broken, and he was having a hard time keeping his left eye open. The collar of his turtleneck was warm and sodden with the blood that flowed from the gash. His left forearm had four even rows of flesh deeply shredded by Zorin's nails.

God only knows what standards of personal hygiene Zorin maintained. If Dalton didn't get killed tonight, which now seemed unlikely, he was going to need a tetanus shot. His head was pounding, and his shoulders still ached from the effort of breaking Zorin's treetrunk neck. Yet he was, as previously mentioned, still inconveniently alive. After he finished with Belajic, there was only a bottle of Bollinger, and maybe the Ruger as a chaser.

He reached the doors of the chapel and stood on the threshold, staring down the long nave to the wooden altar on the far end of an open expanse of marble tiles. The chapel, which seemed as ancient as a pharaoh's tomb, smelled of sandalwood and candle wax and six hundred years of complicated Venetian piety. There was an ornate triptych above the altar, framed in intricately carved cypress wood, possibly by one of Tiepolo's students, taking a serious stab at the Stabat Mater.

The wing panels of the triptych were utterly dreadful, mud-toned, deadeyed cartoon figures marinating in pious self-esteem: probably some medieval merchants making their play for immortality and being badly let down by a journeyman artist. These panels were likely added years after the main panel, which was quite good, a vigorous swirl of jewel tones in ruby, emerald, lapis lazuli, and fire opal, and for once the Virgin, haloed in gold leaf, didn't look like a sanctimonious old shrew—you could feel the maternal grief coming off her in waves as they took her ruined son off the cross. Naked, as gray as a slab of raw fish, Christ nevertheless had the build of an NFL linebacker and looked as if He would have been able to twist Zorin's head off with one hand.

Doric columns marched down the nave of the chapel on either side, and the interior was cast in shadow, half lit by the candles burning on the altar. The pillars seemed to move, in fact, as the flames flickered in the wind from the open doors.

A squat, bent, almost gnomelike figure, neither old nor young, with a round, bald head and a hawklike nose, broken, then badly repaired, was standing at the far end of the nave, his once-powerful arms held low, his twisted hands clasped together over his belly in a kind of sinewy Gordian knot. His black eyes, as hard and sharp as a crow's, were fixed on Dalton.

Mirko Belajic was slumped on the floor behind him, his back up against the Communion rail, his thick legs sprawled out across the green-and-white marble tiles, his Briony topcoat in a heap at his side. In the glimmer of the candles, Dalton could see a sheen of sweat on Belajic's fat cheeks and the rapid rising and falling of his chest. His shirt had been pulled back from the bullet wound in his chest. Someone, presumably the gnomelike figure at the foot of the altar, had put a makeshift compression bandage over the entrance wound. There was, of course, no exit wound.

That was the whole idea with the Ruger .22.

Dalton looked down at the Ruger in the bloody glove on his right hand, did a brief press check, drew in a long breath, let it out slowly, and began to cross the long, bare expanse of marble, the soft leather of his shoes soundless against the floor, his eyes scanning the clerestories above the rows of pillars on either side of the nave, the choir loft at the back of the nave, the lady chapel to the right of the main altar, the modest reliquary to the left, even the confessionals, low and huddled wooden huts hard up against the stone walls.

It *felt* as if they were alone, but he kept the Ruger ready, his attention now centering on the bent figure waiting patiently for him at the altar rail. He knew the man well, and the man knew him, although neither of them spoke until they were a few feet apart.

"Micah," said Issadore Galan, his voice a soft croak, "you are hurt."

Dalton smiled at Galan, whose presence here, although inconvenient, could not have been a surprise. Issadore Galan was Major Alessio Brancati's security chief, essentially the intelligence arm of Brancati's Carabinieri detachment for Venice, Siena, Cortona, and Florence.

Once a member of the Mossad, Galan had come by his crumpled body and battered face during several months of captivity with the

Jordanians in the late eighties. The fingers of his hand had been broken many times . . . broken with hammers. Other obscene atrocities had been performed, not so much for the extraction of useful information—which, from a man such as Galan, was unlikely—but rather for the sheer joy some modern young Islamic men take in delivering pain to a helpless infidel body.

In the course of this torture, they had taken away any hope he may have ever had of giving or receiving physical love again. Perhaps as a result, he tended to flare out at life through small dark eyes wreathed in pain lines and a cold, unsettling smile. After he was released in a prisoner exchange, he studied his naked body in a hospital mirror and resolved never to allow his wife and family back in Tel Aviv to see what he had become. Now he worked for Major Alessio Brancati in Venice and was, in his arid, ruined, and clinically detached way, reasonably content.

The smile he returned to Dalton was genuine; he and Dalton and Alessio Brancati's Carabinieri had just come through a short, sharp war with the Serbian Mafia and, in the main, had won. Dalton, once a CIA Cleaner whose job had been to police up the blood and ruin left by other CIA agents, now exiled by an internal conflict in the Agency, was still waiting for the official call back to Langley that had been promised to him by Deacon Cather, the Deputy Director of Clandestine Services. That call had never come, and waiting for it, Galan believed, was killing the young man.

Dalton touched his cheek, came away with blood on the tips of his glove. A wave of fatigue swept through him, and his vision blurred for a moment.

"Issadore," he said, shaking his head to clear it. "How are you? You look well."

Galan gave him an oddly Italianate shrug, raised his hands.

"You have had a busy night, Micah."

"Almost through," said Dalton, feeling Mirko Belajic's eyes on him.

Galan turned and looked down at Belajic, came back to Dalton.

"I have called the water ambulance. They will see to you as well."

Dalton shook his head.

"Not necessary, but thanks. Now, Issadore, I need you to step away."

Galan lifted his hands. He had no weapon, at least no visible one.

"Micah, you cannot continue in this—"

"Ask him where are my men," Belajic said in a breath-starved whisper. Dalton looked down at him, his pale eyes glittering in the candlelight.

"How many did you have?" asked Dalton. Belajic hesitated, looking crafty, but the black hole in the Ruger's muzzle made it hard to dissemble.

"Four. All I had left."

"I killed every one who came at me."

Belajic stared up at him, his wet cheeks glistening.

"All? Even *Zorin?*"

"If he was out there, Mirko, he's dead."

"Zorin . . ." said Belajic, more to himself than anyone and in a tone of shocked wonder, "he was a . . . *golem*. Even you . . . could not kill . . . *him*. How did he die?"

"I broke his neck."

Belajic shook his head.

"A . . . black lie . . . No one man could—"

Dalton lifted the Ruger, pointed it at Belajic's forehead.

"You can talk it over with him in Hell."

Galan stepped into the line of fire.

Dalton sighed, slumped, gave him a look.

"You know what this *thing* is," he said in a soft voice, meaning the old man on the floor and the snail-slime trail of violence that stretched out behind him for all the long years of his predatory life. Galan nodded.

"Sure. He is . . . a waste. I am here, Micah. I am here for you." He hesitated, and then went on. "For Cora Vasari too, maybe."

Dalton winced at the name.

"Cora's in Anacapri. Her family has her in the villa there. I've tried to reach her. Everything I send drops into a well. But I can still finish . . . this."

"It is *already* finished. And how do you know she doesn't answer? Her family has her isolated. Your messages may not arrive, nor hers leave."

"Issadore, all that's over. Please step aside. If I leave him, he'll just come back at me. Maybe try for Cora again. You know the rule."

"You will not kill him, Micah. You will not kill anyone else in my Venice tonight. Maybe you are tired of Venice. Maybe also Venice is tired of you. Venice makes crazy the people she gets tired of. Or she kills them. Anyway, you have done enough to yourself tonight. Your mind is out of order. Too much drinking. Too much hating. I know where you hope to take this. You hope to die. Like you are on a train. I am here to stop your train. Give me the Ruger and go sit down. You are about to fall where you stand."

Galan's face was rocky. The light behind him was shimmering, going in and out of focus. The pain in Dalton's cheek was intense. More than anything else, he wanted to sleep.

"Dah," Belajic hissed, "kill me . . . *Krokodil* . . . and be done."

The Ruger came up again. Dalton stepped to the left. Galan matched the move, closed in suddenly and grabbed the muzzle of the Ruger in his leathery paw, pressed it against his own chest.

"Pull," he said. "Maybe you do me a favor."

"No," said Dalton, "I won't."

"I know," said Galan, taking the Ruger gently away. "Now, go sit."

Belajic started to wheeze. It took a while for the others to realize he was laughing. Dalton ignored him. Belajic was dead to him. He walked over to the verger's chair and collapsed into it. Galan looked at Dalton for a while and then turned away and put a bullet into Mirko Belajic's left eye. This seemed to come as a shock to Belajic, who found himself in Hell a few seconds later.

Dalton looked at Galan, who shrugged.

"You were right, about killing him," he said. "He would have sent someone for Cora just for payback. These honor killings have no ending. But Venice is my city and I decide who to kill. Not you."

There was a commotion at the door, the sound of boots and the creak of gear. Low, competent voices and the crackle of radio handsets.

"The medics are here, Micah."

"Bugger the medics. I have nowhere to go."

"Yes, you do. You will go back to the Savoia."

"Yes? And do what there?"

"I will send a man to help you."

"Help me what?"

"Pack."

"I'm leaving?"

"It seems that you will have to. Even now, events overtake us. Brancati will explain—"

"Explain what?"

Galan shook his head, his expression becoming fixed.

"No. There is a . . . development. He will lay it out. It is too deep for me. Also, Brancati can protect you from a great deal, but the Prefect will not let you make Venice an arena for what is the term, three letters, I think, in your American army?"

"CQB? Close Quarter Battle?"

"Yes, that is it. Or do I mean MOUT?"

"What about . . . tonight? The bodies?"

Galan smiled.

"Venice swallows bodies up like pythons eat rats. By morning, there will be no sign these men ever lived. And they were the last of Gospic's people. So now hear me, Micah: our private war with Branco Gospic is truly over, yes? And you must go back to the hotel and gather your clothes."

"Where am I going? Can't go back to the U.S."

Galan shook his head slowly, sadly.

"The decision is not mine, it belongs to you, and other parties, and when you know you would be wise to tell no one, not even me. You have some money?"

"Oh yes," said Dalton, through a weary, humorless grin. "Thousands. Everything left over from the thing with the *Mingo Dubai*. Langley never asked for it back. I guess they just wanted me to go, and stay gone."

"Then, Micah, as much as it saddens me, that is what you should do."

"Yes?"

"Yes. Go, and stay gone."

AFTER THE medics had more or less stitched him back together—with his shirt off, Dalton's scarred and bullet-pocked body looked like an aerial map of Antietam—a corporal of the Carabinieri, a rangy young Venetian with the features of an assassin and the air of a kindly priest, helped Dalton to his feet and walked him down the steps of the chapel, clearly meaning to see him all the way back to the Savoia e Yolanda on the other side of the piazza, down along the Quay of Slavs, two bridges east of the Palazzo Ducale.

Dalton stopped to gather himself in the campo outside the chapel, taking a deep but careful breath, looking up at the sky. The clouds were shredding apart in a rising wind off the Adriatic, and the snow had stopped falling. The moon pierced the tip of the Campanile in the Piazza San Marco. The air was sharp and cold and burned in his lungs like chilled grappa. Far in the east, over the black cliffs of Montenegro on the far side of the Adriatic, the indigo sky was shading into a pale pink glow.

"What is your name?" he asked the young corporal.

The lad stiffened into a formal parade brace.

"Sono Corporale Orinaldo Zargozzo, Commendatore!" he barked. Being assigned to walk the Crocodile home was a signal honor. Dalton's role in the defeat of the Gospic *sindacato* in Venice was spoken of in whispers all over the service, but it was also making him nervous.

He had just finished watching the medics clean up what was left of a man named Zorin Vinzcik, found dead in an alcove near the Calligari steps across from La Fenice. It had taken three men to get the corpse on a gurney. The head had been twisted so far around that the body seemed to be looking back over its own shoulder.

The Crocodile was perhaps a touch over six feet, broad in the shoulders, but otherwise built like a horseman, lean and supple, with an air of latent menace, yes, but no match for a creature like Zorin Vinzcik, who reminded him of a rhino he had seen in a zoo in Palermo many years ago.

"Corporale Zargozzo, may I trouble you for a favor?"

"D'accordo! Certamente, Commendatore."

"May I walk home alone?"

The soldier's face was all confusion, unease, regret.

"Mai . . . Il Signore Galan—"

"I promise you, I will go home and pack. But this will be my last night in Venice for a long time. I'd like to walk it alone. *Con permesso?"*

Corporal Zargozzo gave it some thought. The Crocodile was clearly in some sort of bad place in his heart, and Galan, who obviously valued him, had been forceful on the necessity of seeing him safely to his hotel.

On the other hand, there was the dead rhino.

"Please. Tell Issadore I *insisted*. He will understand."

After a moment, the corporal nodded, his dark face conflicted. Dalton offered his hand, they shook, and he turned to walk away. He had gone a few steps when the corporal called out to him. Dalton stopped and looked back at the boy, silhouetted in the warm light pouring from the chapel.

"Signore Dalton, mi perdoni?"

"Yes?"

"Con la grazia di Dio, Commendatore, un giorno, Lei ritornerà a Venezia."

"Will I?"

The young man nodded again, smiled hugely, snapped off a razor-edged salute, spun on a heel, and walked away. Dalton saw him up the steps of the church and then turned back to the darkened streets of Venice.

He made his way back through the Calle 22. Someone had already cleaned Belajic's bloody handprints off the security shutters covering the Cartier store—"Like pythons eat rats," Galan had said—and, in the Calle de L'Ascensione, there was no sign that a careless Albanian bodyguard had caught a .22 slug in the temple just outside the west gate of the piazza.

Dalton stepped through the arch and into the most beautiful open space on the planet, the serene perfection of the Piazza San Marco; flanked on three sides by the ordered cloisters and three-part harmonies of the Museo Civico and the Procurates, paved in intricate cobblestones, closed at the eastern end by the Moorish domes of the Basilica, all of this dominated by the redbrick spire of the Campanile.

To Dalton, the square of Saint Mark's in Venice always seemed to float in a timeless present, as if the whole murderous planet, with all its centrifugal cruelty and whirling insanity, was spinning like a well-balanced top on this one utterly still point.

The floodwaters had subsided during the night, but there were still pools standing in the cobblestones, and they reflected the stars just beginning to show through rents in the cloud cover.

Dalton stepped his careful way around the standing pools, heading for the turn next to the Palazzo Ducale and the short walk along the Riva degli Schiavoni to his suite at the Savoia. His mind was clear, and for some strange reason he felt more at peace with himself than he had in many weeks.

Perhaps he found killing therapeutic. Maybe he should do a paper on it for Cora Vasari, who was a professor of psychology at the university in Florence. On the other hand, maybe not.

When he came abreast of the shuttered windows of Florian's Café, he was suddenly aware of a dark figure seated at a table just beneath the archway. He reached for his Ruger, realizing as he did so that Galan, a prudent man, had kept it in his pocket. There was a motion, a dry click.

Dalton waited for the bullet, thinking that it was typical of whatever old Norse gods ruled him that he would finally get himself shot once he had decided not to die. A flaring yellow light rose up to a blue cylinder: someone was lighting a cigarette in the dark.

The glow of the lighter flame lit up the craggy face and cold blue eyes of Porter Naumann, killed in Cortona some weeks ago and left in a chapel doorway off the Via Janelli to be ripped apart by the village dogs.

Naumann drew in the smoke, blew it out slowly, and tapped on the top of the tippy tin table, his signature drumbeat.

"Micah, my son, take a pew," he said, using his Cartier to light a candle in a glass bowl. Dalton thought it over.

He hadn't seen Porter Naumann's ghost for several weeks, not since Cora had been shot. At that point, Naumann's ghost had been somehow trapped in Cortona and had troubles of his own. Dalton came over and stood by the table.

As far as he could make out by the glow of the candle, Naumann was, as usual, nicely turned out, in a long tan wool topcoat over tobacco-colored tweed slacks, a rich brown sweater, a Burberry scarf, elegant loafers in some sort of deep-brown snakeskin.

And, for whatever demented reason, emerald green socks, possibly silk.

He showed his teeth to Dalton in that same Grim Reaper smile that he had been famous for when he was the top Cleaner at the Agency, before he had gone to England to start up the investment house of Burke and Single, an Agency cover op in London.

"Sit, will you?" he said. "You look like death."

"Do you know you have emerald green socks on?"

"I do," said Naumann. "I think they give me an air of *insouciance*."

"I think they give you an air of being the middle guy in the Lollypop Guild."

"Are you gonna sit down and play nice, or do I have to go all ectoplasmic on your sorry ass?"

Dalton had, after a struggle, resigned himself to the idea, put forward by the medics, that these intermittent appearances of Naumann's ghost were an artifact of his exposure to a cloud of weaponized peyote and datura root a while back, a trap set for him by the same man who had killed Naumann. Once the hallucinogens worked their way out of his system, the medics insisted with varying degrees of conviction, so would Naumann's ghost.

At least, they sincerely hoped so.

Dalton's view was that if the guy in *A Beautiful Mind* could win a Nobel Prize while seeing invisible roommates, Dalton could handle an amiable specter. In the meantime, with nothing better to do, Dalton sat.

Naumann leaned forward and extended a slim gold cigarette case, offering Dalton a selection of Balkan Sobranie Cocktails, absurd creations in deep blue, turquoise, even flamingo pink, all tipped with gold filters. Where Naumann got them, Dalton never knew: Naumann insisted that he found them in a shop in Hell called Dante's— *"Nel mezzo del cammin di nostra vita."*

He picked a blue Sobranie and let Naumann fire it up for him, leaned back in the chair, drawing the smoke deep into his lungs and letting it out slowly, a curling, luminous cloud in what was left of the moonlight. The candle glow lit up their faces, the living and the dead, as they sat there for a time in a companionable silence.

"So," said Naumann, after a decent interval, "you owe me fifty bucks."

"I do?" said Dalton, grinning at him. "For what?"

"My money was on Zorin."

"Was it?"

"Yeah. Nothing personal. Guy was a rhino."

"And what am I?"

Naumann seemed to consider the question.

"You're more of a wildebeest. You know, top-heavy, ugly as sin, bandy-legged but agile."

"I lucked out."

"You fought dirty. I have to say, nobody on my side is real thrilled to have him over here. The guys in the boat—now, that was just plain showy. It was like you were *trying* to get shot."

"Actually, I was."

Naumann made a pouty face, leaning over to pat Dalton's hand.

"I thought so. Poor baby. Got those bad old blue devils, have you?"

"I guess so."

Naumann sat back, shaking his head, raised his hands, palms out.

"Christ, lock and load, will you? Look at *me*. There I am, in the prime of my life, hung like a Valparaiso jackass, the body of a Greek god, the looks of a young Sterling Hayden—"

"Who the hell is Sterling Hayden?"

"—a killer town house in Wilton Row, all my expenses paid by the Agency, I'm adored by all, beautiful women cry out my name in the night—"

"More like a shriek."

"—and along comes some whack-job Indian psycho, he slips me a mickey, I get half eaten by wild dogs in a churchyard in Cortona, and now, in case you missed it, I seem to be dead. Do you hear me whining? Do you?"

Naumann satirically cocked an ear, looking off into the starry night.

"No, you do not. So get a grip. You about through for the night?"

"I think so," said Dalton, stifling a yawn. "Why?"

"Bit of a backlog down in Processing. Central Command wants you to ease up for a while. Too bad it wasn't you. We had a table booked."

"Piazza Garibaldi?"

Naumann nodded.

"Where else? Word is, you're getting the boot."

"Everybody's telling me so, anyway. Last time I saw you, you were stuck in Cortona, and these evil-ass smoke demons were rising up out of the stones to hiss at you."

Naumann shuddered at the memory.

"Hey, don't joke about that, Micah. Naming *calls*. Seriously. I've seen it happen. Those are some very bad dudes."

"So what happened?"

He shrugged, drew on the cigarette, the tip flaring like a firefly in the shadows of Florian's portico.

"Buggered if I know. One afternoon, they all just . . . scarpered. Had something to do with eucalyptus, I think."

"You didn't ask?"

"Ask? Ask who?"

Dalton raised his eyes skyward in a parody of reverent piety.

"Who, Him?" said Naumann. "Hell, over on this side God's as hard to pin down as Barack Obama's ears. Ask me, He's kind of like that big head in the *Wizard of Oz*. Real power's behind the curtain. Probably some saber-toothed power broad like Nancy Pelosi, wears a pearl-gray pantsuit and stiletto heels, a pair of killer ta-tas, has a smile so cold bourbon freezes on her lips."

"You think Nancy Pelosi has killer ta-tas?"

"Hey, you haven't seen her naked. I have."

While Dalton worked that through, Naumann moved on.

"So, about leaving Venice, what are you gonna do?"

"About what?"

"Like I said, you're getting the heave. About time, by the way, you ask me. Tourists will be back in April, and they'll be tripping over your roadkill all around town. Probably find something moldering away in a gondola. You're gonna need some kind of work, Micah. Left to your own devices, you go all wobbly and your wheels come off. You ever hear from Deacon Cather?"

Dalton shrugged, as if the name meant nothing.

Naumann, who knew his man, didn't buy it.

"So, no call? Not a peep? Ungrateful bastard. Typical Cather. Dried-up old Jesuit, but slick as a pickerel's pecker. Always reminded me of Sir Francis Walsingham—"

"Who?"

"Queen Elizabeth I's security guy. Eighty-sixed Mary, Queen of Scots, in one of the first confusion ops? Do you *read*, Micah? Improve yourself?"

"Nope. Reading hurts my head."

"After all we did for the Agency? That Serbian thing in Chicago—"

"*We?* I didn't notice you prancing about the place."

Naumann looked hurt.

"Micah, I'm *always* there. You just don't see me, unless you're totally fucked up. I'm sort of . . . hovering. And, for the record, I don't prance."

Dalton yawned again, mightily this time, drew in the last of the cigarette, stubbed it out on the stones beside the table, pocketed what was left of the butt out of habit, pushed his chair back. Naumann tipped his chair against the walls of Florian's, brought his legs up, crossed his ankles, set his nicely shod feet on the table, and lit himself another Sobranie. The move exposed a couple of inches of his emerald green socks.

"You not coming?" said Dalton, who could have used the company. "I think there's a couple of Bollys in the minibar."

On another level, he was painfully aware of how heroically deranged a man had to be if he was asking a dead man's ghost to come back to the hotel for a nightcap. Naumann shook his head.

"Not this time. You really going back to the Savoia?"

Dalton looked around the piazza, back at Naumann.

"Where else? Florian's doesn't open for another six hours."

Naumann gave Dalton the once-over, as if trying to make up his mind.

"Well, I got something for you to chew on, smarty-pants. You go back to your room, there's a surprise waiting there for you."

Dalton was silent for a time.

"Galan said something about . . . developments. Events. Who is it?"

"You tell me, smart guy."

"Oh no. None of that shit. You're the one thinks he's real. Give."

"That, my lad," said Naumann, "is for me to know and you to find out. Anyway, if I'm right, then you have to admit I'm a real ghost and not some bit of undigested peyote bud stuck, God forbid, in your colon."

Naumann was starting to fade.

"Where you going?"

"Me? I'm gonna cut right along to the next time I see you."

"Where's that? *When* is that?"

"From my side of the mirror, Grasshopper, all those kind of questions sorta run together."

"You haven't got a clue, do you?"

"Want a hint?"

"Sure. Yes. Give me a hint."

"Okay. You'll be in a hurry. Literally."

"I just love it when you go all Delphic on me. One last time. Who's in the room? I'll bet it's just Brancati, dropping by to say *ciao*."

"Like I said, that's for me to know and you to—"

"It's Brancati, and you're *still* not telling me anything I don't know."

"Micah," said Naumann, now almost gone, "*you* don't know so damn much I hardly know where to start. Watch your back. There's more going on than you think. Change is coming. See you around."

DALTON'S SUITE at the Savoia e Yolanda was on the top floor of what had once been a private villa for a lesser scion of the Sforza family, now a high-end boutique hotel. Dalton had three rooms and a small balcony on the top floor, with a view across Saint Mark's Basin to the island of the Giudecca and the Palladian façade of San Giorgio Maggiore. Although Dalton had an Agency flat in London, around the corner from Porter Naumann's old place in Belgravia, this had been as close to a steady home as Dalton had known since his marriage had ended, in tragedy, ten years ago.

Now it looked like just another trap, and he was approaching it that way, coming into the hotel through a delivery door at the rear. He had rigged the lock weeks ago and no one had noticed. Climbing the service stairs all the way up to the third floor, he walked down the service hall to a maid's closet, where he had taken the further precaution of concealing a fallback piece behind a stone slab: a stainless-steel Dan Wesson revolver chambered for .44 Magnum rounds. A hand cannon, but he loved it.

He left the steel briefcase. It contained his alternate ID, a weak but serviceable throwaway cover as a Canadian with the unlikely name of Tom Coward who specialized in stainless-steel polishing systems. The ID would at least get him out of Europe. There was also twenty grand in mixed and nonsequential euros, another ten grand in U.S. dollars, and a small but heavy Crown Royal bag filled with .999 pure Canadian gold wafers. These days he was living on what was left over from the Agency's operating advance during the Chicago thing, almost a half million dollars in a bank in Zurich. This was his get-out-of-town stash. If he needed all this later, it would still be there. If he got killed in the next few minutes, some workman doing a reno twenty years from now would have himself a lovely morning.

The Savoia had a roof-garden café, shuttered and winterized now, but it could still be reached by stepping out onto an old iron grid on the fifth floor that held a refrigeration unit. Using the unit, he was able to boost himself onto the sloping red-tiled roof. The footing was tricky glare ice, and the tiles had a tendency to give way under his step, but he got himself across to the front of the hotel, where he lay down and eased his way to the lip of the roof just above the balcony of his suite.

The balcony was set back into the building but open to the sky above, perhaps five feet deep by ten feet wide, with a small marble table and a couple of garden chairs. The French doors that opened onto it were ajar, and a soft light poured out from the living room, along with an aria from *Lucia di Lammermoor* and the spicy scent of Toscano cigars. A voice called from inside the room, a baritone purr with a Tuscan lilt.

"*Micah, che cosa fai? Tu sei pazzo!* Use the door, like a gentleman!"

The voice belonged to Alessio Brancati, the Carabinieri major. As expected. The next time Dalton saw Porter Naumann's ghost, *he* was going to be the one getting all ectoplasmic on somebody's sorry ass. Dalton, feeling like a complete mook, slipped over the edge and dropped softly onto the balcony, ripping some of the fresh stitches in his side as he landed.

Straightening, trying not to wince, he saw Brancati sitting in one of the leather wingbacks in front of the fire, his feet on the hearth fender, the firelight playing on the shiny black leather of his riding boots and on the thin red stripe running up the leg of his navy blue riding breeches. His white shirt was unbuttoned, his uniform tunic and black Sam Browne draped over one wing of the chair. He had a cigar in one hand and a flute of Dalton's Bollinger in the other, his seamed and rough-cut face cracked in a broad, toothy grin under his salt-and-pepper handlebar mustache.

Brancati, in his mid-fifties, had deep-brown eyes and a ready smile and the general air of a man who was willing to be favorably impressed. He was also a hardhanded and ruthless soldier-cop who had recently designed and executed, with an assist from Dalton, a wildly illegal and entirely covert Carabinieri war against a Serbian gang that had left their leadership dead and their few remaining foot soldiers lining up for anxiety therapy in exotic Third World hellholes with neither indoor toilets nor an extradition treaty with Italy. Brancati had, for reasons buried in their joint past as soldiers and spies, made Dalton's survival a matter of personal interest.

He stood as Dalton came into the light, still holding the Dan Wesson at his side. When he got a better look at Dalton by the light of the wood fire, his expression changed, and all his jovial humor fled in a flash of sudden anger.

"*Bocca al lupo!* Issadore said you were not badly hurt."

Dalton put the revolver down on a small side table and sat down in the other wing chair, leaning back into it with a long, uneven sigh.

"They patched me up. I'll do, Alessio. I'll do. I could use a drink."

Brancati shook himself out of his shock and stepped across to the granite-topped bar that filled one side of the main room, tugging the Bollinger out of an ice-filled silver bucket and carefully filling one of the tall crystal flutes to the brim. He brought it over to Dalton like a man carrying nitro, put it into Dalton's slightly unsteady hand, and stood over him while Dalton put the flute to his lips, his powerful arms folded across his chest.

"So," he said, with grim emphasis, after Dalton had drained half the flute, "now our private war is *finito*, yes? No more of "—he lifted his arms, taking in the room, the city, the *situation*, in one encompassing Italian *abracco*—"your personal *vendette?*"

Dalton sat forward, eased off his tattered blue topcoat, and sat back again. His turtleneck had been sliced open where Zorin's blade had reached him, and fresh white bandages showed through the rent. His face was bandaged and taped. He could feel the stitches in it when he drank, and his entire left cheek from jawline to temple was turning into a Mark Rothko tone poem in bloody blues, smoky blacks, and lurid purples. He was looking forward to a hot bath and a deep, dreamless sleep.

"How did Galan get onto it? I thought I was flying under his radar."

Brancati delivered himself of a kind of eloquent snorting huff and went back to his wingback, poking an iron into the fire with some suppressed anger. The fire flared up and made a gargoyle of his fine Italian profile.

"Galan's radar is impossible to get under. He knows more about me than my wife and daughters. Sometimes I think he knows too much of everything. If he was ever turned—"

"Not him, Alessio. Not ever. He has no . . . handles."

Still staring into the fire, Brancati said "Seriously, Micah. This thing tonight, it *cannot* ever happen again. The Prefect must be . . . handled. I cannot handle him if you cannot handle . . . you. *Capisce?*"

"I know that, Alessio. And I apologize for . . . the inconvenience."

"Hah," he said, with a wry grin. "Five dead men is to you an *inconvenience?* Anyway, it is done. Over. Now we have . . ."

His face set again, the smile fleeting and gone.

". . . I think, Micah, you will have to leave Venice. For a time, anyway."

"Yes. I know that too. Galan explained . . . the situation. He also said something about events? Developments? That you would explain?"

Brancati stopped churning up the flames, sat back and let the fire glow and the champagne ease him into a better humor. He glanced across at Dalton, a sidelong look.

"In a moment. You are . . . in a better place . . . now?"

Dalton caught all the levels in the question and gave the matter some careful thought. Brancati had a right to the truth.

"Actually, yes. I think so. Makes no sense, but there it is."

Brancati nodded, as if his instincts had been confirmed.

"I too find this. There is always this . . . tranquillity? After action, yes?"

"Maybe. I ran into Porter Naumann, on the way back."

Brancati's expression remained carefully neutral. He and Dalton had met during the major's investigation of Porter Naumann's death, which had caused something of a sensation in the superstitious population of Cortona. There had been some talk of a walking demon in a red skin, and one of the elder citizens, a chapel verger, had claimed to have seen Porter Naumann's ghost standing on the Via Santa Margherita, near the Piazza Garibaldi, every evening for a full year before the murder actually occurred. The tale was regularly recounted around the *bacari*, growing more lurid with each telling.

"You are still . . . seeing him?"

"Now and then."

"And he is . . . the same?"

"Since you saw him? God no. He's got himself all put back together. You'd like him. He makes the *bella figura*—"

"*Si, per un cancrenato!* I was hoping this *cancrenato* would go away."

"He will."

"*Grazie a Dio,*" said Brancati, more as a prayer than a belief. It was always possible that this volatile young American was insane, but for Brancati, who knew the man's whole story, a barrier of mild insanity was a sensible response to the experiences he had lived through.

"Micah, about leaving Venice . . ."

"Yes. These . . . events? Galan said you would explain?"

"Not yet. In a moment. No, I was thinking of Cora."

"Then stop. There's nothing left to do. Her people have her—"

"I know. Hidden away in Capri. But she is no *fanciulla*. She's older than you are, a grown woman, and a professor at the university in Florence—"

"*Psicologia.*"

"Yes. And also a witness involved in the trial of the man who shot her."

"Radko's still alive?"

"Yes. For the most part."

Radko Borins had, in his attempt to kill Cora Vasari in the courtyard of the Uffizi, also managed to kill two of Brancati's men assigned to her protection detail. Radko Borins had the bad luck to be taken alive by a man whose ancestors once controlled the prison next to the Palazzo Ducale. They had walked many men across the covered Bridge of Sighs who had never been seen again by their loved ones. Radko Borins had been made to suffer.

"How does that affect Cora?"

"I could have her . . . what is the word? *Summoned?*"

"Issue a *subpoena,* you mean. Force her family to deliver her?"

"Yes. She is almost recovered now. She would want to see you."

Brancati spoke with less than total conviction, since there was no way of knowing what Cora was actually thinking, but, in the absence of a reply in any other form, her silence was eloquent. And reasonable. Her connection with Dalton had nearly killed her. Twice.

"No," said Dalton after a time, "let it go. She's safer that way."

"Can you? Let her go?"

"I already have."

Neither man called the lie. What was the point?

They sat in silence for a while, watching the fire burn down.

Brancati sighed, leaned forward, set his flute on the hearth fender, reached into his shirt pocket, and pulled out a small, rectangular black lacquer box, about eight inches long, intricately inlaid with pale green jade and tied with red silk ribbon. He handed it to Dalton.

"This was found sitting on my desk last Monday morning—"

"On *your* desk?" said Dalton, turning the box. Shimmers of amber light rippled along its sides.

"Yes," said Brancati, clearly upset. His office was on the top floor of the Arsenal, deep in the heart of Italy's military and *spionaggio* establishment—in these years of terror war, a difficult place to reach.

"Last Monday, you said? That was three days ago."

"Yes. It took a while for us to figure out that it was meant for you."

"How did you find that out?"

"Do you not recognize it? It used to have a cigarette holder in it."

Dalton held it in his hand, thinking. Then it came to him.

"Mandy Pownall. She's an aide at Burke and Single. In London. She's Agency. You've met her. I was with her in Singapore, when she got this. As a gift from an SID agent named Sergeant Ong Bo. The cigarette holder inside it was a trap. They tried to say it was drug paraphernalia."

Brancati nodded.

"I remember you telling us the story. Galan looked for tobacco residue in the liner, just to confirm. It is there. There could not be two such as this. And besides, we do not believe in coincidences, do we?"

"How did it get there?"

Brancati made a face, raised his hands.

"When I find out, someone will be unhappy. Open it."

Dalton popped the catch. Inside, nesting in a lining of old emerald green silk, was a long, slender stainless-steel hand tool with a rubber handgrip at one end and a small sharp disk of some dark material at the other, held in place by a tiny axle.

He picked it up, hefted it carefully, his heart shifting beats.

"Do you know what that is?" asked Brancati.

"Yes," said Dalton, the skin along his neck and shoulders tightening and his face becoming hard and set. "It's a glass cutter."

"There is a maker's mark on the underside. Do you see it?"

Dalton held it up to the fire, saw the letters H&R stamped on the shaft.

"And does a glass cutter with these markings mean something to you?

"Yes," said Dalton, already miles away, seeing the rabbit hole opening up under his feet, a blue vein beginning to throb at his temple, "it does."

SAVANNAH

THE MANSION ON FORSYTH

On a misty but luminous sunlit December afternoon in Savannah, at around the same time that Dalton and Brancati were contemplating a glass-cutting tool by the dying light of a cedarwood fire, a woman named Briony Keating was introduced to a tanned and muscular young man with short blue-black hair, prematurely gray at the temples, and a general air of contained aggression that brought the word *duelist* to mind. The young man had a fine-boned, hawkish face, with wide-set and direct topaz-brown eyes.

This introduction took place in the muted elegance of the Lobby Bar in the Mansion on Forsyth, across the street from the famous park where the Old South had once cadence-drilled the flower of her doomed youth. The man radiated intelligence and sly wit, and had a charming if rather predatory smile. Briony Keating, who, at the age of sixty-two, was a seasoned and cynical judge of men, felt his wolfish smile as a kind of warming glow in her lower belly. Aware of a rising heartbeat and a certain shortness of breath, she decided that while his navy blue pinstripe could be Hugo Boss and his flawless white shirt might be from Pink's, his morals were straight off the Serengeti.

He didn't feel gay to her, and she had wonderful antennae for nuances of sexual identity, but she could not rule it out completely, at least not without further investigation. His name, according to Briony Keating's friend, a Bryn Mawr classmate named Thalia Bowering, was Jules Duhamel.

When introduced, sensing a kind of subtle arrogance in him, Briony considered the young man coolly for a long moment without response, allowing the silence to last just enough to create a certain uneasy tension.

The noisy chatter of the women all around pressed in, the *ping-ping-ting* of ice tinkling in cut-crystal glasses, the boy at the piano leaning over the keys with his limp blond hair in his eyes and his pale face set as he worked his way through the "Moonlight Sonata" . . . at last, Briony Keating offered her hand, which Mr. Jules Duhamel took gently in a strong but brief grip, bowing slightly as he did so. His skin felt smooth and warm and dry, and made her think of a stallion's neck. He spoke with a slight accent, not French, someplace much farther east than that . . . Slovenian? Montenegrin?

Was Jules Duhamel, obviously French, not his real name? Interesting. His voice was pitched low, but not at all forced, a natural baritone purr.

"Miss Bowering has been telling me—"

"Please, call me Tally," said Miss Bowering, who was short and blunt and had something of the look of Ayn Rand about her. She was aware of this, and even wore her thick black hair cut short. Her attention, openly sexual, was fixed on the young man. She sent Briony a brief, telling look—*I saw him first, and isn't he a killer?*—and then broke away as Mr. Duhamel bowed again, offering a quick flash of his perfect teeth. He had two rather prominent canines, which seemed to fit his predatory image nicely.

"Yes . . . Tally . . . has been telling me that you were schoolmates together? At . . . Bryn Mawr? I don't know it, I'm afraid—"

"A girls' school, in Pennsylvania," said Briony, trying to throw it away, but Tally would have none of that.

"We were Brecons together," she cut in, her voice trying for a sultry whisper but ending in a dry cough. Briony glanced at her, a look of concern flickering across her well-defined WASP face, her hazel eyes sharp. Tally, a chain-smoker, had mild emphysema. When Briony looked back at Mr. Duhamel, she found him studying her exposed throat with a kind of vampiric intensity and resisted the impulse to lift a hand to cover her neck.

No, she was better than that. She straightened her shoulders, lifted her head, brushed her long silvery hair back from her high, clear forehead, and hooked a heavy lock of it behind her left ear, where a large diamond earring caught the random glare of a halogen spot and sent prisms of rainbow light dancing across her slightly too tight jawline. Duhamel watched her do this with obvious approval and gave her a sly, conspiratorial smile, as Tally Bowering caught her breath and began again.

"Brecon . . . is a residence there . . . at Bryn Mawr, I mean."

She made a sweeping gesture, taking in the gathering of well-dressed and obviously wealthy women, all of a certain age, scattered about the sunlit atrium with the reflecting pool, revealing as she did so the slightly crepey flesh at the underside of her upper arm, look-ing, for a moment, shopworn, even jaded, as if she was being ob-served without the affection she genuinely deserved. With her face turned away as she spoke, Tally missed the glitter of distaste that flashed in Duhamel's lambent brown eyes.

Briony Keating did not.

Tally came back, gasped a bit, and rushed on: "This is actually our reunion class of 'sixty-seven—Bree was our valedictorian—she went on to do something very clever for the government, didn't you, Bree? She's very close about it, if you want to know. I think she was a spy. Although everyone who goes to Bryn Mawr is expected to do something very clever afterward."

Briony, who disliked being called Bree, gave Tally a tolerant smile, waiting for Duhamel to begin some "continental" charade of polite disbelief about her age, but Duhamel only smiled again and shook his head.

"And now you are in Savannah, Miss Keating? Do you live here?"

"No. God no. Too claustrophobic."

"Really? Such a pretty town too. Draped in age, like the moss in the live oaks, yet somehow timeless. Why do you find it . . . ?"

"Claustrophobic? Well, you should remember that Spanish moss is a parasite. It would kill the oaks, if they let it. Savannah is a small town, with all that implies. Everyone knows everyone, and everyone talks about everyone else. The main entertainment around here is a kind of desultory adultery, if you'll forgive the rhyme, with adultery's faithful handmaiden, vulgar melodrama, following close behind. They have a school of the arts here—a ghastly 'avant-garde' sort of postcolonial snake pit. Odd combination of smug and venomous, as the radical left always are. You'll have to drop by. Yesterday they did something called 'GlobalWorming,' which consisted of a lot of unattractive naked young people with tattoos and body piercings writhing around on a plastic sheet covered in motor oil to protest something or other perfectly ghastly that ExxonMobil was doing out there in the Third World."

"It was *olive* oil!" Tally put in. "It wasn't *really* motor oil."

"Please," said Briony with a drawl. "They looked like huge uncooked prawns, rolling about in the grease like that. Dreadfully earnest, the young. Utter bores."

"And you did not . . . protest . . . when you were at Bryn Mawr?"

"Oh hell yes. Protest was part of the Core Curriculum. Along with Good Works. We were all such intense little socialists then, sitting on piles of Grandaddy's money and cursing capitalism like Tartars. Tally here was one of the first Brecons to protest the Vietnam War, weren't you, Tally?"

"Yes. It was a *disgraceful* imperialist adventure. Bree was all for it."

"What? In favor of the Vietnam War?"

"Yes, I was," said Briony. "Daddy was in the Army. It gave you a different view. If there were any imperialists in that war, they were all Russians. After Americans win their wars, all they leave behind is their dead. Anyway, all that's a complete bore. And we were having such fun slanging the art school—"

"I know this art school," said Duhamel, giving her an impish smile. "They have invited me here to Savannah in the first place."

Briony was not discomfited in the slightest, seemed genuinely delighted.

"Really? Well, you'll see what I mean, then, won't you? Poor man. And what was your specific crime?"

"I'm here to discuss a possible photo exhibition later in the spring."

"Dear God, what is it? 'Toward a Deconstruction of Dystopia: Panoramas of Open-Pit Slag Heaps'? That sort of dreadfully urgent stuff?"

"Not really," said Duhamel, clearly enjoying himself. "It's a collection of photographs, taken of older women. I'm something of a collector—"

"Of older women?" said Tally, cutting in. "Well, you've come to the mother lode today, Mr. Duhamel. Doddering Old Bats and Crotchety Crones piled up to the roof beams. Place is crawling with them. What's your slide show called? Not 'Toward a Deconstruction of Dystopia,' I hope?"

"Not at all. The theme is the 'Odalisque in Autumn.' "

"Is it?" said Briony. "How very Ingres. What sort of photos are they?"

"Black-and-white, made with a special gel film. They've been compared to Karsh or Hurrell by people who should know better."

"Are they *erotic?*" said Tally with a tone.

"That depends on the woman in the picture. If she is, so is the shot."

"You find older women erotic?" said Briony.

"I find older women *interesting*. Often that is also very erotic."

"And young women?" asked Briony, probing.

"I find young women—what is the word?—like a young bug. *Larval?*"

Tally laughed at that, with a bit of a smoker's bray but real. Briony liked his answer too and warmed to the man, in spite of that fleeting contemptuous flicker in his brown eyes when he had looked at Tally.

"Well, I'd be intrigued to hear your take on the town after a few days. The whole place reeks of that Women's Institute sort of pious decay. Everyone in Savannah thinks of herself as . . . what is the word, Tally?"

Tally, not happy to have Briony getting all of Mr. Duhamel's attention, provided the word *louche* with a bit of a pout. Briony was on a tear, which was unusual for her. Her normal manner, when out and about in a crowd, was to stand resolutely alone in a corner with a glass of single malt and her trademark what-fresh-hell-is-this? expression firmly in place.

Briony Keating, thought Tally, was . . . *interested.*

"Louche. Thank you, sweet. Where, in actual fact, they're about as racy and decadent as the DAR. And they have mean mouths. The only way not to get slandered in this town is to never miss a dinner party. Everyone feels they have to burn as brightly as . . . fireflies. One gets terribly tired."

"Bree, I've got to . . . you know?"

Have a smoke

"Of course, Tally, you do that."

"Will you still be here?"

Briony looked at Duhamel and then back at Tally.

"Of course! Where would we go?"

Tally, who knew Briony pretty well, gave Jules Duhamel a slow, sly smile meant to convey the possible advantages to Mr. Duhamel of waiting for her swift return, patted Briony on the arm, and made her way through the pressing crowd, passing from shadow to light and back into shadow again as the crowd swallowed her up. Beethoven had come at last to the end of his lunar reverie, and now the young piano player was sitting at the bar, his black tie undone and his rented dinner jacket draped carefully on the back of the stool, watching the elderly barman construct a large vodka martini.

The walls seemed suddenly to close in, and the low, genial conversations of these dear familiar women now hit her ear like a flock of farm geese objecting to a stranger. Duhamel seemed aware of this alteration in her mood. Without appearing to withdraw from the group, he led her to a more private corner, by the long, wood-paneled walkway that led to the lounge.

"Do you have . . . commitments, after this event?"

"Nothing in particular," she said, her throat tightening. "Tally and some of the Brecons are talking about a dinner cruise on the river, but I don't do boats anymore. And you?"

To her mild surprise, he looked at his watch—an antique Breguet—and sighed. "Now that I have met you, I wish I did not. But I have to go to this . . . avant-garde snake pit . . . to meet with the director. This I am told will be over by six. After that, there is to be some sort of dinner with the committee."

"You poor devil. Drink, quietly but steadily. It's your only hope."

"But I am, I admit, feeling rather tired. Jet-lagged?"

"You've just arrived from some exotic shore, have you?"

"From London only, I'm afraid. Are you staying with friends?"

"No. I'm here, at the Forsyth. I leave tomorrow. For New York."

"Manhattan? You live there? How exciting."

"No. I have a little place on the Hudson River, a few miles north. I work at the academy, actually. It's pretty close."

"The academy?"

"The military academy, I mean. West Point?"

He smiled, really one of his best, and Briony, who was already feeling a kind of erotic vertigo, found herself falling right into it, eyes wide open.

"West Point? I am amazed. Where you are this dangerous spy?"

"Where I am this dangerous librarian."

"What a shame. I so wanted to meet a spy. Well, I have to go, whether I wish to or not. Please give my regrets to Miss Bowering. Perhaps we will meet in the bar, later?"

"Not a chance. I'll be in my room, dead to the world."

"I see. You are alone, then? Your husband . . . ?"

"Off in Odessa, I hear, fumbling away at his poxy Ukrainian pierogi."

"Pierogi?"

Briony's smile had deep and bitter roots, from the pain he saw in it.

"It's some kind of doughnut, I think. Dylan picked her up in a chat room, so they tell me. Poor girl. Instead of a rich American, she got my needle-dicked husband, who, thanks to my lawyer, is also virtually penniless."

Duhamel looked a little off balance then, but he recovered.

"Ah, then, of course, your children . . . ?"

"My son's in . . . the military. I'm not sure where he is right now. And my daughter? We are currently not on amiable ground. We do not speak."

"No. What a shame."

"Not really. We have agreed to disagree on the subject of her father. She takes the view that I am too controlling, and I take the view that he's a whoremongering, poodle-faking parasite who crossed me once too often."

Duhamel's expression went through a number of changes, all of which were hard to read. "Would it be . . . terribly offensive . . . if I were to ask—?"

Briony fixed him with a look, but gently, smiling carefully at him.

"I would find it terribly offensive to be gossiped about . . . Jules."

His face hardened imperceptibly, just enough to show his edges.

"I do not . . . gossip . . . Briony."

That brief glitter of cold, hard steel under the velvet did it.

She was gone, she thought.

Quite gone.

"Room 511, then. Around nine. Don't be seen."

Duhamel bowed again, a brief inclination, his eyes never leaving hers. He turned to walk away then, and she called after him, in a throaty whisper.

"Jules . . ."

He stopped, turned, his expression once again unreadable.

"Yes, Briony?"

"If you wish," she said, "you may bring your camera."

LONDON

SHOREDITCH

The only factory left in England where stainless-steel hand tools such as the glass cutter bearing the mark H&R were still being made was a tumbledown redbrick Dickensian sprawl scattered liberally about the landscape along Myrtle Walk. There, Dalton found the ancestral digs of the venerable old firm of Higgins and Robeling, resting in the hulking shadow of Hackney Community College. This was far out in the wilds of Shoreditch; for the uninitiated, Shoreditch is to Belgravia as lime green Crocs are to a pair of Cole Haan slippers.

Dalton set himself up in an improvised OP at one of the local "eateries" provided for the sustenance of the unhappy inmates of Hackney Community College, a dark, dim, dank pit of a place called the Stag at Bay; they even had a large copy of the Landseer etching framed above the bar. It was one of those prefabricated Olde Tyme Pubs that had at one time spread out across the globe to inflict the unique consequences of authentic English cuisine upon an unsuspecting world and which had now, like Pomeranian vetch weed, come full circle to sprout themselves all over suburban London.

He took up his regular position in a booth at the back of the place with lines of sight to every entrance, front and rear, as well as decent coverage of the showroom of the Higgins and Robeling factory across the street. He ordered his usual, a Guinness and a steak-and-kidney pie. This was his third day trailing a wing on the London watch. He settled in with a sigh to watch the rain sheeting down across the phony Tudor glasswork that fronted the pub.

It was after three on a rainy late-December Friday. The old year, laden with grave new alarms in the Far East and on the turbulent borders of Russia, was stumbling toward a well-earned grave in this Sargasso season of the Holy Days, the post-Christmas week. A bank of clouds, as low, damp, and utterly depressing as the underside of the Battersea Bridge, had arrived from the Channel a few days ago and spread itself out across London, the Home Counties, and all the way up the Thames Valley.

Once it got nicely settled in, all comfy-cozy like, it went right to work lashing down a dirty bone-chilling, heartbreaking half sleet, half rain all over the place for days and days and days on end, with no sign of letting up until long after Hogmanay, if ever.

The façade of the Higgins and Robeling shop had once been cheerfully decked out in green-and-red bunting enlivened by several threadbare strings of blinking Christmas lights, but days of unrelenting rain had reduced this brave display to a limp network of moldy gray-green rags and a few plucky pin lights that twinkled on regardless, through the mist and fog, in the best traditions of Old Blighty.

Dalton had checked in, as T. Coward, Purveyor of Stainless-Steel Polishing Systems, Lorne Park, Ontario, Canada, at a small boutique hotel called Blakes, just off the Old Brompton Road. He was staying away from his Agency flat in Wilton Row until the game that was being played grew clearer, although he had his theories. He had also made no attempt to contact either the offices of Burke and Single on Threadneedle Street or the Agency safe house in Marylebone, and he never even went near the U.S. Embassy in Grosvenor Square, not to mention his favorite local, the Grenadier, around the corner from his flat in Belgravia.

THE VENETIAN JUDGMENT 63

The Dan Wesson, sent on by Brancati in a diplomatic pouch to an Alitalia luggage booth at Gatwick that doubled as a dead drop for Italian couriers, was a reassuring but damned uncomfortable eight pounds in a leather shoulder holster that was spoiling the drape of his third-best navy blue pinstripe, but the trench coat he had inherited from Porter Naumann provided a kind of George Smiley–style English cover.

It was also, thankfully, waterproof and warm. He had, a few hours ago, been thrown a little off balance when he found three gold-tipped cigarette butts in the left-hand pocket of the coat. He'd been wearing this same topcoat that last night in Venice, when he and Porter Naumann had shared some of Naumann's Sobranie Cocktails in the Piazza San Marco. If the encounter with Naumann's ghost had been an hallucination from start to finish, where in hell did these cigarette butts come from?

It was an existential conundrum he didn't care to contemplate. Guinness was a great antidote to existential conundrums, so he had a few, and waited, and the hours passed, and the rain fell in steady wind-driven sheets, and the passersby made their molelike way back and forth in the driving rain, with their collars up and their heads down, grimly enduring the rising damp and the ague-inducing chills of a dreary English winter that was making the venerable old town seem like one huge concentration camp smacked down in the middle of a swamp. In other words, utter dank misery, relieved every now and then by flashes of dismal gloom.

THEN CAME *THIS* DAY, the late afternoon of the third day, and the last day Dalton was willing to sit here like a drowning duck: he was considering other more risky tactics to get this game in play, whatever it was, while poking listlessly at something gray and gristly called "bubble and squeak." He suspected that the title of the dish came from the family names of the first two Norway rats who had found themselves included in the recipe. The publican, who had made him two days back as some sort of high-priced PI working the adultery business, suddenly loomed up at the gates of the booth, brushing back his Hitler mustache with one tobacco-stained finger and offering Dalton a cell phone on a battered tin tray.

"'Ere's a caller fer yer," he said in a thick Midlands accent, neither wasting words nor having any to waste. Dalton looked at the phone, and then up at the blunt, fistlike face of the publican, who had a large flat nose that might have been shaped with a mallet and small brown eyes like raisins shoved into a suet pie.

"For me?"

The publican shuffled his hobnails, rearranged his pen wiper again.

"Th'all be a Mr. Pownall?"

Dalton thought it over and then nodded.

"Lef'ti fer yer, din't she? Ba the wif," he said, or may have said.

"The cell phone? It was left here by . . ."

The look on the man's face said, as clearly as if written on his brow, *And I already told yer that, din't I, you daft berk.*

"Gimme a quid, she did, sed'if yed cum ba, I'm to old'er phone, privylike, till she call. And 'ere's yer 'ere, the na, and 'ere's 'er callin', yus?"

"Ah? The wife? *My* wife?"

The publican, who may have reached the conclusion that Dalton was either deaf or retarded, tried to clarify the issue by saying all the same things all over again, only much louder, which was a tremendous help of course.

But he finished with a description that stayed with Dalton for weeks afterward: "Tall bint, wif lorly garms? Very queenly like? Any gate, she's on t'line 'ere now, sor, as I ha' pressed the t'ingy."

"She's on the line right now?" he said, taking the cell phone and putting it to his ear. The publican nodded and took himself off right sprightly, shaking his round, bumpy head and muttering darkly to himself.

"I heard that," said Mandy Pownall. "He called me a bint!"

"True, but he said you had 'lorly garms' and was very 'queenly like.' "

"You got the package."

"Obviously. What took you so long?"

"Someone had to hold the fort while you were moping around in Venice like a lovesick lemur. I gather you're still at that dreadful pub?"

"Actually, I've grown very fond of it. I can't bring myself to leave."

"You're probably stuck to the bench. Wait there."

TECHNICALLY, Dalton did as he was told and waited. Tactically, he did what he was trained to do and moved to a location across the street, a glass-walled bus stop with large red-lettered signs that warned people who boarded the buses that if they didn't take care, they would eventually find themselves at the Old Street tube station, and then where would they be, eh?

After about a half hour, he came on point, as a squat black London cab squelched to a halt by the entrance to the Stag at Bay. He noted the number in case it was one of the Agency's car-pool units, which it was not. The cab, as the most humble cocoons often do, delivered itself of a real Mayfair butterfly.

First came the brolly, a long, slender black tube that shot up out of the cab's interior and blossomed like a time-lapse film of a wet black flower opening, followed immediately by the lady herself, recorded in *Burke's* and the *Almanac de Gotha* as Cynthia Magdalene deLacey Evans Pownall, but known around Sloane Street and Berkeley Square more simply as Mandy.

Today, she was long, lean, and damn-your-eyes elegant in a shimmering black capelike raincoat and high black boots. Long black gloves, of course. The coat, unbuttoned and flaring in a gust of wind, revealed a long, formfitting knit dress in a smoky charcoal hue, the mock turtleneck rising up her graceful neck. At her throat was a strand of large black pearls. The dress clung to her thoroughbred body all the way down, perhaps out of sheer sensual delight, suggesting, to the observant male eye, that she may have been wearing nothing at all under it.

Mandy hesitated at the curb, cool, composed, with none of Cora's earthy fire, a pale English rose compared to Cora's dark blue dahlia, her long silvery hair flying in the rain-sodden wind, her expression intense as she scanned the terrain, fixing quickly on Dalton's figure inside the bus stop.

In spite of her striking presence, Mandy Pownall had managed to adapt to the cloak of obscurity and the reflexive diffidence of an active field officer. None of which was at all in evidence this afternoon.

She had been Porter Naumann's lover and friend, as well as the central pillar of Burke and Single, the London banking house they ran for the Agency. After his murder and the aftermath, she had been drawn into a more active role in the field operations of London Station.

They sent her to Maidenhill and Camp Peary to pick up the essentials of basic tradecraft, and she now worked at London Station, under the lecherous eye of the reptilian Anthony Crane, too fond of the Americans to be accepted by the Brits as one of them and too British to be fully trusted by Langley. Her tradecraft, once uncertain, had improved to the point that she had gotten out of the cab in a driving rain and immediately spotted Dalton, right where she expected him to be.

"Bloody hell," she called out to him, "I'm drowning here, you sod."

Dalton crossed the street while she watched him, her broad smile changing into a disapproving frown as she got a better look at his face.

When he reached her, she shook her head slowly, touched the wound in his cheek, and then ran her hand around his neck, pulled him down to her, and kissed him gently on the lips. A delicate, sensual touch, breathing him in and surrounding him with her scent, something spicy, with citrus and sandalwood in it.

The fact that they had not been—and, if Dalton could hold out, would not ever be—lovers was a touchy issue between them, since Mandy officially disapproved of heroic fidelity, and she particularly disapproved of heroic fidelity to fragile Italian crybabies who couldn't take a simple bullet to the head without getting all pouty and running off to hide out at Daddy's villa in Capri. She released him, stepping back to take him in, her gray eyes troubled.

"I heard you were coming apart. I didn't believe it. Now I do."

"I'm happy for you. Maybe we can dilate on that theme inside," he said, taking her arm and leading her back to his booth at the rear of the pub. The barman came over, perhaps just to get a second look at her "lorly garms," and went away again to fetch her a pot of tea and a mug. When he had come back and gone again, Dalton reached into his pocket and took out the glass cutter.

"I take it there's some kind of trouble with these people?"

Mandy flinched at the open display of the glass cutter, took it, and put it in her purse, snapping the latch with a certain dramatic emphasis.

"Why not put a notice in *The Guardian*? You hapless wretch."

"It's a glass cutter, Mandy. Not a dagger dripping blood. Don't be such a dramatist. I take it there's a problem with the Glass Cutters?"

Mandy sipped at the tea, made a face, and set it down.

"Utter swill," she said.

"And such small portions?"

"You know the Glass Cutters? What they do?"

"I know the essentials."

"Dangerous work, theirs, would you say? Lots of wear and tear?"

"The Glass Cutters? God no. Mind work, but not . . . why?"

"Well, my lad," she said, sipping at her tea, "you may want to revise that view, since they seem to be dying like . . ."

"Flies?"

"Such a cliché," she said, making a face, "but there it is."

"But many of them are . . . getting on, aren't they?"

"Old age has its burdens, I agree," she said, giving him a look over the rim of her cup, "but being tortured to death is not usually one of them. Not in England, at any rate, although I admit that the National Health does all it can."

NEW YORK STATE

Briony Keating's "little place on the Hudson" reminded Jules Du-hamel of Berchtesgaden, although Hitler, who had the Bavarian taste for vulgar excess, would never have built such a Lutheran home: it was a square, slightly stolid stone fortress done in the Federal style, with six bedrooms, maids' quarters, a large book-lined study, an honest working kitchen. Its best feature was a long stone-walled, low-beamed living room that took up all of the home's riverside view.

This open, light-filled, masculine space was filled with old saddle-leather couches and armchairs grouped around a large cut-stone fireplace, with a wall of antique sash windows on either side. A collection of Civil War weapons took up most of one wall, and six rather good oil paintings of the Adirondacks took up another.

The house overlooked the rolling Hudson River valley and the low blue mountains far to the west. It also had a small stone carriage house, built in the same Federal style, that had once been a stable. This was where Briony Keating kept her private office. He had not been shown this office. Yet.

The home rested on a shelflike outcropping of land that had been extensively planted a long time ago, so the entire three-acre estate now stood in a grove of ancient oaks and wind-twisted jack pines.

The house was set squarely down in the middle of a rolling park that led to a steep drop into the broad brown Hudson River, which swirled massively in a long, lazy bend below the edge. All of this was tinted pale amber by the patina of old money that seemed to lie upon it like the soft winter light that bathed it every afternoon.

The house had been built by Briony's great-great-grandfather, a West Point man, she explained, who served with John Buford's cavalry, and had been severely wounded in the first day at Gettysburg. It seemed to be important to her, so he was careful to appear interested.

Duhamel had no idea who John Buford was, and he was a little vague on the details of the American Civil War, although he suspected that Gettysburg was somewhere in Pennsylvania. But he had always been good at looking as if he were listening, and getting Briony to speak freely about her life was important to him.

He listened attentively and with every appearance of intense interest as she explained that the house had originally been built on the site of an old riverside inn that had been a stop on the famous Underground Railway, the route escaping slaves from the South had taken to reach Canada. *Really*, said Jules Duhamel, *how fascinating. Was the railway really underground?*

But he hadn't said that out loud, and he listened with counterfeit attention—his mind wandering a bit as he took in one priceless antique after another—the landscape in the study would need some verification, but it could be an original Lauren Harris—she even took him down to the basement to show him what looked like a massive cast-iron boiler set into a wall of fieldstone but which actually turned out to be the concealed gateway to an underground tunnel running from the main building across to the carriage house. She launched into some tiresome narrative connected to a tunnel collapse at some point and the shocking costs involved in opening it up again. Her voice faded into a kind of soothing background murmur . . . Slaves . . . Pinkerton men . . . An escape to the carriage house by moonlight . . . Even a secret speaking tube that ran from the tunnel up to the kitchen.

Duhamel abhorred tunnels of any kind—wouldn't ride the London Tube or the Paris Metro at gunpoint—and this one was little better than a dank, dark hole-in-the-wall, lined in clotted moss and dripping stones, and it stank of the grave. Briony went on and on, rather too much of this for his taste, but at any rate the house—particularly the treasures it contained—were quite appealing. He felt that things were going wonderfully well so far, and he had to admit that the house was a perfect place to bring a lover. It was made even more private by the fact that Briony had sent her aging housekeeper back to Charleston for the holidays and they were perfectly alone.

If memory served, and there were times when he felt it was badly failing him along with everything else, they had made love all day and every day in practically every open, flat, and reasonably soft space the house provided, and in one or two of the knobbier corners as well.

While this was not strictly true, he recalled some interludes where champagne from Briony's cellars may have been involved, this was how it seemed to him, caught in the eye of this sexual storm called Briony Keating. It was as if Briony had just discovered sex and was determined to get her master's in it by the end of the first week. As for Duhamel, he simply held on for dear life and hoped she wouldn't snap off anything he really needed.

This afternoon, as the pale winter light was fading into the west and the deep cold was rising out of the gorge, they were sitting, naked under fox furs, on an Adirondack-style couch padded with plaid cushions, breathing a little heavily after their exertions and sharing a bottle of claret, when the phone rang. They were about four days and three nights into the New York State part of their affair, and so far Briony had been ignoring phone calls, e-mails, letters, and any other kind of message from the outer world.

But this time she sighed, and gathered some of the furs around her, rising, showing him a flash of her lovely body. She padded across the flagstones and went in through the sliding-glass doors that led into the living room. As she went, Jules Duhamel noted that, unlike the other times this phone had rung, the ringtone was different, as if the caller's number had a special identifying code.

He gathered the silky furs in close, drank some more of the claret, and savored the view across the river. America truly was a lovely country, and here he was, like a blade, deep in the beating heart of it.

LONDON

"Tortured to death?" said Dalton, not really believing Mandy, who could be cinematic if it amused her.

"Yes," she said, without a trace of lightness, her expression suddenly grave. "Tortured. They're saying it's a robbery gone wrong, but there are complicating factors . . . I think something is very wrong with the Agency . . . Look, Micah, I want you to read something, but don't *touch* anything."

She took an envelope out of an inside pocket, turned it upside down, and let the papers inside it slip out onto the table. Dalton leaned forward to read them:

CASE NINETEEN WORKING GROUP

URGENT SURGE QUERY <u>all resources</u> concerning VE-NONA-SUBSET and GLASS CUTTER activities in-house or by neighbors and cousins emphasis on any link to <u>VENONA 95</u> decrypt "UNIDENTIFIED COVER DESIGNATION 19" in *VENONA 8/7/1953* ISSUED 10/9/74 (attached) Report assembly classified UMBRA and EYES/DIAL. Final summary to be conveyed by recipient direct to this sender. <u>No information concerning this audit is to be communicated in ANY FORMAT to D. Cather DD-OPS-NCS pending final audit review by POTUS/DNI/NSC. ENTITIES BREACHING THIS DI-RECTIVE WILL BE SEQUESTERED FORMALLY SANC-TIONED AND TERMINATED WITH PREJUDICE.</u>

EYES/DIAL MARIAH VALE IR/AUDITS/HQ

VENONA

~~TOP SECRET~~

USSR   Ref. No: ▆▆▆▆ (of 18/7/1953)

Issued: ▆▆▆ 10/9/74

Copy No.: 301

<u>3RD REISSUE</u>

"19" REPORTS ON DISCUSSIONS WITH "KAPITAN", "KABAN" AND
ZAMESTITEL' ON THE SECOND FRONT

(1943)

From: NEW YORK

To: MOSCOW

No: 812   29 May 1943

To VIKTOR[i].

   "19"[ii] reports that "KAPITAN"[iii] and "KABAN"[iv], during conversations
in the "COUNTRY [STRANA][v]", invited "19" to join them and ZAMESTITEL'[vi]
openly told "KABAN"

[10 groups unrecovered]

second front against GERMANY this year. KABAN considers that, if a second
front should prove to be unsuccessful, then this [3 groups unrecovered]
harm to Russian interests and [6 groups unrecovered]. He considers it
more advantageous and effective to weaken GERMANY by bombing and to use this
time for "[4 groups unrecovered] political crisis so that there may be no
doubt that a second front next year will prove successful."

   ZAMESTITEL' and

[14 groups unrecovered]

". 19 thinks that "KAPITAN" is not informing ZAMESTITEL' of important military
decisions and that therefore ZAMESTITEL' may not have exact knowledge of
[1 group unrecovered] with the opening of a second front against GERMANY and its
postponement from this year to next year. 19 says that ZAMESTITEL'
personally is an ardent supporter of a second front at this time and considers
postponement

          [Continued overleaf]

VENONA

VENONA

~~TOP SECRET~~

2   (of 18/7/1958)

[15 groups unrecovered]

can shed blood

[13 groups unrecoverable]

recently shipping between the USA and

[40 groups unrecovered]

The "COUNTRY" hardly [9 groups unrecovered] "insufficient reason for delaying a second front."

No. 443   MĒR[vii]

Footnotes: [i]   VIKTOR   : Lt. Gen. P.M. FITIN.

            [ii]   19   : Unidentified cover designation.

            [iii]   KAPITAN   : i.e. "CAPTAIN"; Franklin D. ROOSEVELT.

            [iv]   KABAN   : i.e. "BOAR"; Winston CHURCHILL.

            [v]   COUNTRY   : U.S.A.

            [vi]   ZAMESTITEL' : i.e. Deputy - therefore possibly
                                   Henry Agard WALLACE, who was
                                   ROOSEVELT's Deputy (Vice-President)
                                   at this time: later he is referred to
                                   by the covername "LOTsMAN".

            [vii]   MĒR   : Probably Iskhak Abdulovich AKhMEROV.

Dalton read all three pages quickly, and then again much more slowly. When he had finished, Mandy used one of the pub's stir sticks to get the papers safely back into the envelope. "They're reactive-dye-marked and touch-sensitive. I have to get all this back into Pinky's lockbox by tomorrow."

"They're isolating *Cather*? Why in hell?"

"Not just him. Vale has a short list, but he's on it."

"Who else is on it?"

"I can't get at that. Given the inference that if the other people on it are all in Cather's age range in order to have any connection with the original Venona cable intercepts, there can't be more than five or six at the outside."

"That's a small base. Can't you work back from that? Take the roster, limit the search profile to only those who fit the parameters, add in a limiting factor for access—"

"Yes, that's the thing: access to what? We don't know what triggered this audit, other than the fact that it had something to do with a Glass Cutter operation. I only know Cather's on it because I side-lined this encryption."

"How did you do that? There's no way you're on her distribution loop."

"No. We're too close to Cather. Pinky decrypted it for Tony—"

" 'EYES/DIAL' means the recipient deciphers it himself—"

"Tony couldn't decipher a finger jammed into his left eye. Pinky always does it for him. Pinky knows he has to do whatever Tony tells him because Tony knows he's a latent perv and could burn him whenever he wanted to. And he would. Pinky also leaves his office unlocked whenever he's in the loo scrubbing away at his flippers. I nipped in and rigged his lockbox codes—"

"Why? Did you *expect* this memo?"

"No. But I knew there was something in the wind when Tony Crane told me to stop copying 'DD Clandestine' on the Operational

Summaries. Cather was always in that loop and now suddenly he's not? Tony was vague about it, gave me some nonsense about not cluttering Cather's desk with trivia. What struck me was that I never heard from anyone at Cather's end, you know, asking about the summaries, where were they, that kind of thing. I made up some reason to call Cather's office, and Sally Fordyce answered—"

"Sally? She used to be with Jack. How's she doing?"

"Well, after what happened with you and Jack Stallworth, they really put her through the attar press, but Cather vouched for her and took her onto his staff. Anyway, Sally mentioned some routine thing she saw in that week's London summary, and I didn't know what the hell she was talking about."

"So what they've done is construct a quarantine screen around Cather's office, make it look like he's still getting all the real stuff—"

"Including composing fake OpSums from London Station—"

"That's what they did to Aldrich Ames," said Dalton, stunned that things had gotten that serious. "That kind of quarantine operation would need top-level approval. Right from the Director of National Intelligence. He'd have to inform the President, and maybe his cabinet as well."

"That's what I thought too. And I knew Tony wouldn't isolate Deacon Cather unless he was sure he could get away with it. And he'd want it written down in a formal memo, so he could use it to cover himself if Cather somehow survived . . . whatever it was. So I've been hitting Pinky's lockbox almost every day for the last month—"

"Why take that risk? And why cover for Cather? He's a grown-up."

"I know how you feel about him. I know Cather promised to bring you back in, and then he never called. I do think he meant what he said, and I think he's left you out in the cold right now because he knows he's under some sort of a shadow and doesn't want you dragged into it. Anyway, there's no way in the world that Deacon Cather is a mole. *If* there is a mole at all, which I doubt. Mariah Vale is using this as a way to step all over the operational side, that's all. She hates it when anybody at Clandestine Services actually goes out and *does* things in the real world. If she had her way, everybody in Clandestine would sit around in the Bubble listening to Yanni and visualizing world peace. Anyway, this memo turned up two weeks ago. When I saw it, all I could think of was to warn you—"

"Me? Why?"

"You were, *are* one of his Cleaners. If Mariah Vale was trying to hobble Cather, then she'd start by pulling in all his Cleaners and running them through the ringer. Porter always said, in any audit one way to find out what the target is trying to protect is to find out what sectors he never seemed to be interested in at all. So what he did with the Cleaners Unit would be one way to help build up a total picture of what Cather was thinking and doing, and when. You know the drill: find the mole by finding out what the enemy knows and when he knew it and work backward through the possible sources of that information. Look for points of intersection, contact opportunities, travel itineraries that might coincide with major tactical shifts in the opposing intelligence operations. Watch for our sources going silent or doubling and run that backwards to see if that coincides with something the mole might have done, a trip he might have taken. Build up a complete map of the mole's influence and you will eventually get him. That's how MI6 finally got Philby and how we got Ames. That's exactly what Vale is doing. She's already called in Dewey Strickland and Javier Souza and Miles Terry—"

"I thought Miles Terry was on the *Orpheus?*"

Mandy winced at the mention of the ultrasecret floating CIA

prison disguised as a hospital ship that Porter Naumann had set up for Cather a couple of years back, using the Burke and Single banking house as a cover for the operation.

"He is. Or was. The *Orpheus* was in the eastern Med, off Rhodes. They sent a Sea King to take him off. He was pretty ticked because they had just taken on a new houseguest."

"Houseguest? You mean a *defector*?"

"That's the rumor. One of the old Moscow Center guys. Spent fifteen years as a *Rezident* in D.C. They didn't name him but Pinky had made a note beside the decryption. 'Y. Kirensky'—mean anything?"

"You don't mean *Yitzak* Kirensky! Christ, he's famous. He's one of the biggest old thugs in Moscow Center! Don't tell me he came in?"

"Yes. I think that was the name. He must be pretty old by now. He came in to the station officer in Athens. They got him onto the *Orpheus* the same day. The guy had some kind of pacemaker, and it was malfunctioning. Kirensky, he was pretty fragile and seemed anxious to talk. Miles felt they were right on the edge of a—"

"Man," said Dalton, thinking of the Yurchenko defection in 1985, "I really hate defectors. They're either making stuff up to justify a huge payout and an estate in Maryland or they're part of some Confusion Op."

"This guy seems legitimate. He had already given them some material on Russian negotiations with the Iranians about nuclear technology. Langley cross-checked it with other sources, and the data was solid. Could only have come from someone high up in the Kremlin."

"How do you *know* all this stuff?"

"I'm a sneaky little minx. And it all goes through Pinky's lockbox."

Pinky was Stennis Corso. He was called Pinky only behind his back. Tony Crane's XO was a small, round seal-like man with slicked-back blond hair and tiny ears, very shy, definitely pink, who could not bear to be touched and who washed his soft, pudgy pink hands obsessively, perhaps with good reason.

Corso contained in his formidable mind almost all of the secret histories of London Station going back to the Cold War. He was the station's chief archivist and also its resident expert on the Balkans and any issues that touched on the Adriatic and the Aegean. This required the talents of a Princeton historian, which he had been, as well as an ability to calmly consider the tactics and strategies of the region's worst people without anger or prejudice, seeing them in the clear—a priceless asset to a CIA station.

He was therefore London Station's most valuable analyst, so critical that his latent pedophilia, never acted upon once he had left Cambridge and apparent now only in the care he took to conceal it, was, if not overlooked, then at least tacitly tolerated. Still, the Minders kept an eye on him.

"That's a serious security weakness in London Station. What if you get taken up by the Reapers? They'd have the Agency by the—"

"Now, that's the odd part, come to think of it. We've been monitoring the Russians here, as always, and they're not doing much of *anything*: no KGB thugs pretending to read the catalogues at the Tate Modern, no velvety Slavs cruising the fetish clubs looking to snap up another ambassador's ADC, not even the usual god-awful Trade and Commerce bun-fights that they used to throw to try and cuddle up to embassy sources. I mean, when you think of it, that's all pretty strange, isn't it? Even the Reapers, who are usually active in London, they've all been woolly bah-lambs for months now."

"They've just shaken up the Kremlin," said Dalton. "Putin's nailing down his base. Once he's got that done, they'll be back out in force. He wants to rebuild the USSR. I'm afraid these are the early days of Cold War Two."

"Yes, so am I. I hope the new guy is up to it. If he's another Jimmy Carter, Putin will have his googlies for cuff links. Anyway, we're wandering. I figured you were Mariah Vale's next victim, and from what I was hearing—"

"Hearing? About *me*? Hearing from whom?"

"Issadore Galan. He was worried about you. He got in touch with me—"

Dalton sat back, staring at her.

"How? When?"

"After Chicago, when Cather didn't bring you to D.C. and you went back to Venice. He took one look and figured you were running off the rails. He contacted me—"

"How?"

"Sent me an invoice from Spink and Son, on Southampton Row. The gold coin people. I don't owe Spink and Son anything. But the invoice amount looked like it could be a time marker. And he was there."

"Christ, Mandy, it could have been anyone. There could have been a Reaper crew in a white van ready to take you right off the curb."

"I know. But I told you, they haven't been active lately—"

"They'd have made an exception for you—"

"Dear boy, you flatter me. Anyway, the invoice was for a set of Venetian florins, so I sort of made the connection. And I was right."

"How'd Galan get into London without Portcullis tagging him?"

"I asked. The old dwarf just smiled. I think he has a crush on me, by the way, although from what I hear he's no threat. Anyway, we set up a two-way system, which I'll explain later, and he kept me informed about you and how you were swooning around Venice, pining for that Florentine ninny-hammer—"

"I'm aware of your feelings about Cora, okay? The point, please."

"The point is, when I realized you were probably going to get picked up by Mariah Vale's evil minions, I sent the cigarette case to Galan."

"You couldn't just pick up the phone? Or get Galan to say something?"

"I wasn't going to mention the Glass Cutters to Galan, was I? And I wanted it to be something only you could figure out. Without employing any method that Vale could intercept. I don't think she's corrupted FedEx . . . yet."

"Galan put your cigarette case on Brancati's desk."

"Did he? Why not just give it to you? I guess he just likes being Byzantine. Or he doesn't like to do anything behind Brancati's back. The point is, you're here, and now we have to do something—"

" *We?* What do we have to do? Why us?"

"Micah, dear boy, do you *really* think Cather's some sort of mole?"

"Look, Mandy, whatever Cather is—and, no, I don't think he's a mole—this is not our problem. You're an officer at London Station, a long way from Langley, and I'm as good as off the roster entirely. And, not to be too petty, I don't owe Deacon Cather a damn thing."

"It's not *about* Cather, you manky git. This audit has derailed Clandestine. Until the DD gets cleared, our whole operational arm is crippled. With men and women in the field. In wartime. Don't you care about that?"

"Yes, of course I do. But, like I said, I'm on the outside look-ing in."

"We'll see about that. Do you have any money?"

"Yes, pretty much the whole budget from the Chicago thing."

"Zowie! So, we are in funds, my sweet?"

"*We?* What happened to all *your* money. Isn't your family—"

Mandy's mood changed a bit, a look of sadness flitting across her face like the shadow of a swift flying overhead.

"Not anymore, my lad, I'm cut off. Poppy's gone off us Yanks since that bun-fight in Iraq. Gave me a bloody ultimatum, he did, the old teapot. Quit the Company or be thrust into the outer dark-ness to wither and die."

"What did you say?"

Mandy made a show of looking about the booth, under the table.

"I'm here, am I not? In the sinfully silky flesh?"

"But penniless?"

"For the nonce. I have the Agency pittance, sufficient to sustain a kind of grinding penury—rather like a monk but with silks and gar-ters. Anyway, yes, I do mean *we.* So, Micah, my darling lad, hero of the hour, last hope of the West, will you do it? Will you help me? For the motherland—"

"The *motherland?* You were born in Knightsbridge, Mandy. You're only an American citizen because your mother was from Santa Fe."

"Yes, so in my heart I'm really a Girl of the Golden West. Come on, Micah, please don't make me beg. Pleading's bad for my com-plexion."

Here she rolled out one of her famous up-from-under looks. Dal-ton always felt that look of hers in his lower belly. Many lesser men, when exposed to it without a welder's mask on, had simply burst into flames.

Nevertheless, Dalton wanted very much to say no.

It looked as if the Agency was once again ripping itself apart over internal security issues, as it had in roughly five-year cycles from the fifties to long after 9/11. Everybody at Clandestine knew the horror stories: the Jewels cipher machines being compromised by U.S. Marines at the Moscow embassy; Jimmy Carter and Stansfield Turner firing eight hundred and fifty experienced intelligence officers in the Far East and Asia in 1978, in the process deliberately wrecking Clandestine Services; Iran-Contra and the disastrous long-term effects of the Church Commission; the fallout at the NSA and the CIA from the FBI's Power Curve investigation; Howard and Pelton in 1985, which set them up for the Poison Pill gambit the KGB pulled off with the defection of Vitaly Yurchenko later that year, a Confusion Op worthy of Viktor Fitin himself.

The Yurchenko "defection"—he gave his CIA debriefing team the slip in November of 1985 and turned up back at his old desk in Moscow a Hero of the Revolution—resulted in the exposure, grotesque torture, and eventual execution of fifty-six high-value CIA sources in Russia and across the Soviet domain while sowing mass confusion and distrust throughout the entire espionage structure of the West. The Yurchenko affair created lasting rifts between the CIA and MI6, the French DGSE, the Syrians, the Mossad, the German BND, not to mention the FBI, the RCMP, and the NSA.

Bill Clinton, a man with a ferocious ideological antipathy for the Agency, took advantage of the general condemnation of the CIA in this period, along with what he called the "Peace Dividend," to gut its budget by thirty percent, to cull seasoned staffers from almost all the foreign stations, to forbid any Agency contact with what he called "unsavory sources" abroad, and to harry the CIA's very best Middle Eastern and Indonesian agents into forced retirement. Then, in 1995, as a kind of coup de grace, Clinton instructed Deputy AG Jamie Gorelick to forbid the FBI from exchanging intelligence with the CIA, or, for that matter, over the cubicle partition between the law enforcement side of the FBI and the intelligence-gathering side of the same damned agency, creating the infamous "wall" that effectively blinded the U.S. intelligence community just as militant Islam was on the rise.

Next came Aldrich Ames, Harold Nicholson, and of course all the famous, feckless, interagency cluster fucks that paved the way for September 11, the gross miscalculations about Iraqi WMDs . . . Taken all together, these events constituted a series of almost mortal blows to the Agency's professional credibility and to American Humint and Sigint operations worldwide.

Dalton, who saw the Agency clearly and understood it as well as any man alive, knew that this record appeared to be far more terrible than it actually was, since most of the Agency's successes—and there were literally thousands of them—never reached the public's eye in the first place. But these internal convulsions had almost wrecked the CIA, and now the whole self-defeating process seemed to be starting up all over again.

Not to mention the additional risk of getting involved in a mole hunt with a head-office carnivore like Mariah Vale at the other end. Attempting to conduct a parallel inquiry into the Glass Cutter case without her knowledge would be like trying to pluck a kitten out of a wood chipper.

On the other hand, what were his options?

Sooner or later, if his pattern held, two bottles of Bollinger and the Ruger for a chaser? Naumann was right: if he didn't have work, his wheels started to come off. And, in the end, there was also that pesky concept called "duty, honor, country." He'd sworn an oath with those words in it at one point, hadn't he? They rang a bell, anyway.

"Okay, what the hell, I'm in."

"Thank you," she said. "You won't regret it."

"Ha! Do you really believe that?"

She reached out, patted his cheek, the one without the bullet scar.

"Goodness no, dear boy, not a word of it."

NEW YORK STATE

Briony Keating, in the living room, holding the fur wrap over her breasts and belly, leaving the rest of her to shimmer in the warming light of the fire, picked up the phone and said the name that this caller needed to hear. His name was Hank Brocius, the AD of RA for the NSA and at one time, a long time ago, her lover for one brief summer in Rockport. Brocius made the correct reply, and gave her his report.

"Full name: Duhamel, Jules Thierry Dassault. Brown eyes, black hair going slightly gray, about five-eleven, runs one seventy-five. Born in Chantilly des Bains, France, November twenty-three, 1973, to Lucien and Celeste Duhamel. Catholics, duly registered him in the baptismal record two days later, although the originals—take note—were destroyed in a fire in 'seventy-nine, so this comes from the National Records instead. No siblings. No birth issues. Always been healthy, other than some childhood problems with asthma. Parents, both deceased—looks like a car crash in Bilbao when he was ten. He was okay but got some burns on his back, which were repaired by cosmetic surgery when he was sixteen. Can't see his back from the shots you sent, so be sure to check, will you? By the way, as Fernando Lamas used to say, 'You look mahvelous, dahling.' I know, I know, I'll delete them. Or post 'em on Facebook. Anyway, the father owned a big chain of photo shops called Kiosks Lumières in Paris and Cannes, and the boy inherited a lot of money. He was sent by an uncle to live with relatives in Montenegro—he's some sort of minor Montenegrin royalty, is the word—I guess this is where he got the accent you were asking about. Educated in Paris, majored in visual arts and art history, spent time at the Sorbonne but did not graduate. Established a gallery in, get this, Saint Petersburg—I mean, the one in Russia—called Atelier Dassault. Very successful, according to the tax returns he files. Runs it under a numbered corporate shelter based in the Canaries. They sell to all the major houses. Concentrates on fine-art photography, and is well thought of as a shooter himself—had shows in Vienna, Prague, Paris—but is not well known in the U.S. other than that thing in Savannah. Nothing against him in any database. No known bad habits. Credit's fine, liquidity excellent. Healthy, no STDs—guy in Russia described him as 'serially monogamous.' Keeps in shape, obviously, from the shots you sent along. The DNA came back with all the right numbers for his nationality. I called a lot of people in Montenegro, other locations where he does business. Spoke to the girl who runs the gallery in Saint Pete. She said he was gone for the holidays—wouldn't say where—but he would likely call in soon. So, it all checked out—"

"And you think . . . what?"

"I think . . . I think he probably is what he says he is. Although I don't like the church-records fire, or the fact that his parents are dead. Also no siblings, no wife—not even engaged. And there are some shots of him—the Paris Station sent me his visa photo, for example—where he looks, I don't know, wrong. But who looks good in those shots? If you actually look like your passport shot, you're too sick to travel, right? I really worked that stuff, and there was nothing all that hinky, just the usual chaotic mess of a normal life. Point is, what do *you* think? I mean, he's right there in the house, isn't he? That's not like you, taking a risk, right? You want, we could flake him somehow, take him in on some phony visa gig, questions about his declaration. He's a foreign national—he's *French*, for chrissakes—we can heat him up, see if he shows any cracks? No muscle, no bruising, just a few hours of hard-ass interrogation by some steroidal federal thugs. I got just the guys. More I think about it, more I like the idea. If he comes through clean, we can set it up that you used your pull with ICE to get him sprung. Then it's all polka dots and moonbeams for you and the little frog prince, right?"

Briony stared at the fire for a while.

"I think you've done very well."

The man's voice was heavy with disappointment.

"So, no flaking a beef? You sure? Come on, just a *teensy* one?"

"No, I think I'm . . . satisfied . . . with the results. Very relieved."

"Too bad. Would have been fun. Do I send you the hard copy?"

"Yes. Send it to my office at Pershing Hall."

"Okay. Anything else?"

"Not now. Will you be accessible?"

"I'm off the grid for a while . . . that thing in London?"

"Yes. Terrible. I knew her. We all did."

"Well, the spanner's hit the spinners. Agency's trying to muscle in, but I'm not going to let them near this. Pack of seditious old kiddy diddlers slipping state secrets to the *Times*."

"Yes, I have heard your views. Have they decided anything?"

"Looks like a simple home invasion that went postal. I have follow-up people inbound right now. First Response said there was no sign that it had anything to do with her profession, no incursion attempts on the grid, no attempts to hack in anywhere so far. She had a lockboxful of jewels, gold, bearer bonds, and they got the numbers to open it, which supports the torture-for-robbery idea. Still, you sure you don't want some of our security crew up there with you?"

"No. I was rather worried about this one issue, which now seems to have been resolved, but other than that I'm fine."

"Yeah, well, I hope so. This guy checks out, I guess, but I don't like the idea of you making a brand-new friend at the same time that we lose Millie Durant. I don't like . . . coincidences."

"Neither do I. That's why I had you check it out. And you did."

"Yeah, okay, I'll stand down. By the way, you hear from Morgan lately?"

"No, I haven't."

"Last I heard, he was at NAS Souda. How long since you had a call?"

Briony tried to keep her fear out of her voice. Her son, Morgan Keating, was a twenty-six-year-old U.S. Navy medic. He had been sent out to the Naval Air Station at Souda Bay on the island of Crete a year ago. The base was isolated on the northwestern end of the island, so isolated that service there was pay-rated the same as duty at sea. Morgan had managed to get quarters off the base, which he shared with a couple of E4s. According to his last e-mail, thirty days ago, he was even dating a local girl. Briony didn't like to hover, so she hadn't been pushy about e-mail replies. But thirty-plus days was not at all like him. She had told herself—often—that there was a war on and that his silence could have any number of legitimate explanations.

"Oh, it's been a while now."

"Yeah? That's not like Morgan. That young man loves his mother. Want me to look into it? I got a guy with the Sixth Fleet. If he's on a medical deployment anywhere in the Med, I could probably find out."

"Oh, that's not necessary."

"You're being pretty oblique. The little frog prince around?"

"Possibly."

"Look, I'm gonna find out where your kid is, okay? There aren't that many places they can hide a Navy corpsman. I'll call back when I know something. You still got that little Sig P-230 around?"

"Yes, I keep it close."

"Good. Keep it *real* close. Nothing settles a lover's quarrel faster than a coupla Black Talons in the chitlins. You take care, you hear me?"

"I will. Thanks again."

When she set the phone down, Duhamel was standing in the open doorway, naked, with the last of the winter light a corona around him. Although he looked splendid, his face was in darkness, and there were only two small yellow sparks of firelight reflected in his deep-brown eyes. For a moment, she felt a shimmer of unease ripple through her.

"I'm sorry," he said from the shadows, his baritone purr carrying a note of concern, "but I could not help but overhearing something about *results*? That you are *relieved*? I do not mean to pry, but are you not well, Briony?"

She heard the note of genuine concern in his voice, and it warmed her. She was too old to fall in love, but you're never too old to be loved.

"No, nothing, just the usual woman stuff. Came back negative."

"Good," he said, relief flooding his voice, his posture changing. "I am not ready to lose . . . to lose your company. You are . . . important . . . to me."

Lovely words. She'd heard them before and believed them. Could she believe them now? All men were gifted liars in the early days. Getting laid seemed to inspire them. She was about to say something droll and cool when he stepped into the fire glow and she saw him in that golden light. She let the blanket fall and for a while stopped thinking about anything at all.

LONDON

THE STAG AT BAY, SHOREDITCH

"So . . . let's review," said Mandy, relaxing into the booth now that she had made her kill. "It all starts with the Glass Cutters, doesn't it?"

"Looks like it," said Dalton, reaching for his cigarettes, realizing as he did so that England, like all the nanny nations of the West, had banned smoking in public bars. Feeling a tad aggrieved, he called for a Guinness.

"What are they doing right now?"

"They're still working on all the Venona subsets," said Mandy. "All the intercepted cables from the Cold War and later. You knew that, didn't you?"

"I know what the Glass Cutters do, more or less. Decryption's not my thing. I suck at math and I hate crosswords. But I thought they wrapped up the Venona project in the eighties. Moynihan had all the Venona decrypts made public in 'ninety-five. Nobody even noticed, although the cables confirmed that Joe McCarthy was dead right about Alger Hiss and his Harvard—"

Mandy rolled her eyes, reached over, and patted his hand.

"What*ever*. Let it go, Micah. Ancient history. You're in danger of turning into this saggy old sorehead, pounding the long bar at the

Hicksville VFW until your false teeth pop out: 'Lissen up, sonny. Joe McCarthy was a gol-dern hero, I tell 'ee, ba tunderin' Jaysus!"

"He *was* a hero, a Marine combat vet, and I am *not* a saggy old—"

"Perhaps not yet, Micah, but you're well on your way. Can we get back to *my* subject, please? The Glass Cutters picked up where Venona left off, and now they're working their way through all the intercepted cables that Venona couldn't crack, as well as new stuff from the seventies and eighties. They're triangulating the cipher codes by using archival communiqués from places the Russians pulled out of when the Evil Empire collapsed. The Ukraine, Georgia, Latvia, Estonia, what used to be East Germany."

"What's this 'Venona 95 Unidentified Cover Designation 19' thing?"

"Yes. I saw that reference, and I admit I have no idea. From the context, I'd guess that Stalin had a source close to Roosevelt who was never exposed. They only know him as 'Unidentified Cover 19.' People who looked into it a few years back figured this 19 guy could have been Harry Hopkins, but he died of cancer in 'forty-six, so there wasn't a lot of attention paid. Other people said he was Eduard Beneš, and others were dead certain he was Owen Lattimore, or that it was code for Alger Hiss, although he worked for the GRU, not the KGB, and his code name was 'Ales.' So, it's still up for grabs. Find out who he was and then maybe you open up the box a bit—"

"You can bet they're trying," said Dalton.

Mandy nodded.

"Yes. As far as the decrypt itself, it looks like a report to a Soviet control officer named Viktor on talks Roosevelt and Churchill were having with Stalin about opening up a Second Front. Dated May 29, 1943."

"Cather was only ten in 'forty-three. He got to West Point in 'fifty-two, I think. Missed Korea. MOS was G2, Military Intelligence.

Worked against Castro, and *may* have been in Bolivia when the military shot up Che Guevara in 'sixty-seven. Did Vietnam, from 'sixty-eight to 'seventy-one. Served in Eye Corps, out of Anh Khe, up near the DMZ. Stallworth used to say he was probably MAC-SOG, and, if he was, he went the distance too, three tours in the open and a lot of black work. Did Phoenix in Laos and Cambodia. ADC at the Paris Accords in 'seventy-three. Got the Beirut watch after Hezbollah butchered Bill Buckley. May have done something with the Taliban after the Russians invaded Afghanistan. His whole era was the Cold War, Vietnam, up to the Soviet collapse in 'ninety-one. He was right in the middle of all of it. The link to some Agent 19 in a Venona cable from 1943 sure doesn't jump out."

"Not yet," said Mandy, "but the name Fitin rings a bell. Wasn't he the GRU colonel who specialized in making deep legends for his people?"

"Viktor Fitin was an espionage genius. They still teach him at Peary. Say the name Viktor to anybody in the trade, they'll know who you're talking about. Look, about the Glass Cutters, they're NSA, aren't they?"

"Technically," said Mandy, "but they're not working *at* Crypto City. The AD of RA at Fort Meade runs them. You remember him?"

"The ex-Marine with the burn scars on his face?"

"Yes, Hank Brocius. He hates the CIA, thinks we're all a gaggle of treasonous pencil necks. He didn't like the Glass Cutters being too near Langley, so he broke them up and scattered them all over. They stay in touch through shielded servers at Fort Meade. But whatever is going on, the Glass Cutters must be making *somebody* nervous."

"How do we know this?"

Mandy gave him her lifted-eyebrow-and-curled-lip look.

"Because, as I may have mentioned, somebody just killed one?"

"Yes. I meant, how do we know that all this is *connected*? You said they were calling it a random robbery that went bad. Where did this go bad?"

"Here. Right here in London. At her flat on Bywater Street in Chelsea."

"Jesus, who's got it, the Bobbies? The FBI? The Yard? MI5?"

"No. She was NSA, so Brocius wants his own people on it. Some NSA field agent named Audrey Fulton. The FBI raised hell, but the DNI made it happen. They're telling the Yard and MI5 that Fulton's crew is FBI, but actually they're part of Crypto City's security detail. London Station is to provide logistical resources only and otherwise to stay the hell away. As I said, Brocius hates the CIA."

"Then how are *we* involved? I know, duty, honor, country, and all that. But there's something else going on, isn't there? Something *personal*."

Mandy looked at Dalton for a while as if she were about to do something difficult that she knew she was going to have to do eventually and now the time had come. Her mood shifted abruptly, all the light leaving her face: "Yes, there is something . . . personal."

Dalton sat back, took in some Guinness.

"Okay. I thought there was more going on than you were saying."

Mandy considered Dalton for a time as if taking a reading on his mental state. Then she reached into her purse, took out a small digital camera. She did not hand it to him immediately but held it in her bone-china hands, looking down at it.

Her expression, normally mobile, reactive, with a quiver around her lips that very easily became a teasing smile, turned still, even grave. Watching a somber mood come over a person as innately sunny as Mandy Pownall was like watching a vandal spray-paint a stained-glass window.

Dalton braced himself for what was coming.

"I'm going to show you a file of digital shots, Micah. I wish I didn't have to. I wish I hadn't seen them myself. But I think you need to see them. They're from the crime scene . . . Micah, I really *do* hate to do this to you."

Mandy was deadly serious.

He felt his breathing alter, tried to get his adrenaline back down.

She was silent for a time, gathering herself.

"Well, let's get this behind us, then. The woman in the pictures had a name. Her name was Mildred Durant. They called her Millie. She was one of the original women who worked on the Venona Project under Colonel Carter. She had a long, full life, served her country well. She had children and grandchildren, and lots of people who loved her. You understand me?"

Dalton understood that only too well. Working as a Cleaner was like being a homicide cop, a priest, and an executioner. He had seen many photos of what was left of one of their agents or what an agent had done to someone else. Pictures of the victims caught in the obscene sprawl of violent death, of deliberate murder, impose a special burden on anyone who must look at them. The victim needs to be honored, to be recognized as a human being, and, for a moment, held in your own heart, as much as you can, as she was held in the hearts of those who knew and loved her in life.

You owed them that much.

Mandy passed the camera over to Dalton. He pressed the ON button and looked at the wide LCD screen. There were thirty pictures on the chip, taken from several angles. It was brutally clear from the shots that they were taken by the killer, or killers, before, during, and after the murder. Looking at what was being done to the frail nude body of an elderly woman was like looking into the sun. It couldn't be done for long, and Dalton was no different.

There was a long silence between them after he set the camera down. Mandy picked it up and put it in her purse again, handling it like poison, which it was. Dalton knew he would never forget those shots, that they'd come back to him every now and then for the rest of his life, that he was not the same man now that he had been a few seconds ago.

Mandy, knowing this, feeling it herself, reached out and put a hand on his wrist, not to comfort him so much as to touch another human in the midst of such a cold place.

"Micah, I have to tell you this part too. Whoever did this sent copies of the shots to everyone on the victim's e-mail list. Her kids. Her grandchildren. Her brother. College alumni. Hank Brocius too. Sound familiar to you?"

Dalton was staring at her, his expression setting like concrete. Mandy held his look.

"Yes, I thought it might."

Dalton looked out at the rain streaming down the pub windows. Night was coming on, and the little pin lights across the street were bravely blinking on in the storm. You could almost hear Vera Lynn singing, he thought: *When the lights go on again all over the world.* Then a procession of mole people passed by the windows of the pub, blurred brown figures hunched against the driving rain, braced against the coming of the night.

"But what about this home-invasion angle? I mean, taking the photographs? Sending them out to the family? Are there any records of that kind of thing happening in London—hell, anywhere in the U.K.?"

Mandy shook her head.

"Nothing *remotely* like this. Lots of things *as* weird: this *is* England, isn't it? We gave the world Jack the Ripper. But the . . . methods here? The extreme violence, the way it was . . . prolonged? I've seen crime scene shots like these only in one other place and that was when we were in Singapore."

Dalton was still struggling with it.

THE VENETIAN JUDGMENT   109

"I mean, didn't they find his body in the water off Santorini? Strangled with a scarf. Cut up. Sexually mutilated. Do you really think it's him?"

She considered it for a while, staring at her cold tea, listening to the rain. Finally, she said, "I really don't know for sure. What I do know is that the Glass Cutters stumbled onto something that brought Mariah Vale down on Deacon Cather's head, and now one of them is dead. And either the killing was random or it wasn't. And, if it wasn't, the NSA isn't going to let us poke around at their end, so we need a line of our own. And, as far as I can see, this is the only one we have."

"Kiki Lujac," said Dalton, "is he alive or is he dead?"

"And if he's alive, why is he in England killing Glass Cutters?"

Dalton made one last attempt to slip his cables, not because he didn't want to know the truth but because he didn't want to put another woman for whom he had real affection out on the firing line. His record in that area was rotten: two dead, one still missing, one badly wounded and currently recovering in Capri and not taking his calls.

"We *could* save ourselves a lot of trouble by simply telling Hank Brocius about Lujac. The photographs. Singapore. We just stay the hell out."

Mandy looked doubtful.

"We could. But we're Agency. Without any real proof, he's just as liable to tell us to go to hell. He'd think we were just trying to elbow our way in. We need to have something solid to show him. Anyway, Kiki Lujac was working for Gospic, and Chong Kew Sak, and that horrible fat little policeman—"

"Sergeant Ong Bo."

"And did Kiki Lujac not do his best to get us all killed in Singapore?"

"Yes, he did," Dalton said, resigned now, giving in to fate.

"So, if he's still alive, don't we *owe* that psychopathic little shit?"

There was no other answer to Mandy's question.

"Yes, we do."

He stood and offered Mandy his hand.

"Shall we?"

Mandy smiled, reached for her purse and gloves, and took Dalton's hand as he helped her out of the booth and then held open her cape.

"Yes," she said, slipping into it, "we shall."

part **two**

SANTORINI, THE AEGEAN SEA

FIRA

They were inbound to Santorini on an Olympic Airlines airbus, flying in wave-top low because a major storm was lashing the Aegean from Athens to Rhodes, and the heavy plane was taking one hell of a beating. From where Mandy was sitting, wedged in tight between the pale and the queasy, the island of Santorini looked like the jagged base of a shattered amphora sticking up out of an angry coal-black sea, ringed in by lashing surf, apparently uninhabited, although there were signs of clustered dwellings running along the saw-toothed cliffs that ringed the lagoon in a rough semicircle.

All in all, the place looked nothing like the travel brochures she had cheerfully picked up in Heathrow and which were now stuffed, crumpled and forgotten, into a slot next to the airsickness bag, an item that now held much more significance for her immediate future. She watched the ocean tilt as the plane lurched heavily into a banking turn, riding a crest of wind like a sailboat quartering a cross-cut sea.

Mandy closed her eyes and swallowed carefully.

"What do we know about this bloody island?" she asked, mainly to distract herself. "It looks like a hellhole. Have you ever been here?"

"No, but I pulled an Agency brief off the website."

"Anything useful?"

"Not as useful as this," he said, holding up a *Lonely Planet* guide. "What would you like to know?"

Mandy swallowed again, her cheeks damp, managing somehow to evoke images of both Ophelia and Camille.

"Just enough to keep my mind off how bloody ghastly I feel."

"Fine. As you are indisposed, I will read aloud . . . 'The island that is now called Santorini first came to the attention of the rest of the ancient world by blowing the living daylights out of itself about sixteen hundred and fifty years before Jesus got his first tricycle—' "

Mandy opened one eye.

" 'Tricycle' seems a bit glib, don't you think?"

"It's pithy. At *Lonely Planet,* they strive for pith. Pith is their policy. Shall I go on, or would you prefer to editorialize?"

"God, no. Continue. *Pleathe.*"

"Thank you . . . 'The island was known at the time as Strongoli, which means "the round island." Strongoli became the center of a vast trading empire based on the vast trading of . . . stuff. Unfortunately, it was also the center of a huge volcano, a feature of the landscape that the Minoans probably should not have overlooked since, when this volcano finally blew itself thirty miles into the upper atmosphere, it also blew the Minoan civilization, which had up until then been pretty hot potatoes, to smithereens.'"

" 'Smithereens'? They actually say smithereens?"

"Right down here in Helvetica Bold. Apparently, it's an old Theban word meaning 'pieces too small to pick up with tweezers.' Since the island was no longer quite so round, they renamed it Thera, which means 'no longer quite so round.' Now *this* is interesting. The famous Homeric expression Ἱερά Ἥη! Τί εστί ἐκεῖνοσ δυνατόσ θόρυβοσ?, which, as I'm sure you will recall from reading Greats at Oxford, means 'Holy Hera! What was that really loud noise?,' may actually date from this period."

Mandy, sighing theatrically, plucked the book from his hand, looked at the text through red-rimmed eyes.

"It doesn't say any of that anywhere, you hound. And I, a dying woman."

"I was summarizing," said Dalton primly, "giving you the essentials. Are you going to be okay? You look a bit . . . puce? Or do I mean ecru?"

Mandy went back to staring out at the churning whitecapped ocean.

"God, look at all that angry water. And Athens, what a bloody mess. It looked like a huge ashtray with a cheap model of a Greek temple stuck in the middle. This *cannot* be the real Aegean."

"This is the winter, Mandy, as you may have noticed, and this is what the Aegean is like in the winter. You should see Venice right now: it looks like an Art Nouveau ice-cube tray. It's all in the timing. If you showed up at the Royal Opera House at four in the morning on a bank holiday, you wouldn't expect to see the Bolshoi leaping about the place, would you? Your nose needs some attention, by the way."

Mandy, searching her purse for a tissue, said something unladylike, and the woman in the seat ahead of them turned around to give her a stern look, which resulted in Mandy saying something unladylike to her as well. After a bit of a row, in which she gave as good as she got, Mandy got up and went staggering off in the direction of the τουαλέτα. She was still in there when the bell went off for the final approach, at which time an unsuspecting flight attendant made what would have been *her* final approach toward Mandy's locked bathroom door had Dalton not headed her off.

"But she needs to come out," said the young Greek girl. "It's not safe."

"And it's not safe to go in there after her," said Dalton. "Really!"

The girl, a stumpy brownish little thing with close-set black eyes who looked to be about eleven, made a pouty hall-monitor face and went off to put Mandy's name down in the *Great Big Book of Very Naughty Passengers.*

They were on the ground a few minutes later, Mandy wrapped in Dalton's trench coat and Dalton still in his third-best navy blue pin-stripe, fighting the wind and the sleet and their luggage across the stony terrain that led to the low neoclassical pile that marked the spot where one day, God willing, a real airport would get built.

There was a thin vulturine man standing by a large black Škoda, a limp hand-rolled cigarette in his blue lips, his hands stuffed in the pockets of his military fatigue jacket, his collar up, watching with interest as they made their way across the tarmac. When they reached him, he straightened up and bobbed his head, simultaneously spit-ting the cigarette into the wind and offering a gloved hand to Mandy, who had come to a halt and was looking at the little man as if he were a village yobbo here to see about the drains.

"I am Sergeant Valentin Keraklis, Deputy Prefect of the Port Police."

Dalton redirected the man's hand away from Mandy's midsection and shook it firmly, first once and then once again, fixing the man with a look.

"Thank you for meeting us, Sergeant. I'm William Pearson. May I present my wife, Mrs. Dorothy Pearson?"

Sergeant Keraklis, who may have needed glasses, was squinting at Mandy with a myopic grimace that Dalton realized was probably his best seductive smile. It wasn't working, but Mandy took his hand anyway.

"Lovely to meet you, Sergeant."

"Well," said Keraklis, reeling as a gust of wet wind came in off the whitecapped expanse of the Aegean, "you are not seeing Santorini at her best, I am afraid. I am to take you to your hotel, if you please.

You are at the Porto Fira Suites, are you not? The best place in Fira, I promise. Much is closed as this is the off-season, as you can see. Captain Sofouli has set aside the rest of the afternoon for your requests, if that is convenient."

"That's terrific," said Dalton, stuffing their bags into the trunk of the Škoda and easing a still-queasy Mandy into the rear seat. The Škoda smelled of stale Turkish tobacco and Sergeant Keraklis in roughly equal proportions. Mandy rolled the window down and tried not to breathe any more than absolutely required.

They bounced and jounced over the rocky, twisting saddleback roads that climbed up the bony spine of Santorini, revealing with each S-curve another sprawling vista of the storm-tossed seas that had given Ulysses so much trouble. The island seemed to have absorbed so much history that it was cracking under the weight of it, but Dalton found the wintry desolation perversely attractive. Fira itself, the capital, spreading itself out across the top of the caldera wall, was a postcard-perfect example of a picturesque Grecian town, overflowing with jumbled-up villas and odd little shops and crowded blocks of apartments, all of it fluttering with awnings and curtains and, madly, ornamental vines of every color, some of them carrying blossoms even in this vile weather. There were few people out in the streets, but Dalton recalled that the entire population of the Greek isles was less than ten million in the off-season—it spiked to thirty million in July.

Sergeant Keraklis delivered them to the portico, helped with the bags, grimaced at Mandy once again with a similar effect, and puttered off back to the station after securing Dalton's promise to come no sooner than was necessary, and repeating that Captain Sofouli was looking forward to meeting him.

The Porto Fira Suites turned out to be a rambling all-white Art Deco pile perched helter-skelter on top of the spikiest of the jagged peaks that rimmed the caldera wall. In the summer, the views from its flowered terraces and stepped gardens would have been stunning.

After doing a sweep for bugs and cameras and finding none, as he expected, he got Mandy more or less undressed, halting, with some regret, at the outer limits of decency, taking a moment to consider the enduring enigma of women's lingerie, namely, that the more expensive it was, the less there was of it, and that Mandy's must therefore be worth its weight in rubies.

She was still feeling perfectly ghastly but, with a bleating protest, finally settled into the king-sized bed in their open, airy, and again, somehow, in this bitter season, flower-strewn rooms. She lay there, still in her Ophelia/Camille mode, staring glumly out the window.

Dalton, following her look, thought that the view across the windswept bay to the ragged islands of Thirasia and Nea Kameni had a grand North Atlantic wildness to it. And the sea really was "wine-dark," just as Homer had described it.

Mandy summoned herself and took his hand, holding him in place.

"What if he just simply believes you and lets it go at that?"

"We'll think of something else."

"What if he's a complete berk?"

"You read his record. He got the Santorini assignment as a reward for ten years with their antiterrorist squads. He goes back as far as the colonels. If he survived the sixties in Greece, he's no berk."

"You do understand that we could end this evening in a cell?"

"I have no intention of letting that happen. You'd look lousy in handcuffs."

"What could you do to prevent it? Where could we run to? We're on an island."

"I'll do something clever and daring and dazzle you senseless. Remember, fortune favors the brave. Isn't that your family motto?"

"No. Our family motto is *Cogito sumere potum alterum*."

"Which means?"

"I think I'll have another drink."

"Very witty, I'm sure. Would you like one now?"

"Maybe when you get back . . . *if* you get back. Now, kiss me and go."

He pulled a soft crazy-quilt blanket up over Mandy's body, kissed her gently on her forehead. She smiled weakly and pushed her way deeper into the pillow. He went out into the main room, furnished in spare but well-done blond woods and Art Deco glass and floored in muted mosaic tiles, where he deciphered the phone instructions and called the front desk for a cab.

His command of the modern Greek language was limited to a few lines from *Shirley Valentine* and the last name of Archbishop Makarios. Fortunately, most of the island spoke serviceable English. He brewed up some coffeelike liquid that seemed to have been derived from coal tar. Oddly, it was excellent. He threw some water on his face, put a fresh bandage on his cheek, changed into a new suit of clothes—tobacco browns and tans, in honor of Porter Naumann's current winter ensemble, but without the emerald green socks—and looked in on Mandy, who was sound asleep. He was standing, trench coat belted, under the broad portico of the Porto Fira a few minutes later when his cab arrived.

The office of the Port Police—the only constabulary on the island—was on Fira Martiou Street, the main drag. The building itself was a cement-block structure with barred windows, a Third World police bunker of the type Dalton had seen all over the world. The interior was lined in patched plaster and stucco, lit by a bank of fluorescents that made the duty officer behind the counter look like a three-day-old corpse: another wiry, vulturine fellow—Keraklis's brother? The officer got to his feet as Dalton came in through the glass doors.

"Mr. Pearson? Captain Sofouli is waiting for you."

He led Dalton down a narrow, half-painted hallway to an office in the rear, a large enclosed space marked off by rippled-glass panels. The door was open, and the space it defined was pretty much completely taken up by Captain Sofouli himself.

Crisp and correct in British Army–style black-and-tans, complete with a polished Sam Browne and a big Beretta in a worn leather holster, he looked as if he could have been Alessio Brancati's older and very much larger brother, a heavy-bodied, sallow-skinned man with sharp Grecian features, shaggy salt-and-pepper hair, and a grip that was like getting your hand caught in the trunk of a Buick.

His smile was careful, a cop's smile, and he offered Dalton—aka Mr. William Pearson—a coffee, which Dalton accepted. He asked for Dalton's—Pearson's—ID and passport, flipped through the pages, and handed the papers back. They sipped at their cups—small, delicate, Turkish, with a complex Moroccan motif—while the wind howled and banged the shutters. Sofouli set his cup down, made an apologetic face, and handed Dalton a clipboard with a single sheet of paper on it.

"If you would, Mr. Pearson, fill this out for me. It is just a formality. Name, home address, and a way you can be reached while you are in Greece. Also your passport number, as you can see there."

He offered Dalton a pencil, which Dalton accepted, but the lead cracked as he began to use it. Sofouli looked about for a replacement, but Dalton pulled a cheap ballpoint pen from his own pocket and used it to fill out the form. Then he slipped the pen under the clip and handed the form back to Sofouli, who scanned it briefly and set the board aside, leaning back into his chair and hooking his hands over his belly.

"So, I am sorry to hear the business that brings you here. You have lost your son, I am informed."

"Yes," said Dalton, "I brought some recent photos," setting the cup down on the edge of the captain's desk and drawing a set of snapshots out of his breast pocket. Sofouli took them in his thick-fingered hand and spread them out on the green leather pad that covered his desk. He put on a pair of reading glasses and looked down at the shots, five colored photos of a sunny-looking young American boy in his mid-twenties, taken alone and with friends, at some seaside resort that looked vaguely Adriatic. The boy was olive-skinned and had long dark hair, bright green eyes.

Mandy had selected the shots from a file of over sixty thousand facial types on file at the Agency, searching the characteristics based on known photographs of Kiki Lujac, of which there were none to be had, not even on Google—Mandy noted this decidedly odd phenomenon at the time—so she guesstimated the essentials of his height, size, and weight, according to his Montenegrin medical papers.

The boy in the shots was a real person, last name Pearson, who had actually disappeared from Ravenna last August. The details of his disappearance had dictated the structure of their cover as his parents, a real family called Pearson; it was a good short-term cover, stronger than a snap cover but not a real legend, which would be fully supported by a team of other Agency staffers ready to take verification calls and back up the fieldman in any way they could.

Mandy had called their cover "NOX," which was Agency jargon for "Nonofficial Cover." It would not hold up under a suspicious and thorough vetting by a hostile agent. It should hold up with Sofouli, however, long enough to get Dalton through the interview, which was all they really needed.

And as long as Sofouli hadn't already made a call to the real Pearsons, who, Mandy had determined, were incommunicado at a beach house on the Oregon coast, still mourning the loss of their son. Using their genuine loss this way was cruel, mean, despicable, horrid, and effective. The whole idea was to look plausible, and then, on a second look, not so much.

"He is a very handsome lad," said Sofouli with sympathy.

"Thank you. His name is Luke. Short for 'Lucas.' "

"These shots, where were they taken?"

"He was in Ravenna, on the Adriatic. You can see the old *castello* in the background there."

"His age at this time?"

"Thirty-one. These shots were taken in August. He was on a vacation with friends, as you can see. He disappeared later the same day, just . . . vanished. He told his friends he was going for a gelato with a girl he had just met and that he would meet them later on the Ponte L'Espero. He never showed up. At first, they thought that he had gone off on a tear with this girl, but no girl was ever identified. The Carabinieri did all they could, and we brought in private investigators—"

"You spoke with these . . . friends, I imagine?"

"Yes. Not personally, but the police did, and later our people."

"And now you have come to Santorini because of this body we found here a few weeks ago?"

"Yes. I know it's a long shot, but we can't let anything go . . . My wife, she still hopes. For myself, less so. But we do . . . whatever it takes."

Sofouli kept his head down, looking at the shots far longer than was necessary. Then he sat back, the wooden chair creaking under his weight like a tall ship tacking hard. He tented his large fingers and looked at Dalton over their pink-skinned tips.

"Your son, he does not look like you. I have not yet met your wife, so I assume she is the dark-haired beauty I see reflected in your son's face?"

"Yes, he takes after her, fortunately."

"This will be hard for you. I must ask you, how tall is your son?"

"He's a little under six feet. Five-eleven. He weighs about one hundred and eighty pounds."

"He was fit. 'Well-knit,' as you say?"

"He played football for Washington State. Not your kind of football."

"Yes. The American helmet-bashing, bloody-nose kind. I like it very much. Soccer, these poncey-boys tripping over shadows and writhing like stuck piglets on the . . . Well, I am wandering. You would wish to know about the body that was found on the far side of Thirasia, then, earlier this fall?"

"Whatever you feel you can tell me."

"May I ask, what is your profession?"

"I'm a teacher. A lecturer, actually, at Portland State University."

"You have received an injury to your face."

"Yes, kicked by a horse. Caught the edge of his shoe on the bone."

"Kicked very hard, I see. You are a lucky man. You ride, do you?"

"Bystanders might argue with that."

"You look fit. Are all teachers in America so fit? You look more like a soldier than a teacher, Mr. Pearson. Have you been in the service?"

Dalton, trying to recall if the real William Pearson had done any military service, was finding Sofouli's methods instructive. He managed to radiate an odd combination of friendly interest and jovial threat.

"I was in the Navy for a while. Years ago."

"I see. You do not seem to be the teacher type, Mr. Pearson . . . But, let us set that aside. If you wish to see the photos of the body that was pulled from the sea, I will allow it, although you will not like what you see. The body was that of a young man, very fit, of about the same weight and height as your son. Around the same age, according to the bones. Did you happen to bring some dental charts with you?"

"Yes, they're at the hotel."

"It will not be necessary since they had all been pulled out."

"Pulled out? By whom?"

Sofouli shrugged, reached for his coffee, sipped it with surprising delicacy, set the cup down.

"That, we do not know. But the cause of death was murder. Other signs of violence were on the body, we think before death, but most of the damage that had been done to the corpse happened after it had gone into the water. The sea is full of life, and all of it feeds on whatever it finds. Many fish found this body. Also he was—do you know the term?—*adipose*. It refers to the fatty tissues of the body. After long exposure to water, the flesh begins to shed. The body turns into an unpleasant waxy thing, Mr. Pearson, swollen, grotesque, a horror. That is the thing we took pictures of. It did not resemble a human at all."

"The body was male?"

"It was not female, that much could be told."

"The eyes, the color?"

"There were no eyes, I am afraid."

"Anything about the skin, the body hair?"

"There was little skin left, and, of course, with the skin goes the hair."

"Were you able to obtain some DNA?"

"Yes, degraded, but enough to establish that the body was that of a Caucasian male, with Nordic ancestors. Would that describe your boy at all?"

"Yes, but I am afraid it would also describe half the boys in America. Would there be any chance that I might obtain some of this DNA? We have some very fine labs in the U.S. and perhaps they could narrow the field—"

"We have many fine labs here too, Mr. Pearson. But I cannot say yes to your request . . . There is the matter of procedures . . . jurisdictions. You are an interested party, but you have no legal standing. I have done what I can for you, but, beyond this interview, I must decline. I have not the power."

"I understand."

"Did your boy have any broken bones when he played sports?"

"Yes, he broke his fibula and his femur."

"Left or right?"

"Right, if you mean the femur."

Sofouli looked at Dalton for a time, clearly thinking him through.

"There was no broken femur on this body. Do you know the name of Kirik Lujac?"

"I know the body you found was identified as someone named Kirik Lujac. They called him Kiki, and he was some kind of fashion photographer."

"That is all?"

"Yes. Why do you ask?"

"Well, you see, I am troubled . . . The report we filed mentioned that no bones had been broken in this body. And now you have come all this way to ask about a body with no broken bones and yet your son had broken bones."

"I see," said Dalton, trying to look nervous and succeeding. "Well, we were just following any leads no matter how unlikely. Sometimes the report is incomplete. I'm not sure I understand you . . . ?"

Sofouli looked at Dalton for a while longer.

"Regarding the body, we are satisfied that the person identified as Kiki Lujac was the body we found. The body is not the only evidence we have. Mr. Lujac was last seen here in Fira in the company of a young man named Marcus Todorovich, who was known by the Athens police to frequent the gay nightclubs around the islands, especially Mykonos. He had a reputation as something called 'rough trade,' and a long police record."

"Do you know his location at all?"

Sofouli said nothing for a time, his expression hardening.

"I am interested to know why you would ask that."

Dalton let his eyes wander away from Sofouli's hard look as if he were trying to think of some excuse. Then he came back.

"Well, if this . . . Marcus . . . ?"

"Marcus Todorovich."

"Was known as a kind of predator—"

"Was your son gay, Mr. Pearson?"

"Gay? No. I mean—"

"Marcus Todorovich preyed on gay men, Mr. Pearson. If your son was not gay, then I am afraid there is nothing else that I can do for you."

He set his big hands on the desktop, pushed himself up, sighing heavily, and stood looking down at Dalton, his face now hard. Dalton stood up, and they faced each other across the desk. The air in the room seemed to be slightly charged with a vague threat.

"Well," said Dalton, gathering his photographs and slipping them into his case, "I want to thank you for your time."

"Certainly."

Sofouli pressed a button on his desk. Sergeant Keraklis appeared in the doorway. "Sergeant Keraklis will drive you back to your hotel, if you wish."

"Not at all," said Dalton, looking over his shoulder at Keraklis, whose face now wore a kind of chilly official blankness. "I would like to walk the town a bit. My wife is a little under the weather."

Sofouli said nothing, and did not offer his hand as Dalton turned to leave. Dalton was at the door when Sofouli said, "What is your subject?"

"My 'subject'?"

"You are a teacher. What do you teach?"

Dalton was stuck with what William Pearson actually taught.

"My field is cultural anthropology. I lecture on the effects of Christianity on pre-Columbian Mesoamerican cultures."

"And what was the effect?"

"Oh, terrible," said Dalton, feeling like a complete horse's ass and wondering if he was really going to be allowed to leave. "Their culture was wiped out. Disease and war and pillage—the usual European imperialism—"

"Did these natives not cut the hearts out of living men?"

"Well, that formed a very small part—"

"I am Greek Orthodox, Mr. Pearson. What are you?"

"I guess you could say I am an . . . agnostic."

"Agnostic? So you are 'undecided'?"

"Yes, I suppose so."

"So you are undecided about the cutting out of hearts?"

"Well, from a cultural perspective, we have to avoid . . ."

Sofouli nodded dismissively at Keraklis and sat down again.

"I am not undecided, Mr. Pearson. Not at all. Good-bye."

UNLESS THEY WERE very good, no one followed Dalton back through the narrow, tangled streets of Fira to the hotel. Night was coming down on the little town, and the streetlamps glowed pale blue in the mist. The wind had died away while he was talking with Sofouli and, with it, the bone-cracking chill. He could smell the tang of ouzo and Turkish tobacco in the air as he passed by an open taverna. The tinny Grecian music had a Moorish feel, the wild, insistent rhythm and the clashing of brass on brass pouring out into the stony streets.

He felt a chill running up and down his spine, and his chest was tight. He wished for a weapon, and wondered what quality it was that Sofouli possessed that made an interview with him seem so dangerous.

Mandy was awake, showered, and dressed in tan slacks and a crisp white shirt, seeming much recovered. She was sitting on the couch, her normal glow back, with a hot, thick coffee on the table in front of her. The windows were open to the sea, and the scent of salt and seaweed was strong. In the distant west, a faint glimmer of golden aura flickered on the curved knife-edge of the island of Thirasia, and the whole bay was filled with a soft violet light.

Mandy had something Moorish and sensual playing on the hotel's CD system. She had also ordered food, an elaborate room-service feast of grilled lamb in a red wine sauce, seasoned rice-filled cabbage rolls smelling of lemon and eggs, various salads and side dishes, and a large bottle of Vinsanto, apparently a Santorini invention. The food smelled of garlic and wine and lemon and spices, and Dalton realized he was starving.

"How are you?" he asked, filling a small plate and settling in.

"I live," she said, smiling. "Where life is, hope there also dwells."

"You had airsickness, Mandy. It hardly ever kills."

"Perhaps it should. Have some wine. You look peaked."

Dalton accepted a glass of Vinsanto, tasted it, made a face.

"God, I didn't see a cat around."

"I grant it's a little strident," said Mandy, leaning back into the cushions with a cup of coffee and a phyllo pastry. She watched Dalton tuck in with an indulgent smile, happy to see some flesh coming back onto his sharp-planed, almost haggard face. He looked . . . younger, and not so hunted.

"Tell me, Micah," she said after some hesitation, "do you still run into Porter now and then?"

Dalton paused with a tomato fritter halfway to his lips, gave Mandy a sidelong look, which she held well. He set the *domatokeftedhes* back down and considered her pearl-pink skin and large hazel eyes.

"Yes," he said. "Saw him a few days ago, in the Piazza San Marco."

She smiled the kind of smile that isn't reflected in the eyes.

"What did he have to say for himself?"

Dalton shrugged.

"The usual Porter line. He was wearing emerald green socks with a tobacco-brown tweed suit. Seemed in good form. Called me a 'whiner.' "

"Did he say why?"

"He thought I was trying to get myself killed."

"Galan told me about that night. And was Porter right?"

Dalton stared at his hands, running that night over again on the screen at the back of his skull.

"Maybe. I don't really know. I felt pretty good afterward. Serene, you know? Which I guess means I'm totally bats. In that vein, I have to admit I was actually happy to see him. I was in the mood for company, and he was always good company—"

"You *do* know he doesn't exist, don't you?"

"He's pretty convincing, you ask me."

"Does he ever ask about me?"

"All the time," Dalton lied.

"You're a lying hound, aren't you?"

"Moi?"

"This isn't really all that funny, Micah. Are you coming apart at the seams? Are you up to what we're doing? Really?"

"Hey, you dragged me into this. I was doing just fine in Venice—"

"Oh yes. Other than suicidal, single-handed vendettas—"

"I don't do well without . . . work. I just don't like being cut off."

"From the Agency, you mean?"

"That, yes, and . . . from the States. To be honest. I miss it."

"You wouldn't miss it right now. The market is in ruins."

"Not the current events. I miss the country itself. Everything in

Europe is so damned close to everything else. I was brought up in Tucumcari. Country was so flat, you could watch your dog run away for three days—"

"My mother used to say that all the time."

"Yes, she was from Santa Fe, wasn't she? How'd she end up in London?"

"Changing the subject, are we?"

"If it works, yes. If not, then no."

"Galan thought you were like a man who had jumped out of a very high window and somehow missed the ground."

"He say that in Italian or Yiddish? It sounds Yiddish."

"He said it in English. Is it true, Micah?"

Dalton looked at her face, at the worry lines around her eyes and the tension in her neck and shoulders. She was an extraordinary women, truehearted, smart, occasionally dangerous, crazy brave, with a powerful sensuality and a fine loving heart, and her life was racing past her while she sat in this still, silent place looking at a man who had nothing left to give to anyone. He felt a fish hook tug under his ribs, and a kind of slow-burning shame. She could be loved, he realized, and she should be loved.

"Mandy," he said, "you need to get yourself a *real* man."

She smiled back at him, raised an eyebrow.

"I don't want a *real man*, Micah, I'd rather have *you*."

"You had Porter, didn't you?"

"Frequently, in one sense. Not at all in some others."

"Then I'm the last thing you need. Can we let this go?"

Mandy held his look for a time, long enough for the tension to build between them, long enough for him to want very much to take her to bed right now and bury himself inside her for the rest of the night. Then she broke it.

"For now . . . Now, eat. Then I have something to show you."

Dalton caught her tone, poured out some more Vinsanto for both of them, and sat back on the couch.

"I can eat later. What did we get?"

Mandy reached into her purse and set a shell-pink BlackBerry on the table beside his plate, tapping the screen with a polished nail. Dalton gave her a look, picked the BlackBerry up, clicked it on, and hit a series of letters and numbers that bypassed the ordinary functions of the machine and activated the high-powered radio receiver embedded in the casing.

The receiver was tuned to the CCS Ghost Series nanotransmitter hidden inside the tube of the cheap ballpoint pen that Dalton had used to fill out the form Sofouli had handed to him. Dalton had taken three versions of it to the interview, one in a ballpoint, one embedded in a wad of rubber made to look like gum, which could be stuck to the underside of a chair, and a third hidden inside a pencil.

The nanotransmitter could pick up voices in the next room, but it could also detect the electronic tones produced when someone dialed a phone number or the radio signals emitted by a wireless keyboard when someone typed. The ballpoint was configured for voice and phone. In a moment, he was looking at a long list of phone numbers, along with time markers. There were twenty-six numbers on the readout but only five had markers.

Mandy, speaking as if the room was miked in the unlikely event that Dalton's sweep had missed something, said, "I went down through the list and thought these places might appeal to you."

22860 22849	1821 hours
22860 24428	1830 hours
9239224	1835 hours
503 823 0044	1841 hours
90 212 560 41 10	1854 hours

Dalton recognized the first number. It was the main desk of the Porto Fira Suites, where they were staying. Sofouli had called right after Dalton left his office. There was a vox icon next to the number, which meant that whatever Sofouli had said on his end during the call had been recorded. Since neither Mandy nor Dalton had a useful command of Greek, and the Agency's language-translation module was, to be honest, an utter waste of time, they were concentrating just on the numbers themselves.

Dalton tapped the second number.

"This place looks interesting, dear."

"Yes," said Mandy, "it's a place called Franco's Bar, on Martiou."

He moved his finger to the third number, gave her a look.

Mandy handed him a piece of hotel notepaper.

The Tourist Police Office in Athens

Dalton gave that some thought, tapped the fourth number, and then looked at the next note Mandy handed him.

The Portland Oregon Police Department

"Well, I'm not sure that appeals to me," he said.

"I didn't think it would," said Mandy, lifting an eyebrow.

"How about this last one?"

"Oh, that one's really interesting. I got their brochure."

She handed him a third note, almost a letter.

The Ataköy Marina Hotel. It's in <u>Istanbul</u>, for God's sake! I played the VOX recording, and it was all Greek to me (get it?), but I don't think the man calling was Sofouli. I think the caller was Keraklis. That whiny voice! He said one word three times. He said *subito*. That's Italian for "quick," yes? But isn't it also the name of Kiki Lujac's boat?

Dalton stared at the note for a time, his mind working. Mandy was sitting forward on the couch, watching him do so with gathering intensity.

"Well, what do you think?"

"I think," said Dalton, "we should get off this island."

At that moment, the phone rang. Mandy tensed, picked up the receiver, said a few words, and then listened for a time. She said yes and thank you and good-bye and set the phone down again.

"That was Sergeant Keraklis. He says that Captain Sofouli has some new information for us, about our son's disappearance, and would it be convenient for us both to come back to the station?"

"And you said yes."

"I said yes, as you heard. They're sending a car. Now what?"

"He wants us both?"

"Yes. He put some stress on that. I admit, I don't like the timing."

"You sure it was Keraklis who called you?"

"Yes. And it was the same voice on the VOX transmission. He made that call to Istanbul, to the Marina. I'm sure of it. His voice reminds me of a dental drill. That stays with one."

"And he said he was calling from the station?"

"Yes."

Dalton picked up the receiver, showed Mandy the screen. She

leaned forward and looked at the last number dialed from that location, 22860 22232. That call had been made almost thirty minutes ago. No other call had been made from the police station since that time.

"That's not this hotel number, is it?" she said. "I think it's for the Atlantis Hotel, on the other side of the island. What do you think?"

"He could have been calling from a cell phone."

"Yes, there's that possibility. Do we take that chance?"

Dalton did not hesitate.

"No, we don't. I think that either Sofouli found the transmitter—"

"If he had, he would have left it in operation while he called, just to keep us in place while he sent a team over."

"Yes, good point. Which leaves us with the alternative . . ."

Mandy studied Dalton's face, her eyes widening slightly.

"Sergeant Keraklis is lying?"

"Yes," said Dalton. "And he's on his way over here."

"And if he's any kind of field operator—"

"His containment team is already here."

SEASIDE, FLORIDA

SEVENTY MILES EAST OF
PENSACOLA NAS

On the inland side of Scenic Highway 30A, on the Gulf Coast of the Florida panhandle, there is a carefully planned little town called Seaside, a charming collection of highly stylized, compact wooden homes that are all built in the same classic Florida coastal style and painted in the officially approved colors of white or blue or red or teal and, if a special permit has been obtained, lime green or pink, and they sit in environmentally sensitive sand-and-gravel gardens trimmed in white picket fences, and every house has a veranda and every veranda has flower baskets, all overflowing with magnolia and bougainvillea and palmetto. The narrow cobblestoned streets are sheltered from the glare of the summer sun and the scouring winds of the hurricane season by towering live oaks and tough old Georgia pines. All the folks are good-ole-boy, shoofly-pie, down-home neighborly. Cars are not allowed, but just about everyone has an electric golf cart made up to look like the surrey with the fringe on top, which is just as cute as cute can be, and everything is done exactly the way it's supposed to be done, or else.

On the seaward side of Scenic Highway 30A, a large barrier dune runs for miles along the pristine shoreline of what is called around here the "Emerald Coast," and the very best homes in Seaside sit atop this immense dune and look out from shaded balconies and palm-tree-lined terraces upon the shimmering blue-green eternity of the Gulf of Mexico. Most of the homes in Seaside have been given pet names by the enormously wealthy retired people from Georgia and Louisiana and Alabama who have their summer homes down here, names such as KATY-DID-IT and KIT 'N' PRETTY and HEAVEN FOR BETSY, but the large stucco-walled and storm-shuttered Tuscan-style villa that sat high up on the barrier dune at the outer edge of the town line had no name at all, and the number plate had been taken off when the new owner moved in a year ago, around the same time that a tall wooden barrier fence had been constructed around the property.

Nobody knew very much about the owner, which, in a tight-knit little place such as Seaside, was a difficult state to achieve and required some concentrated effort. The people on either side of the villa knew only that the owner seemed to live alone, had a gleaming white forty-five-foot Hatteras motor cruiser named *Conjurado* docked at the marina in Destin Harbor, spoke with a strong Tidewater Virginia accent, was tall, tanned, lean as whipcord, with vivid blue eyes and deeply etched lines around his eyes and a long silvery mane of perfectly convincing hair, and that he carried himself ramrod straight and had the air of a retired military man who had made a whole lot of money in the private sector.

His name was, oddly, not available. The owner of the villa, as reported to the Rate-Payer Registry of the Incorporated Village of Seaside, was a corporate entity known as Conjurado Consulting, registered in Wilmington, Delaware. When directly addressed by an elder townsman, a retired lobsterman named Dub Kingman, who was a curious sort and not at all shy, the mystery man had introduced himself simply as Jack Forrest.

Dub Kingman had gone online to generate the further information that the mysterious gentleman might be related to Nathan Bedford Forrest, the legendary Confederate cavalry commander. At one time, the U.S. Army had carried on its roster a man born on the same date, October 4, 1926, with the same name, James K. Forrest, who had served in various capacities with the U.S. Army's intelligence branch, and who had been awarded, among lesser honors, the Vietnam Service Medal, the Bronze Star with a V for Valor, and the Purple Heart. James K. Forrest had retired as a major general in 1999. Information regarding the particulars of his service—which country, which units, which campaigns—was listed as "TNA" on the Army website: "Temporarily Not Available."

Dub Kingman duly relayed this information to the rest of the village elders. From that point on, they began to regard the taciturn and uncommunicative resident of the former Morley Silverman villa on the East Dune Breaks with the kind of wary affection that old soldiers hold for crusty commanding officers such as George S. Patton or Vinegar Joe Stillwell. They sensed his chilly silence and cold distance were qualities he had rightfully earned in hard service somewhere lethal and were to be gratefully honored by the better angels of the village.

So "Colonel Jack," as he came to be known, was accepted into the tight little community of Seaside with a degree of quiet pride and a general determination to protect the old soldier's privacy from sundry outsiders and local busybodies. Many may have wished to know more about the man who had taken up a great deal of the available ocean frontage and who had not spoken more than a dozen words to anyone in the village in the sixteen months that he had been in residence. Well, they all agreed, weirder folks than Colonel Jack were to be found all along the Emerald Coast, which was known by the residents as the "Redneck Riviera," and all agreed that nothing good ever came of being a nosy parker.

All of this is recorded as a kind of preamble to the arrival of a Federal Express truck at the barred gates of Jack Forrest's villa at three p.m. Seaside time, which was ten at night on the island of Santorini, where Micah Dalton and Mandy Pownall were considering tactics while awaiting the imminent arrival of Sergeant Keraklis.

The driver put the vehicle in park and pressed the buzzer beside the solid wooden gates. In a moment, a soft male voice came on the intercom, asked him to state his business, and reminded him to lean out of the window of his truck so that the overhead cameras could get a good look at him. This the driver did, since he had done it many times before all along Scenic Highway 30A, which was well populated if not downright infested with privacy-obsessed people behind heavy gates.

In a few minutes, a small side door clicked open and the man known to the locals as Jack Forrest appeared, tall, wiry, dressed in a starched khaki shirt and white linen pants and barefoot, his glance moving quickly about the terrain before settling on the face of the young black man behind the wheel, who, as always, was struck by the wintry chill in those pale blue eyes. No small talk was exchanged, as the man signed for and accepted a sealed envelope. The truck backed out onto the highway again, and the man known as Jack Forrest went back inside his gated compound carrying the envelope in both hands, his body erect and stiff, climbing the stone steps to the villa slowly, either like a football player with very bad knees or like a man who had once been shot several times in the back.

The open and airy interior had been sparsely furnished in dark wooden Shaker-style furniture, clean lines, all rectangles and screens, with a long teak desk that looked like it had been salvaged from a sailing ship taking up the entire width of the villa in front of ornate leaded-glass windows with a fine view out over the broad, churning sea.

This monastic simplicity contrasted oddly with the Romanesque arches and the Murano-glass lighting and the intricate marble floor the Morley Silvermans had installed at great expense the year before

Mrs. Morley Silverman, born Agatha, had been diagnosed with an inoperable brain tumor. Forrest crossed the large room to his desk, pulled the chair back, and sat down in front of a gunmetal-gray Sony laptop, dropping the envelope onto the desk and reaching for a pack of Gauloise cigarettes sitting in a large crystal ashtray at his right hand.

He lit the Gauloise, drew in the smoke through thin pursed lips, a knot of corded muscle convulsing at the right side of his leathery neck as he did so, creating the unsettling impression that a very large tarantula lived right under the skin. His colorless eyes squinting against the burn of the smoke, he leaned back into the creaking wooden chair and considered the FedEx envelope as it lay unopened on the battered surface of the desk. A sticker on the cover said that the envelope had been sent by:

BEYOGLU TRADING CONSORTIUM
SUITE 5500, DIZAYN TOWER,
MASAYAK AYAZAĞA,
ISTANBUL, TURKEY

The packet showed signs of having been opened at one point, possibly at the U.S. port of entry, perhaps by the Turks themselves. The customs declaration stated that the contents were ELECTRONIC DOCUMENTS/NCV and not insured. Jack Forrest's face, as he studied these exterior details of the packet, was closed. The fact that the package had been sent by a public courier indicated a number of things, first among them that the sender had been motivated primarily by haste and not by security. Otherwise, a personal courier would have been sent. This carried implications that would have to be dealt with, sooner or later.

Forrest exhaled a cloud of smoke, looked out at the light changing on the glittering shoreline as a chain of pelicans drifted past, in a

single, sinuous line, uncannily snakelike, each bird gliding motionless, skimming the whitecaps. They looked prehistoric, like pterodac-
tyls, and had the dead-black eyes of sharks. Crushing the Gauloise in
the crystal ashtray, Forrest picked up a military dagger, a Fairbairn-
Sykes, and used it to open the envelope. He tilted the envelope to
empty its contents onto the table: a sheet of paper with some handwriting on it and an eight-gigabyte armored flash drive. There was
nothing else in the envelope. He picked up the paper, a smooth,
heavyweight vellum with the BEYOGLU watermark embedded in the
fibers.

On it, a strong hard hand had written in Russian:

Перейти рассказать спартанцев

"Go tell the Spartans," he said half aloud.

Forrest smiled to himself, although the effect on a watcher would
not have been heartwarming. The lines of the epitaph played in his
mind: *Go, tell the Spartans, stranger passing by, that here, obedient to
their laws, we lie.*

Although the flash drive looked ordinary, it contained a glass vial
of sulfuric acid connected to a microscopic spring-loaded titanium
spike. If anyone tried to read the contents of the drive without first
entering the correct password, the plunger would break the vial, and
the acid would destroy the drive's memory chip. Sulphuric acid had
an advantage over an explosive because it would not set off a detec-
tor. Freezing the flash drive to render the glass vial useless would also
destroy the contents of the memory. If anyone tried to decode the
password by attaching the drive to a decryption program using asymmetric algorithms, the drive would be destroyed. And, as a final bar-

rier, the correct password had to be typed in *once only,* without a single error, within ninety seconds of being requested by the drive or, again, it would destroy itself. Forrest inserted the flash drive into the Sony's USB port, waited as the computer brought up the drive's password bar.

Counting off the seconds, he pulled a book of prime numbers off the shelf next to his desk. Since Herodotus, who wrote the most well-known history of the battle at Thermopylae, was a Greek, as, for that matter, was Leonidas, he flipped through to the list of the Euclidian primes, another Greek creation, and typed in the sixth one in the series —20056049013—because he and Piotr had agreed a long time ago that the password prime would always be the number in the series that had no more than nineteen and no less than eleven digits. Since each prime number in all of the seventy-seven categories of primes increased exponentially, anything higher than nineteen digits would have been too long to be accepted by most civilian password systems, and both agreed that anything lower than eleven might be successfully attacked by a powerful computer generating primes.

After all these years, Forrest had grown used to the way Piotr's mind worked, and when the flash drive finally opened up and the MPEG it contained began to play, he understood the grim humor in his reference to the famous epitaph to Leonidas and his three hundred Spartans—*here, obedient to their laws, we lie*—as he watched a naked man sitting in a cheap metal chair bolted to the floor in the middle of a large sheet of clear plastic.

The chair sat in a pool of hot-blue light, but the rest of the scene was in darkness. The man in the chair, in his fifties, with a full head of lank brown hair, was pale and thin, with prominent blue veins all over his torso: he had been bound to the chair with plastic cable ties, bound so tightly that the ties had dug into his wrists and elbows and ankles deep enough to draw blood. The man in the chair was Antonijas Palenz, a Latvian police official who had lost his position in Riga after the fall of the old Sovietski and who was now Piotr's chief "talent scout" for Athens and the Aegean.

Anton normally wore glasses, but they had been taken away, and now he blinked out into the darkness all around him, his face wet and his bony chest working very hard. The questioner, not visible, was a woman with an English accent and a soft, persuasive voice. The questions were in English.

"Tell us again, how you explain what your man did in London."

Anton tried a smile, but fear twisted it into a grimace, and when he spoke his voice was hoarse and raw, as if he had answered the same question many times before, which, Forrest knew, would be the case exactly.

"I followed your instructions. Truly. I told him that it was to look like a robbery. That is what he did. What we wanted him to do. Truly. And he got the list, as we hoped he would. May I have some water now. Please. And where is Maya? Maya, are you there?"

"Maya is not here anymore."

Anton's breathing grew rapid and shallow.

"Where is she? Please, she is not a part of this . . . Please . . ."

"She is being questioned in another room. What happens to her will depend on what you say in here. Again, how do you explain London?"

The man worked at his wrist bindings, clearly on the edge of a breakdown, and tears began to flow down his sweaty cheeks.

"Maya . . . I need to see Maya."

There was some muted talk off camera, and then a man stepped forward into the glare of the light, his back to the camera, a massive hulking shape with the kind of Mohawk cut favored by veterans of the Kosovo Army. He held a large sheet of paper up in front of Anton's face. Anton peered at the paper, jerked his head away, and began to sob, his chest convulsing.

The big man stepped back from the chair, and for a time the only sound was the distant hum of an air conditioner or a generator and the deep wrenching agony of the man crying. Forrest lit another Gauloise and turned the volume up a bit so he could get an idea of where they were. The chair looked like something found at a market anywhere in the Middle East. The plastic was generic. The bolts that held the chair to the floor looked old and badly made; the plastic restraint cuffs looked like the ones the Turks used. Turkey, likely, or maybe Bulgaria.

The interrogation resumed.

"You've seen the pictures he put on the net. He sent these pictures to everyone on her list, and to the head of their NSA as well. Was this part of your instructions to him? Was this to help make the murder look ordinary?"

Anton made an effort, got his crying under some control.

"You knew what he was. He has done this before, many times. He *likes* to take pictures. He did this in Trieste, and in Athens, and in Kotor and Sveti Stefan, and possibly in Shanghai two years ago, and we think once in Singapore in the fall, and he was doing it in Santorini on the very day I reached him. We knew this. We *all* did! We agreed on the risk. I am not to blame. We chose him because he already had a legend and could move freely in the West. We chose him because there was no one else we could train in time. We chose him because he has courage and does not panic, and he is able to adapt and innovate. We took his legend and made it unbreakable. Even now we maintain it—"

"It is still in place for only one reason. He is next to the target already. What do you suggest we do if he repeats this error?"

"What can we do? We have no one to send in his place. We have not enough time! We have to let him work."

"Do you wish what is happening to Maya to stop?"

"Yes. Please."

"Then you will go to America and control your man."

Anton shook his head.

"You don't *know* him. At Kerch, he could be controlled. But now that he is in America, we have no choice—"

"You will go to America. You will either control him until he completes his mission or we will give Maya to the Chronic Ward."

"God, she's a child . . . a child. We are not this kind of people—"

"We are you, Anton, and you are us. You will go to America and control this man, and when his work is done you will kill him or we will give Maya to the men in the Chronic Ward. What is your answer?"

Forrest, watching this, had slowly straightened up. What the hell was Piotr thinking? Anton was no fieldman. Was there no one else?

No, there was no one else because the agent in place would kill anyone else who contacted him and then abort the mission. That was the rule. You only spoke to your controller. And Antonijas Palenz was this man's controller.

"Yes," said Anton after a long, breathing silence, "I will go."

"Good. You will not go alone. Bukovac will go with you."

Anton's face sagged and his eyes widened.

"I would . . . rather not work with Bukovac. He is . . . extreme."

"Yes. That is why he will go with you. To be extreme."

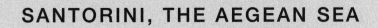

SANTORINI, THE AEGEAN SEA

THE PORTO FIRA SUITES

Insistent knocking on the door of their room brought Mandy into the hallway, her throat tight, her heart racing, her arms folded, her face composed. "Who is it?"

"Police. Please, open door."

"Is Sergeant Keraklis there?"

"He is in car. You are to come down. Please, open."

The voice was low, almost a whisper, but packed with tension. Mandy went to the security peephole and looked through. Two men—one short, stocky, with long curly brown hair and the furtive air of a fallen priest, the other large, blunt, with a hog's face made for glaring—both in rumpled brown suits and open-necked, greasy white shirts, were standing shoulder to shoulder staring back at her. The large man, older, clearly the one in charge, sported the standard-issue large black handlebar mustache favored by cops and thugs all over the eastern Med.

"Please show me some ID," said Mandy, her heart rate bumping up a bit. She took a few careful breaths to get her adrenaline back down and forced herself to move slowly, to wait for the moment, to let the thing play out. The large older man lifted up a battered black wallet, flipped it open, and plastered it forcefully against the peephole. It was impossible to read it, and the man knew that. He jerked it away, then leaned in to bang with the side of his fist against the door, shaking it in the frame.

"Please to open, miss. We are police."

Mandy slipped the chain off, cracked the door, and stepped back as the two men pushed their way through the door and into the hall, the big man brushing past Mandy and rushing on into the main rooms of the suite, the other standing in front of her, a diffident smile on his face but still blocking both her view and her retreat from the hall. Shorter than Mandy, the younger man stared into her face with obvious appreciation, close enough for her to feel the heat off his unwashed body and to smell the reek of Turkish cigarettes on his suit jacket. His partner was back in the hall in a few seconds, his hambone face now knotted like a fist.

"Where is Mr. Pearson?"

"I have no idea. He went out a few minutes ago. What is your name?"

The man looked surprised at the coolness of her question.

"I am Pappas. Where is Pearson? He was told—"

"'Told'? No one told us anything at all. He went out. He'll be back. You may wait in your car or out in the hall. Now you will leave my rooms."

Pappas's expression went through some changes as he struggled to hold his temper in the face of Mandy's chilly self-containment. Before he could speak, the younger man, who had an air of weary resignation, stepped in.

"I am Corporal Nouri. This is Sergeant Pappas. We wait here. Please sit, Miss Pearson."

Mandy considered telling him to insert and twist but did not.

"Suit yourselves. I do not invite you to sit down."

She swept past both men and went into the main room. The windows were open to a starless windy night, and the sound of the sea rose and fell slowly. The air was heavy with spices from some nearby kitchen, and under that the salt tang of sea air. Mandy picked a book off the table, settled into a chair by the open glass doors that led out onto the terrace, crossed one ankle over the other, and proceeded to ignore the men standing in the middle of the room, both looking uneasy, both shifting their weight from foot to foot.

The younger man—Nouri—looked at Pappas and tapped his watch. Pappas took out a small police radio and pressed the talk button, said something unintelligible that included the name Keraklis. The radio hissed and popped, and then the sound of Sergeant Keraklis's voice came back. Pappas listened, his face blank, then he said what Mandy assumed to be Greek for "Okay, roger that," and put the radio away.

"Miss, Sergeant Keraklis coming now."

Mandy looked up from the book, raised an eyebrow.

"Isn't that peachy," said Mandy, going back to her book, leaning into the pool of light from a tall, heavy-looking brass reading lamp on the table beside her. Pappas frowned at her tone but said nothing more.

In a few moments, there was a firm knock at the door. Nouri looked at Pappas, who gave him a curt nod. Nouri shuffled off down the hall. Mandy heard the door latch turn. Pappas took a position in front of Mandy, staring down at the top of her head and breathing heavily in order to convey to her the depth of his disapproval, so he missed Corporal Nouri backing into the room with the muzzle of his pistol—a butt-ugly Croatian semiauto HS95—pressed up against Pappas's forehead and Dalton's glare burning a hole in his left eye. Mandy set the book down and smiled up at Pappas just as Dalton shoved Nouri into the middle of the room.

Nouri hit the coffee table and went over it backward, scattering flowers and shards of pottery. Pappas went for his own pistol, getting it halfway out of his belt holster before Mandy kicked him just behind the left knee and, as he fell, struck him very hard across the skull with the heavy reading lamp that had been on the table next to her. The lamp hit Pappas across the base of his skull with a disconcerting crunching sound, and the lightbulb blew out. Apparently, so did Pappas.

He continued his journey earthward without further comment and landed on his face and upper body, bounced once on the tiles, and lay still, blood seeping slowly through a large rent in the skin over the back of his head and turning his black hair a sodden purple.

Something about the way he went down and the way he was sprawled sent a ripple of nausea through Mandy's body. She knelt down beside him and put a finger on his carotid artery. She stayed that way for a while, and then she stood up again, her face now gray, a vein at her temple pounding.

She caught Dalton's glance, shook her head very slightly just once, her lips pressed tight. Dalton's glance flicked away again, his face impassive, holding the blue-steel HS pistol fixed on a point between Nouri's suddenly very large black eyes.

"Why do you both have Croatian pistols," he asked in a flat tone.

Nouri blinked up at him, his face working.

"What?"

"Greek cops carry Beretta 92s. This HS is a piece of Croatian shit. No self-respecting Greek cop would use something like this for a doorstop. Therefore, you are not a Greek cop. What are you?"

Nouri tried to find something forceful to say, failed.

"Where is Keraklis?" he managed, in a bleat.

"Resting. Dorothy, please dig his ID out and toss it over."

Mandy, making a face, stepped over the body of Sergeant Pappas, bent down, and dug into the sour recesses of Nouri's sticky wardrobe with obvious reluctance, coming up with a limp black ID case that she flipped over to Dalton, who caught it with his off hand, glanced briefly at it, and then went back to Nouri.

"This ID is also a piece of shit. What are you?"

Nouri rallied a bit, shook his head as if trying to clear it.

"Fuck you, Ami. You no nice guy. Go shoot me."

"Dorothy?"

Mandy trembled once, and then steeled herself. She had an idea what was coming. They had discussed this element in detail. There were two ways to interrogate people: the slow, gradual deconstruction of the prisoner or a short, sharp demonstration of readiness to kill. The speed with which things got deadly in this business was a little unnerving. On the other hand, she was ninety percent certain that Pappas was already dead. This made it a little easier for her, but not much.

"Yes?"

"If this kid doesn't answer my next question, put a couple of rounds into the back of that man's head."

Nouri, on the floor, jerked his head around, stared at her for a second, saw the pallor of her skin, the tightness in her body.

"No. You play a game—"

Mandy picked a pillow up off the chair, knelt down beside Sergeant Pappas, placed the pillow over the back of the man's head, pressed the muzzle of the pistol up against the pillow, and looked back up at Dalton expectantly.

Nouri looked at her and then back up at Dalton.

"Once more," said Dalton. "What are you?"

Nouri opened his mouth, closed it, and looked around the room for an exit strategy and came up with nothing that didn't involve being dead.

"Who the *fuck* you people? You CIA?"

"Wrong answer," said Dalton, looking briefly at Mandy

"No . . . wait . . ."

Mandy, still kneeling, resisting the urge to turn her face away and close her eyes, squeezed the trigger—once, twice, three times—a series of muffled cracks. Pappas's body jerked with each impact. There was hardly any blood, just leakage from the exit wounds, which meant his heart had already stopped. Mandy began to have more confidence in the idea that she had just executed a dead man.

The pillow was smoldering, a thin column of white smoke rising. Mandy got up, dumped a pitcher of water on it, and went across to the window, still holding the pistol, her face bone white and her gun hand shaking. Nouri's breathing was short and shallow, and his skin was wet. A urine stain was spreading out from his crotch. He stared up at Dalton, hyperventilating now, his black eyes huge.

"Who *are* you?"

"Last time," said Dalton. "I don't need you. I can get all this from Keraklis."

"No. You kill me, anyway. And I talk, they kill me."

Dalton's face looked like a mask, and his pale eyes were in shadow. Mandy wasn't looking at him now, which was just as well since what was in his face was not something she would have wanted to remember later.

"I'll try again. What are you?"

Nouri's eyes were red as he looked up at Dalton. What he saw there was his sudden death.

"We are"—he looked to be struggling for the English word—"we are—how you say?—*za nayam?*"

"For hire?"

"*Dah,* for hire. He, him—the one you killed—he is my godfather, Uncle Gavel Kuldic. I am—my real name is—Dobri Levka—"

"You're Croatian?"

"Yes. Both of us. We are from Legrad, near border from Hungary."

"You work for Branco Gospic?"

Levka's face went convincingly blank.

"Who—"

"Never mind. Why are you here? In this room?"

Levka went inward, working it through, then brightened.

"Sergeant Keraklis call us. Said you ask about this body they find, supposed to be your son. But the boss—"

"Who?"

"Captain Sofouli—Keraklis boss—he think you are not . . . kosher? He tells Keraklis to check you up."

"Where is Sofouli now?"

Levka made a face, lifted his shoulders.

"He has woman. He goes to dinner with her, then *bim-bim-boom*?"

"Dinner where?"

"I don't know. He made a call, I think, to Franco's Bar? After that, he is gone with his woman."

Dalton looked at Mandy, who nodded.

He went back to Levka.

"Is Sofouli part of this?"

"Sofouli? No. He is"—Levka made a gesture of dismissal—"how you say?—bored too much. Once he was a big-time terror cop. Now like retired. He likes his girls, his big dinner, his *bim-bim-boom*. So long as Keraklis takes care, he is okeydokey. Keraklis tells him he look into it, then he calls big boss somewhere—"

"Where?"

"I don't know. Kerch, maybe. We are just to be muscle. After he talks to boss, he calls us and says we are to take you two out of hotel."

"Take us where?"

Levka looked a little greener now. He licked his dry lips, looked down at his hands, and then across to Mandy.

"Look, is business only. No personal thing."

Dalton and Mandy exchanged a look, and Mandy's face got some color back into it. There is cold-blooded killing, and then there is killing a killer. The difference is often small, but it is important to the one doing the killing.

"Do you know why Keraklis wanted us dead?"

"I . . . it got something to do with a Russian. Todorovich."

"Marcus Todorovich?"

"Yes, I think this is his name."

"Where is Marcus Todorovich?"

"I think he is in Istanbul. Keraklis says we are to get his boat, me and . . ."

Levka glanced over at the dead body again and swallowed hard.

"Do you live on Santorini?"

"No. Last month, we were in Kerch, in Ukraine. No work for us, now war is over in Kosovo. We can't go home because they're hunting all of us. For war crimes. Which I never do. We are looking for maybe work on fishing boat or in big coal plant there. We are in bar by the docks. Double Eagle. A man shows up one day, says he has work for good old soldiers. Says he is a good Croat. He knew man we knew."

"What man?"

Levka shrugged.

"He say his name is Peter. No last name. Not Croat. I think Russian, or maybe Ukrainian."

"What did he look like?"

"Like . . . nothing. Like everything. We called him *Siva Čovjek*. Gray Man. He is maybe six feet, not big, not small. Big belly like Buddha. Soft, fat hands. Fingers like sausage. Old. Bald. Has small eyes, black, sharp like a bird, but big red lips, like big fat worms. He is man hard to remember later, you know? Voice is soft like girl. He gives us money, sends us here, to Santorini, to work for Sergeant Keraklis."

"Did Sofouli know about you?"

"Sofouli knows we are here. We are no trouble, stay away from girls, stay quiet. We speak Greek pretty good, so Keraklis tells him we are fishermen, faraway cousin to him. We maybe get work in tourist time. We no trouble, he does not care."

"You said Keraklis called the big boss. Is that Gray Man?"

Levka shrugged again, looked over at Gavel Kuldic's body, and then back to Dalton. "Maybe Peter is big boss. Only Keraklis know this."

"Keraklis told you to kill us?"

Levka looked pained, swallowed with difficulty, then nodded.

"And what about our bodies. This is an island. Mostly rock."

"We are to take you off island. Keraklis knows Sofouli doesn't want any trouble. No dead tourists all over. You gone is okeydokey with him."

"Take us off how?"

Levka shrugged.

"In boat maybe. Or maybe in helicopter. Sofouli have one."

"What kind of chopper?"

"I . . . I saw them in Kosovo, in the war. *Jastreb crno*. Blackbird?"

"A *Blackhawk*? Not a chance. The Hellenic Air Force flies Super Pumas. Or those crappy little Bell 47s. There's no way in hell there's a Blackhawk on Santorini."

Levka nodded vigorously.

"But *is* Blackhawk. I know from Kosovo. Believe me, I know. You getting shoot at by one, make big picture in mind, no foolings."

"Whose is it?"

"Got markings: UNPROFOR? Old machine. UN logo. Big red cross on both sides. Twenty years, maybe. Keraklis thinks Sofouli keep it for to sell someone."

"You're telling me that Sofouli has an old United Nations mede-vac Blackhawk for his personal use?"

"Not for personal. Sofouli in private business, buy and sell guns and ammo and radios to Bulgaria people, also to Romanians. Big black market for Turkey. This one come in three weeks ago. Sits there, tied down under big camo tarp. Nobody know how to fly. Kind of beat-up. Paint pretty bad. But is Blackhawk, okeydokey. Full up of gas."

"How do you know?"

"Keraklis show us."

"Does it have external tanks?"

"Like big bombs with points? Stick out from bottom, at sides?"

"Yes, that's right."

"Were they full?"

Levka shook his head.

"Do not know. Who can tell?"

"What about Keraklis, could he fly it?"

Levka made wry face, shook his head.

"Keraklis cannot drive fucking Škoda. Maybe Sofouli?"

"Get up," said Dalton, stepping back.

Levka did not want to get up but he did, slowly, like a corpse ris-ing, which in a way he was. He straightened his suit jacket and looked down at his soaking crotch, a fleeting spasm of self-loathing crossing his face. He stood in the middle of the room, a forlorn presence, waiting for a bullet. He stared into the middle distance, went inward. He was a feckless and unlucky man, thought Dalton, watching Levka steel himself for death, but he was no coward. Dalton shifted the muzzle of the Croatian pistol, indicating the body of his cousin. "Can you carry him?"

Levka seemed to come back from another place. He blinked, looked down at Pappas, and then back at Dalton.

"Yes. Often. He drinks too much."

"Roll him in a carpet and bring him with us."

Levka held Dalton's look for a moment longer.

"A suggest I make, okay? No shooting."

Dalton nodded. "Go on."

"Is balcony out there? Three hundred feet to rocks. Storm all night too. In morning, maybe no body anywhere."

"Fine. Do it."

They watched as Levka did just that. He must have been telling the truth about carrying Kuldic home drunk, because he managed to get the other man up off the floor and into a fireman's carry, although the effort made his face turn blue and he staggered under the body's deadweight all the way out to the balcony. Kuldic went over the edge without a psalm, dropping into the wind and the eternal Aegean with only a slight flutter from his coat.

For a time, Levka stood there, staring down at the dim churning of the distant surf, at the jagged rocks along the shoreline. Dalton came up behind him, looked down at the black water, saw nothing at all. The wind sighed and moaned, the surf boomed, and the air was full of salt tang. There was music from a nearby bar and a faint scent of frying fish.

"Okay," said Dalton, "let's clean the place up and go."

Levka looked at Dalton, his expression altering.

"Look, Ami, I dead man. So why I have to go somewhere else only for to die anyway. You shoot me now, okay? I go down there with Uncle Gavel. Be quick, yes? Easier for both of us."

Dalton raised the pistol.

Levka crossed himself and closed his eyes, waited for the bullet.

Dalton, for reasons he could not work out, was not fully committed to squeezing the trigger on this odd little soldier of fortune.

Levka, sensing a hesitation, spoke up.

"Wait, Ami, I got idea."

Dalton held the pistol on Levka's face.

"What is it?" he said.

"You kill me, you got two dead bodies down on the rocks, yes?"

"Yes."

"Two bodies harder to disappear than one. Even for great big sea."

"Possibly."

"So instead of kill me, you hire me."

"*Hire* you?"

Levka shrugged, actually managed a smile.

"I got no job here now. You hire me, I work for you. You man who kills much, got that look, no offense. So maybe you make more bodies later. With handy service of Dobri Levka, you don't have to bust big fat dead men around place all by self, ruin good suits like you got."

The kid had a point.

He was a lunatic, but he had a point.

"I killed your godfather. Your uncle. Croats believe in the vendetta. Sooner or later, you'll have to try to kill me."

"Look, is true. But Gavel, he kind of jerk, you know. Mean drunk. Also, filthy habits—"

"I don't think we want to hear about that."

"Look, okay, Uncle Gavel dead. Lots of guys dead. Vendetta for all dead guys, life too short. I not in favor of vendetta. In favor of live Dobri Levka. Okeydokey?"

"Can I trust you?"

Levka looked hurt, stiffened, straightened his shoulders.

"I am *soldier*. Like you, I think. My word good. Only nobody want me back home. I am *nitko nema čovjeka u zemlji*. You understand?"

Dalton shook his head.

"I think," said Mandy from the open doors, the yellow light behind her pouring out onto the windblown terrace, "I think he's saying he's a no man in no-man's-land. At least, I think so."

Levka nodded, grinned, showing a set of teeth that belonged on a mongrel dog on the other side of a chain-link fence.

"Yes! Miss is right. I am no man. You hire me, I am *your* man."

"I can't use you," said Dalton.

"Yes. Yes, can use me! For once, I can lift heavy stuff, like old dead Uncle Gavel. For twice, I speak Greek, Turkey too—okeydokey?—a little bit Ukraine. And, for thirds, maybe I can finds you Gray Man."

"How can you do that?"

"He finds me. So we go backward to Kerch, find him, yes?"

Dalton had an image of Sergeant Keraklis at the bottom of the empty swimming pool at the side of the hotel. Dalton's interview with him had been brief. It had been Dalton's plan to lock him up, deal with the goons, and crack him wide open later to see what he knew. But Keraklis, panicking, had started to scream, and that had to stop. Keraklis was more fragile than he looked. So he was now dead. And without him, there was no direct way to drill back up the chain. Dalton lowered the gun. The Croat had nerve—he'd give him that much. And he hadn't begged or whined or sniveled, which took sand.

"How much?"

"What?"

"How much to hire you? What's your rate?"

Levka broke into a huge grin, and it seemed for a moment as if he would try to hug Dalton, then he looked down at his soaking pants.

"Maybe for now," he said tentatively, "new suit?"

GARRISON

There was a swinging gate made of cavalry lances down at the end of the long treed lane that led to Briony's house, and every weekday at around four in the afternoon a square red, blue, and white van would pull up to the gate and place the daily mail in the large brass cartridge box that Briony's grandfather had set out as a mailbox.

This day was no different. The truck ground its way up the gravel path and lurched to a stop and a gangly kid, wearing the uniform of the United States Postal Service about as badly as it could be worn, stuffed a large sheaf of letters bound with a blue rubber band in the box. As he had each day since he had arrived, Duhamel resisted the temptation to wander down and look at the mail, under the pretext of saving her the walk. It wasn't necessary. When the letter he was waiting for arrived, he would know. In the meantime, he played his part in their quiet country life, doing much of the cooking and all of the shopping in the absence of her housekeeper. It was a principle of his that a houseguest should always make life easier by his presence until his time came to . . . become more clear.

Each day at noon, Briony would emerge from the gatehouse, where she kept her "office." She would work a solid five hours without a break, during which time, she had tactfully informed him, she would rather be left alone to do her "annotating," part of a much larger work undertaken by the academy—she never called it West Point—that would one day become a six-volume tactical history of the Philippine Insurrection of 1899 and the years of guerrilla insurgency that followed it.

Dry old stuff, she said with a smile, but worth doing well.

Each morning, she would emerge after work and wander around the house and the grounds until she found Duhamel. Usually, she would come upon him taking pictures: views of the Hudson, panoramas of the blue mountains in the far distance, detailed studies of the way a knotted burl of tree bark had slowly, over a hundred years, worked its way into, around, and through a section of wrought-iron fence.

Briony liked the young man's intense and solemn dedication to this work and often stood a little distance away so she could watch him without disturbing him. She had a great affection for him. Their fires were still burning, although now they were more warming than searing, and although she was something of a solitary type she was enjoying this transient period of domestic calm.

She was under no illusions that they would still be together in the spring, although she found that life with this strange man had a kind of taut stillness to it, a kind of meditative calm, which seemed to come from someplace inside the essentially unknowable recesses of his soul. He was smart, funny, well read, loving, gentle, inventively sensual, and a closed book to her.

That was part of his appeal. She was old enough to appreciate that it is not in "the bright arrival planned, but in the dreams men dream along the way, they find the Golden Road to Samarkand." In other words, with men the journey is always better than the arrival.

Today, the weather was sharp and cold, and the light so clear that the bare black branches of the oaks looked etched into the crystal blue sky. Ice had formed in long, gliding, spear-shaped islands on the broad brown back of the river bend, and in the evergreen trees along the far shore a murder of crows had taken up residence, their harsh cries ringing faintly in the air. Duhamel had taken to lighting a fire in the great room every day at noon, and a white plume of smoke was curling from the chimney, its scent drifting across the lawn, biting and spicy. Duhamel, kneeling in the dry grass, focusing in tight on a piece of birch bark, looked up at her as she crossed the lawn and came to him, his dark face breaking into a delighted smile, as he always did when they met at the end of her day.

" 'Home is the hunter' . . . ?"

" 'Home from the hills,' " she said, finishing their little exchange. "Care for a drink? I'm utterly parched."

He got up and took her arm in his.

"I took the liberty of opening one of your Montrachets. I hope you don't mind."

It intrigued Briony that Duhamel's oddly ambiguous French-Montenegrin accent had slowly diminished and now he spoke colloquial American with only a slight trace of something foreign in it. He was rather like a chameleon, she thought, a very charming chameleon.

"Lovely. What year?"

"I think it was an 'eighty-five."

"Before you were born, then?"

Duhamel smiled but did not rise to the taunt. They made their way around the house, and he waited at the front door while Briony walked down the drive to get the day's mail. Each day when she did this, a shiver of anticipation, vivid and sexual, would begin to burn inside him. *Perhaps today*, he thought to himself, lighting a cigarette, one of Briony's menthols, long and slender and tart, like the woman herself. *Perhaps today.*

In a few minutes, she was back, carrying the sheaf of letters bound with its blue rubber band, smiling so openly at him as she came up the stone steps, her silver hair shining, her eyes bright, lips and nails as red as taillight glass, so magnificent in brown leather boots and tight jeans and a vivid red fox coat in all the tones of autumn that he felt a strange sense of gratitude to whatever pagan god that made him that, no matter how beautiful it might be, he was born without the weaknesses that forced other people to care about any living thing.

She got to the top of the stairs, already leafing through the mail, and he led her through the open door and down to the long granite bar in the kitchen, where he had already set out the Montrachet and two glasses. She sat down at one of the tall barstools and spread the mail out in a fan, chattering away at him about something or other. He found it hard to listen attentively because there was a letter in the pile that had the kind of look he had been told to expect.

She glanced at it as she accepted a glass of wine, they touched glasses together gently, savoring the ethereal *ping* of the crystal, and then, as she always did, she began to go through the mail, her head down, her bell of silvery hair shining in the downlight, her fine long-fingered hands moving gracefully as she slit each envelope open with an old K-Bar knife that had the letters USMC etched into its blade.

"Bills . . . bills . . . Here's one from Tally . . . You remember her? . . . She's asking if I ever heard from you after the reunion . . . I'll say no . . . Should I say no? . . . Yes, I should say no . . . ."

"Perhaps we could send her a picture?"

"Jules! Don't even think about it. You're a . . . degenerate."

"Am I?"

"Absolutely. And may you never change. What's this . . . ?"

She picked up a letter—blue, with a London postmark, the address done in a spidery handwriting in turquoise ink—stopped, held it in her hands for a time without looking up. A stillness came over her, and she seemed to have stopped breathing. Duhamel put a hand on her shoulder, and she looked up at him.

"It's a letter . . . from an old friend."

"You do not want to open it?"

She looked back at the letter in her hands, hesitated, and then opened it gently without using the knife. There was a fine linen card inside, which she pulled out and opened. On the cover was a black-and-white photo of a couple standing in front of a fireplace, the man very tall and slender and elegant in the mess kit of an officer in the Blues and Royals, a legendary British cavalry regiment, and, on his arm, a chic woman with fine features, wearing a formal gown, her hair in a Veronica Lake fall, lovely, soft eyes, but a firm, ripe mouth and a set to her features that suggested determination and force.

"How regal," said Duhamel, looking at the photo. "Who are they?"

Briony said nothing for a time, her silence filled with some strong emotion. She opened the card, and in the same spidery script, copperplate but weak and thready, was the greeting:

> *Dearest Briony,*
> *Thinking of you as always this Christmas.*
> *My very best to Morgan and to Cassie as well.*
> *All my love, Mildred*

After a long silence, Briony spoke, her voice a strained whisper.

"This is from my friend Millie Durant. She . . . died . . . a few days ago . . . just before Christmas."

"She was an old friend?"

"Very . . . A truly lovely woman."

"I'm very sorry, Briony," he said, touching her hair, caressing it, seeing in his mind the last few minutes of Mildred Durant's life. It hit him with a shock that if he had been a little less careful, he might have sent Briony some of those very same shots, taken as Mildred approached her ultimate boundaries.

He was aware that he was becoming aroused at the memory of that exquisite afternoon in Mildred's eccentric little flat on Bywater Street in Chelsea. The sound of the traffic on King's Road had been a muted whisper in that solid old building. She had a copy of this very same picture on the night table beside her bed.

Duhamel had a clear memory of drops of her blood running down the picture's glass like the rain that had been running down the ancient leaded-glass windows in her front room. The flat had smelled of a coal fire, fresh flowers, old-fashioned floral perfume, and burned toast. At the end, she had lashed out at him, but he caught her hand.

"Are you all right, Jules? You look . . . odd."

He gathered himself.

"I'm sorry. The photo on the front reminded me of my parents."

"Your parents? Yes, you never talk about them, do you? And you never talk about yourself at all."

"Really? I suppose I bore myself. I know all my stories and none of them are very clever. This letter is from London. Did she live there?"

"Not until the last years. She was from Maryland, actually. Worked as a"—Briony caught herself, tried to cover it—"clerk, I think. Some kind of war work, I guess. In those days, everyone was doing war work."

"How did you come to meet?"

She recruited me was on the tip of her tongue.

"She was an alumna. At Bryn Mawr. She sat on the board of re-gents. For a while, I was her liaison with the student assembly. She took a liking to me, I guess . . . After I graduated, she sort of took me on as project. I was a little wild—"

"Briony, not *you?*"

"And she found a way for me to put that to use."

"As a librarian, Briony?" said Duhamel, teasingly, but she did not rise to the taunt. A darkness had settled on her, and she seemed to be almost completely closed to him. He let her drift, sipping the wine.

Darkness had come down outside as well, and a wind had risen up off the river valley, bringing a fine, cutting snow from the mountains in the west. The old house ticked and groaned like a ship settling into a long voyage. The rest of the house was dark and sunk in the gloom of a northern winter afternoon, except for the dying flicker of the wood fire in the great room.

After a time spent in what must have been a very sad place—he could only guess, from the expression on her face and the way she suddenly looked her age in the half-light coming from the halogens overhead, dark shadows where her eyes should be, her cheeks lined— she finally shook herself and set the letter aside, picking up a long business-style envelope, heavy navy blue paper with little flecks of gold in it, obviously expensive, no return address, and sent, according to the stamps, from Crete.

Duhamel felt his chest begin to tighten as Briony turned it in the light, studying it. It was perfectly flat and had no distinguishing marks. The handwriting, in black ink, was coarse and heavy.

Mrs. B. Keating
15000 Bear Mountain Beacon Hwy.
Garrison, New York
USA 10524

"From Crete?" asked Duhamel, keeping his voice steady.

"It was franked there, anyway," said Briony, thinking that NAS Souda was a lot closer to Crete than Garrison was. This letter could be from Morgan, although the writing was in no way like his.

"You don't know the handwriting?" he asked.

"No, I don't."

"Are you going to open it?"

She didn't answer. Unmarked envelopes from foreign places with unrecognizable handwriting and no return address triggered her professional caution, especially in light of what had happened to Millie Durant in London. She set it down on the counter, walked over to the kitchen drawer, and, to Duhamel's surprise, took out a small digital camera, came back over, and took several shots of the envelope, front and back, turning it each time not with her hand but with the blade of the K-Bar knife. Duhamel, watching her, realized she might not be as easy to deal with as Mildred Durant had been.

"You are nervous . . . about this letter?"

She smiled, waved it away as nothing, but continued dealing with the envelope as if it might contain an explosive.

"The Unabomber, I guess," she said by way of explanation, which for Duhamel explained nothing. Still, he nodded, looked grave.

"Do you want me to open it for you?"

She looked at him, frowning, laughed shortly, and handed him the knife. "Yes, you open it. If it blows your hand off, I'll have film."

She was smiling but serious. Using the tip of the blade, she edged the envelope across the countertop toward him and stepped back a few paces.

"What if I am killed?" he asked, smiling at her.

"I'll have my favorite bits pickled and bury the rest of you in the garden. You did love the view across the river. Go on."

She raised the digital camera, pressed MPEG, and waited.

"You are not a good person," said Duhamel, still smiling.

"You should hear what my ex-husband thinks."

Duhamel took a fork out of the silverware drawer, pinned the envelope to the counter with it, and carefully inserted the sharp tip of the K-Bar into the narrow opening at the end of the flap, thinking *Anton, have you decided to punish me for what I did in London?*, which was not out of the question. He had, as he liked to think of it, exceeded his mandate somewhat.

He slipped the blade in and slowly drew it along the edge of the envelope. Nothing happened—no flash of white light, no rising cloud of white powder—nothing at all.

Sighing a little, he used the knife and the fork to tip the envelope up. A blank rectangle of white paper the size and shape of a business card slipped out onto the granite. Taped to the middle of the card was a small black plastic square, very thin. Along one edge of the square ran a row of tiny gold bars. It was a memory chip, with no maker's mark of any kind.

Briony kept the digital camera focused on him as he slipped the tip of the K-Bar under the chip, carefully pried it up, and held it out to the camera on the end of the knife. She clicked the button, then stopped filming and stepped in closer.

"It's a memory chip," he said, keeping his voice level.

"So it is," said Briony. "What do we do with it?"

"I have my laptop. It has a reader."

"What if the chip is full of viruses?"

"You didn't worry about that when I put my chip in your reader."

She looked at him, laughed, and let her breath out in a rush.

"Well, yours was a much bigger chip. Okay, let's go stick this in your machine and see what happens."

Duhamel's machine was in the great room, next to a large leather wingback chair that had become his by default. It was next to the fire, beneath a lovely old Art Nouveau lamp that Duhamel, with his thief's eye, had pegged as an original Gallé.

They flipped his laptop open, inserted the chip in the card-reader slot, and waited for the program to open it up. A few seconds later, the screen went black and then dark blue, and they were looking at a single string of numbers in red and a cursor icon blinking beside it.

408 508 091

Briony stared at the numbers in silence, her expression closed and wary. Duhamel watched her for a while.

"Well," he said, "I have no idea. Is it a password?"

"No," said Briony with a chill, "it isn't."

"What is it, then?"

She was quiet for a while longer.

"Maybe I should take this into my office."

She was talking more to herself than to him.

"Why? How does that help?"

She looked at him steadily, working it through.

"Jules . . . I don't know what . . . to do with you."

"With me?"

"Yes. I don't really know you, do I?"

"I think we have known each other pretty well, no?"

His accent seemed to come back under stress. She felt a surge of affection for him—she could either shut him out or bring him in a little further. Hank Brocius had vetted him thoroughly, and Hank was one of the most untrusting men she knew. Yes, he was closed. But perhaps that just meant he was uncomplicated. He could be exactly what he seemed. And she wasn't ready to shut him out of her life yet. Besides, she had already let him see too much, he was already involved.

"These numbers, Jules, do they mean anything to you?"

Duhamel studied the screen.

"Are they a series perhaps?"

"They could be. But I don't think they are. I think this is just one number. That's the way these things are done."

A seam. A crack, an opening, after all this time.

"What . . . 'things,' Briony?"

She went inside herself then and stayed there for almost a full minute, clearly struggling with a difficult decision. Duhamel found that he was holding his breath—this single moment was the fulcrum upon which all their calculations turned. Which way would she lean? Inside her silence, she could not know that her life was also in play. If she chose wrongly, Duhamel had clear instructions on how to continue, and overwhelming brutality would only be the beginning. He himself did not know which outcome he was favoring. It didn't matter. In the end, she would be his.

She looked up at him, as if trying to read his mind, and then sighed.

"Look . . . Jules . . . if I wanted to send you something in a strongbox and I didn't want anyone to know that we knew each other and I didn't want anyone to be able to open it, how would I do that?"

"You would lock the box."

"When you got the box, you would have to unlock it. How?"

"We would have the same key maybe?"

"Then at some point, I would either have to send you the key or have someone else give you a copy. Either way, our connection is open to exposure, right?"

"Yes. If you insist we have no contact, then there can be no key exchange. I don't see how this can be done without a key to open the box, do you?"

"Yes. There is a way to lock the box without exchanging keys. I send you the box with my lock on it and then you put your lock on it and send it back to me. On both trips, no one can open the box because it has two locks on it. Not even me when it gets to me, because you have put your own lock on it next to mine and I don't have that key."

"Yes," said Duhamel, seeing it at once. "And then all you have to do is to take off *your* lock—"

"Leaving yours in place—"

"And when I get the box back, I take off my lock and the box is open. Brilliant, except for all the going back and forth with the box."

"Not a problem, if the box is really just a string of electrons."

"A 'string of electrons'? You mean a coded message?"

"Yes."

Duhamel considered her for a while.

"Briony, in Savannah, Tally said you did something—"

Very clever for the government. "Yes."

"Are you a spy after all?"

"No, I'm not."

"But you are not a librarian either, are you?"

"No. I can't say any more, and don't ask me. But I know about things like this, and the fact that someone has sent this chip to me . . . is a problem. I should take this in to my employers and let them deal with it."

Anton had seen this moment coming. They had discussed the psychology of the subject, what they knew of her character. In the end, they had formulated this reply: "I agree! Completely. Whoever they are—and I do not want to know—give this to them, and you and I can go back to being . . . quiet. I like this time with you, and I don't like to see this worry in your face."

She reached out and touched his hand, but her mind was elsewhere.

Crete, she was thinking, *Morgan is on Crete. And he has not contacted me in more than thirty days. What if there's something in here that has to do with Morgan. If I give this to Hank Brocius, who will he take care of first? Morgan or the NSA?* She knew the answer as well as she knew Hank Brocius.

"What are you thinking, Briony?"

"I think . . . I need some practical advice."

"Off the record?" he said with a disarming smile, softening her resistance to him. She poured out another glass of wine for herself and one for him, sipped it, thinking hard.

"Yes," she said with a note of decision in her voice. "Look, my son Morgan, I told you he was in the military?"

"Yes. But you did not know where."

"I was being careful. America is at war and . . ."

" 'Loose lips sink ships'?"

"Morgan is in the Navy. And I *am* a little worried about him."

"Of course, that is only natural for a mother in war—"

"No, it's more than that. He's always been great about staying in touch—phone calls, e-mails, sometimes a postcard . . ."

"But he is at sea, is he not?"

His accent was all the way back, she noted, and forgot it at once.

"No, he's actually on a land base. He's stationed at a Naval Air Station. It's called Souda, and Souda is—"

"On Crete," said Duhamel, his expression altering.

"Yes, on Crete. My worry is—"

"That he is in trouble of some sort. And if that trouble has to do with this chip, and you take it to your boss, then what happens to your son will be out of your hands, yes?"

"Yes. I just want to . . . know. I have to take this to . . . my boss, anyway. But I want to know first."

"Briony, is your . . . boss . . . in your government?"

"Yes," she said after a struggle.

"Okay, I must now speak as stranger. Briony, I am here on a visa, I am a French national, and if there should be problems with your government connected to this . . . whatever it is . . . I run a greater risk than you think. I do not wish to appear craven, but if you are concerned about this package and what it contains, I would not wish to complicate your life by forcing you to explain a foreign national."

"My boss is not a fool . . . but . . . I don't know what to do."

"I do. You must take this to him now. Without touching this thing anymore. Your son is a grown man. If he is in trouble, he should face it. If you try to protect him, you might destroy yourself. Then what can you do for your son? For that matter, you do not really know that this involves your son in any way. You are making a nervous conjecture based on facts that could be . . . totally unrelated, yes?"

She looked miserable.

Duhamel tried to imagine what she must be feeling. He knew it as a concept, but misery as a *feeling*? He had been cold, sick, angry, sometimes worried. But misery? He did not know it. He kept his face in order and hoped that his tactic worked.

"But they're *not* totally unrelated."

"How do you know this?"

"Jules, how good are you at math?"

"I am, in a word—two words—*a cretin*."

"Then I'm not going to try to explain asymmetric encryption to you. Let's just say that this number here is like that box I was talking about."

"The one with all the locks?"

"Yes. But this number is also the *key* to the box."

"It is its *own* key?"

"In a way. All encrypted messages now are actually numbers. The original message—we call it a 'plaintext'—is encrypted using—"

"Please, recall I am a cretin—"

"Using what we call a 'one-way function.' A one-way function does something tricky to a series of numbers that can't be reversed. To put the lock on the box, we turn the plaintext message into a series of numbers, and then we do something tricky to these numbers that can only be undone if the receiver has the keys to it—"

"And now my head begins to throb."

"Have some more wine . . . Good . . . Yes, me too . . . Okay, how that is done is that everyone has access to the receiver's 'public key'— a number like this—made by multiplying two prime numbers. So anyone can send her a message using this public key number and an encryption program, but only the receiver can decipher the message because only the receiver knows the two primes she used to create her public key number—"

"Like the box?"

"Yes. For reasons too irritating to go into, we use prime numbers for this kind of encryption. On this chip, the number here is a public key made by multiplying two secret primes. To open it, we need to know—"

"What the two secret primes were. Okay, so we use a computer—"

"Yes, it's called 'factoring.' Want to know how long that would take factoring this number?"

"Yes, please."

"About eight hours. This isn't really an encryption attempt here. The number's too small. For a real encryption, the number might be in the trillions. It would take all the computers in the world five years to factor out the primes for a really large number. This isn't an attempt at encryption, it's a *message* to me personally, and the message is that the person who sent this has an understanding of asymmetric encryption—"

"And that he knows you do too?"

"Yes."

Duhamel looked at the screen.

408 508 091

"Do you know what the two secret primes are that make this number?"

"Yes: 18313 and 22307. Both are prime numbers. Multiply them together and you get 408508091."

"That's amazing! How did you do that?"

"Morgan is like you: he hates math. I once tried to teach him what I'm trying to teach you."

Duhamel was quick, Briony thought, but the speed of his reply was surprising: "And this is the number you used, yes?"

She looked at him without expression, and his chest began to tighten, seeing for the second time the steel under the velvet skin.

"Yes. That's . . . amazing. You missed your calling."

"I should have been a spy, you mean?"

"Maybe . . . Anyway, now what do we do? I know this has to do with Morgan. There's no other explanation. The number makes that clear. So, what do we do?"

"As I said, take it to your boss."

Silence, and her large gray eyes on his, unblinking.

"I can't. I can't take that chance. I need to know."

"To know, and then to decide?"

"Yes."

"Do you want me to go away?"

She softened, her shoulders slumping, her eyes glistening.

"No, I don't. I should, but I *can't*."

"I will leave, if you wish. But to know, you must open it."

She stared at the thing, her face full of dread. Duhamel reached out and touched her hand. She looked up, her eyes glistening.

"Then, for now, do nothing. Perhaps in the morning things will seem more clear. Why hunt grief?"

She sighed, and a shudder ran through her. Duhamel got up, took her hand, and led her upstairs. Duhamel knew what was in the memory chip, knew that after she opened it things would change between them.

But not just yet.

UH-60 BLACKHAWK CHOPPER

155 MPH, ALTITUDE 6,000 FEET,
304 MILES NNE SANTORINI

INBOUND OVER TURKEY

Mandy, in the copilot's seat—cold, tired, her entire body throbbing
to the complex beat of the aging Blackhawk's rotors and the deafening howl of its turbines—was watching, without enjoyment, the
strobing lights of the two Hughes OH-6 Cayuse choppers that had
picked them up as they crossed the coastline of Turkey about an hour
and a half ago. Also known as "Little Birds," they were small egg-
shaped machines, each bearing the marking TURKISH AIR DEFENSE SER-
VICE, each with a machine gun visible in its open bay door.

They had one chopper on their port side and another on their
starboard, which created in Mandy's mind the image of a pair of
crows harassing a condor. These Little Birds had made radio contact
with the Blackhawk when they were ten miles off the Aegean coast
of Turkey, a young male voice asking, in accented English and with
cool efficiency, who they were, why they were flying a chopper with
the markings of the United Nations, what their intentions were, and,
finally, why they had filed no flight plan. All excellent questions,
thought Mandy at the time.

Dalton had told them they were UN medical officers inbound for
Istanbul on an emergency mission to the Hastanesi Children's Hospital in Beyoglu, that they were carrying a donor heart for an urgent

transplant case, and that they had filed a formal flight plan as soon as the heart had become available.

Reactions to this statement varied.

From the coolly efficient pilot of the Little Bird on their port side—Mandy's side—there had been a prolonged silence followed by an order to maintain level flight, to make no evasive maneuvers, and to await further instructions.

From Dobri Levka, sitting on one of the two gunners seats—in his case, the starboard—fondling the rusty pintle-mounted 7.62mm machine gun in the bay, there was shocked silence, and a kind of sinking dismay that his new employer had turned out to be a suicidal lunatic, followed shortly by a typically Balkan acceptance of the fact that fate seemed determined to see him either dead or in a Turkish prison before dawn. He patted the pockets of his medical corpsman's BDUs, found in one of the lockers and into which he had happily changed, being painfully aware that peeing in your pants had a chafing effect on the inner thighs, and extracted a bottle of ouzo from a case that had also been hidden in the locker. He downed a third of it in one go, which helped tremendously.

Mandy, for her part, simply stared at Dalton for a while, shook her head, and settled into the copilot's seat a little deeper, trying without much hope to find a way to be comfortable in it, which was not the maker's intent. Her silence was eloquent, as was the taut tense way in which she was resisting the meager military comforts of the pipe-and-canvas chair.

The interior of the Blackhawk's cockpit had been painted matte-black—"Helps with the night vision," Dalton had offered, to a cool reception—and the control panel was a migraine-inducing array of red, green, yellow, and amber lights coming from the altimeter dial, the compass and horizon indicators, the RPM indicator slides for both engines, and the large multifunction display panel in the middle. A pale green glow shone down on Mandy from the lights in the breaker systems arrayed overhead. Through the overhead window, she could see the blurring fan of the rotors and, beyond that, a starless, moonless sky.

A few minutes later, there was a burst of static, and Little Bird 1 came back on the air to inform them, in vaguely accusatory tones, that the night-desk nurses at Hastanesi Children's Hospital in Beyoglu had no record of any heart-donor flight scheduled to arrive from anywhere in Greece.

Dalton replied, with righteous indignation, that the recipient, a three-year-old girl named Asya Hamila—this brought a sidelong look from Mandy, who knew the man was slick, but where did *that* name come from?—was being brought in by Red Crescent Air Ambulance from an outlying village in Turkey, the name of which he had not been told, that he knew for a fact that all proper arrangements had been duly cleared with Ankara, that this was, after all, a medical emergency, with a child's life hanging in the balance, and not the time for bureaucratic meddling, and did Little Bird 1 now wish him to throw the donor heart overboard, turn around, and go home, and let the United Nations, the Red Cross, Ankara, Reuters, the Associated Press, and Little Bird 1's immediate superiors sort out who was to blame for the needless death of an innocent girl?

More radio silence followed.

Then, eventually, a rather stiff reply: a decision had been made to allow them to cross Turkish airspace under close escort, to avoid passing over any built-up areas, to stay at least fifty miles away from Ankara, and to land at Atatürk Field in Istanbul, where, if their story checked out, they would receive a police escort to Hastanesi Children's Hospital, and, if it did not, they would then be invited to enjoy the gracious hospitality of the Turkish Military Police.

This conversation had taken place approximately three hundred miles back, and little else had been said in the pilot cabin since then. It would be reasonable to describe the atmosphere in the copilot and pilot's section of the chopper during this period of onrushing travel as "frosty," while in the stripped-down cargo section the atmosphere, now rich in ouzo fumes and the scent of one of Levka's Turkish cigarettes, was much more festive.

Through the windshield, in the formless dark, under a starless sky, the lights of a town could now be seen; the lakeside city of Bandirma, according to the GPS array in the control panel. To the north, beyond the scattered grid of town lights, a vast darkness—the Sea of Marmara, and on the farther side of that, fifty miles over black water, the ancient and storied city of Byzantium, for now just a pale glow on the northwestern horizon, but racing toward them like a verdict. Mandy, watching the lights of Istanbul shimmer in the distance, set her cold coffee down in the holder and clicked on her headset mike, switching the com-net from CREW to PILOT ONLY mode.

"Micah, darling, may I raise a tiny issue with you, at the risk of seeming to whinge?"

"Please. You know how I adore your voice."

"Do you? Well, that's lovely. 'Absolutely *peachy*,' as Porter would say. My question is—and I ask this in the full expectation of a wonderfully comforting reply, knowing your remarkable skills, your ineffable tradecraft, your matchless derring-do—just *precisely* how will our being buggered hourly in a Turkish prison speed our plow? Of course, as you have not had the advantages of an English public school education, being buggered hourly may be a new experience for you and one to which you may take a fancy. But it *does* seem rather a distraction from our main mission, does it not? Just asking, dear boy."

"You're starting to sound like the Queen Mum, you know?"

"I could do worse. At least she found great consolation in Tanqueray. I await your reply."

"Speed."

"Speed?"

"*Speed* is what this is all about, Mandy. We have to get inside the decision cycle of whoever is running this operation. Keraklis called Istanbul and mentioned the *Subito*. He called"—Dalton checked his watch—"at 1854 hours, a little before seven in the evening. It's now almost two in the morning. Sofouli won't find Keraklis and the missing chopper until he gets up. Whoever was running Keraklis will be wondering why he hasn't heard back. But it's a good bet that he won't get really concerned about it until the morning. By then, we'll be right in his face, exactly where he won't be expecting—"

"Whoever *he* is—"

"Yes. In short, we'll be inside his decision cycle—"

That put Mandy over the top.

"Oh *bugger* his decision cycle. Couldn't we have taken a civilian flight? Or do you just like commandeering things?"

"Even inside the EU, they ask for papers at the airports. Which travel documents would you have used? The Pearson passports, which, by the time we got to Athens, would have set off alarms all over the airport? Our personal papers, which would kick off triggers back in Langley. Or would we just tell them we were CIA agents on a goodwill tour to Turkey? You know how well we're getting along with Turkey these days. You heard Keraklis talking to someone at Ataköy Marina about the *Subito*. That boat's a crime scene, supposedly the scene of Kiki Lujac's murder, and I want to go over it before they put it somewhere we'll never find it—"

"We don't know the *Subito* is at this marina—"

"And we don't know it isn't, but if we stay inside the decision cycle—"

"If you use that phrase again, Micah, I swear I will strike you. We will also be *inside* a Turkish prison, as I have pointed out—"

"No, we won't."

"No? Now I'm all aflutter. Why not, pray tell?"

"We're going to lose our escort."

Mandy gave him one of her raised-eyebrow looks, but since it was quite dim in the cabin and he couldn't see her face, he was able to survive it.

"Oh goody," she said. "I just *knew* you'd have a plan. How *are* you going to lose our little friends? Really?"

"Do you want to know? Really?"

"No, not really. Well, yes . . . yes, I do."

Dalton told her straight out, and since then she had been, for her, unnaturally silent. Now, with the lights of Bandirma under their feet and the black void of the Sea of Marmara eating up the rest of the forward universe, the time for acting was growing very short.

Dalton got on the CREW com-net to Levka.

"Levka, how are you doing back there?"

His voice came back, a little oversprightly but coherent.

"I am good, boss. I have machine gun working, if you like?"

"How'd you do that?"

"Found oil can in locker. Also big box of 7.62. You want I shoot up a Turk soldier for you? I never liked Turk soldiers."

"Not right now. What else is back there?"

"Hard to say. All the medical stuff is ripped out. Rest is all tied down. Looks like maybe life raft, flares, blankets, gas cans—junk, boss, only junk."

"But it's all tied down, nothing loose?"

"No, boss. All tight"—*Including Levka,* he thought but did not add.

"Okay. For now, what I want is for you to buckle up. I mean, strap in real solid. You follow?"

Levka was silent for a moment while he worked out the implications.

"Okeydokey, boss," he said, cinching his straps in and stuffing the ouzo bottle into a zippered pocket. "I follow. We are going for ride?"

"We are," said Dalton. Then he looked across at Mandy, checked out her straps and his, checked them both again, gave Mandy a look that said *Brace yourself,* and then clicked the com-set to open.

"Escort Six Actual, this is Medevac, come back."

"Medevac, this is Escort Six."

"Six, I'm looking at my starboard engine temperature readout and it's saying I'm running at over red line. This may be an instrument malfunction since all my other parameters are nominal. Can you drop back and take a heat signature off my starboard engine?"

A pause.

"No, we cannot, Medevac. We are not equipped. Do you have redundant sensors?"

No infrared detection on board.

"Negative. This old bird is very tired. Taped together. Our avionics are ten years old. Do you have night vision capabilities?"

A pause.

"Negative. We are on approach to Atatürk. ETA, thirty minutes. Do you need to turn back and try for Bandirma?"

And no NVGs.

"Negative, Six. This heart is too urgent. We have to try for Atatürk. Can you drop back and see if I'm losing coolant?"

More silence.

Six Actual was a wary flyer. Young but smart.

"Yes, Medevac. We will drop back and do a visual on your starboard engine housing. Please hold your course and maintain altitude."

"Roger that. Appreciate it, Six."

The three choppers flew level for another few seconds, and then the Little Bird flared up slightly and dropped back, gaining altitude but losing speed. At the same time, taking his mind off the game, the pilot of the port Little Bird chopper let his ride drift a few degrees farther away. Dalton had his hand on the collective, waiting for his moment.

"Medevac, this is Escort Six. I am in your slipstream and cannot see any coolant leakage. Repeat, you are not losing—"

Dalton hit a flip-top button marked EMERGENCY FUEL DUMP. The multifunction display indicator started to flash bright red with the warning STARBOARD AUXILIARY FUEL DUMP. There was a hissing sound, and a vapor cloud of JP-6 fuel began to stream out from the starboard auxiliary tank, a teardrop-shaped bolt-on clamped to a stub wing.

Little Bird 1 was right in the cone of the fuel spraying out from the Blackhawk's slipstream. The pilot's reaction was quick but not quick enough.

"Medevac, this is Escort Six. You are losing fluid! I am in your stream, and you are losing coolant. Repeat, you are—"

But it wasn't coolant. It was high-octane aviation fuel, and it promptly did what JP-6 likes to do: it found a hot spark in the Little Bird's engine, there was a red flash, a blooming white light. Little Bird 1 caught fire and, a moment later, blew itself to pieces.

The concussion wave hit the tail boom, knocking the Blackhawk forward and into a yaw. Dalton, fighting to regain control, hit the com-set and radioed Little Bird 2.

"Escort Two, I am losing power. Repeat, I am losing—"

The com-set speaker crackled into life with a frantic burst of cross talk in Turkish as the pilot of Little Bird 2 radioed the news of the midair explosion to his base, wherever the hell that was. Right now, as what was left of Little Bird 1 was raining molten steel and burned body parts down onto the town of Bandirma, the pilot of Little Bird 2 was not thinking about the United Nations Blackhawk at all.

Dalton, seizing the moment, cut the radio off abruptly, at the same time that he turned off all the exterior airframe lights, including the rotor-hub strobes and the navigation lights under the nose and tail boom.

He hit the collective and shoved the Blackhawk into a controlled shallow dive, checking his parameters. He shut off FUEL DUMP, waited two seconds for the flow to tail off.

Then he pressed CHAFF/FLARE.

A spray of shredded aluminum foil and four red Very lights popped out of the flare pod and rocketed backward into the vapor cloud of fuel that was still drifting in the atmosphere behind them. In a moment, another blue-white light blossomed, illuminating the sky, followed by a dimly felt concussive boom. They heard a burst of panicky Turkish from Little Bird 2 on the com-set, a brief, terrified shout cut off abruptly.

Mandy, twisting to look through the side window, saw Little Bird 2, a thousand feet above them, watched it veer sharply up and to the south, trying to avoid flying into the second fireball burning in the cold night sky.

Dalton, knowing that the pilot of Little Bird 2 would get his nerve and his bearings back in a moment, kept the Blackhawk in a steep descent, right at the operational limits. The altimeter display was winding backward, the two RPM indicators were well into the red zone, and the PARAMETER alert was going off, a deafening klaxon wail.

Mandy watched the surface of the Sea of Marmara coming at them, glanced over at Dalton, whose tight face was locked and grim as he fought the collective and watched the control indicators. The rotor vibration was intense, shaking the airframe brutally, with things rattling around the floor of the cockpit, and the engines were shrieking.

At a thousand feet, Dalton pulled back on the stick, finally leveling the laboring chopper out at less than two hundred feet above the surface of the sea. They were still running dark, although the glow of her twin turbines would have been faintly visible against the water. The rotor wash was kicking up spray, and the windshield was streaming.

Dalton slowed the shuddering old machine to a near hover, looked out his side window, then through the glass overhead. He saw a faint strobe blinking far above them, the other Little Bird, circling aimlessly, probably on the radio calling in his position and scrambling a rescue chopper.

Mandy broke the short silence.

"Did you know that was going to happen?"

Dalton looked over at her.

"Yes, Mandy, I did."

Mandy looked away.

"Those poor kids."

"Yes," said Dalton. "And that's what we do. You understand that?"

She flared back at him.

"Yes. I started this, didn't I? I shot a dead man in the back of the head a few hours ago, so I imagine I can handle this."

Dalton held her look for a moment, and then got on the CREW net.

"Levka, you okay?"

Levka had lost his bottle of ouzo in the dive. It was rolling around the floor of the cabin, and he was trying to retrieve it. He jerked back in his straps and hit the squawk button.

"Yeah, boss. Okeydokey."

"I'm going to hover here for sixty seconds. I want you to open the bay door, pop that life raft into the water, and dump everything we have back there into the raft. You copy that?"

"Everything? Also luggage of miss?"

Dear Saint Boris, not the ouzo!

"No. Not the damned luggage. And not the camouflage tarp. But everything else!"

Dalton held the machine in hover. Through the boards, they could feel Levka dragging cargo to the open bay, and they could hear the splash as matériel hit the waves. The open door let in a cold, wet wind and the smell of diesel oil and dead fish. Dalton and Mandy spent the minute trying to see where Little Bird 2 was—so far, still circling at six thousand feet, judging from the position of the blinking strobe on its belly.

Down at this level, they could make out the hulls of freighters crowding the entrance to the Bosphorus, a constellation of navigation lights blinking on the horizon, their black masts silhouetted against the low-mounded glimmering of Istanbul. Levka was back on the headset radio.

"All okay, boss. Now what?"

"You keep one of the flares?"

Levka swore to himself.

"No, boss, sorry. You say dump everything!"

"Got a match?"

"Yes, boss."

"Still got some of that ouzo left?"

"Ouzo, boss?"

"I can smell it up here. Grab a bottle, stick a rag in it, light the rag, and toss it into the raft. Do it!"

Levka, sighing, did what he was told. The bottle, fire flickering at its neck, tumbled into the raft, shattering into licking blue flames just as Dalton put the chopper into a forward glide, skimming the top of the waves. They were a hundred feet away when the flare box went up. And then the ammunition belts cooked off, a fireworks display that could be seen on the shoreline a mile behind them. It lasted a few moments, and then, as the raft burned and deflated, winked out, there was nothing but darkness.

Dalton was hoping that brief flare-up against the black plain of open water would be taken as the UN Medevac chopper crashing.

The water depth off the coast of Bandirma was over six hundred feet, and the bottom was littered with iron wrecks from Gallipoli and two world wars, so any sonar scan would be pretty inconclusive.

Dalton lined the nose of the Blackhawk up on the misty lights of Istanbul and pushed the collective forward. The chopper picked up speed, its wheels just brushing the waves.

"Levka?"

"Yes, boss?"

"You know Istanbul?"

"Pretty okay. I know good whorehouse in Aksaray—"

"I need to put this machine down somewhere out of sight. If the military don't buy the idea that we crashed off Bandirma, they'll tear the town up looking for this chopper. And they'll find it sooner or later. On the GPS charts, there's open land on the east side of Atatürk Field—"

"Yes. Is soccer stadium. Across from airport parking lot. Next to that is sewage place. Big open field, but no good to hide chopper. Too much people all around."

"Okay, I'm open to suggestions."

Levka gave it some thought while they swooped in toward the lights of the city. The mist on the water coated the windshield. Freighters and tankers and container hulks were all around them now, some of them close enough for the rows of porthole lights and the rust on the hulls to be seen as they ghosted past them, most of them moored in the shallow waters, showing only navigation lights. The rotors churned up the water as they drifted over it, sending a large circular fan of ripples outward, dragging it along behind them like a white lace net on a black velvet tablecloth.

"Micah," said Mandy during the pause, "there's only one place where a helicopter won't stand out and that's at an airport. Is there another one around, maybe a small private one?"

Dalton hit a few buttons on the GPS chart screen and a list came up, along with lats and longs and bearings from their position.

"There's another big public one on the Asian side, at Sabiha Gökçen . . . There's a little one, Samandira, looks like mainly private planes. Not used much, according to the data file, but it's a long way east of our position—twenty miles, anyway—and it's seven miles inland. Over a lot of towns and villages. Levka, you copying?"

"Yes, boss?"

"You know a private airport on the Arab side of Istanbul east of the Bosphorus, seven miles inland, called Samandira?"

"No, boss. But is *private* field? On Asia side of Bosphorus? Not on Europe side?"

"Yes, looks like it."

"We have money?"

"We have money."

"Then Asia Istanbullus have good word for this. *Vermek* is word."

"*Vermek*? What does it mean?"

"Means 'bribe.' "

"Would a straight bribe be enough to get them to take a risk like that? If they got caught with a chopper involved in the deaths of Turkish military personnel, they'd be lucky to just get shot."

"Asia side hate Europe-side Turk soldiers. Arab side lie to Turk soldiers for free. With big smile on. *Vermek* is for them honey on top of pretty girl's belly."

"I'm not sure I get that, but *vermek* works for me," said Dalton.

"*Vermek* work for *everybody*," said Levka. "Is proof God love us."

NATIONAL SECURITY AGENCY

FORT MEADE, MARYLAND

THE BLUE BOX, CRYPTO CITY

The AD of RA's office, in the large blue-glass cube in the center of Crypto City, was a stripped-down corner suite with a view out over the barren ochre forests of Maryland in winter. The office interior echoed this wintry austerity: wooden floors, a long wooden desk of no particular style, a sideboard from Crate and Barrel. The only impressive fixture was a Sony plasma screen hanging on the wall facing the desk, on which were running several simultaneous feeds from news operations and intelligence services inside the American security matrix.

There was a U.S. flag with military-style gold fringe in one corner next to a framed photo of a platoon of U.S. Marines moving carefully through a jungle clearing. Judging from the style of their BDUs, it was sometime in the mid-eighties. The jungle could have been anywhere from Central America to Malaysia. The young Marine LT on point, in itself unusual for an LT, was a large-bodied artillery shell of a man with clear-cut features, deep-set eyes, and a wild piratical look about him.

A few years later, an older version of this young Marine would have an Iranian-made shape charge detonate against the side of his armored Humvee during the taking of Fallujah, rocking it onto its side, mortally wounding the driver and setting the interior on fire. The hatch gunner on the .50 got his sleeve tangled up in the gun-mount swivel as the ammo started to cook off, and he would have either been burned alive or riddled with .50 caliber rounds if the third Marine in the Humvee, a lieutenant colonel by then, hadn't gone back into the flaming vehicle to drag the boy free, getting a faceful of fire for his efforts.

The .50 gunner lived to fight again, the driver DOA at the TOC, and the lieutenant colonel—a brigade-level G2—got a Silver Star and a mandatory early out due to facial disfigurement and the loss of one eye.

The man now sitting at the unremarkable desk in this Zen room was that same man, Hank Brocius, ex-USMC, and now the AD of RA for the National Security Agency, dressed in a fine gray pinstripe, the jacket neatly stowed on a hanger on the back of the door.

Brocius, one side of his face covered with a masklike burn scar from temple to chin, and the other side, an older and more battered version of the same Marine in the framed jungle photo, was leaning back in an armless wooden swivel chair with his back to the window, his hands folded behind his neck, as he directed his one-eyed but highly approving consideration upon the lovely young woman sitting in the rail-back chair on the far side of his desk, a classic, full-bodied Italian heart attack in the style of Isabella Rossellini, whose name was Nikki Turrin.

Ms. Turrin was reading from a decrypted communication sent by the London field team investigating the torture killing of Mildred Durant, once a mainstay of the Venona Project and, up until her death, a kind of unofficial adviser to an NAS decryption team, known generally as the Glass Cutters.

The work of the London investigation team was complete, and Nikki Turrin, chief assistant to the AD of RA, was relaying the summary of their findings in a flat, toneless voice, much unlike her normal speech, which was bright, quick, lively, and delivered in a soft soprano lilt. Nikki's tone now was unvarying, Brocius was well aware, because she thought the field team's report was, from title to appendices, a load of utter horseshit.

". . . and the toxicology report came back with nothing other than some alcohol traces in her blood—"

"Millie loved her gin and tonic," said the AD of RA.

"And of course the meds she was on were all represented. But nothing in that was, they say here, 'indicative,' whatever that means. Why can't Audrey simply say they didn't find anything useful? Never mind. She goes on here about the state of Mrs. Durant's health, several paras of that—"

"Does she ever cut to the chase?"

Nikki looked up, tossing her long brown hair as she did so, her dark eyes full of the winter light streaming in through the blinds behind Brocius.

"As far as I can see, sir, Audrey and her people have no actual 'chase' in them. Her conclusions are laid out in the summary page. Do you want me to read the rest or just go there?"

"Just give me the summary."

Nikki put the documents into a lockbox on the AD of RA's desk with a Post-it on it reading REDDIT? SHREDDIT!, sat back in the uncompromising chair, crossed her legs demurely at her ankles like a good Italian girl, and gave Brocius a smile that was completely devoid of humor.

"Sir, to be brief, she concurs . . . God, I'm starting to talk like her . . . She *agrees* with the findings of the First Response forensic unit when they got on scene, namely, that the intruder was male, possibly in his mid- to late forties, based on the results of the witness canvass, quite strong, that he must have presented an appearance to Mrs. Durant that was acceptable to her or she would never have unlocked her door to him—no sign of forced entry—that he took control of Mrs. Durant immediately upon gaining entry—she had a medic-alert alarm on a chain around her neck and it was never used—"

"Never found either, right?"

"Yes, sir. The initial assault took place in the front room, based on the pattern of scrape marks on the hardwood . . . She was picked up and carried into the bedroom, where the assailant proceeded to—"

"Oh my no. Stop there, will you? I'm not up to all that again. None of us are. What does Audrey say about the thing with the pictures?"

"Part of his fetish—that's the word she uses—she's let Oprah and Dr. Phil completely screw up her mind—part of a *humiliation ritual with Oedipal subtext*—" She stopped, sighing heavily.

"Christ, sir, this is all boneheaded crap—"

"We can editorialize later, Nikki."

"Fine, you're the boss. Basically, Audrey and her team have reached the conclusion, based on all the evidence they could avoid—"

"Nikki!"

"Sorry. That Mrs. Durant was the victim of a sadistic predator who had two motives in the assault, the first was the complete domination and destruction of his victim—penetrative sex did not occur, apparently—and the second was something she's calling 'fetish robbery.' Items taken from the victim's body that would serve later as masturbatory aids as the fantasy replayed in his . . . I mean, what the hell is a *fetish* robbery? Is that like armed robbery only instead of a gun you brandish a dead chicken? Anyway, the assailant obtained the entry codes to Mrs. Durant's safe—a Victorian-era Whitney embedded in the bricks of her house that would require a pound of plastique to dislodge—and took from that various items which, from the insurance policies she had, included rings, bracelets, necklaces, assorted loose jewels—rubies, sapphires, emeralds—possibly three thousand pounds' worth of old Bank of England notes, a man's antique Breguet wristwatch—her husband's, I guess—some bearer bonds, perhaps a diary . . . It goes on, but all of it's basically what you'd expect to find in a wealthy woman's flat—"

"And the hard drive?"

"The killer used it to upload the digital shots. It's where he got all her e-mail connections, the nasty little prick. We got the entire machine here two days ago, and the Gearboxes went through it bolt by bolt. And there was no subsequent attempt at an intrusion into the Glass Cutter network that the Net Watchers could find. So Audrey's conclusion is NEA—"

"No Enemy Action—"

"Right. Just an unlucky collision between a lovely old lady and a walking demon from the deepest pits of Hell. Too bad, but there it is, life is hard, lah-dee-dah, sometimes bad things happen to good people—"

"And you don't agree? With any of this?"

She shifted in her very uncomfortable chair—one day she was going to sneak into this office and install a whole new suite of furniture, it so looked like a military monk lived in this barrack—folded her arms across her chest, and cocked her head to one side, giving him a look of affectionate exasperation.

"Sir—"

"Nikki, we've been *sleeping* together for weeks."

She gave him a lovely smile but shook her head.

"Not in this office, we haven't."

"Yet."

She looked around at the sharp-edged furnishings.

"And we never will. Sir, if you ask me, Audrey sees what she wanted to see."

Brocius wasn't persuaded.

"Audrey's been right most of the time, Nikki. And I agree with her that no foreign intelligence agency would indulge itself in the kind of elaborate vivisection that happened here. Nor would they invite a phalanx of *federales* down on them by sending pictures of the attack out to all her friends and colleagues. I have to think—"

"Sir, do you remember a CIA Cleaner by the name of Micah Dalton?"

Brocius, under stress, often stroked his cheekbone just under the patch over his missing eye. He did that now.

"Christ yes. How could I forget him? He fast-talked me into doing a unilateral TEMPEST shutdown of half the communication grid in the Balkans. I ended up in the Oval Office in front of the DNI and the President."

"That TEMPEST intervention also saved the nation from a Serbian stock swindle that could have sunk the American commodities market for ten years."

"Yeah, yeah. And the market tanked, anyway, didn't it? This is me waving a tiny, invisible flag. I don't have stocks. I have a rapacious ex-wife and a penny jar. Anyway, what about him? Cather never called him back in, did he? Last I heard of him, he had gone back to Venice to sit around and sulk in some stinking pink palazzo."

"I doubt that man sulks very much. Did you read his AAR?"

"I didn't have to. I had it read *to* me, by the DNI, at the top of his lungs."

"Do you remember what it said there about this Montenegrin national named Kiki Lujac?"

"Yes, I do. Some kind of fashion shooter who was using his day job as a cover for freelance intelligence work. Supposed to be connected with Branco Gospic, the guy Dalton eighty-sixed in Kotor. Lujac turned up dead, a floater somewhere in the southern Aegean, I think it said."

"Yes, sir. Off the island of Santorini, actually."

"Okay, good riddance. Probably the Croats, cleaning house. Or Dalton, who, if you don't mind my saying, is a serious whack job.

One of our stringers in Trieste said the Carabinieri were jumpy as hell just having the guy hanging around Florian's."

"I didn't think he was all that bad when I talked to him on the phone. He seemed competent. Calm. Had a sense of humor. And some grace. I had some news for him about a woman he was involved with, Cora Vasari, she had been shot in Florence. When I told him she was going to be okay, you could hear the relief in his voice, thanked me from the heart. Doesn't sound like a whack job to me. And I met the woman he was working with in Singapore—"

"That English babe? Pownall? I saw a picture of her, made . . . I mean, she made quite an impression on me. What about her?"

"She thought the world of him. And from the little time I got to spend with her, she was in no way a fool."

"Fine, I stand corrected. The chicks all adore him. Even you, sounds like. Isn't that special. You have an actual point here?"

"She talked about this Lujac guy, the photographer. She said that he had done something pretty kinky to a cop in Singapore—"

"Good for him."

"And that afterward, he had taken pictures of it—"

"Okay, now I see where this is going."

"Digital pictures—"

"Geez."

"And sent them to his superiors, to the local press in Changi—"

"But not to his Facebook page?"

"You know very well what I'm saying—"

"Yes. You're saying that somehow this guy Kiki Lujac rose from the dead in the Aegean, strapped on some Hermès sandals—note the classical reference—flew himself to London, where he managed to weasel his way into Millie Durant's flat in Chelsea. Nikki, I knew Millie, and I'm pretty sure she would not have opened her door to a dripping-wet partly decomposed corpse no matter how nice his shoes were."

"It pleases you to be droll."

"It pleases me to . . ."

He stopped, his expression altering, thinking suddenly of the little frog prince.

"Nikki, what did this guy look like?"

"Lujac? We can get shots from his website—"

"Can you? Get me one, will you?"

"Right now?"

"Yeah, please, if you don't mind."

Nikki got up without a word and went back into the outer office. Alice Chandler, secretary to the AD of RA, was a rather severe-looking but greathearted older woman with shining silver hair swept up behind and sterling silver reading glasses that she wore low on her aristocratic nose. She worked whatever hours her boss worked, having no life outside the NSA and no desire for one. Tonight, Nikki and the AD of RA were working until well after midnight, therefore so was she.

"Alice, can you click onto a website for me?"

Ms. Chandler, who knew very well that Nikki Turrin and the AD of RA—that's what she called him, and, after a while, so did everyone else except Nikki—were having an affair. Alice Chandler had known the AD of RA's wife before she was an ex—the woman had left a fifteen-year marriage because she couldn't deal with the man's burn scars!—and she highly approved of the poor man's new relationship.

"Certainly, dear, what is it?"

"I think it's kikilujac.com."

Ms. Chandler keyed it in, waited a heartbeat. A site not found popped up on the screen.

"Are you sure that's the right one, Nikki?"

"Positive. Can you just Google the name Kiki Lujac?"

"Of course."

Seconds later, she shook her head at the screen.

"Not a thing. Some writer used the name in a novel, but, other than that, there's no return for Kiki Lujac at all."

"Can you try his full name, Kirik Lujac?"

Ms. Chandler tried that too.

"Not a thing, sweetheart. Nothing at all."

Nikki frowned at the screen.

"But that makes no sense at all. He was a well-known fashion photographer. There would have been hundreds—thousands—of references to his work all over Europe. He shot Madonna, for heaven's sake."

"With a gun?" said Ms. Chandler, who deeply disapproved of Madonna and all her works and days.

"With a camera, I imagine. I don't get it. How could this be?"

"Well, if you wanted to have someone hunt down every reference in Google and try to get it pulled, I guess you could do it that way."

"That would take . . . No, it's just impossible. There'd be thousands of references—websites—many of them buried in other sites that you couldn't hack into if you . . ."

Her voice trailed off.

"Do you think someone hacked into Google in some way?" asked Ms. Chandler. Nikki was silent for a while and then shook her head.

"No . . . I don't know . . . no. The whole thing's impossible. Thank you, Ms. Chandler . . . really."

"That's fine, dear. Always happy to help. Do you two want some coffee?"

"Please, that would be terrific," said Nikki, going back into the AD of RA's office. She found him on the phone, listening intently to someone on the other end of the line. He smiled at her, pointed to the same damned chair. He was still on the line when Ms. Chandler came back with the coffee, but he ended the call as she was leaving.

"Thank you, Alice, just what I needed."

Ms. Chandler let her beatific smile shine upon them both, like the blessing of a saint upon the marriage bed.

Nikki caught the smile on Brocius's face.

"Does she know about us?"

"Alice?" said Brocius, his face a mask of innocence. "Goodness no."

"You never say 'goodness.' "

"I do when I'm lying. What did you get?"

"Odd," she said. "Really odd. There's not a trace of him anywhere on the Web. It's as if someone scoured the Internet, wiping out every reference to him. I mean, that isn't possible, is it?"

Brocius didn't smile.

"I don't know. If I don't mind spending the rest of my life in Leavenworth, I can shut down the entire communications net of a foreign country with a couple of keystrokes."

"But why . . . why would someone do something like that? And think of the resources you'd have to have. I mean, the guy's dead. What would it matter?"

"If he was such a fashion celebrity, there'd be pictures of him—hard-copy shots—in all the high-style magazines like *GQ* . . . *Vogue* . . . um . . . ?"

"*NASCAR Week*? *Guns 'n' Ammo*?"

"Well, excuse me. I'm sorry I'm not quite up to speed on the fashion scene. I think I'll put one of the kids in Research on that."

"You looked like you were thinking of something specific. I mean, something to do with Lujac?"

Brocius said nothing for a while, running his background check of Briony Keating's little toy frog through his mind. He had done it himself so he would know that it had been done properly. And it had been. There were a couple of things that had bothered him: the parents dead early, the fire at the records hall. And Briony had never confirmed that the burn scars that were supposed to be on this guy's back were there.

But on everything else, the guy was rock solid.

And something else: he and Briony had gotten a little tangled up—more than a little—in Rockport, Massachusetts, for a few memorable weeks one long-ago summer—by then, both their marriages had been cratering—but the story of Briony Keating was one he didn't feel like cracking open with Nikki Turrin just yet.

Maybe the best thing to do would be to take the shuttle up to La Guardia, drive on up to Garrison, and just . . . pop in. Just like old friends do. See the guy for himself. Yes, he'd go tomorrow. Which reminded him of something else: he had promised Briony that he'd find out where in the eastern Med her son Morgan was stationed. So far, his guy at the Navy Yards hadn't gotten back to him. So wrap that up too and take it all up to Briony in the morning.

Nikki was waiting for a response. He made a dismissive gesture, looking down, playing with some papers.

"Yeah, but it was nothing, a dead end."

She smiled, aware that Brocius had just set something aside, something he didn't want to talk to her about at any rate. That was fine. She didn't *own* the man. "Okay, who were you talking to just now?"

"Nikki, do you like to travel?"

"I know this one. You ask me if I like to travel and I say yes and then you say 'Do you like sex?' and I say yes and then you say 'Well, why don't you fuck off?'"

"Is that a real line?"

"I've used it to get rid of creeps in bars. Who were you talking to?"

"You got me thinking about Lujac. I called a guy in Santorini, where this Lujac guy is supposed to have died. I reached a cop named Sofouli. He was a little worked up. Want to know why?"

"Why?"

"Somebody killed his sergeant and stole his helicopter."

"Why is he telling you this?"

"Because he thought I had something to do with it."

"And why did he think that?"

"Because I was calling from the National Security Administration, which to him is the same as calling from the CIA. Actually, the way he phrased it, that would be the *facking* CIA, pardon my Greek. And Captain Sofouli is convinced that it was somebody from the CIA. He described the man—in fact, it was a man and a woman. They were both Americans. They claimed to be a couple from Portland, Oregon, by the name of Bill and Dorothy Pearson. Had the passports to prove it, which tells us something. But when Captain Sofouli put a call in to the Portland police, they sent a cruiser around to Mr. Pearson's home and—bingo!—there they were, and, according to them, there they had been for about three months. Would you like to know what brought these Portlandish Pearsonians to Santorini?"

"I would love to."

"They were there, in Captain Sofouli's view, to ascertain— now I'm talking like Audrey—to ascertain the identity of a corpse that Captain Sofouli's people found floating in the waters off the island."

"Would that corpse be the corpse of Kiki Lujac?"

"Correct. Your prize is a lollipop. Do you want it now or later?"

"Later. Did he get any pictures of these people?"

"He did. He's e-mailing me their visa shots now. Oh look, here comes the lovely Alice right on cue."

Ms. Chandler came in with two-color printouts in her hand. She smiled at Nikki and put them down in front of the AD of RA. Then she smiled at Nikki again—unlike her opinion of Madonna, she was totally in favor of Nikki—and drifted out of the office on a lilac-scented zephyr.

The AD of RA looked down at the Greek visa shots, taken at the customs desk at Athens International, and then turned them around so that Nikki could get a good look.

The woman was fine featured and beautifully boned but rather imperious-looking, with milk-white skin and cool gray eyes and a damn-you twist to her sensual lips. Nikki knew her quite well.

The other picture was a lean, cut young man with a sharply defined jawline and prominent cheekbones—one of which carried a deeply scored, raw-looking scar, almost a slash, looking quite recent—hooded eyes of an unnerving pale blue—killer's eyes—a firm but not entirely cruel mouth, and pale blond hair, swept back from his face and long enough to reach his shoulders. This picture radiated a kind of predatory sensuality that she could feel in her . . . Well, it was none of anyone's business where she could feel it.

She tapped the shot of the woman.

"That's Mandy Pownall. Which probably means—"

"The guy is Micah Dalton? That's him. I've got his shot on file from the Agency. That's Micah Dalton in the creeping flesh. Like his looks?"

Nikki gave the question some serious thought, which bothered the AD of RA a little. He had just uncovered a long-dead emotion called "jealousy." He didn't like it and was working very hard at burying it again.

"He looks like a guy you'd want around if you had a problem with an ex-boyfriend who needed scaring off. And he has a nice smile somewhere inside there. You can see the lines around his eyes and mouth. And he looks smart. He doesn't have that deadeyed hating look that you see in some professional killers . . . ?"

" 'The enemies of reason have a certain blind look,' " said the AD of RA, quoting Ridley Scott's film *The Duellists*.

"Yes, I call it the 'Mohamed Atta face.' That's not what you see here. I'll bet he has a good mind, but he's a little damaged. I would love to know his whole story. What did his file say?"

"Mainly classified. No next of kin listed, not even a sibling. Married once, wife suffered some sort of stroke and was in a vegetative state in a hospital in Carmel. Died a while back. Buried with their only child, a baby girl, killed in a domestic accident a few years earlier. Pretty young, considering his operational experience: Somalia, Central America, Afghanistan, Tora Bora, when they were trying to get Bin Laden. Word in the halls is, he's resourceful, a great fieldman. Smart."

Nikki considered the man's face for a time.

"I would guess that women like him. A lot. Mandy Pownall certainly does. And that Vasari woman seemed to be important to him."

"Yeah, well, in the meantime why are these two in Santorini asking questions about Kiki Lujac? And whatever they're doing, they're playing hardball. This sergeant who got killed? They found his body in the bottom of a swimming pool. His neck was broken. According to his file, that's a Dalton trademark. He likes to get in close, to kill with his hands. He was Fifth Special Forces before he came on with Clandestine Services, and they still talk about him around the non-com mess at Fort Campbell. They called him the 'Crocodile.' Last fall, he killed some psycho Indian medicine man in southeastern Colorado, hacked his head off, and mailed it to a cop in Butte, Montana. Yes, that's right, Nikki, that got your attention. That's what they're *like* at the goddamned CIA. They're either a pack of nancy-boy, left-wing college profs mincing around the hallways leaking state secrets to—"

Nikki rolled her eyes theatrically, sighed heavily.

"The goddamned *New York Times* . . . I know, sir. We all know."

"Well, it's the simple truth, isn't it? That's on one side. Over on the paramilitary side, they're a bunch of living-dead night stalkers, just like this guy, shape-shifters and dark-of-the-moon vampires who eat their dead and lick their blades clean after every kill."

"Now, there's a lovely image."

Brocius ignored her.

"Look, I don't like this *coincidence*, Nikki, not one little bit. You tell me you have a feeling Kiki Lujac could have done this Durant thing. Now it looks like the CIA's in Santorini on the same guy's trail. I don't believe in coincidences, but I do believe in your instincts. You're fresh. You haven't been inside long enough to start thinking like Audrey Fulton. You did great work in Trieste. So maybe it's a good idea to send you—"

"Maybe?"

"Look, this is serious. Hear me. I do not want the CIA *anywhere near* this Millie Durant investigation. Or near the Glass Cutters in general. CIA types just complicate things. Look at this Agency harpy Mariah Vale, runs their Counter-Intelligence Analysis Group. Last fall, at an interagency briefing, which was just a courtesy, she took a vague, unsourced, and completely unverified reference we *might* have found in one of the Riga intercepts—it might even be a sorting artifact—"

"What is that?"

"Decryption's a matter of number-frequency sorting. Depending on the language you think the message was encrypted in, you try to assign a frequency value to every possible letter. In English, for example, letters often appear in pairs or threes, so if you get a *t* followed by two other letters, you have a statistical basis for thinking the other two are *h* and *e*. Once you're sure you have those three letters identified, you try to see where a similar number string occurs. Letter by letter, gradually over time, you get whole words, then phrases, and, theoretically, you have the entire message decrypted. Different languages have different letter groups, letter frequencies. You sort out the letter-frequency possibilities with the mainframes, but now and then things screw up and you get a sort of false positive. A string of words that look like a phrase—and it may be—but it's not a real part of the actual message, it's just a 'program artifact.' "

"Like the infinity of monkeys typing a Shakespeare play."

"That's it, sort of. Only, in this case, it's just a few words running together. The problem is, the words running together looked like an indirect reference to a long-term mole in a certain sector of U.S. intelligence."

"Did anybody try to tell Mariah Vale about this 'artifact' issue?"

"I did, personally. I told her what I just told you. Several times. But she's so freaked out about moles she's come down with the Jesus disease."

Nikki had read a brief on the man last month and was pleased to let Brocius know it. "James Jesus Angleton. After Philby bolted, he got completely obsessed with the idea that there was still a mole in the Agency. But wasn't he finally proved right?"

"Christ, who knows? Depends on which KGB defector you be-lieved, Golitsin or Nosenko. They told completely conflicting stories. Angleton's own assistant, Clare Petty, was pretty convinced at the end that Angleton *himself* was a KGB agent. I mean, who did Jim Angleton ever expose? Nobody. Mostly, he wrapped the CIA up in a tangle of flat-out paranoia until Colby finally sacked him in 'seventy-six. He couldn't have screwed up the Agency more if he *had* been a KGB mole. That's the kind of swamp they swim in over there. And now this Mariah Vale broad—woman—now she's got intelligence in a virtual war with the National Clandestine Service. She's started a full-blown counterespionage audit looking for a mole that probably doesn't even exist. The whole Agency's paralyzed all over again. In-cluding Deacon Cather. You ever meet the guy?"

"I talked to him on the phone during the Chicago thing. I've seen a picture of him. Six feet two, long, horsey face, teeth like tomb-stones, bald, skin like a lizard's, and the coldest black eyes I've ever seen. Reminded me of one of the meaner Medicis. Dalton works for Cather, doesn't he?"

"Hard to say. After Chicago, it looked like Cather was bringing him back in. But Dalton was still in Venice last week. And now he turns up in Santorini and people get killed. I think I really need to know what's going on."

"So, do you want me to go to Santorini and talk to this cop?"

"Last time, I sent you to Trieste and you almost died."

"But I didn't. And it was Muggia, not Trieste."

"Look, if I let you go, I just want you to be a back-channel asset, and you report only to me, okay? Here's your mission from which you *will not* deviate, hear me? You fly to Santorini as a declared representative of this Agency, you have a chat with this cop, he proves to you that Kiki Lujac is dead, you confirm for us that the two Americans who came to see him were actually Dalton and Pownall, you say thanks, you spend the night in a snazzy hotel, maybe soak in a Jacuzzi—*alone*—have a nice meal, you fly right back home in the morning. And Nikki, above all, you stay *aeons* away from this Dalton guy. *Light*-years. All I want you to do is put this Lujac theory to bed and then come back here and we go on with our quiet little lives. Could you do that, and *only* that?"

Nikki was, for once, stunned into silence. Traveling *declared*. With ID. This constituted a *major* promotion. At least two pay grades.

"I'm . . . dazzled. And complimented."

"Just don't do anything nuts. Have a talk with Sofouli, then come home—*straight* home. Understand?"

"Heard and understood. How am I traveling?"

"You *could* have one of our Gulfstreams."

"I thought we weren't trying to attract attention?"

"I know. I just thought it would be—"

"Safer? Thanks, but no. How about I just fly a public carrier?"

"Okay, but not back there with the herbivores. First class. Full diplomatic protection. None of that covert crap. I want the NSA crest tattooed on your . . . your luggage. Your carry-on. Whatever."

"What do I say I'm doing?"

"Consulting with other agencies. If they press you at any port, have them call Alice and she'll page me and I'll rip their lungs out."

"I accept. With heartfelt thanks. I mean, the whole assignment."

"Yeah, you're welcome. Just don't get hurt, okay?"

Nikki gave him a hard look and then softened it.

"I need to make my *own* name here. Not just as your—"

"Anybody saying that?"

"Not to my face."

"I get wind of any of that, time I'm through with them they'll look worse than I do. Now, go. Go, and then come back."

ISTANBUL

ÇENGELKÖY, THE ASIAN SIDE OF THE BOSPHORUS

Dawn was a faint rose-colored tint on the black night in the hills behind them as the gypsy cab turned near the Bosphorus Bridge. They cleared a line of trees, and across the water the city of Istanbul opened up before them, a panoramic sweep of shimmering light from the northern suburbs all the way down the shoreline to the jutting headland of Sultanhamet, the skyline pierced in numerous places by the needle-tipped minarets of hundreds of mosques. There was no way Istanbul could ever be mistaken for a Christian city.

Kipling aside, this was the city where East and West really did meet, a city that had been the crossroads of the world ever since the place was called Byzantium. As they made the long sweeping curve north through rolling parkland, the far shore, beyond the spotlit hulk of the Ortaköy Mosque at the water's edge, was a wall of lights that filled up the low rolling hills of the city all the way to the crest, where a black starless night sliced them off abruptly. In the extreme south, they could just make out the illuminated domes of the Topkapi Palace and the four slender minarets of Hagia Sophia.

It was the coldest part of a January night, and a veil of coal smoke and sea mist lay over Istanbul, giving it a pale aura and an ethereal beauty that, as ethereal beauty often does, vanishes in the cold light of morning. The air smelled of car fumes, coal fires, cooking oil, and under that the wet-stone-and-seaweed reek of the Bosphorus.

Their cab, a rusted-out hulk that might once have been a Benz, was being driven by a fatally bored young man in a woolen watch cap and a Korn T-shirt who had listened to deafening techno-house on an iPod and chain-smoked little black cigars all the way from the tiny airfield at Sandirma. He was a terrible driver, jerking and jinking and horn-blasting his way through the mad swirl of jitneys and trucks and motorcycles that filled up the lunatic maze of Istanbul's streets even at this unholy hour.

Levka, up front with the driver, had his boots braced against the dashboard and had long since given up trying to engage the kid in small talk. Now he was staring out the passenger window at the storefronts and milling crowds hurtling past while nursing a paper cup of black tea. Mandy and Dalton were sitting close together in the rear, aware of the heat of their bodies, staring stoically out the side windows and breathing through their mouths.

They had left the Blackhawk at Sandirma, rotors folded, wheeled into a hangar and covered with the tarp, for a rack rent of a thousand American dollars a night, paid in cash a week in advance to a shriveled little gnome in grease-stained mechanic's overalls and an oil-soaked kaffiyeh, who had scowled at them out of a face so wizened and wrinkled it looked like a dried apricot, until the dollars got counted out on top of his toolbox.

Then his face had opened up like a lotus, as he displayed a set of snaggled teeth that were a standing indictment of Turkish dentistry, and solemnly swore by the Sema of Sufi that not even the imps of Shaitan would sniff a whiff of its presence. Then he dragged out a truly appalling *nargileh,* fired the bowl up with something that looked like compacted mouse dung, and insisted on passing the water pipe around three times to settle their business. But, thanks to Levka's contagious criminality, it *had* been settled, and, to Mandy's lasting amazement, Dalton's wild ride had not ended in a Turkish prison but in the backseat of this Benz with Istanbul spreading its infectious charms out before her like a *houri* shedding veils. Dalton, hip to hip with her, felt her shiver slightly and folded her hand in his.

"Are you okay?" he asked in a low, warm whisper, the heat of his body and the scent of him—dry grass and tobacco smoke and spices—filling her up and sending a flood tide of post-traumatic lust through her body.

"I'm fine," she said, leaning softly into him. "I'm tired. I need to be taken to bed. What is this place we're going to again, the Sumatra . . . whatever?"

"The Sumahan. You'll like it. It's a five-star hotel in Çengel village, right on the waterline, with a view across the strait. You can see all of Istanbul from your balcony. Trust me, it's up to your standards. I wouldn't put an English noble into a ratbag, would I?"

She moved in closer, nuzzled into his neck, inhaled deeply, breathing him in, his heat, his scent. She moved his right arm closer to her left breast and held it there.

"And what are your *plans*, dear boy, when we get there?"

She got the answer she expected, but not before he kissed her in a not entirely brotherly way on the side of her mouth, his dry lips open slightly.

Progress, she thought.

"You are going to get some rest. Levka and I are going straight to the Ataköy Marina. It's on the European side, down on the Marmara coast, a couple of miles from Atatürk Field. About fifteen miles by car. I want to get there before full light."

"And what am I doing?"

"Sleep. Have a bath, get some breakfast. Then I need you to find a waterfront rental with a boathouse. A big one. Big enough for a fifty-foot cruiser. Close to the hotel. Ask the concierge. Tell them you want to rent a villa, a furnished one, but it *has* to have a boathouse. One that's available today. It's a tourist area, lots of water-front homes all along the shore. It's a very wealthy area. And it's not the high season. We can pay top dollar, which never fails. Somebody will have something."

They had turned off Yaliboyu and were cruising along Kuleli now, through a neighborhood of large private waterfront homes, gated, heavy with palms, fig trees, and frangipani vines, the soft, warm light of money spilling from leaded-glass windows and intricately carved Moorish screens and vine-draped Juliet balconies. The street ran in a long, curving glide through tree-lined avenues, past an open park, a brand-new luxury development now coming up on their right, huge white-stone mansions in the Italian style, built along a cresting hillside, with red-tiled roofs and swimming pools, and now coming up on their left, the waterfront side, a long Frank Lloyd Wright fa-çade in stone and steel and glass that ran for several hundred feet along the edge of the Bosphorus. A large glass-and-steel sign had been set into a limestone wall—SUMAHAN—their Turko-Goth driver rolling up to the glass doors and slamming on the brakes, still deep into his techno-house.

They were promptly besieged by uniformed attendants. In a mo-ment, Mandy and all their baggage had been swept into the hotel, leaving Dalton and Levka alone with the driver, who seemed to feel that his part in their little excursion had come to an end and that it was time for a hard-earned and life-altering gratuity.

Levka leaned into him, plucking the earpod free with a sticky pop, said a few soft words in pidgin Turkish, close enough to the kid for him to feel the large pistol in Levka's belt. The kid sat up straight, stared back at Levka, and nodded several times, his brown eyes open so wide Levka could see a ring of white around each iris.

Levka patted his cheek, not gently, stuffed a fat wad of Turkish lira into the neck of the kid's T-shirt, and in a Turkish trice they were back on the road again, this time heading south, with the lights of the suspension bridge on their right floating like a chain of fireflies in the hazy air, Istanbul glimmering on the far side of the strait. The driver had dumped the iPod and was now driving with great care, his thin body rigid.

Dalton, from the back, leaned forward, tapped Levka.

"What did you say to him?"

Levka beamed at Dalton.

"I motivate him, boss."

"Really? How?"

"I explain him situation. I tell him you are big man in Swedish Mafia. If he don't take iPod out of ear and drive like human, you will cut his balls off, cook them in lingonberry sauce, and eat them."

"Lingonberry sauce?"

"You know, like Swedish meatballs?"

Dalton nodded, sat back, thought it over.

"The *Swedish* Mafia?"

Levka shrugged, looked back at Dalton over his shoulder.

"Look at you, boss. Long blond hair. Ice eyes. Look like killer Viking. What I gonna say? You dago don from Sicily?"

There wasn't much to say to that. The rest of the trip passed uneventfully, although the kid seemed to be having some trouble breathing. But he drove wonderfully well, gracefully negotiating the hectic four-lane traffic swarming across the Bosphorus Bridge, dealing gently with the packed causeway that ran along the Galata shoreline, and basically handling the Galata Bridge and the clogged arteries of Sultanhamet just like a limo driver in Vegas. As they rounded the causeway curve below the high hill of Sultanhamet, the minarets of the Sultan Ahmed Mosque silhouetted against the sky, a lemon yellow winter sun crested the low black hills far away to the east, and the first gleam of dawn struck the Sultan's turret in a shaft of light, just as it said in the *Rubáiyát*.

They reached the Ataköy Marina on Kennedy Caddesi a few minutes later, a former Holiday Inn—and it looked it—a row of stolid chevron-shaped buildings, looking a tad down-at-the-heels, nowhere as severely posh as the Sumahan, more of an airport hotel for business travelers such as you'd find near any huge national hub from Frankfurt to La Guardia.

They passed through the lobby, barely drawing the attention of the half-asleep attendant behind the counter, heading for the long dining room that fronted the marina and the pool deck. At the entrance to the dining hall, Dalton stopped by a newsstand, still shuttered, to look down at a wire-bound stack of papers called *The New Anatolian*, apparently published in English since the headline, in large screaming-scarlet letters, read:

MIDAIR COLLISION OVER BANDIRMIA
TWO CHOPPERS DOWN
MASSIVE SEA SEARCH FOR SURVIVORS
DEBRIS AND BODY PARTS LITTER SHORELINE

Levka and Dalton exchanged a look but said nothing, and went out the waterside doors onto the pool deck, a large, open space looking south across the Sea of Marmara, now a vast plain of sparkling-blue water fluttering with wind-whipped whitecaps that looked like shark's teeth and the strong, dank graveyard reek of old, deep water. The pool deck was lined with white wooden recliners laid out under fake-palm-frond *palapas*. Beyond the deck, out in the marina harbor, the masts and rigging of luxury sailboats stitched the pale sky down to the rugged shoreline.

The marina itself was huge, sheltered by a man-made seawall that defined a D-shaped harbor about a quarter mile in length, inside which there were seven wooden docks each about four hundred feet long. Even in winter, the marina was reasonably full, holding at least three hundred craft of various sizes, from runabouts to sixty-foot trawlers, although most of the boats had been shrink-wrapped in blue plastic and sealed up for the winter.

Dalton stood there for a moment, running his eyes over the array of pleasure craft, looking for the low sharklike cruiser he had last seen in Venice.

Levka stood a little behind him, facing the hotel, looking for watchers and seeing no one, although any of the shuttered rooms that overlooked the marina could hide a man with a scope.

Dalton made a short muffled sound, and Levka turned around.

"You see it, boss?"

Dalton nodded toward a long, sleek Riva motor yacht, a stream-lined fifty-footer with a white cabin and upper deck, lots of brass and mahogany and teak, silver handrails, and a navy blue hull, with a thin line of red paint separating the blue and white a foot below the deck. She was tethered at the far end of the third inner dock, half covered with a plastic tarp that made her look like a swan tangled up in picnic trash.

Levka followed Dalton's look.

"So, she still here."

"Yes. They'll try to move her today. We got here too fast for them."

"Pretty boat. I not seeing guard at all. What we gonna do?"

Dalton didn't answer for a while, and then he turned and looked back at the hotel. In the dining room, a few waiters were beginning to pass among the tables, laying out dishes and silverware for the early breakfast crowd.

He looked at Levka—still in his air-crew khakis, unshaven and rather shopworn. And then down at himself, wearing the pants to his navy blue pinstripe, a pair of black wingtips, and a reasonably clean white shirt, no tie. They both looked a little on the scruffy side but presentable enough for a second-rate Turkish hotel in the off-off-season.

"You hungry?"

Levka showed his teeth, not to his advantage.

"Boss, I could eat horse."

"Let's settle for bacon and eggs."

THREE MEN CAME in midafternoon, a trio of small but solidly built button men with a military cast, ranging in age from twenty to forty, with the oldest man, who was also the shortest, a tough-faced thug with a Kosovo Marine cut and a trim black goatee. Dalton, watching him, thought he carried the unmistakable burden of non-com leadership. The Top Kick look.

They were all wearing bug-eyed sunglasses, faded blue jeans, brown leather boat shoes, and heavy turtleneck sweaters that bulged around their waistlines, clearly hiding weapons.

They passed through the dining room in single file, looking neither right nor left, staring straight ahead like Sagger missiles homing in on a target. They went right past Dalton's table without giving either of them a sideways glance, banged out through the swinging doors, and headed at speed in the direction of the dock where the *Subito* was tied up.

Dalton gave Levka a wry look, tossed some new Turkish lira on the table, and stood up. He didn't look back, but he knew Levka was right behind him as he cleared the doors and walked out onto the pool deck. He was a little nervous about going into this with Levka at his back. This was very likely their first tactical contact with the crew being run by Levka's Gray Man, and Levka's loyalties might be under some strain.

In a few seconds, the three men had reached the *Subito,* Top Kick stepping onto the rear deck while the other two started peeling back the plastic sheeting. They had the sheeting off, folded and stowed away inside the cruiser in a couple of minutes, while the older man moved around on the deck, checking the ship out. There was no doubt they were getting ready to take her out of the marina.

"So, boss," said Levka, "how you want to do this?"

"Quietly, for starters. No gunfire. Still got your piece-of-shit pistol?"

Levka made a face.

"No offendings, boss, but is not a piece of shit, okeydokey?"

Dalton smiled at that, keeping his eyes fixed on the deck of the *Subito*.

"Okeydokey, Levka. You look like a guy who could be working on a boat. See that box over there?" he asked, indicating a cardboard box full of rags that sat by the pool filter. Levka nodded. "Okay, pick it up, slip your not-a-piece-of-shit pistol into the rags, start carrying it out to the dock there. I'll follow at about twenty feet—"

Which puts you in front of me when the action starts.

"Don't look at the men on the *Subito*. Take your time. Look busy. They won't be taking the lines off for a couple of minutes. You follow?"

Levka did. He picked up the box without another word, fumbled with something at his waist, and then started out along the jetty, ambling casually, looking to Dalton as if he were about to start whistling, which he did not actually do. Dalton picked up a copy of the *New Anatolian* that was fluttering on a nearby table, folded it in half, and eased his Beretta into the fold, pushing the paper under his left arm.

Then he began to stroll slowly along the same dock, stopping to look at a runabout here, a gaff-rigged ketch over there that looked as if it belonged in Nantucket, a forty-foot matte-black Kevlar cigarette boat farther along the jetty, four huge Mercs on the stern, which fairly shrieked of smuggling . . . Up ahead, Levka had reached the berth beside the *Subito,* where a large sports fisher with a flying bridge, closed up tight, was rocking gently in the sea lift, her rigging clattering in the onshore breeze. He set the box down on the sports fisher's fantail, extracted a rag, and began to scrub vigorously on the brass letters affixed to her transom: MEVLEVI. Dalton had the vague idea it meant "dancer" or "dervish."

One of the younger men on the rear deck of the *Subito* had come up from below and was now standing on the stern board, staring hard at Levka, his face like a knot and his unibrow beetled.

Dalton was now about fifteen feet away, still wandering. The man stepped off the stern, came up to Levka, leaning over him now, his suspicions flaring up. He nudged Levka, saying, "Эй мудакчто ты делаешь," which Dalton, who recognized it as Russian, interpreted to mean something along the lines of "Hey, asshole, what are you doing?"

Dalton ambled past just as Levka looked up with a *Hello, fuck you* grin and said, in pretty-good Russian, "Сосать мою dick," which needed no translation at all. The man's face turned dark red, and he reached for Levka's collar just as the barrel of Dalton's Beretta slammed off the back of his head. He went down on the dock, hit hard, and looked like he'd be there for a while.

Dalton left him with Levka, vaulting up onto the stern board of the *Subito* just as the second inside man, perhaps feeling the dip as Dalton hit the swim ladder, stepped out of the darkness of the pilot cabin, squinting into the sunlight, his eyes widening as he realized he was staring right into the muzzle of a large blue-black semiauto.

He opened his mouth to warn the Top Kick, who was still inside, but Dalton managed to persuade him not to by shoving the pistol's muzzle into the man's open mouth and then, after a brief introductory grin, kneeing him in the nuts *very* hard. The impact lifted the man up a few inches, causing him to shatter a few front teeth into bloody stumps on the muzzle of the Beretta.

He folded himself into the teak deck, holding onto his nuptials and making a thin hissing sound through his bloodied front teeth. Levka was on the stern board now, his pistol in hand, as Dalton stepped lightly through the open gangway into the pilot cabin.

He found himself in a trim, beautifully appointed, and profession- ally laid-out cabin with a panoramic view that took in the entire marina. Leather chairs were arranged around a small teak-and-brass coffee table, a navigator station off to the left, and a large wood-and- leather pilot seat faced a control panel filled with every conceivable electronic option a wealthy young shooter could imagine.

Unfortunately, Dalton was quite alone in this lovely space.

He froze, checked his six, saw no one. In the forward section of the pilothouse, a gangway led down to the cruiser's main salon. Pre- sumably, there'd be a master stateroom up in the bow and a smaller sleeping cabin off the main salon. A couple of heads, a galley.

A lot of places to hide and wait.

Dalton stepped to one side, his pistol up and ready, ducked warily down and gave the main salon a quick once-over. Again, no one.

He was pretty confident that Levka, who was still on the deck dealing with the other two men, would have seen Top Kick if he had scrambled out of the forward hatch and jumped to the mole. For that matter, Top Kick didn't look like a guy who would cut and run.

Which meant he was somewhere in the cruiser, armed, waiting. This was a tactical situation that called for some delicacy.

He felt a step behind him, pivoted, and saw Levka standing there staring back at him, an odd expression on his face, his Croat pistol in his hand. Levka lifted his left hand up, touched his index finger to his lips, and then pointed straight down at the deck in front of him, his eyes widening.

Dalton looked down, saw a silver ring set into the teak boards, and realized they were standing over the engine-room hatch cover. It was a little off-seam, as if it had been pulled shut but not locked.

A nice move, he thought.

Wait for the searchers to move on down into the main body of the cruiser, pop up behind them, and kill them both. Levka followed his look and then grinned at Dalton. He bent down and reached for the silver ring, but Dalton put out his hand and signaled for him to stop.

He motioned for Levka to stand back and cover the hatchway, and then he stepped over to the cabin wall beside the navigator's station. There was a red fire panel there, with a series of breakers and gauges. There was also a yellow-and-black checkered lever with a plate above it that read:

ENGINE ROOM FIRE SUPPRESSION
CAUTION: CARBON DIOXIDE
RISK OF ASPHYXIATION

Levka saw the sign, nodded vigorously, braced himself. Dalton tripped the lever, a klaxon alarm began to blare, and there was a distinct hissing sound from under the floorboards as the fire-suppression system released a cloud of carbon dioxide vapor into the engine room under the pilot deck.

Two minutes later, the hatch cover flew open and Top Kick popped up like a jack-in-the-box, gasping, his face blue, his eyes running, waving a large blue-steel Colt .45.

Dalton stepped in, took the muzzle in an iron grip, jerked it viciously upward and back, trapping the man's index finger inside the trigger guard and breaking it, a muffled but audible snap as the Colt came loose.

Levka stepped forward, stuck the muzzle of his HS hard up against Top Kick's cheek, and grinned fiercely down at him.

Well, that settles the issue of Levka's loyalty.

"What about the other two?" Dalton said, not taking his eyes off Top Kick, who was holding his right hand in his left, pain in his weathered face, as he dealt with a badly broken trigger finger, so badly broken that a bloody stump of jagged pink bone had ripped its way through the flesh and was now sticking out sideways about a half inch.

Levka was breathing a little hard, but he got his answer out anyway.

"In the stern. Found cable ties in fishing box. They trussed up good. One you knee in nuts, he not a very happy boy. Other one still out. Maybe for good. You hit pretty real hard, boss."

Dalton recalled Levka's jaunty offer while waiting to be shot in the head—*"With handy service of Dobri Levka, you don't have to bust big fat dead men around place all by self, ruin good suits like you got."*

"Anybody on the pool deck see any of this?"

"No, boss. Don't think so."

"Go make sure."

Levka was back in two minutes.

"All quiet. What about this one?"

So far, Top Kick had uttered not one word.

"Get him out of that hole."

Levka reached down and lifted Top Kick out of the engine compartment by the collar of his sweater, set him down in front of Dalton. The man stood there, swaying a little, sweat on his face, a five-by-five granite block of obstinate hate, his black eyes cutting from one to the other as he waited for the inevitable bullet he had learned to expect in his trade.

Dalton glanced at Levka, who took a cable tie out of his pocket, jerked the man's thick arms around, crossed his wrists behind his back, wrapped the tie around them, and tugged tight. It must have hurt like hairy hell, but Top Kick didn't make a sound. He just went on glaring sudden death at Dalton. Dalton gave him a big, cheerful grin, reached out, and patted his cheek affectionately.

"Aren't you just the maddest, baddest dog in town. What's your name?"

"Kiss my ass," he said in a guttural, Slavic snarl.

"Really? All one word or do you hyphenate? Levka, did the other two have cells?"

Levka shook his head.

"No. Got two wallets and some money, also watches," he said, holding up a wad of euros, two cheap leather cases, and what looked like a pair of Soviet-era military watches.

"Then I'll bet Kissmyass here has a phone. Search him."

Dalton stepped clear, keeping the muzzle of the Beretta trained on the man's left eye while Levka did such a thorough hands-on search of his body that Dalton felt he ought to buy the guy flowers afterward.

Levka came up with a wallet, some crumpled papers, stripped the guy's watch off his wrist—like the other two, a black-faced Russian army timepiece with Cyrillic markings.

Levka finished with a comprehensive grope around down in the guy's shorts that Dalton wouldn't have performed for an oatmeal cookie and a long, wet kiss from Charlotte Rampling. Levka's face changed—*No wonder,* thought Dalton—and he came out with a tiny black flip phone.

"Man, you should go boil your hands, Levka."

Levka gave him a queasy look, nodding.

"Is that phone on?"

Levka opened it.

"Yeah, boss."

"See when he made the last call on it."

Levka thumbed a few tabs.

"Minute and half, boss."

"How long was the call?"

"Says seventeen seconds."

Top Kick's face was getting a bit tight, but he still wasn't talking.

"You understand English?" asked Dalton.

"Dah," he said, making it sound like a goat coughing up a turnip.

"Who'd you call?"

Kissmyass bared his teeth. He had some periodontal issues.

"Motherfucking Teresa."

"Levka, what number did he call?"

"Ahh . . . two-one-two, two-eight-eight, eight-five-one-five."

"Find out who has that number."

"Okay, boss. Ahh, like . . . how?"

"Call the operator. Tell her you are trying to reach your daughter, she called from that number, upset, got cut off, now you're worried sick."

"I not that damned good in Turk talk, boss."

"Do your best."

Levka hit a number, put the phone to his ear, and moved back out onto the fantail deck. Dalton could hear him talking, a burst of rapid-fire chatter with a panicky edge, some silence, and then more chatter.

Dalton and Kissmyass stared at each other all through this, each man deciding that he really did not like the other one and that maybe one day he could kill him. Levka was back in a couple of minutes, his face shining.

"Got it. Beyoglu Trading. Dizayn Tower, on Masayak Ayazağa."

"Which is where?"

"Here, boss, in Istanbul. Europe side, across the Galata Bridge. Right next to Diamond of Istanbul."

"That pointy blue-glass thing in the north, looks like a skating trophy?"

Levka worked it through, realized Dalton was right, and nodded.

"Okay. Can you drive this boat?"

Levka looked around, took it in.

"Fancy-pantsy, but is still boat."

"Any pelicans out there on the mole?"

"Pelicans? All over Istanbul, boss. Garbage birds."

"Okay. Does that cell have a GPS function?"

Levka's face went blank, and then bright red as he realized he hadn't thought of that possibility. He studied the cell screen, found the little GPS icon and the + indicator beside it.

He shot Kissmyass a look of injured reproach.

"Yes, boss. Has fucking GPS turned on right now."

"Leave it on. Find some plastic wrap, seal the thing up tight, and toss it to a pelican. That might buy us some time. Then cast loose and get us rolling. I have a feeling Mother Teresa is on the way and she's not coming in happy."

"What about this one?"

"Kissmyass and I are going to get to know each other a little better."

"Bite me," said Kissmyass.

Dalton beamed down upon him like the newly risen Christ, only blond and not quite so loving, with a bullet scar on one cheek and no intention at all of turning the other.

"Oh, I don't think it'll come to that."

GARRISON

It was long after sunrise by the time they had exhausted each other. Briony lay beside him, her chest heaving, her eyes shining in the half-light of a cloud-veiled sun pouring in through the windows. She turned to him.

"Jules, I have to open it."

"In the fullness of time, sweet. Let it wait."

She shook her head, sighed, and sat up, reaching for her robe. He rolled out of the bed and stood, looking down at her. In the normal course of his affairs, women were not his first choice, nor even his second, but she had been splendid, and now it was coming to an end. He felt the first electric stirrings of the more unusual aspects of his libido.

"I'll put some coffee on."

"No," she said. "For this, I'll need some champagne and orange juice."

They went down together. In the winter the old stone house was always dim, the leaded-glass casement windows and the trees blocking all but the setting sun in the evening. Duhamel turned on some lights and this time opened some champagne: it seemed right to celebrate the end of an affair and the beginning of a much more *intimate* understanding between them.

He poured her a flute and set it beside her, enjoying the way the halogen light played with the bubbles in the glass, sending little fireflies darting over the countertop and hovering on her cheek. He didn't bother with the orange juice, and she didn't seem to care.

She sipped the champagne, set it back down, looked up at him once, and then slipped the memory chip into the reader on the side of his laptop. It took a few minutes for the decryption program to unlock the MPEG on the chip. Since Briony suspected that the tape was very likely programmed to erase itself after one play, she also set up her digital camera on a tabletop tripod beside the screen, switching it to MPEG so she could at least have a record of the video. Duhamel, watching this, raised his appreciation of her skills another couple of notches. When the video finally started to run, Briony wished it had taken a week to load.

Duhamel took a chair on the other side of the bar where he could not see the laptop screen. He felt that this would make Briony more comfortable. It didn't matter to him. He had already seen the footage.

He sipped at his champagne and watched Briony's face change as the first few frames began to run. It was like watching a time-lapse documentary of a magnolia dying. He resisted the temptation to get his own camera and take a shot of the metamorphosis, sensing that Briony might find that a bit callous. There'd be time for the recording of metamorphoses later.

He was a connoisseur of change. He had once read a monograph by a doctor who had been present at the execution of a prisoner in Paris who had been sentenced to the guillotine. The doctor had retrieved the severed head immediately after the falling blade sliced it from the body, placed it upright on a block, and sharply called out the man's name. The eyes, at first unfocused, became much sharper, the pupils dilated, the eyeballs moved, and the doctor was completely convinced that the man was responding to his name. The doctor let a minute pass, during which the eyes slowly became unfocused again. He then called the man's name, seeing the eyes sharpen, turn again to seek him out, and settle on him: the doctor knew that the man was looking at him, seeing him, was fully aware of him.

Five minutes passed in this way, and then the light of this awareness drained away from the eyes, they glazed over, and the severed head responded to nothing after that.

Duhamel had watched many people die what he sincerely hoped was an excruciating death, but he had never tried this intriguing experiment with a severed head.

It would be interesting, professionally, to sever a head from a victim, place it in a position so that the person could see her severed body, and then to take a film of the encounter, concentrating mainly on her eyes, zooming in very close to catch whatever was in there.

Someday, perhaps. Maybe with *this* one. She has a strong mind and a very powerful life force. Compared to her, Mildred Durant had been a firefly, snuffed out after a dying flutter, her departure much too fast to really savor.

But Briony Keating was of another order entirely. If anyone could stay alive through such an experiment, no matter how briefly, and then show him what she was going through, the realization of that ultimate horror that would be in her eyes as he leaned in close to inhale and *become* her final horror, it would be this splendid woman.

He felt his blood rising up, his breathing changing, and he looked down at his glass to hide his eyes in case she looked across at him at that moment. If she did, she would see what he was.

He was finding it hard to stay inside this Duhamel carcass. More and more, the need would intrude, the impatience, the tectonic-plate shifting he could feel deep inside, the building pressure to . . . surface, like a great white rising up from the deep.

But he was a professional—and the men he was working for were at least as dangerous as he was, having been at this kind of thing longer than he had been on the planet—and he intended to survive this brief commission and go back to being wildly wealthy and free to move in the upper world.

So he would wait a while longer. As *Les Juifs* used to say, the few of them who were left, "Next year in Jerusalem."

Watching Briony's face, and to calm himself, he tried to imagine what Briony might be *feeling*, sitting there, watching her son making clumsy, handless love in a squalid hostel room across the bay from the Souda naval station. From the way her pupils had narrowed, she wasn't at all happy. But she didn't look away.

A very powerful mind.

Full of promise.

ON HER SIDE of the screen, Briony Keating wasn't really taking in what she was seeing. According to the buffer indicator, the MPEG had another ten minutes to run, so she contrived to unfocus enough to stay calm while she waited for what she feared was coming.

She looked around the edges of the image, taking it all in, trying to get an idea where this was happening. It was clearly a surveillance film, taken by a hidden camera, from an angle someplace near the ceiling, in a corner of the room or perhaps behind a ventilation grille, in a position to see the whole sordid little room. The film had been taken in color, but the only light in the room was a yellow glow from a small lamp on a table by the bed, so the image quality was poor—grainy, blurred, indistinct—but clear enough that there could be no mistake about the identity of the two people tangled up in the sweaty sheets.

The bed was a single, old, with a pale yellow wrought-iron bedstead—it creaked rhythmically as Morgan and his companion approached the crescendo—and the furniture in the room was spare and functional, the sort of shabby chic you would find in cheap backpacker hostels all around the Mediterranean. Thin gauze curtains drifted like cigarette smoke in a faint breeze blowing in from a pair of open glass doors that led out to some kind of balcony. A section of old wooden railing could be seen, painted in bright primary colors, and beyond it a row of streetlamps, pale globes with light mist around them, that sickly, energy-efficient, blue-tinted corpse light that was making European public spaces from the Piazza San Marco to Hagia Sophia look like Hell's Waiting Room.

Briony had the impression that somewhere beyond the streetlamps there was an ocean, perhaps because of the mist or the distant dim sighing sound in the background that could be surf breaking on rocks. The quilt that had slipped off the bed earlier in the encounter had a bold floral pattern that looked Greek, or at least Mediterranean, and the picture above the bedstead was a gaudy amateur gouache depicting a harborful of fishing boats silhouetted in black against a lurid orange-and-pink sunset sky that had never occurred in real life anywhere on this planet.

There was a dresser on the far wall, with candles still flickering but dangerously low, two bottles of what looked like Metaxa, empty, on top. Clothes were scattered on the floor, the classic farcical sequence of jeans, skirt, blouse, socks, panties, indicating a mad stumble-dance to bed. If the sounds being produced were any indication, things were moving toward a brisk and, for Briony, and probably for the girl, a far-too-prolonged conclusion.

God help her, she thought, as Morgan hammered away at the poor thing as if she were a block of marble he was trying to pound into something human, his head raised and his neck-muscle cords standing out. *He could use some lessons from a grown woman,* she thought, thinking of a turtle she once watched on an island in the South Pacific, neck stretched out in the same reptilian way, mouth open and eyes blank as he humped away at a female turtle braced on a hot flat rock.

This was just . . . *punishment.*

She could see the girl's face—she was fierce and dark, and had a fan of wild fake blond hair spread out on the pillow under her head. Her black eyes were fixed, almost snakelike, on Morgan's throat, which he was presenting to her in the way victims are said to offer themselves to vampires. It came to Briony that the girl was exactly that, some sort of snake, and the phrase *honey trap* came floating up from somewhere in her dormant professional self.

Before the final moment came, the scene jumped—a hard, jarring cut—and now the couple were lying side by side in the bed, sharing a small, twisted hand-rolled object that was probably what the younger generation was now calling a "spliff."

She realized that the previous scene had been included by whoever had sent this chip only in a spirit of sadistic aggression. There had been no need to subject Briony to the sordid experience of watching her young son make bad love to a Greek tart.

It had been done to please the sender, and to force himself into a kind of sleazy partnership with her, the beginning of an extortionate seduction, as these things always are. Briony braced herself for what was now to come, and was not in any way disappointed.

This was the whole idea, after all.

There must have been a mike somewhere close to the bed. Under the bedside table. Shoved up that little bitch's . . . Well, somewhere close, because the sound now dialed up, and Briony could hear their pillow talk—low, breathy, spaced out between long, luxuriating pulls on the twisted cigarette. Morgan was talking about his job at the base, his boyish voice dry and hoarse and a little drugged by whatever was in the cigarette.

"No, like, Crete's boring as shit, actually . . . I mean, except for you . . . But if I stay in for five years, we can get stateside, maybe Walter Reed—"

"You wouldn't never leave me, would you?"

This required a kiss, of course, and some muffled saccharine exchanges that Briony was thankful the mike could not pick up. The girl rolled away and plucked a glass from the floor beside the bed, drank some of the liquid, passed it over to Morgan, who drained it, making a face.

"Christ, Melina, what's in that? It tastes like vinegar."

"It's raki, I think . . . But you get paid so bad in the Navy . . . What about your mother? Couldn't she get you a job in the government somewhere?"

"Sure, she's got all sorts of pull . . . if we're married. She'd insist on that, Melina—"

"So would I, Morgan. I'm not whore—"

"I know . . . I think Mom would like you—"

"She work for a library?"

Morgan laughed, sucked on the joint again, held it for a full thirty seconds, blowing it out through pursed lips.

"Oh yeah, she's a librarian. That's what she tells people . . ."

Melina made a pouty face, crossing her arms over her breasts.

"I don't see how librarian could help me go to America—"

"You're marrying an American! And she's not just this librarian, anyway. She's, like, this superspy—"

"Like Brangelina?"

"Who? No, not Brangelina. She's more like this secret-code breaker—"

Melina pushed him almost out of the bed, apparently angry.

"You always tell me bullshit, Morgan. You are big bullshitter, like all Navy boys. I think I should throw you out and take another boy."

"I'm not a bullshitter. It's true. She works for this big spy agency—"

"Sure. With Matt Damon and James Bond."

"No, it's like the CIA, only more secret . . . Really, I'm not lying."

"Bullshitter."

"No, listen"—another long pull, passing it between them—"you ever hear of the"—Morgan made a comic show of looking around the room, even under the bed, and then, in a stage whisper, as Briony's heart sank within her chest, said—"the NSA?"

"The *Ennessay*? What is this *Ennessay*?"

"Not *Ennessay*. NSA. In Maryland. She works there. Or used to, before they moved her up to West Point—"

The girl Melina reacted to that.

"West Point? West Point is where Army teaches soldiers, isn't it? I saw a film once about this West Point. She truly is librarian there?"

"That's her cover . . . Well, look, the thing is, she has *lots* of pull, and—"

Briony watched as what she was expecting to happen happened. From the camera angle, it was hard to see where the men came from, but there was a loud bang as the door to the room was kicked open and the room filled with big, fast-moving armed men in cheap suits, screaming at Morgan and Melina in English, with Southern accents, loud cop voices braying at them—"Military Police. Do not fuckin' move. Military Police"—while Morgan and the girl lay in frozen shock on top of their tangled sheets.

Another jump cut.

Morgan, now dressed, limp, haggard, exhausted, pale, sitting in a bare wooden chair in a bare, windowless room, with a U.S. flag on its staff in the corner and a picture of the President on the wall beside it, a table littered with coffee cups, an ashtray filled with butts, smoke hanging blue in the air. Two large men in shirtsleeves, military brush cuts, their backs to the camera, one standing and one sitting in a wooden chair and tilting it backward, his size-twelve shoes on the table, his beefy arms folded behind his neck, speaking softly to Morgan in a lazy Texas bass.

"Thing is, kid, you're on the tape—that's the whole problem here—"

The standing man broke in, angry, aggressive.

"Mike, I don't know why we're playing hide the floppy with this fucking mutt. He's a traitor. We're in a goddamned war. He sold out his mother for a cheap piece of Turkish skank. He's going to Leavenworth for the rest of his fucking life—"

The man in the chair held up his left hand, made a calming gesture.

"Brad, leave the kid alone, will you? Go take a piss or something. You're scaring the crap outta him, okay? Get a fucking cruller or something."

Brad stood with his huge furry arms crossed for a few seconds longer, glaring down at Morgan, looming over him like an avalanche.

"Hey, fuck it. You wanna play nice with this asshole, be my guest."

He left the room, there was a brief silence, and then Mike sat forward, placing his forearms on the table and leaning in close to Morgan.

"Look, Morgan, forget Brad. Okay, you talked loose around a Turk broad. Yeah, she's got a background. Yeah, she was a whore for a while—"

Morgan rallied a bit at that.

"She's not a whore."

"That's never *all* they are, kid. But the part that's a whore is how you got into this fix. She's been seeing the wrong guys, why we had her room wired, guys with connections to drug dealers, guys who've been selling dope to our people—stand-up patriotic kids just like you—and I'm a military cop, and it's my number one job to take care of dumb young gullible pukes like you. So when I'm sitting there watching you start to shoot your mouth off about your mother and the NSA and all that shit, I figured enough's enough, and in we go. You were digging yourself a hole, and I wanted to give you a chance to shut the fuck up. Do you a favor."

"Favor?" said Morgan, his skin wet, and his eyes hunted-looking in the shaft of light from the ceiling fixture. "I'm going to Leavenworth."

"Maybe . . . maybe not," said Mike.

A silence, during which Morgan's expression altered, showed a glimmer of hope coming like a thaw to the red-rimmed eyes.

"Maybe not?"

"Don't have to go that way, kid. Could go another way."

"It could?"

Mike lit a cigarette, took a pull, blew out a dense cloud that roiled in the still air, and leaned forward into Morgan's space, his tone cold and grating, like someone scraping ice off a windshield in a Minnesota winter.

"Look, I'm gonna let you in on something, you ever shoot your mouth off about it to anyone—I mean *anyone*—I will flake your case so huge that the admiral himself will personally shoot your ass into the heaviest block in Leavenworth. You'll get punked out before your heels hit the ground, spend the next fifteen years getting passed around behind the blanket wall like a rubber chicken, and if you ever get out you'll be wearing Depends the rest of your sorry fucking days. And Melina will get sent back to Istanbul so loaded down with contraband that the Turks will bury her deep in Arkasoy Pits, and not even the roaches will be able to find her then. She'll be fucking gone forever. My word on that, Morgan, as a United States Marine. Am I making myself totally fucking clear?"

Morgan could only nod, his bony chest working. Briony, watching in mute horror as this fatal farce unfolded, was torn between wishing him safe home and wishing him dead.

Mike, having said his piece and gotten the response he wanted, leaned back out of Morgan's space, tossed a pack of Camels across the table, waited while Morgan, his hands shaking, took one out and put it in his mouth. Mike threw him the lighter, a pink plastic Bic, waited with massive stillness while Morgan lit it up and exhaled a shaky plume.

"Okay," said Mike, "here's what I can tell you. You know NAS Souda is a fucking backwater, right? Not even run by major brass. Just fucking noncoms and swabbies like you. Only claim to glory is it's overrun with stray cats. It's the asshole of Crete, nothing to do but smoke and drink and chase pussy and go fucking bats with boredom. War going on anywhere but here, guts and glory for everybody but you."

Morgan drew on the cigarette, his attention focused on Mike's face.

"But what else has NAS Souda got? I'll tell you. Souda is two hundred and sixty miles south-southeast of Izmir, in Turkey, and Izmir is the fucking Emerald City of fucking drugs. That shit you were puffing with little Melina? Laced with hash oil straight from Izmir. How does it come from Izmir to Melina's cockroach cottage in Souda? Go on, ask me."

"How does it come—"

Mike slammed the tabletop so hard the cups flew into the air, and Morgan jumped a yard.

"Your fucking Chief Strahan, that's how."

That rocked Morgan. The cigarette, halfway to his lips, froze in midair. He started to shake his head slowly back and forth.

"Chief Strahan? Chief Strahan is running drugs?"

Mike nodded heavily, his face turning into a scowl.

"Damn well told us he is. He's running your medical supply unit, ordering up gear, meds, has them brought in by Sea King from the Persian Task Force Support Group, right? Also by supply hulls out of the mainland."

"Yes, but—"

"Kid, we got this asshole locked down. Case file is longer than my dick. Not a lot of shit, just enough to make him rich. Moroccan hash oil by way of Izmir, meth from an ethanol distillery in Kerch, shit from all over the eastern Med, and a lot of it's running right through Strahan's AO—"

"No. Chief Buck's stand-up. He wouldn't do—"

"Chief Buck Strahan is a puke, is what he is, Corpsman, and we only need one thing to take him down for good."

Another silence while Mike let the message percolate through Morgan's panicky haze.

"What . . . What do you need?"

Mike leaned forward, setting the hook in tight.

"We need to know where the fucking money is."

"But can't you—"

"Shut up and listen. Brad gets back here, he has the push to jerk you onto a C-130 going stateside this evening, he gets pissed enough. I don't have time for a back and forth on this. We've got his whole system, but if we can't lay the money on the table in front of the JAG-offs, he'll get a tap and go, and I want serious time for this puke. Here's where you come in. You got one shot and one shot only. You either take it or you're gone this afternoon, and your mommy will never see you again, except maybe through a piece of chicken-wired bulletproof glass. And she won't like what she sees. You with me?"

"I am. Christ, I am. What do you want me to do?"

Hooked . . . Hooked and gaffed, thought Briony.

Mike took a USB flash drive out of his pocket, laid it on the table between them, used the tip of his index finger to nudge it closer to Morgan.

"You have access to Chief Strahan's personal laptop, right?"

"His *personal* one? No, I don't. He keeps it in his briefcase, locked up. Has it with him all the time. I mean, it's his own machine. He uses it mainly to MSN with his family back in Shreveport. Nobody gets near it."

"Yeah. Ever wonder why?"

"No . . . No, I guess not."

Mike sat back, leaving the flash drive on the table, his face closing up. "You guess not? You guess not? Well, start fucking guessing. You either find a way to get this flash drive into Chief Strahan's personal laptop for fifteen seconds or you go to Leavenworth. We been all over the guy's hooch, his office, his office desktop, his pay books, and can't find the money trail. Laptop's gotta be it. Nowhere else. Fifteen seconds is all we need."

"What's in the flash drive?"

A massive shrug from Mike.

"Fuck if I know, kid. Comes right from where your mommy works, the NSA. My guess, it's some kind of undetectable surveillance program, does a stealth scan of the entire system. Next time Chief Buck goes online, everything on his machine gets copied to Fort Meade. Don't fucking ask me how, I'm no techno-geek, I'm just a cop. All I know, you can move around Chief Buck's office, we can't. So it's gotta be you who finds some fucking way to get this flash drive into Chief Buck's machine. You gonna try or not?"

Silence, the smoke rising, both men breathing audibly. A man's voice, muffled through the walls, a harsh, braying laugh, coming closer.

"That's Brad. Got his doughnut and now he's coming back. You in or out?"

A slow zoom from the hidden video camera, coming in tight on Morgan's face, so close Briony could see his eyelashes and the sheen of sweat on his pale cheek, see the child he had been and the son he had become, and the ruin he was about to make of his life. Her heart burned into a cinder and died, but none of that changed the outcome in the slightest.

"Yes . . . Yes, I'm in."

A jump cut, as Briony expected.

Morgan, unshaven now, looking utterly spent and exhausted. He was in the same room, now missing its flag and its portrait of the President, and the table was bare except for the flash drive and a sheaf of computer paper neatly stacked beside it. There was a different man sitting in the chair opposite Morgan, back to the camera, a slope-shouldered lumpish shape with a squat neck and a roll of fat flowing over the collar of his dirty white shirt, his pale gray suit jacket wrinkled as if it had been slept in, sweat stains showing under the armpits. He was leaning forward under the cone of downlight, speaking to Morgan in a thick Eastern European accent—possibly Ukrainian or Georgian, or some kind of Russian-inflected dialect combining both of them and neither at the same time. His voice was low and calm, seeming to have been electronically distorted, and he spoke in short, unadorned sentences. He gave the general impression of being neither dead nor alive, present nor absent, real nor imaginary. He was neither black nor white but very gray, and decidedly lethal.

Briony, who knew the type, knew him for what he was.

A KGB officer, probably at or above the rank of colonel, and, given the classic nature of this honey trap, working for their Second Directorate, which handled Internal Security and Counter-Intelligence. The fact that he had his back to the camera and that his voice was being electronically altered told Briony that he might be identifiable, a voice and a face known to the West. She studied his general body shape, burning it into her mind. No matter what else happened, she was going to find out who this man was.

The man reached out a fat sausage-fingered hand and tapped the pile of papers in front of Morgan.

"This will go to your Office of Naval Intelligence in a simple Federal Express package, along with the video of your confession—"

Morgan, flaring out, his neck muscles corded and his face red. "I've told you and told you, they were fucking MPs. They told me—"

The Gray Man—Briony had given the nameless man a name—interrupted, calm, in control, in a flat tone, his pudgy hand raised.

"The evidence presented will show you accepting this device and undertaking to introduce it into the personal laptop of your superior officer. The evidence will show that the program introduced in this way was able to penetrate this officer's desktop when he transferred personal photo files of his children sent by his wife in Shreveport to his desktop as a screen saver. And, in a while, the program sent this—we have printed it out for you to consider—which is a sampling of the logistics and materials systems for much of the Fifth Fleet and peripheral operations in the eastern Mediterranean. Have you read this?"

"Fuck it."

"I repeat, have you read it?"

"Yes. Fuck yes."

"And you recognize that having obtained this material for us places you in a very difficult position?"

"No, I'll just tell them what really happened."

"And that it also places your mother in a very difficult position?"

"My mother?"

"Yes. How will the charges of treason and espionage against her son affect her standing within the American intelligence community?"

"She had nothing to do with this. You set me up."

"You cooperated with a foreign agency and obtained classified—"

"None of that's classified—"

"It's not considered to be secret, but tactical information concerning your Navy's logistical and materials-routing systems is always useful, perhaps in the resale market. And the fact that this stealth program remains resident in the Souda Base computer system is also an asset. It has other uses besides key counting and file copying. And it was placed there by you."

Morgan, pushed to the limit, found his steel at last.

"Look, I'm tired. What the hell do you want me to do? I'm not doing anything more to help you. I think you're KGB, and I'm not a traitor no matter how you try to make it look that way. I fucked up. I'll pay the fare. Put a bullet in me or let me loose. Up to you. Kill me, let me walk. I don't really give a fuck anymore."

The Gray Man sat back, sighed, reached into a breast pocket, brought out a small stainless-steel pistol, laid it on the table in front of him, turned to someone off camera and said something in an Eastern bloc language that contained "Melina."

At the name, Morgan jerked upright, opened his mouth, and closed it again. The room was filled with a taut silence, and nothing happened for a time. There was a commotion, the sound of a door being thrown back, and the man who had called himself "Brad" came into the room, dragging the young blond woman named Melina by the arm. She was crying, her hair matted, her clothes filthy, her face bruised and bloody. She knelt there, breathing heavily, looking at nothing. The Gray Man lifted the pistol, placed the muzzle against her temple, looked across the table at Morgan.

A moment passed, and then Morgan said, "Fuck her too. She's probably one of yours."

The girl called Melina lifted her head up, stared at Morgan.

"Morgan, please—"

The Gray Man squeezed the trigger. There was a sharp, cracking pop, a puff of smoke, a spattering of blood and brains on the wall beside her, and she dropped out of the camera frame. Morgan stared at her body on the floor, and then back across at the Gray Man again, his face slack, stunned. The Gray Man lifted the pistol, pointed it at Morgan's head, squeezed the trigger—and the screen went black.

The black screen held for a moment, and then light came back, a tight shot of the pistol on the table and the voice of the Gray Man speaking.

"Miss Keating, your son is still alive. We have not yet decided our next course of action concerning him. He can be exposed to your Office of Naval Intelligence as a spy and sent to Leavenworth, which may not destroy your career but will certainly limit it. Or, to use an American term of art, he may undergo 'rendition' to a third party, such as Al-Qaeda in Iraq, the Taliban, or the Iranian secret service, where he will be subjected to the most extreme forms of interrogation they can devise. He may eventually make an appearance in a terror video at some point, where he will be inexpertly beheaded on camera by some clumsy jihadist while he cries out for your help in his last terrible moments. All these things may happen or none of them. It is up to you. His fate is in your hands. Your organization is in possession of a collection of archived cable transmissions between certain Soviet station agents in Paris and their superiors in Moscow. This collection of paper documents was unearthed quite recently in Riga, Latvia, by a joint task force of American and NATO intelligence officers. These paper transcripts—let us call them the 'Riga Transcripts'—which are in code, have been delivered to your superiors at Fort Meade and are now being addressed by your particular department, a group of decryption experts known internally as the Glass Cutters. I am about to give you a date range. Please secure a pen, since this video will automatically erase itself. Have you a pen?"

Briony looked up at Jules, her eyes hunted, looking suddenly haggard and old. He held a pen out to her, along with the pad she kept by the fridge to write out shopping lists. She was reasonably certain that the little Sony digital camera she had set up to record a backup of the image on her screen had enough capacity to hold the entire video, but she wasn't going to leave anything to chance. She jerked it out of his hands and spread it out on the counter.

The Gray Man's voice rolled on. "I will assume you now have a pen. The date range we are concerned with is from the twentieth day of April 1973 to the nineteenth day of June 1973. Do you have that?"

The Gray Man repeated the dates another three times.

Then he went on to his final statement.

"I will assume you have the dates clear. Please make certain that you also write down the following instructions as well. We are aware that as the Senior Coordinator of the Glass Cutters, you are in a position to review progress and assign certain sections of these cables to specific subgroups for more efficient decryption operations.

"Here are our instructions. They are quite simple.

"In your Venona transcripts, you make frequent reference to 'x number groups unrecovered,' as in 'fifteen groups unrecovered' or 'forty groups unrecovered.' You will see to it, Miss Keating, that in the Riga Transcript that you have in your possession now, on a specific transcript you have docketed as 'Riga one five seven dash alpha hotel'"—Briony's pen was racing—"on that particular transcript, you will find that *very* few number groups are recoverable. Very few, less than fifteen percent. Find whatever procedural excuses or justifications are persuasive. But you *will* ensure that outcome. I will repeat this section again."

He did, and then closed with:

"Now, I know you are a patriot, Miss Keating, and this will run against all your instincts. I can tell you in complete honesty that we are dealing with ancient history here. There is *nothing* in this cable that can have any effect on our modern world in any way. It is our desire to protect the reputation and legacy of one of *your* most respected intelligence officers. His was not an act of betrayal but rather an inadvertent disclosure. But his exposure would have some peripheral consequences that would not be in the interests of *either* of our countries.

"Come, Miss Keating, do not be excessively fastidious. These accommodations are made between agencies all the time. They are called 'realpolitik.'

"This man is far from a threat to your country or ours. But the orders have come from my own superiors, and I must, as you must, obey orders.

"Our methods are forceful—perhaps too forceful. If I had been left to my own methods, I would have been far more subtle. Such is not the case. We are, to use an American phrase, 'under new management.'

"I beg you, as a Christian man, to carry out this simple request, and I give you my word as an officer that you will do no damage to your nation in any way, and that by carrying out this mission you will also save the life and honor of your brave young son. Such a sordid game we find ourselves in, and for what? I cannot say. Perhaps one day, we will find ourselves in a better world, yes?

"Finally, I am directed to warn you that if you fail in this mission, events in the real world will play out in such a way that we will know that you have failed. At that point, your son's fate is out of my hands.

"Good-bye, Miss Keating. And may God bless our nations."

A snap to black, a flicker, and then a single bar line that read MESSAGE ERASED.

Briony closed the machine lid softly, sat in silence for a time with her head down, and then looked up at Duhamel, her expression unreadable.

"My God, Briony," he said, "what will you do?"

"Do?" she said, her voice faint but clear. "I will save my son."

"But your job . . . your obligations? And if you do this, they will own you. These . . . people . . . they will never let you go if you do this."

"I know."

"And if you are exposed, you will go to prison. You know that?"

"Yes, I know that."

"So you have only two roads in front of you: your son will suffer or you will become a traitor."

"That's right."

"Then what will you do? What *can* you do?"

"Take the third road."

"The 'third road'? What is that?"

Briony looked up from the screen, unsmiling, her expression wary, slightly veiled.

"I think, Jules, you should leave in the morning."

Duhamel kept his expression mild, although inside him a dark thing was starting to uncoil.

"I would not want to leave you like this. In this trouble."

"You can't help me with this. And I can't do what I'm going to do with you around. You said it yourself. You're a foreign national. This is a National Security issue. You can't be anywhere near it. I wish it were different, but I can't make it so. You'll have to go."

"But you've already brought me into this, haven't you?"

She looked uncertain for a moment, but then she settled into certainty.

"What you know so far, it is not dangerous to know. Most people in my trade know the same things. Much of it is already in the public domain."

"I know your son is being held hostage by . . . Russians, I think."

"Yes. And if you love me, if you really want to help me save him, then you need to go. You can't be near this. You have a gallery in Saint Petersburg. You could go back there and wait. When this is over, I'll fly out and you can show me your world."

Don't tempt me, he thought but did not say.

It was clear that Briony had made up her mind on this.

Duhamel, trying to remain professional, was about to make some final attempt at loving persuasion. But if it failed, then by the terms of his commission, in the Gray Man's own words, he was free to use "his own *methods*." This arrogant woman on the far side of the counter was about to meet the *real* world that Jules Duhamel lived in, the world Mildred Durant and others before her had seen. He felt the heat rising in his belly, his heart pounding in his chest, the coming release all the more sublime for being so long delayed. He set his glass aside, leaned forward with a look of counterfeit concern, and the telephone rang three times, a silence, and then three more times—rich, deep bell tones—reverberating through the house.

They exchanged puzzled glances, and then Briony got up and walked over to the wall phone next to the stove.

"Hello?"

"Briony, it's Hank."

Unaware of her movement, she had turned her body away from Duhamel slightly. She put her hand on the receiver, looked back at him.

"It's the office," she explained in a hoarse whisper.

She turned away to the phone again, pitching her voice low.

"Is there a problem?"

"Okay, I take it the little frog prince is right there?"

"That's true. So what's the problem?"

"I heard from my guy in the Sixth Fleet. Briony, you really want this now with the guy sitting right there?"

"You called, I'm listening."

"Okay. It's not good. Get ready. The reason you haven't heard from him is he's AWOL. Navy didn't want to let it out until they were sure. He's been off base for five weeks now. They knew he had a girl in the town. Figured he'd just taken an unofficial vacation. The MPs started looking for him in earnest three weeks ago. By now, they've torn Crete apart. He's not on the island. They have no idea where he is. Have *you* heard from him?"

She tried to keep the lie out of her voice.

"No, not at all."

"Damn. I was hoping . . . Look, this isn't good. They find him now, he'll be in the brig for weeks. If you have *any* idea where he is, anything at all—"

"I don't. None at all. That's why *you* have the file."

Brocius said nothing for a time.

"I don't like this whole thing, Briony. Something's not right. I can feel it. Something's going on here."

"I see. What will you do?"

Another long silence.

Brocius had . . . antennae. She could feel his mind racing.

"Your guy there, I have to say, he's . . . bugging me. I don't know why. Something's . . . hinky."

She saw that he was on his cell.

Where was he calling from? Was he close? she wondered.

"How close are you, Dianne? To getting this done?"

"Close? I'm on the Taconic. Don't talk about this to *anyone*. You follow?"

"I follow."

"You'll hear from me . . . soon."

"That would be good."

"Yeah, real soon, Briony. You still got your fallback option?"

"Yes, I do."

"Good. Maybe you should use it right now."

"If you feel that strongly about it, then it's okay with me."

"I do."

The line went dead. She set the receiver back in the hook.

"What did they want?" asked Duhamel.

"They had a problem with the sorting thingy. A technical thing."

She was lying to him, she realized.

About Hank Brocius.

Why?

The lie hung in the air between them, and she felt Duhamel's dark eyes on her, a look in them that she had not seen before, a cold, remote appraisal.

I don't really know you, do I? she thought.

"You look strange, Briony. What's wrong?"

The question was asked in a loving tone, but there was no light in the young man's eyes. They looked like black holes in a mask. She thought about a few things she should have thought about much sooner:

"You've just arrived from some exotic shore, have you?"

"From London only, I'm afraid. Are you staying with friends?"

Just arrived from London.

With an antique Breguet watch, just like the one Mildred Durant's husband used to wear. And what had Brocius said, about some scars?

"Parents, both deceased, looks like a car crash in Bilbao when he was ten. He was okay but got some burns on his back, which were repaired by cosmetic surgery when he was sixteen. Can't see his back from the shots you sent, so be sure to check, will you?"

She knew this man's back very well. It was as strong and smooth as a horse's neck. And it had never been scarred.

"You know," she said, "I think I need to pee. And I think we're going to be up for a while. Would you put on some coffee?"

"Do you still want me to leave tomorrow morning?"

The question was asked in a soft tone, a gentle pleading note in it, but there was nothing in his face that looked anything like softness. He looked like a gundog her father used to have, taut, primed, trembling, waiting for a grouse to explode out of a hedge. She shook her head.

"No, I don't."

Duhamel softened visibly, seemed to come off point.

"You're sure?"

She gave him her bravest smile.

"I'm sure. Maybe I'm just being . . . dramatic. I . . . just want to have some coffee. Talk a bit. Get my mind clear. Maybe there's some way out of this I haven't thought of. That *we* haven't thought of. Maybe there's a movie on cable, or we can watch a DVD. We can figure out what to do about all this in the evening, okay?"

"Yes, that would be fine."

"I need to freshen up. Will you go see what's on?"

He smiled at her then, and it was one of his best smiles, like the one that had pulled her in and held her in Savannah. Hank's words played in the back of her mind as she smiled sweetly at him.

"You still got that little Sig P-230 around?"

"Yes, I keep it close."

"Good. Keep it real close. Nothing settles a lover's quarrel faster than a coupla Black Talons in the chitlins."

"Yes," he said, "maybe one of those old black-and-white films?"

Gaslight.

She thought of it immediately but could not say why.

She turned and left the kitchen then, more in a glide than a walk. She felt his eyes on her until she reached the corner and melted into the winter shadows of the old stone house.

Duhamel stared at the black rectangle of the door for a time, his expression unreadable. Then he walked across to the wall phone. It had a caller-list screen. He keyed up the last call: 443-479-9560.

The area code for Garrison, and for West Point, across the river, where Briony said the call had come from, it was 845. In another part of his mind, he was thinking about the compact seven-round Sig Sauer pistol that he had come across in Briony's night-table drawer a few days back. Since moving it would have been hard to explain, he had left it in place. With a thick wad of tinfoil rammed up the muzzle, the plug shoved well out of sight with a pencil. If she fired it now, the weapon would take her hand off.

He himself had brought no guns to America.

Why would he?

He was in a kitchen right now, with the all tools of his trade laid out in front of him. He slid open one of the drawers and considered the array of knives. They were very fine knives, all of them, and well maintained. They shone in their blue velvet coffins like quicksilver. He felt a soft, burring sensation in the pocket of his robe, reached in and extracted his cell phone. He had a text message: cq.

He stared down at the letters, his vision blurring briefly, trying to take in the implications. The code was childish for a reason: complex codes announced themselves to the NSA computers.

He hit reply and typed in: ?ru.

The answer came back at once: ?ur+3n-c cqcq.

Three miles north of where you are. In a car. Emergency.

Anton was *here*, in Garrison.

Their protocol for a flash meet such as this was to text back a specific time and then make a reconnaissance run forty minutes before the time set. In this case, Anton was likely in a car three miles north on the parkway. If there was no *tell* in the area—a chalk mark at the location, a cat's-eye marker stuck into the ditch nearby—then the actual meet would take place ninety minutes *after* the announced time. If there *was* a tell, the meet would take place in the nearest church at eleven the next day. But why? Why was Anton *here*?

Duhamel looked out through the doorway into the shadows of the old house. He had not heard the upstairs toilet flush. You could always hear it, or at least hear the water rushing in the ancient pipes.

The silence felt *wrong*.

The whole house felt *wrong*.

And where was Briony?

ISTANBUL

NORTHBOUND THROUGH THE BOSPHORUS

They had rounded the high, tree-covered northern cape of Sultan-hamet, with Hagia Sofia and the Topkapi Palace glowing in the slanting light of a setting winter sun, and now they were cruising northwest into the windswept channel of the straits, heading back to Çengelköy.

Waiting for them there, at this very moment, was Mandy Pownall, fresh from a nap, a long, luxurious bubble bath, a thorough full-body massage from a green-eyed Turkish girl—who had, in the final six minutes of the massage, earned every Turkish lira of her tip—and then a mad round of spending Micah Dalton's money in the hotel's wonderful shops. Mandy was now gracefully arrayed by a table on the marble wharf in front of the Sumahan Hotel, at one with her world, an icy G and T in one hand and a gold-tipped black Balkan Sobranie cigarette in the other, her fine-boned face turned just so to catch the fleeting warmth of the winter sun on her cheek. Service to country had its consolations, she felt, however fleeting they were.

The *Subito* was just now coming level with the Maiden's Tower, a small island in the channel on their starboard side a few hundred yards off the Asian shore, with nothing on it but an ancient stone temple with a tall, turretlike tower. On their port side, a quarter mile up, was the long, neogothic façade of Dolmabahçe Palace, sitting right on the waterline and looking very much like the Houses of Parliament in London without Big Ben.

The cruiser was burbling smoothly along at five knots, cresting the swell and gliding like a white heron through the shipping along the way, the hazy air filled with the muttering and snarling and popping of boat engines, small planes buzzing overhead, tugs and rusted freighters growling along, big props chopping up blue-black water into dirty yellow foam. Crowded and dilapidated ferries, their hulls streaked with rust and river grime, butted their way from the Asian side to the European side and back again, like loom shuttles weaving both halves of Istanbul together.

Flotillas of pug-ugly grain and oil tankers steamed north, heading for the ports of Georgia and the Ukraine, the Black Sea and the Sea of Azov, passing their heavy-laden sister ships coming back down the waterway. And from the far shore, the tape-recorded chant of the Muslim call to prayer, blaring out from every minaret along the channel. And, under that call, like the half-heard roar of a great ocean, was the sound of the city of Istanbul itself, filling the sky and echoing back from the hills all around.

Packing the slopes on either side were the crowded warrens of red-roofed apartment blocks, narrow switchback alleys, side streets and dead ends, unexpected leafy little squares, squalid factory blocks with plumes of black smoke rising up, and here and there, in the northern distance, tall blue-glass office towers set out on the hilltops—the tallest, the Diamond of Istanbul, a towering arrowhead glittering in the last of the sunlight.

Covering the slopes in between, like tumbled clay bricks, were miles and miles of tightly compressed houses and flats and shops, pressed into every nook, and all crammed tight together under the palms and fig trees, then pinned in place by the black hairnet tangle of overhead power lines.

If not for the spearheads of the sultan's towers and the needle-sharp minarets that pierced the skyline everywhere you looked, and the romantic veil of coal smoke and sea fog that lay over it all as the day ended, Istanbul might have been any one of a hundred over-crowded Third World hellholes like Kowloon or Port Said or Valparaiso.

Levka, at the helm of the *Subito,* was enjoying the kaleidoscopic panoramas of Istanbul immensely, sitting at ease inside the lemon-oil-scented cabin. With all this shimmering mahogany and highly polished brass, the cabin reminded him of the mandolin his mother used to play for him back in Legrad.

If he were a man given to reflection, which he was not, he might have stopped to ponder the capricious currents of life that could take you in just twenty-four hours from the brink of a grubby little death, in pee-soaked pants on a hotel balcony in Santorini, to sitting here with a glass of tea in one hand and the wheel of a million-euro yacht in the other.

Although for Dobri Levka life was sweet, for Kissmyass and his one surviving colleague, whom Levka had christened Numbnuts, life was considerably less so.

The third man, Vladimir Krikotas, according to the ID they found on his body, had succumbed to his severe cranial fracture and its consequent massive subdural hematoma, slipping into a stertorous coma and later being consigned, not quite dead, to the loving embrace of the Sea of Marmara, slipping quietly over the starboard side with a short quote from Dalton about "the sea giving up her dead" and the ship's spare Danforth to see him quickly to the bottom of the bay.

Levka had, a while ago, tuned the radio in to a local station that specialized in a kind of "techno-arabesk" music, a sinuous North African threnody, accompanied by driving *djembe* drumming and the tinkling clash of finger cymbals. This music served two purposes: it nicely caught the exotic flavor of this contradictory town, part Asian hellhole and part hashish-induced illusion, and it helped drown out the sounds Levka was expecting shortly from the galley, where Dalton was about to begin what Levka, based on his brief but compelling experience with the man, was reasonably certain would be an aggressive and bloody interrogation.

Down in the galley, Dalton, fresh from his shower, shaved, and, wearing a navy blue V-neck sweater he had found in the closet off the forward stateroom that went very well with his navy pin-striped pants, had both men, trussed and naked, sitting side by side on a section of the plastic sheeting they had used to cover the *Subito* back at the Ataköy Marina.

Neither man looked very happy about this, but neither was saying much about it, Kissmyass because he was a snake-mean bastard and Numbnuts because he had a mouthful of bloody teeth.

Dalton, sipping carefully at his cup of steaming black coffee, had gone through all the items Levka had taken from the men and had learned a few useful things, starting with the fact that Kissmyass was not actually Kissmyass's real name, although he would forever be Kissmyass to Micah Dalton. His real name was Anatoly Viktor Bakunin, and, according to his international driver's license, he was born in Krasnodar, Russia, in 1962. His profession was listed as "shipping facilitator."

He had a bank card issued by Credit Suisse, and a credit card from there, and five hundred odd in greasy euros. In his back pocket, Levka had found a wad of crumpled receipts from various bars and hotels in and around Aksaray, Istanbul's red-light district, and one for a bar called the Double Eagle, in the Ukrainian port town of Kerch. The other man, the younger one, had an ID in the name of Vassily Kishmayev.

Kerch, Dalton recalled, was where Dobri Levka and his late uncle

Gavel Kuldic had first been approached by the Gray Man. Therefore, Dalton surmised, being a highly trained CIA officer, that this receipt was a *clue*. To exactly what, he wasn't sure.

He looked over at Kissmyass, who was watching Dalton go through his things with a level of adrenalized resentment so extreme that Dalton feared for the poor man's endocrine system.

"Hey, Kissmyass, says here you were at a bar in Kerch on the nineteenth of December. Place called the Double Eagle. What were you doing there? I mean, aside from getting utterly gored on vodka gimlets?"

Kissmyass said something in Russian that cannot be accurately translated into English, Russian colloquialisms being a bountiful trove indeed for the dedicated cultural etymologist. Dalton, not being a dedicated cultural etymologist, stood up and dumped his entire cup of steaming hot coffee on Kissmyass's genitalia, with gratifying results. Next to him, Numbnuts writhed away from the splatter, his brown eyes bugged out, and so much raw horror in his young face that Dalton actually felt a twinge of pity for him. Up in the pilothouse, Levka, wincing, turned the volume up another notch on his techno-arabesk.

Dalton walked back over to the stove, refilled his cup, sat down again, and looked over at his captives with a thoughtful expression on his rough-cut face, his lips thinned, a pale witch light in his almost colorless eyes.

"Know what I think, lads? I think I could spend all bloody day scalding your naughty bits and chopping off your extremities and all I'd get for my troubles would be a pair of perfectly good Allan Edmonds ruined and a galley covered in spit and spatter. You two are a pair of grunts, is what I think. I used to be a grunt, so I know whereof I speak. You're muscle—not very good muscle—and taking you down was like me winning the hundred-yard dash at the Special Olympics. Not much of a challenge, is what I'm trying to say. Anyway, grunts you are and grunts you shall remain. Question is, what do I do with you? Do I dump you into the Bosphorus, wrapped in heavy chains, like your friend Vladimir? Or do I ask you, as officers and gentlemen, to hand over your sabers and retire from the field of honor, swearing sacred oaths to fight no more forever? It's a quandary, isn't it? Kissmyass, you following any of this?"

Silence from Kissmyass.

He and Numbnuts exchanged a look.

Finally, Numbnuts spoke, apparently for both of them.

"Fuck you, Yank. You do what you have to do."

"So that's it? Death and glory, and let's hear it for Mother Russia?"

Both men shut their mouths, let their heads fall back against the cupboard, and closed their eyes. A little blood was running down Numbnuts's cheek, and although Dalton had reset and bandaged Kissmyass's fractured thumb, the fact remained that he was right now leaning back on it and it had to hurt like hell. They may not have been great contenders but they weren't whiners, not by a long shot. Tough little buggers.

Dalton was quiet for a while, considering the two men sitting on the floor. Dalton did not know it, since he had never seen it, but he was wearing his killing face. Most of those who *had* seen it were dead. Mandy Pownall had glimpsed it only once and had never forgotten it. The simple truth was that Dalton was bone tired of killing second-stringers and hapless grunts.

But there was no way he could just . . . release them.

He stood up, looked down at the two men, and pulled out his Beretta. Hearing him move, they opened their eyes, went a little pale but said nothing.

Dalton checked out the backstop behind their heads, not wanting to blow a round into a fuel line or out through the hull. He decided to put the round straight down through the tops of their heads, let the center mass take the freight. He moved over to Kissmyass, put the muzzle hard up against the dome of his skull.

"Hold on there, buttercup—"

He spun around on a heel and saw Porter Naumann lounging on the leather couch across from the galley counter looking quite pleased with himself. He was wearing blue jeans, deck shoes without socks, and a shell-pink crewneck cashmere sweater. At least, it looked like cashmere.

"What the hell are you doing here?" said Dalton, ignoring the stares of the two men on the galley floor. This was understandable, since, from their perspective, he was talking to a couch.

Naumann shrugged, offered a lopsided grin.

"Didn't I say I was going to run right along to the next time? Well, this *is* the next time. Got here just in time too."

"Porter, I'm always delighted to see you, you know that—"

"Don't worry, I'm not staying. I just wanted to chat for a bit."

"You can see I'm sort of busy?"

Naumann leaned out and took a look at the men, shook his head.

"I see that. You planning to shoot them, are you?"

"I was toying with the idea."

"But you're not *happy* about it, are you?"

"All due respect, Porter, this is not the time for some of your half-baked postmortem psychoanalytical heebie-jeebies. How about we—"

"I just don't think you should cap a guy if your heart isn't in it."

"You didn't say that in Venice, and I'd just capped five guys."

"Three. Zorin, you ripped his head off. And Galan popped Belajic."

"Okay, three—"

"Remember what Zorin said while you were doing it?"

"No, I was a little distracted at the time, what with trying to not get killed and all."

"He said, *'Aspetta, Krokodil . . . per Dio . . . Aspetta.'*"

"Okay, maybe he did."

"That means 'Wait, Crocodile . . . for God's sake . . . Wait.' He was begging you not to kill him. *Begging.* That didn't *bother* you? A teensy?"

Dalton shook his head.

"Not at the time. If I lost that fight, was he gonna give *me* a break?"

Naumann shrugged, running a hand across the flat of his stomach, stroking the cashmere in an idle way.

"Maybe it didn't bug you *then.* Seems to be bugging you *now.* If you were okay with it, you'd have lit up these mooks ten minutes ago—"

"These mooks a special case, are they? Massacre of the innocents? Calling for divine intervention?"

Naumann looked over at the men again, considering.

"Nah, I've read their files. They're rotten rotters through and through. World is a better place, you cap them off. If they live through this, so I hear, they go on to perform pernicious prodigies of predaceous persiflage—"

"What the hell is 'persiflage'?"

"Hey, I'm freewheeling here. Point is, instead of capping them off, you're standing around blowing the gaff with a dead man. Think about it."

"For chrissakes, Porter—"

Naumann lifted his hands, palms out, smiled gently at him.

"All I'm saying, Micah . . . All I'm saying is, it's your call. See you."

And he was gone. Dalton stood blinking at the couch for a while and then turned around and looked down at the prisoners, both of whom were staring up at him, their expressions a mixture of dread and puzzlement.

"How about you two? Anything to add?"

It seemed, from their continued silence, that they did not.

Dalton stared at them for a while, then tucked the Beretta away and left the galley. He found Levka up in the pilot cabin, listening to very loud music and staring fixedly out at the Bosphorus. They were within a half mile of the Bosphorus Bridge and even at that distance the air was full of the roar and rumble and clang of the traffic streaming across it. Levka sat up straighter, offered Dalton one of his own Sobranies.

Dalton took it, lit up, and stood for a moment watching the river traffic churning and chugging all around them, the tree-filled eastern shoreline gliding by on their starboard side, the little island with the Maiden's Tower on it slipping sternward.

The *Subito*'s long, sleek bow rose and fell gracefully on the cross-cutting chop. Sunlight sparkled on the blue water. Gulls and terns and herons and pelicans wheeled and shrieked in the chilly air. The stench and burn of diesel fuel thickened as they got closer to the smoky haze drifting down from the bridge deck.

"You hear from Mandy yet?" he asked.

"Yes, boss. She have house all ready. Maybe half mile up from Sumahan Hotel. Big white house with pillars all along the dock, she says. Red-tiled roof. Green awnings. She say we can't miss it."

"Got a boathouse big enough for this barge?"

"Boss, is no barge, is like swan. Best boat in whole world!"

"I apologize. Big enough, anyway?"

"Yes, sir, sixty feet. Has big electric door comes down."

Dalton nodded, thinking about the two men down in the galley.

Levka seemed to follow his thoughts.

"So, what to do with Kissmyass and Numbnuts, yes?"

Dalton said nothing, looking out at the hills on the western shore, at a pale blue glimmer of glass far to the north.

"Look," said Levka, a bit nervously, "no offense, I can . . . take care of this . . . for you."

Dalton looked at him and came to a decision.

"This Dizayn Tower, it's right by that Diamond up there, isn't it?"

"Yes, boss."

"There's a wharf just ahead here, on the port side. See it?"

Levka shaded his eyes from the glare off the water, squinted.

"Yes, by Dolmabahçe Palace."

"Put me ashore there."

Levka looked uneasy.

"You gonna go to Dizayn Tower all by yourself?"

"Yes. I want you to take the boat up to wherever Mandy is, get it out of sight for a while, and go over this boat, see if you can find anything on it that connects to the night this Lujac was supposed to have died. I don't know what it might be, but Mandy's done that kind of thing before."

"We wait there for you?"

"No. I don't know what I'm gonna find at this building. Maybe nothing. But Kissmyass had a bar bill on him from the Double Eagle. You know it?"

"Yes. Is wharf bar in Kerch. Uncle Gavel and me, we drink there."

"And Kerch is where you ran into the Gray Man."

"So we going to Kerch?"

"Yes, but not by chopper. It's not safe to go back there. The Turks will have found it by now—"

"Is true, boss. On radio just now, they saying no chopper found off Bandirma. Big search now for UN Blackhawk stolen from Santorini."

"Yeah? Well, that settles it. We'll take the boat."

"Boss, is five hundred miles across Black Sea to Kerch! Also icy cold as trout nipples. Lots of open water too. No place to hide."

"No help for it. Have the boat stocked and fueled and ready to go by midafternoon. I'll call you and tell you where to pick me up."

"And if no call?"

"Then Miss Pownall's in charge. You're working for her. Do whatever she tells you. And you keep her safe, Levka. Keep her *safe*. You follow?"

Levka met his eyes, held his look without wavering.

"I follow. I keep her safe no matter what. Word of soldier. How about those guys down there?"

Dalton turned and squared up with him.

"You see that little island back there?" he asked, pointing at the Maiden's Tower, its lights beginning to glow against the twilit coast behind it. Levka nodded, looking puzzled.

"Sure. Nothing there but old tower. Nobody goes there in winter. All shut down."

"After you drop me off, take them back down there, uncuff them and drop them off. As they are, butt naked. No papers, no ID, no cash. Turks aren't going to like a couple of naked Russians flitting about one of their tourist sites. It'll take them a week to sort it all out. By then, we'll be long gone."

Levka shook his head, looked uneasy.

"This will be problem, boss. If they talk good, be back in business pretty quick. Know all about us. Should do the smart thing."

"I didn't shoot you. Was that a smart thing?"

Levka took that in.

"No. You not shoot Levka. Maybe we gonna hire these guys too?"

Dalton shook his head.

"No. But I'm not gonna kill them either."

Levka said nothing and had an odd look in his eyes.

"Know what, Levka?"

"Yes, boss," he said, not making eye contact.

"Maybe we better drop these guys off *first* and then you put me on shore, okay?"

Levka looked hurt.

"You do not trust Levka?"

"I do not trust Levka not to tip these boys over the side as soon as I'm off the boat."

Levka looked over at Dalton, gave him a sudden smile.

"Okeydokey, boss. No offense taken."

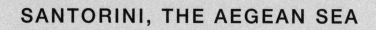

SANTORINI, THE AEGEAN SEA

SANTORINI FIELD

Until he actually met her, Captain Sofouli had not been very happy about having an American official, especially a *female* American official, dropped smack into the middle of the worst professional embarrassment he'd had since Costa-Gavras had based a character in *Z* on him. But when Nikki Turrin had climbed down the ladder of the Hellenic Air Force Super Puma that had brought her from Athens to Santorini and he had gotten a look at her in the cold light of the winter sun, he had a change of heart.

He had been expecting an angular and bloodless young careerist such as he had seen on American newsreels, striding purposefully down the corridors of power in D.C. in pencil skirts and blouses, firing along on sensible heels, their faces as sharp as Chippewa hatchets. This was not at all what stepped out of the hatchway of the Super Puma.

Sofouli watched with profound masculine appreciation as a supple and shapely young auburn-haired woman wearing a long tan trench coat over a navy skirt, a crisp white blouse, and outrageous blue high heels, emerged from the chopper, assisted by two very attentive young flyers, who escorted her down the steps and walked on either side of her across the windswept tarmac, reluctantly surrendering Miss Nikki Turrin, of the American NSA, to the care of Captain Sofouli, Prefect of Tourist Police, Santorini Division, with crisp salutes.

Nikki, shaking Sofouli's hand, liked what she saw: a large, weather-beaten older man, trim in a black police uniform, with deep creases around his eyes and mouth, intelligent black eyes with a blue spark deep inside them, and salt-and-pepper mustache setting off strong white teeth, as he smiled down at her and offered his hand, which was strong yet gentle.

"I am Captain Sofouli. Welcome to Santorini, Miss Turrin."

"Thank you," said Nikki, pausing to take in the shimmering plain of the Aegean stretched out below the cliffs, dazzling in the setting sun, and the jagged rocks of the islands across the lagoon.

Sofouli turned and indicated the jumble of white buildings scattered across the clifftops to the west, pointing to a low, white Art Deco hotel a few miles distant.

"That is the Porto Fira Suites. We found the body on the rocks below it. Would you like to see the room they stayed in?"

"Yes, I would."

She ended up in Sofouli's black Benz, the middle car in a convoy that followed the switchback highway as it climbed up toward the western edge of the caldera wall. As they bounced over the rocky terrain, Sofouli, sitting beside Nikki and enjoying her scent immensely, managed to stay professional, filling her in on what had taken place so far.

"It seems that one of my men, a Sergeant Keraklis, was corrupt. I make no excuse for myself. I made the mistake of thinking myself in an easy posting, and I have paid for my lack of attention. The man in the water—you may see the body if you wish, although I do not recommend it—was a man named Gavel Kuldic. He was identified by Interpol as a Croatian criminal, born in Legrad, near the Hungarian border. There was another man with him, named Dobri Levka, also from Legrad. They were what you could call 'soldiers of fortune,' I guess, taking whatever work they could find. For reasons I do not yet know, my sergeant—"

"Keraklis?"

"Yes, Zeno Keraklis. For some reason, he brought these men to my island, telling me they were cousins. To my shame, I did not check this. The night in question, after my interview with the two Americans . . . I am right that they were with your Central Intelligence Agency?"

"I can't confirm that at all, Captain Sofouli. Our two agencies are not on good terms with each other lately—"

"Yet here you are, from the National Security Agency yourself. You will admit that there is a connection at least with American intelligence. I was a part of that world myself, Miss Turrin, many years ago. I know how these things work. I know you would not be here at all if this did not touch upon American interests at the highest level. Please do not . . . condescend."

Nikki considered the man for a while, thinking this through.

"Okay, I won't condescend. Personally, I think these two individuals, whose names I cannot confirm—"

"Certainly not Pearson, at least."

"Yes, certainly not Pearson. I think they were acting as private citizens—they showed you no official ID, never implied that they were American intelligence officers?"

Sofouli nodded.

"I think—my Agency thinks—that they were acting as private citizens, and that they were trying to confirm the death of a man named Kirik Lujac and that you confirmed this for them. Is that correct?"

Sofouli looked out the window for a time. They were rolling down the main street of Fira now, the convoy making a left turn toward the Porto Fira Suites, far out on a promontory overlooking the Aegean.

"I think first we will look at the evidence and then we will talk. Come, let me show you the room where they stayed."

Although the suite was now the domain of a Greek forensic unit— an area by an overturned table in the front room had been marked off with blue plastic tape—Nikki thought the room itself was quite beautiful, clean and spare and very Zen, with a wonderful view over the glittering blue basin to the dark islands in the western seas. The room smelled of disinfectant and cigarette smoke and the salt-and-seaweed bite of the Aegean. A chilly wind ruffled the gauzy curtains, bringing with it the smell of garlic and flowers.

"Here," said Sofouli, indicating the area marked off by blue tape, "we found traces of blood and brain matter. The victim, Gavel Kuldic, was killed here—three shots into the back of his head as he lay facedown on the floor—and these marks of shoe heels here . . . and here . . . indicate that the man was then picked up and carried out here . . ."

Sofouli led her onto a broad stone terrace jutting out over the cliffs that sloped away steeply to the white ribbon of surf far below them. The air was full of clear evening light, and Nikki felt that she was standing on the edge of the ancient world, like Penelope scanning the sea for Ulysses year after endless year. Sofouli let her take it in, and then gently caught her attention.

"Down there, where you see the blue tape, we found his body, much broken and battered. There was a storm yesterday, as you may have heard—"

"Who killed him? Sergeant Keraklis?"

Sofouli shook his head slowly.

"No. We believe that Sergeant Keraklis was killed before this man.

We found his body this morning, in the swimming pool at the side of the hotel. His neck had been broken."

Nikki fell silent, thinking that this kind of senseless killing did not fit with her impressions of either Micah Dalton or Mandy Pownall. If she was right, then neither Dalton nor Mandy Pownall did these killings, or the killings were not senseless.

"Why do you think Sergeant Keraklis was killed, Captain?"

Sofouli stood beside her at the railing, staring down into the surging breakers, listening to the eternal roar of the sea and the wind.

"I think Keraklis may have started something he could not deal with. I think it had to do with this Kirik Lujac fellow. I knew that man—"

"Lujac?"

"Yes. He came here often, in the high season mainly, but sometimes, as he did last month, in the off-season. He owned a large Riva motor cruiser, one of the most beautiful boats ever to moor off Santorini, but he was not a beautiful man. Physically, he was perfection itself, a Greek god, but he was . . . not liked by the people of the town even though he spent a great deal of money here. He was . . . He gave the impression of being, inside, a spider and not a man. When it seemed that he had been killed by one of his own kind, no one in Santorini was very unhappy. Not even the boys who go all over the Aegean trading their bodies for the high life, not even these parasites missed him. Lujac was a predator, I think, and although he did nothing in Santorini to which I could object, I have reports of him from places like Kotor and Budva and Venice that are not so good to hear."

He was silent then, still looking out over the water.

"Captain?"

"Yes, Miss Turrin?"

"You found a body in the water a month or so ago?"

"Yes. Well, not I. A fisherman saw him, and we sent one of our boats across the lagoon to investigate."

"Who did you send?"

Sofouli gave her a sideways look.

"Sergeant Keraklis."

"I see. These stories about Lujac, from Kotor and Budva, did they involve possible murders?"

"Yes. And they had other . . . elements."

"'Elements'?"

"Yes. I will not tell a young woman these stories."

"I understand. May I tell you one?"

Sofouli looked at her.

"Should we sit?"

"Yes," said Nikki, "we should sit."

Nikki told him what she knew of Lujac's time in Singapore and of his connection with a Croatian syndicate boss named Branco Gospic and what he did to a young Muslim police corporal in a hotel room in Changi Village in eastern Singapore, including the sending of graphic digital pictures. Sofouli listened patiently, interrupting only to clarify a detail here and a sequence there. Nikki could see that he was inferring far more than she was saying and guessing the connections pretty well, but she set that aside, finishing with a detailed description of what had been done to an elderly woman in London just a few days ago. When she had finished, Sofouli sat back in the deck chair overlooking the sea, and, offering her one first, lit up a long black cigarette and drew the smoke in with a thoughtful expression.

He leaned forward, set his elbows on his knees, and looked sideways at her, his sharp eyes glinting in the afternoon sun.

"And you think this . . . killer of a woman in London . . . you think this might be Kiki Lujac?"

"I don't know. That's why I'm here. To ask you."

"It has been officially decided that the body we found in the water was the body of Kirik Lujac," he said with an air of finality.

"Yes," she said, "I know, officially. What about unofficially?"

He frowned, drew on the cigarette, blew out a wavering plume through pursed lips.

"I begin to think—"

His cell phone rang, a high, chattering beep. He took it out, spoke a few words in Greek, paused for a while, his face changing as he listened to a tinny voice on the other end. He said another few words in Greek—they sounded like a command—and then he shut the phone off and looked across at Nikki as if making a decision about her.

"What is your . . . brief . . . in this matter, Miss Turrin?"

"How do you mean?"

"I mean, your orders . . . from your boss . . . what are they?"

"To come to Santorini, talk to you, confirm Kiki Lujac's death, then to go back to America."

"I see. And if we cannot confirm Kiki Lujac's death?"

"I would have to consult with my boss."

"You would go back to America to do this?"

"No, I would talk to him . . . What's going on, Captain? What was that call about?"

"My missing Blackhawk . . . they have found it."

"I see. Where?"

"In Istanbul. I am to go and consult with the Turks."

"You're leaving now?"

"Yes," he said, smiling hugely at her. "Our Super Puma is return-ing. It will be here in an hour. We leave at once."

He reached out, set his bear paw on her hand, leaned in.

"I think our courses run side by side for a time. You ask me if I still think Kiki Lujac is dead. I begin to think not. Perhaps we can find out something in Istanbul. Do you wish to come along?"

She stared at the man, thinking about the AD of RA's clear instructions: *"All I want you to do is put this Lujac theory to bed and then come back here, and we go on with our quiet little lives. Could you do that and only that?"*

If she took his instructions *literally*, then she could say with some degree of honesty—*Not much,* said her conscience—that "this Lujac theory" was still in play, and that by going to Istanbul with Sofouli she was only extending her mandate a little in order to complete the mission . . . Furthermore . . . Well, to cut to the chase, she was in a Hellenic Air Force Super Puma and heading for Istanbul a few minutes later.

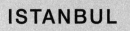

ISTANBUL

ÇENGELKÖY, THE ASIAN SIDE OF THE BOSPHORUS

The Dizayn Tower was a slab-sided, black-striped monolith set down in the middle of a square mile of office towers and banks and business plazas that had sprung up in the last five years on a hilltop at Istanbul's northern limits, all of it now shining in the evening sun. The sector was dominated by the immense curved-glass spear tip of the Diamond of Istanbul, at a thousand feet the tallest building in this part of the world. A biting cold wind was slicing through the open ground in between the buildings, and Dalton was chilled through and through by the time he got into the lobby of the Dizayn Tower. A young black-haired, brown-eyed Turkish girl in a guard's uniform was sitting behind a tall, bunkerlike desk, and she watched him as he came across the polished granite floor.

"Yes, sir, how may I help?"

"I'm looking for Beyoglu Trading. Suite 5500?"

She looked down at something behind the desk wall, frowned.

"There is no Beyoglu Trading listed, sir."

"Can you tell me what firm is in Suite 5500, then?"

"Yes, sir," she said, her intelligent brown eyes flickering over his rather casual outfit. The Turks take business pretty seriously and dress for it as well as anyone in New York or London.

"Yes, sir, it's the Russian Inter-Asian Trade and Commerce Bureau. But I see they are closed for the day, I am afraid."

Dalton, sensing her vague disapproval of his casual look, did not ask to go up anyway. He put on a politely blank expression.

"That's odd. Do they usually close midweek?"

"No, sir. According to the note here, they just closed the office this morning. A sudden illness, it says. They'll probably be open tomorrow."

Dalton thanked her, and walked off toward a flight of stairs that, according to the signs, led down to a concourse with shops and restaurants. The escalator brought him into a large subterranean mall, filled with upscale shops and restaurants, crowded with office workers and shoppers.

He found a store selling trench coats and bought a long blue woolen topcoat and a navy blue silk scarf with white polka dots, along with a short brown quilted ski vest and a brown woolen watch cap. As he was paying, he saw exactly what he had been hoping to see: a "tail," a middle-aged round brown man with a doughy face and aggressively ordinary sunglasses, milling aimlessly around a newsstand and looking everywhere but at Dalton.

He seemed to be alone, but Dalton decided to put him through the paces to make sure. He stepped into a changing booth, stuffed the blue topcoat in the bag, put on the brown watch cap and the quilted vest, and walked quickly out into the mall heading for the escalator. After a moment of confusion, the tail folded a newspaper under his arm and followed him, keeping a distance of about fifty feet, angling slightly away as if he were going to a different area of the mall.

Dalton stopped at the foot of the escalator, patting his pockets and shaking his head, and then turned around and headed back the way he had come. The tail nearly broke an ankle making a hard right turn back toward the newsstand, keeping his back to Dalton as Dalton passed by less than twenty feet away. There was a walk-through coffee shop at the far end of the mall, and Dalton headed straight there.

The mall was a hard place to tail anyone since it was literally a hall of mirrors, plate glass, and highly reflective plastic everywhere you looked. Dalton could see the tail reflected in a shopwindow.

By now, Dalton was reasonably certain that the man was working alone, which could mean these people were not professionals, since a single-handed tail is nearly impossible to maintain without getting burned or losing the target, or it could mean that Dalton was drilling back up their chain of command so fast and so effectively that their organization was still off balance, struggling to get on top of the game. Time to up the stakes, then.

Dalton bought his coffee, stopped at a turn in the hallway to sip some, looking around for a doorway or a storage room as he did so. There was a sign indicating washrooms on the wall and an arrow pointing down a corridor. Dalton threw the cup into a trash can, hesitated as if he were unsure of his next move, and then strolled down the corridor in the direction of the washrooms. The women's washroom door came up first and then the men's. Dalton slipped into the women's—empty, he hoped, or at least the open area seemed to be clear. He heard a rapid squeak of rubbery soles going down the corridor, stopping outside the men's room.

He took off the watch cap and the vest, stuffed them in a garbage can, and slipped into his long blue topcoat. He cracked the door, looked up and down the corridor, came out into the hall, ran to the end of it, and managed to get back out into the mall, almost fifty feet away, mixing in with the crowds, when the brown man popped out of the corridor, his face a little red, looking this way and that, obviously agitated. Dalton, his back to the man, watched the man's reflection in a sheet of plastic covering a map of the concourse. The man looked right at him and then moved on, scanning the crowd.

The man came out into the main concourse, stood for a moment, looking unsettled, his head going this way and that, seeing no one in a woolen cap and a brown vest, and then he pulled out a cell phone, punched in some numbers, his stubby legs working hard as he crossed an acre of gleaming granite heading for an escalator.

Dalton came out of the hall, slipping his blue topcoat off and folding it over his arm to change his appearance again. He picked a newspaper out of the trash—*The New Anatolian,* as it turned out, the headline once again in bright red letters, STOLEN GREEK BLACKHAWK FOUND; he didn't have time to read the rest—and held it out in front of him as he walked but kept his eyes on the round brown man.

The tail reached the escalator, stopping at the foot of it, the cell still at his ear, as he turned to look back across the concourse, his head moving as he scanned the crowd again. Dalton got himself mixed in with a group of office workers queueing up at a sandwich shop and watched the tail through a glass wall. The tail hovered there for a time, still on his cell, and then he turned and went up the escalator toward the main entrance.

Dalton hung back, giving the man time to reach the top, and then came up the escalator two stairs at a time, reaching the top just in time to see the brown man pushing through the revolving doors and out onto the windy open plaza. There, he met a second person, this time a woman, short, also round, black hair in a severe bob, wearing a long black coat, a large black bag hanging from her shoulder. She and the round brown man spoke for about thirty seconds, and then she made a gesture, cutting off something he was trying to say with a sideways slice that convinced Dalton she was in charge.

The brown man, slumping slightly, nodded, and came back in through the revolving doors, heading straight for the escalator again, failing to see Dalton standing by the elevator bank.

Dalton watched the woman in black as she crossed the plaza and walked down a flight of wide concrete stairs, where she stood for a time, obviously waiting for a cab, her head turning this way and that, trying to spot one in the streaming traffic.

The cold wind ripped at her coat, and she pulled the collar up to shield herself from it, which also shielded her from Dalton as he came out of the Dizayn Tower. Again he slipped on the blue topcoat and moved quickly across the open plaza toward her.

At that point, she saw a bright yellow Honda taxi and stepped out into the street to flag it down. The cab darted out of the stream like a carp going for a water bug and came to a rubber-burning halt at the curb. The woman leaned into the open passenger window, talking to the driver in an agitated manner. Dalton had heard that riding in a cab in Istanbul was a risky proposition and required clear agreement about destinations and routes and fares and tips *before* you let the cab pull away with you inside it.

In a moment, the deal was sealed, and she tugged open the door, slipped in, and to her surprise found that she not only had a very handsome blond man slipping into the cab beside her but also had the muzzle of a pistol shoved into the side of her rib cage.

Dalton leaned in close as the cab took off with a roar, lancing back into the traffic, the young Turkish driver oblivious, listening to some talk radio station and chattering happily into a cell phone.

Dalton nuzzled her ear—she smelled of cigarette smoke and burned coffee, and, from the skin on her cheek and neck, was older than she looked, in her forties at least, with a blunt face and wearing too much makeup, the unvarying black of her hair coming straight from a bottle—and he hissed into her throat, "Twitch, and I'll kill you."

He felt her body tense, rammed the pistol in tight. She sagged against the seat back, took off her sunglasses, and looked straight ahead, her eyes wide, her breathing short and rapid, her skin turning bone white under the thick coating of makeup.

Dalton kept the pistol where it was and used his free hand to lift the black bag at her feet off the floor. He dumped it out on her lap, a little landslide of feminine accessories: a set of keys on a large plastic ring, a pack of Gauloise cigarettes, a cheap plastic lighter with a skating scene on it, an orange fake-leather wallet with a mix of currencies in it—euros, lira, even some Ukrainian gravniks—a stubby little black semiauto pistol, a Russian-made PSM, a Nokia cell phone, turned on but without a GPS function that he could see, and a couple of used tissues. She looked straight ahead as he went through her things, and he could feel her heart pounding through the muzzle of his Beretta. She was clearly terrified, which told him she was probably not Moscow Center KGB or even GRU, unless they'd lost a lot of their game since the Great Collapse, which seemed unlikely.

He flipped open the orange wallet, riffled through the cards, dug out an ID with her picture on it that said she was Gretel Pinskoya, lived in Saint Petersburg, and was an attaché of something called the "Russian Inter-Asian Trade and Commerce Bureau."

Dalton flipped her things back into the bag, keeping the nasty little PSM pistol, the keys, and the phone, dropped the bag back at her feet, and took a moment to see where they were going.

As far as he could tell, they were headed north, out of the city, in a stream of heavy traffic—cars, scooters, jitneys, diesel trucks—moving through open country with rolling farmland stretching away into the coming night on their left and acres of brand-new housing tracts on their right. He saw a street sign as they whipped across an intersection: BÜYÜKDERE CADDESI. He leaned forward, keeping the pistol rammed in tight against the woman's ribs, tapped the driver's screen.

"Yes, sir?"

"How long till we get there?"

"*Sariyer,* sir?"

Dalton had no idea where that was.

"Yes, how long?"

The driver, a kid really, looked a little shifty, and Dalton realized he was thinking about his tip and whether or not he'd make more if he just drove around in the hills for a while until he got the tab up where he liked it.

"Oh, maybe ten miles. Hard to say in all this traffic."

Dalton pulled some euros out of his pocket, held them through the partition window. The driver eyed them and literally licked his lips.

"Get us there in half the time and this is yours."

"Okay, sir!" he said, punching the gas and accelerating around an oil tanker, darting back into the lane again, as a transport went by in the other direction, horn blasting.

Dalton leaned back and looked at the woman beside him, who so far had spoken not one word, which impressed him.

"So, Gretel, how the heck are you?"

The woman's lips were blue and tight, and for a moment Dalton thought she was going to pass out. She was not used to this kind of thing, but she knew enough about it to know her chances of still being alive by sundown were slim.

"Who are you?" she finally got out after a couple of attempts.

Dalton gave her a large and unsettling grin.

"My name is Micah Dalton and I work for the Central Intelligence Agency, and I am here to totally fuck up your world. Lovely to meet you."

"What . . . What do you want?"

"I want to know who's waiting for us, Gretel."

"Waiting for us where?"

"Wherever we're going."

Her skin was almost powder blue now, and her lips were white.

"Goodness, Gretel," he said, pulling the Beretta out of her ribs and resting it on her elbow, "you'll faint. Breathe, sweetheart, breathe."

"I am an attaché of a Russian trade office, and what you are doing is kidnapping me. There will be very serious reper—"

"Gretel, sweetie, save it for *Pravda*. By the way, Vladimir's dead."

Gretel couldn't control her reflexive gasp, but she clamped down on it a second later, the muscles along her jawline clenching and her lips set.

"I do not know a—"

"Didn't mean to, actually. Cracked him across the back of the head back at the Ataköy Marina. Had a skull like a paper cup, I guess. Never came to. Dumped him into the Bosphorus. Was he a dear friend?"

She blocked herself off and tried to retreat inward.

"Where's the rest of your crowd, by the way? Can't just be you and the little brown man back at the mall."

In spite of her efforts, something flickered in her eyes. A secret?

"Maybe they're all off tracking us with Anatoly's cell phone? Closing in like avenging harpies? Sorry. Anatoly doesn't have it anymore—"

She flinched at Anatoly's name.

"You know Mr. Bakunin, do you? Little dwarf of a guy? Hung like a hamster?"

She flared at that, her cheeks red, turning to hiss in his face.

"Viktor is—"

She stopped abruptly, shutting down again. But it cost her.

Dalton decided to let her cook for a while, leaning forward to tap the driver's shoulder. The driver had an iPod in his ear—didn't anyone under thirty ever worry about still being able to hear when they were forty?—and he popped it out with a large, gap-toothed grin. Dalton's promise of multiple euros had made them boon companions . . . for now, at least.

"What's that address again? Where're we going?"

The driver looked down at a notepad on the seat beside him.

"Three-six-seven Meserburnu Caddesi, sir."

"Okay, thanks."

"We'll be there in five minutes, okay?"

Dalton sat back again, smiled at Gretel.

"So, Gretel, what's at 367 Meserburnu Street? What's waiting for us there?"

She turned her face away, staring out the side window, probably, Dalton thought, to hide her reaction to the question. Which meant that whatever was waiting there wasn't going to be good for Dalton. He smiled at the side of her head for a time and then tugged out his own cell phone. The line beeped for a while and then Mandy's voice came on, a low, purring vibrato.

"Micah, where are you?"

"Ask our guy if he knows a place in the north called Sariyer?"

There was muffled exchange, and then Mandy was back on.

"Yes. It's a port town, kind of a fishing village, about six miles from the northern end of the strait. On the European side."

"Okay. Where are you?"

"We're . . . just coming up to a bridge . . . Levka says it's the Sultan Mehmet Bridge. Hold on. Are you in Sariyer?"

"Just about."

"Levka says it's about five miles up the strait. We can be there in thirty minutes, if we open the boat up."

"What's the risk?"

"He says there's a ten-knot speed limit in the strait because the wake erodes the shoreline."

"Risk it. Did you find anything?"

"Yes. You want to talk about it in the clear?"

"No. Does it help?"

"Oh my yes. Lujac is alive, and we can prove it. Are you all right?"

Dalton looked over at Gretel Pinskoya, who was simmering away like a little teapot and harrumphing audibly every few seconds.

"I am."

"What's in Sariyer, Micah?"

"A surprise, I expect."

"You should wait until we get there."

"I can't. Speed counts here. Look for me at the main dock."

He flipped the phone shut, sat forward to look through the windshield. They had come down out of a range of low, tree-covered hills and were now racing along a waterside causeway—PIYASA CADDESI, according to the signs—past some very elegant waterside villas with red-tiled roofs and colonnaded balconies, windows glowing with wealth and ease, parks and walkways running along the waterside, mothers jogging with their kids in those big-wheeled strollers, a load of ancient tourists stumbling out of a large blue bus with MINOAN TOURS painted on the side. The kid was slowing down now, counting the numbers, as Piyasa turned into Meserburnu. The trees thinned out, and now they were moving through what looked like a more industrial section of the little town. Fishing boats filled a small marina on his right. The road curved east, and the driver, at a slow crawl, brought the cab to a stop beside what looked like a cannery or a warehouse, about a hundred feet long and perhaps twenty-five deep, sitting out on a concrete wharf.

The driver pulled through a narrow gate in a tall concrete wall and into a small enclosed parking area, which was empty. He turned around to offer his gap-toothed grin to his passengers. If he thought anything of the obvious tension between the blond young man and the teapot woman, he wasn't showing it.

"Here we are, sir. Make good time, yes?"

Dalton thanked him, paid the fare, and gave him a fifty-euro tip on top of it, which caused his young face to break into an ear-to-ear grin. He forced a business card onto Dalton as Dalton got out, bringing Gretel Pinskoya out on his arm in what looked like but was not a chivalric gesture.

She came unhappily but offered no resistance, and they stood together in the fenced-off parking lot for a moment while Dalton considered the solid-steel doors and the blank windows, dirty with dust, closed off with slatted beige blinds like the cataract-whitened eyes of a very old man. The place had a general air of decay and felt empty. Behind the low building, above its corrugated-iron roof, gulls wheeled and dipped, and a single pelican, roosting on the peak, squawked at them indignantly. Maybe, thought Dalton, he was the pelican who got fed a cell phone earlier and had now come back to bitch about it. Probably not.

Nothing for it but to push on, Dalton decided, although he intensely disliked walking into seemingly deserted buildings without backup and maybe air cover. He tugged Gretel into motion—she had lapsed into a kind of slack, sullen resistance—and they got up to the door. Dalton looked around the doorframe for alarms or triggers or any kind of telltale sign, saw nothing.

"So what do we do, Gretel? Do we open the door and get blown out of our panty hose? What should we do?"

Gretel shrugged, stared back at him for a moment, then looked quickly away, but not quickly enough to conceal the tiny glitter of hate-filled anticipation in her flat-brown eyes.

Dalton took out his Beretta, stepped to one side, and then rapped on the door three times—short, sharp blows. There was a silence then, during which even the sound of the traffic flowing behind them faded into stillness and there was only the ripple of the waves lapping against the pylons of the wharf. Dalton waited another sixty seconds and then took out the key ring, riffled through the choices, and settled on a large triangular one that looked like it suited the lock.

He was about to insert the key when he realized that Gretel was now backing away from the door. Dalton heard a distinct metallic click, then reached out and caught Gretel, jerking her to the ground just as there was a series of deep, thudding booms, five huge holes blasting out through the walls at waist level, first on the far left, then near left, then through the center of the door, the near right, then far right. The shooter paused, perhaps to assess damage or to reload his Godzilla shotgun. Dalton stepped in, fast and low, and fired nine quick rounds through the hole in the door. He heard a strangled yelp, and then the clatter of a weapon falling on concrete. Gretel had gotten to her feet and tried to waddle away as fast as she could, but Dalton caught her by the wrist and held her as he fired the Beretta again, taking out the door's upper and lower hinges. He booted what was left of the door and it slammed backward into a dark space that was filled with smoke still hanging in the air from the shotgun discharge. The afternoon sun was lighting up the wide, dust-filled interior, which was bare except for a few sticks of office furniture. There was a huge KS-23 shotgun lying in the rectangle of sunlight, a spray of fresh blood making a fan behind it, and a pair of military boots, splayed out and still, half hidden in the shadows. Dalton pulled Gretel in front of him and shoved her through the door. She staggered a few feet and went down on her hands and knees, her head down, her body shaking.

Dalton changed out his mag, slapped a new one home. He stepped quickly through the open door, checked six, checked right, checked left, checked above, got his back to the wall, covering the large open space. The smell of cordite hung in the air, the coppery bite of fresh blood, along with something else . . . something he did not quite recognize.

He looked back out into the parking lot, expecting to see it filling up with cop cars. But there was no sign that the gunfire had been heard over the booming of the waves. He shut the door, found a light switch, and a series of tired fluorescent bars gradually flickered on, filling the long open space with unsteady shimmering blue light and a buzzing electric whine.

Dalton stepped over the young man, weapon at the ready, and looked down at his shocked features. Fresh-faced, the man had a military crew cut; he was wearing jeans, combat boots, and a white turtleneck sweater.

He also had four bloody black holes stitched across his chest and was obviously dead. The four-gauge KS slide-action shotgun—a Russian military piece designed for their Special Forces, with a pistol grip and a massive barrel—lay a few inches from his right hand, with five ejected casings scattered around the floor behind him. Dalton bent down, picked the shotgun up, checked the chamber, slipping the Beretta into his belt. He looked over at Gretel.

"There was a *tell*, wasn't there?"

She said nothing.

"It was nothing you did, so it was something you didn't do. I guess the cell, right? If you showed up without calling first, the kid knew he should light up whoever was in the door. That was almost you, my dear. I saved your skin. Remember me in your will . . . Okay, Gretel, on your feet."

Still on her hands and knees, her shoulders shaking, she looked at him, her eyes smeared with running mascara.

"No. Shoot me here."

He walked over, grabbed her by the shoulder, jerked her to her feet.

"Anybody else here?"

Gretel shrugged, but now there was a blankness in her face that had not been there before. He pushed her ahead of him, and they went through the warehouse together. There *was* no one else there, and most of the space was empty except for a card table and a cot, where Dalton figured the young soldier he had just killed had slept, and a large rusty fish freezer, still muttering away, where the kid probably kept his food and beer. Next to the cot was an ammunition box, open, full of shells for the shotgun. Dalton, reloading the weapon and filling his pockets with spare shells, saw something sticking out from under the cot, a black triangle of wood. He used his shoe to drag it out from under the bed and found himself looking into the eyes of the President of the United States, the glass shattered, as if the picture had been stepped on. The President grinned up at Dalton, apparently delighted to see him. Dalton kicked the frame back under the cot and walked away.

He found a small, windowless room in a far corner that looked as if it had just been built. The exterior walls were made of new spruce two-by-fours, carelessly hammered together, obviously hasty construction. There was a solid-steel door set into one wall, with a heavy glass window reinforced with chicken wire in it. Dalton looked through the glass, saw a steel table, a wooden chair behind it, a lightbulb hanging down over the table. The table was covered with circular brown stains where coffee cups once sat, and there was a large glass ashtray in the middle overflowing with cigarette butts.

Dalton stepped away, walked back to Gretel, who stood in the middle of the warehouse, her shoulders slumped, staring dully at him. He pulled her over to the cot, pushed her down onto it.

Her eyes grew very wide.

"Hey, I'm not going to rape you, lady. That's a Russian thing."

He found some wire left over from the construction of the little room and trussed her up as gently as he could and left her there. He went back to the door, tripped the light switch on the outside.

A lightbulb, large and painfully bright inside its wire cage, came on, casting a harsh glare all over the room. Dalton opened the door slowly, looking right and left and above, before he entered.

The interior of the room had been walled with thick panels of

Sheetrock and then painted institutional colors—pale green over dark green—and had been treated with something to make the walls look old and dirty. The windowless room smelled of cigarette smoke, stale urine . . . and blood.

On the left-side wall, about halfway up from the floor, there was a large black-spattered stain with bits of lumpy material stuck here and there, mainly in the center. Dalton touched the stain, looked at his finger. It was blood, all right . . . old blood.

The table was made of steel and had been bolted to the floor, and the chair behind it was also screwed down tight. There were U-bolts set into the concrete, as if whoever sat here had been chained to the chair. He sat down in the chair, looked around the room from that perspective, and saw a small grate in one corner of the room at ceiling level.

He leaned forward and picked one of the cigarette butts out of the pile of ash. An American cigarette, he realized, a Camel filtertip. He rolled the cigarette between his fingertips. It was still soft, the filter stained almost black.

Whatever had happened here, it had happened a while back, maybe a month ago, maybe less. He got up, went outside, got a chair, and used it to take a closer look at the grating in the wall. He could see that something had been screwed in place there, probably a camera.

Dalton stepped back down, walked around the walls.

"They made this room look like a police interview room, Gretel. Why did they do that? Who was in this room?"

Gretel said nothing, lying on the cot, her eyes closed.

Dalton looked at her for a while, knowing that he wasn't going to get anything out of her without force and not quite ready to use it. He stood in the empty space, trying to get a sense of what had been going on here. The warehouse was probably leased, but by whom?

The Russian trade mission? But now that Dalton was burning up their network, they were dismantling everything and pulling back. But to where?

Kerch?

A sudden wave of exhaustion rolled over him. He hadn't slept since they had flown into Santorini. How long ago was that? A week? A day? He drew in a long breath, and that *scent* was there, faint, hard to detect under the stale cigarette smoke and the reek coming from the bathroom on the seawall side. Where was it coming from?

He followed the smell across the room, ending up by the fish freezer near the sliding steel doors that opened out onto the wharf. He stood over it for a while, staring down at the rust-streaked lid, at the thin stream of brown water running out from underneath it and pooling by the sliding doors. He looked back at Gretel Pinskoya and found her staring back at him, her expression fixed and white.

"What's in here, Gretel?"

He didn't expect an answer. He opened the lid. A white fog rose up from the inside of the freezer. Huddled there, wrapped in what looked like a tattered American flag, was the frozen corpse of a young girl, her black eyes wide and glazed with hoarfrost as she stared upward at him, her mouth a little open as if she had died struggling for air. The left side of her skull had been blown open by some sort of heavy round. There was a star-shaped entrance wound on the right side of her skull, which meant that the weapon that killed her had been pressed right up against it when the trigger was squeezed. She was wearing jeans and a thin T-shirt, and her blond hair, stiff with blood and matted in a frozen tangle, looked fake, tawdry. She had been crying when she died: her fogged eyes were streaked with black. She may have been thrown into the freezer moments after she died. What looked like tear tracks were still visible on her cheeks, thin silvery trails running sideways down her face. He turned around and went back over to stand beside Gretel Pinskoya, no longer feeling quite so chivalric.

"Gretel, what the *hell* have you people been up to?"

She stared up at him, shook her head several times.

"I had nothing to do with . . . that."

He was about to describe to her what he was going to do to assist her memory when he heard a big boat engine, deep and powerful, muttering, burbling, closing in on the other side of the steel doors that opened onto the wharf—Levka and Mandy with the *Subito*?

How did they know he'd be—he heard a big bolt racked back, a sound he knew too damned well—and hit the concrete just as whatever was on the other side of that steel wall opened up. There was a deep shuddering roar and a hail of large-caliber bullets that shredded the doors, the air full of the clatter and hammer of the rounds zipping and zinging around inside the warehouse like bees. He could feel the thudding chatter of the machine-gun rounds striking the concrete in a shower of red sparks, a row of rounds stitching sparks across the floor. The slugs found Gretel cowering on the cot, tearing her to bloody bits in a split second.

The weapon tracked on, sweeping back and forth, pouring hundreds of rounds into the side of the warehouse, ripping the building apart. Daylight was streaming in through hundreds of holes in the doors and walls. A spray of rounds caught the freezer and ripped it to shards, spilling the torn carcass of the young woman stiffly out onto the floor.

Another slicing ribbon of rounds caught her and chipped away at her like someone hammering a block of ice, parts of her skittered across the concrete, spinning crazily like ice cubes across a bar.

Dalton belly-crawled across the floor, feeling a ribbon of lead chattering up the floor inches from his hip, stinging pain as chips of concrete tore into his flesh, still crawling, ears ringing.

He could see the door into the parking lot, see the body of the man he had killed, dead but jumping and jerking as stray rounds and ricochets pumped into his corpse. Dalton grabbed the frozen girl, his hands slick, and shoved it in the line of fire between him and the machine gun out there, huddled behind it, feeling rounds chipping the ice, trying to make himself as small as what was left of her.

By now, the steel doors of the warehouse were hanging on their hinges, and he could see a large fishing trawler idling just beyond the wharf and a man in the cabin, gritting his teeth as he worked a Russian PK machine gun.

The machine gun chattered to a halt—a jam, time to change out a superheated barrel, or the end of the belt—and the silence was stunning, immense. The gunner took a moment to toss a satchel charge through a rent in the steel, and it skimmed across the floor and slammed into the far wall, its fuse hissing white smoke.

Dalton scooped up the KS shotgun, racking the slide as he got to his feet, charged at the hanging steel doors. The gunner looked up from the breech—he'd been trying to change out a hot barrel. Dalton raised the KS shotgun and blew the man's head into pink mist.

Behind Dalton, the satchel charge blew, and a white-hot flower of phosphorus opened up behind him, the sudden blast of heat scorching his neck and shoulders. Whoever was at the wheel shouted something in Russian, and the trawler heaved around and powered away, leaving a deep white wake as the props dug in. Dalton got a glimpse of the name painted across the stern: акула.

He ran out onto the wharf just as the warehouse caught fire, fired off five more slugs, the heavy shotgun bucking in his grip as splinters flew off the stern boards.

A navigation light shattered in a spray of red glass, and three ragged holes punched into the boards just at the waterline. The pilot pushed the throttle to max, and the stern buried itself deep into the Bosphorus, heading at speed for the open water of the Black Sea.

Dalton heard a klaxon horn sounding from the river on his right, saw the huge blue bow of the *Subito* plowing directly toward him, white wings curling out on either side of the cutwater, Mandy out on the bow with a line, Levka's white face behind the helm in the cabin.

Levka wheeled the boat into a sharp curve to starboard as the cruiser heeled dangerously and white water boiled up along her port side. Mandy staggered, caught herself on the railing, the *Subito* rushing in past the wharf, her engines thudding, Mandy racing along the rail, her wide gray eyes fixed on Dalton. Levka reversed the motors, and Dalton, holding the shotgun in one hand, his eyes on Mandy, set himself . . . and jumped.

GARRISON

THE TACONIC, NORTHBOUND

Brocius, doing a hundred miles per hour northbound on the Taconic, hurtling through a blinding snow squall, caught a glimpse of the bright green I-84 exit sign and nearly put the rented Escalade in the ditch as he swerved across the lanes just in time to lean it into a long right-hand-curving loop and up onto the westbound lanes.

He had picked up the Escalade at La Guardia, intending to take Highway 6 westbound at Shrub Oak, which would put him on 9D, the highway that ran parallel to the Hudson just north of Peekskill, but when he reached the turnoff there was a New York State trooper patrol car parked across the ramp. Highway 6 was closed due to heavy snow coming down from the Hudson Highlands. He had been forced to take the long way around, going north to 84 and then west to connect with Route 9 north of Garrison.

Settling back into a steady seventy—the highway was oddly empty at this midmorning hour, and a major snowpack was building up in the outside lanes, leaving him just one bare lane to follow—Brocius picked his cell phone up again and flipped it open. His thumb hovered over the 911 button for six long seconds while he thought it over—the signal was very weak, barely one bar, this *damned* storm—and flipped the phone shut again.

Briony was in trouble, that was clear enough, and the fact that she had worked pretty hard to keep the frog prince from understanding their exchange on the phone had set off serious alarms for him, although they had been ringing faintly in his subconscious for days.

But what *kind* of trouble was she in?

Brocius figured it had something to do with Morgan's disappearance, and, if it did, would dragging in the New York State patrol guys make the situation better or worse? Worse, he decided.

And when he thought about it, what could he really say that would justify sending a couple of cruisers out into this nasty winter storm? Assuming they had any to spare on a miserable day like this.

Hi, I'm Hank Brocius of the NSA, and I think one of my people is getting . . . nervous . . . about her . . . houseguest? Can you send a car?

Oh hell, sure thing, Mr. Brocius, we're on it like lawyers on a widow. Look for us in the springtime with the darling buds of May.

Briony had the Sig, and she had her fallback position. She knew the drill in an emergency—the Agency trained them all for this kind of event—and the Glass Cutters had all been put on official warning right after Mildred Durant's murder. He didn't know what Morgan's disappearance meant from a tactical point of view, and, until he did, he was going to keep the problem inside the Agency where it could be controlled. But his chest was tight and his mouth was dry as he hammered the Escalade down through the driving snow, watching the exits. A few miles west, there was the sign.

ROUTE 9 SOUTH
NELSONVILLE, COLD SPRING, GARRISON

Garrison was ten miles south, but at Nelson's Corners he'd have to cut west toward the river on Indian Brook and then fork to the left on Avery, which would take him eventually to 9D, known in Garrison as Bear Mountain Beacon Highway. Briony's house was on the bluffs above the Hudson, number 15000.

That depended on whether or not he could use Indian Brook and Avery at all, both narrow, two-lane roads that switchbacked and twisted over the Hudson Highlands separating Route 9 from the towns of Cold Spring and Garrison. Huge flakes of snow were tumbling down in a mad spiral of driving fleece, and his visibility was down to fifty feet. And the weather was getting steadily worse as he came south on 9, until he was plowing through the blizzard at twenty miles an hour.

Even if he didn't lose it on a curve or simply get bogged down in a drift, he was sixty minutes away at least. Maybe more.

A hell of a lot could happen in sixty minutes.

AS A PRECAUTION, Duhamel went to the main board where the phone lines came into the house—he had already established its location, in the pantry off the kitchen—and disconnected the panel, cutting off both the house line and the work line, as well as the high-speed wireless Internet connection that ran throughout the property. Then he walked over to the bottom of the stairs and looked up into the warm light of the second-floor landing. The stillness was profound, as if the old house was literally holding its breath.

"Briony?" Duhamel called her name as he came up the stairs, the blade tucked into his belt in the small of his back, his hands empty and innocent, his tone worried, puzzled—exactly how a human would sound.

He reached the top of the stairs, paused at the landing, looking down the corridor that led to the master bedroom. Although the hallway was in darkness, there was a sliver of light at the far end, a soft yellow glow where the bedroom door was open a few inches.

"Briony?"

No answer.

He stepped onto the carpet and began to walk down the hall toward the bedroom door. He was not afraid—if he was feeling anything, it was anger at the unexpected way this thing was playing out—and a strong sense that he had better have Anton and whoever was with him under control before he settled down to his long-delayed exploration of Briony Keating.

He wondered, idly, who Piotr would have sent.

Bukovac?

Would Piotr risk sending someone like Bukovac to America?

Yes, Duhamel decided.

To win this game, he would risk that.

Well, first things first: locate Briony if possible, then deal with Bukovac when and if he turned up.

Moving lightly but not so lightly as to seem to be stalking her, Duhamel came down the hall, checking the cupboard door on his left as he did so—clear—and then looking into the guest bathroom on the right—also clear. "Briony, sweet, where are you?"

He reached the bedroom door, put out a hand, gently pushed it open. It was a large, low-ceilinged room, done in pale green, with thick wooden beams across the ceiling and a stone fireplace. The heavy mahogany sleigh bed, which had withstood a lot of punishment, was empty, the bedding still tossed and warm from their last—final?—encounter. The room was in shadowy darkness, the curtains still drawn against the cold light of this last morning together, one bedside lamp burning low.

He saw that her cell phone was still lying beside the charger. He picked it up, checked the battery: RECHARGE NOW. This might explain why she hadn't taken it with her, wherever she had gone.

"Briony, this is not funny. You're *worrying* me. Where are you?"

He bent down to look under the bed, feeling slightly ridiculous—nothing. The door to the bathroom was open, and cool white light spilled out onto the dark green carpet on the bedroom floor.

He moved around the bed and walked across to the bathroom door, pushed it open carefully, half expecting to see Briony cowering behind it. This room was also empty.

He came back into the bedroom, stood for a while in the center, using his photographer's eye to see the dimensions of the floor, the room, in relation to the space outside it.

He held his breath for a time, listening carefully for her breathing. Nothing at all, other than the insectile hiss of his own blood in his ears. He walked back to the entrance to the bathroom and stood there, looking at the lines of the built-in closet—fairly recent construction, he thought—comparing the dimensions of the closet to other parts of the room. Then he walked to the leaded-glass windows, pulled back the curtain.

It was snowing—quite heavily now—but there was a pale silvery sun gliding through clouds, and it lit up the broad expanse of lawn that sloped down toward the river, a gray hillside with a glint of pale light here and there on the frozen drifts that lay on the river.

There were no tracks in the snow, no tracks leading across the lawn to the coach house where she kept her office, and he would have heard her trying to start the car—trying, because he had taken a moment to pull the cap off the distributor—he was grateful that she had an *old* car, a large burgundy Cadillac Fleetwood that she had inherited from her father.

Well, he knew one thing for certain: Briony was inside this house, and she wasn't going to get out without being seen. She had gone to ground—probably somewhere on this floor—and now she was waiting for . . . what?

For *rescue*, of course.

The two o'clock caller with the Maryland cell phone number.

He turned back to consider the room and decided there was one way to clear up any ambiguity concerning the situation. He walked over to Briony's night table, pulled the drawer open. The indigo scarf was still there—he had once been very fond of indigo scarves but had not wanted to use this one on Briony because a short while ago an indigo scarf had almost gotten him killed—but there was nothing under it. Briony's lovely little Sig Sauer P-230 was gone. That clarified the nature of this game.

Duhamel—he paused for a blessed moment to shed that name as a snake sheds its skin—shuddered a little as Kiki Lujac came back up from a long way down and stood before him in the mirror next to the bed.

Lujac stared back at himself, running his hands through his short black hair. When this was over, he would grow it long again. He would find the *Subito* and go somewhere warm and sunny. He felt he had lost much of his hard-earned tan in this frigid, sunless place. North Africa was beautiful this time of year, with some of the very best surfing in the world off Casablanca. Marcus Todorovich had told him that once—poor, sweet Marcus. He leaned into the mirror, squinting a little. There was something very wrong with his reflection. Yes, the brown contact lenses.

He leaned over and plucked them out of his eyes, one at a time, threw them onto the rug, where they lay like discarded scales. He leaned close into the mirror, admiring the jade green jewels of his own eyes, a color someone had once described as "Moroccan green."

"Hello, Kiki," he said, baring his perfect teeth. "I've *missed* you!"

"And I've *missed* you," said Kiki Lujac. "Duhamel was such a bore, a complete cold fish."

Lujac agreed.

"And rutting around with that . . . cow . . ."

Lujac held up a hand, closed his eyes.

"Please, don't dwell. The gorge rises."

"On the whole," said Lujac, "I don't really like this work at all."

"Espionage, you mean?" said Lujac, raising an eyebrow.

"Yes. Why the hell did we get into it anyway?"

Lujac shrugged—a very Gallic shrug—his mouth pursing briefly.

"Let ourselves get talked into it, didn't we? By that fucking Piotr."

"The *slug*. I mean, I swear that man leaves a trail."

"I wouldn't doubt it."

"And those lips, like a plate full of squirming earth—"

"Please, no similes on an empty stomach."

"I apologize, forgive me. But . . . now what?"

Lujac gave the matter some thought, raised a finger.

"First, we find that fucking cow—"

"And her little pistol?" put in Lujac.

He shook his head, frowned in mock disapproval.

"Such a hazard, lying there, and in an *unlocked* drawer."

"And *loaded*."

"I mean, what if there had been *children*?"

"Exactly. Handguns in the home are five times as likely to—"

"Kill the owner?"

Lujac nodded.

"Very responsible. We fully approve."

"So do we. Any sensible adult would have done the same—"

A low, melodious bong rippled through the silence of the house, paused, then sounded again, this time more urgently. Lujac smiled hugely at Lujac, his green eyes showing a deep-yellow spark.

"The doorbell?"

"The doorbell."

"Company?" he said, his face opening into a delighted smile.

"I believe it is," said Lujac, smiling back.

"Shall we?" said Lujac.

"We shall."

LUJAC SWEPT down the stairs, feeling a little like Scarlett rushing to meet Rhett, the long thin knife still in his belt. Having shed the stifling cocoon of Jules Duhamel, he felt . . . liberated . . . exultant . . . at one with his world. He wondered idly who might be ringing his doorbell—excuse me, the cow's doorbell—but in his joyful heart he really didn't care.

Whoever it was, he would be delighted to see them.

Delighted.

He stopped at the door, glanced at his reflection in the hall mirror—what can one say when one sees *perfection?*—turned the latch, hauled the massive slab back on its hinges, and saw in the snowfall on the step a huddled figure, wrapped in a North Face squall jacket, a pinched, gaunt face with wet, hunted eyes staring back at him from under a snow-dusted hood.

"Anton," he said, pulling the door open and clearing a path, "what a thrill! To what do I owe the . . ."

Anton shuffled into the hallway, snow drifting off his shoulders, and stamped his booted feet on the flagstones.

"She is . . . where?" he said, looking furtively around.

"Sleeping soundly," he said. "You're alone?"

Anton gave him a reproving look, his red nose running, his skin blue, the lie steaming off him like a cold breath in the winter.

"Of course. I got your signal. What's wrong?"

Lujac had almost forgotten. As soon as Briony had gone missing, he had decided to bring Anton and whomever in close where they could help, if needed. Or be handled, if necessary. So he had sent out a text message on the cell: cq911cq.

Which, according to their code, meant "Get here now."

And, in accordance with their laws, here was Anton the Latvian.

Lujac now had only two minor problems left to deal with.

Where was Briony?

And where was . . . whomever?

"Come in, Anton," he said. "You're freezing."

Anton pushed the door closed behind him, shuffled a little farther into the room, his gaze flicking about the entranceway, peering off into the dim interior of the large main room, seeing the pale light shining in through the wall of windows that looked out over the Hudson. The room smelled of wood fire and cigarette smoke. To his right, the kitchen counter was an island of light in the shadows, with light shining down on Lujac's laptop, the red letters still glowing vividly on the blue background:

MESSAGE ERASED.

Anton squinted at the laptop screen and then moved in closer to look down at the message. Lujac glanced back toward the door and realized that Anton had contrived to leave the latch open an inch, which cleared up one of his problems. He stepped back a little into the hallway, slipping an umbrella out of the stand by the door.

Anton, thinking that his theatrical interest in the laptop would have pulled Lujac along with him, heard the umbrella being pulled out of the rack, sensed Lujac's move, and turned around, opening his mouth to say something. The heavy door slammed back. Lujac caught it with a shoulder, as a large, bulky figure in a black leather jacket and jeans butted through and lurched into the hall, a pistol in his gloved hand. Bukovac, his battered white face wet with melting snow, his darting black eyes blinking through the wet, saw Anton standing there, stunned, his mouth hanging open.

"Behind—"

Bukovac moved fast and well, dropping to one knee and pivoting, his pistol up and tracking to his right. Lujac stepped inside the arc, kicking Bukovac's pistol hand to one side with his left foot.

Bukovac, still on one knee, brought his left hand up. There was a flash of silver, and a grating slither as Lujac deflected the blade with the umbrella. Lujac stepped in low, bringing his right hand up in a silvery arc and jamming all ten inches of slender filleting knife upward through the underside of Bukovac's chin.

The blade pinned Bukovac's tongue to the roof of his mouth, punching all the way through it and into his brain, deep enough that Lujac could feel the bristles on the curve of Bukovac's unshaven chin, feel the man's blood rushing down his wrist.

Lujac held that position for a long, exquisite moment, moving Bukovac's head just a touch to the left so the light from the halogens could shine directly into his eyes as he died.

Lujac held Bukovac pinned in place, watching him go through the changes in a matter of heartbeats—*Lujac . . . parry . . . hurt . . . dying? . . . dying!*—it took almost a full minute for Bukovac to complete this process, and, when it was over, Lujac had to resist the urge to kiss the man on the lips.

That, he thought, withdrawing the blade and stepping back as Bukovac slumped onto the stone floor in a welter of fresh blood, was *perfect*. What do the Americans say? Better than sex?

When he shook off the hypnotic spell of it all, he was not surprised to find that Anton had disappeared. He wiped the blade off on Bukovac's coat, turning it to see it glitter in the light, and then moved off into the darkness of the great room. He stopped in the middle of it, listening carefully, and heard Anton's rapid, shallow breathing on the other side of the room.

He came over and found him huddled under one of the casement windows. Anton made a sound rather like a lamb bleating and turned his face into the stones, covering his head with his arms, his bony knee trembling.

Lujac put a gentle hand on his shoulder, moved his arm away.

"Anton, I'm not going to hurt you."

Anton's face came away from the wall, his eyes wet.

"Why not?"

"I need to know why you came."

"Piotr sent us. I had no choice. They said they'd put Maya in with the men in the Chronic Ward."

"Okay," said Lujac, his tone low and soothing, "I can see that. You had no choice. But why did Piotr want you to come over in the first place?"

"The woman, in London. You sent *pictures,* Kiki."

Lujac sat back on his heels, folding his arms over his knees.

"Yes, I did, didn't I? Naughty me. So what?"

"So what? Kiki, we are supposed to be doing this *carefully.*"

"Tell me, did *anything* come of it? Anything at all?"

Anton looked uneasy and then shook his head.

"No, not yet. They think it was a robbery that went . . . strange."

Lujac sighed, patted him on the shoulder.

"See? Nothing. And now look what you made me do to Bukovac."

Lujac stood up.

"Well, now that you're here, you can at least help."

"Help?"

"Yes. Go do . . . something clever . . . with that *mess* in the hall."

"What will you do?"

Lujac showed his teeth.

"Do you know what a 'panic room' is?"

"Yes, I think so."

"There's one in this house."

"Do you know where it is?"

"Yes, I believe I do."

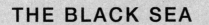

THE BLACK SEA

THE *SUBITO,* OFF POYRAZ

The sun had gone down long ago, sinking into the low green hills
to their left, taking with it the temperature. Dalton steered the *Subito*
north, passing the long concrete jetty of Poyraz on the starboard
shore. *The last Army outpost on the Nung,* thought Dalton, watching
the little village drift by: beyond it there was only Kerch . . . On either
side, the sloping hills fell away into the lingering twilight while ahead
of them the endless sweep of the Black Sea opened up, calm tonight,
moonless and cold, a few early stars showing, five hundred miles of
black water between them and the Ukrainian peninsula.

Up ahead, they could see the glimmering lights of an oil tanker,
already far out to sea, steaming north by northwest for Kerch and
the Sea of Azov, the sound of her engines a faint murmur coming
over the water, barely audible above the steady rumble of the *Subito*'s twin diesels. The radar screen under Dalton's left hand glowed
green, a yellow line sweeping around the circumference, passing over
tiny red blips far out at sea: the freighter up ahead, a smaller red blip
that was probably a fishing boat, and, two miles dead ahead of that,
moving at fifteen knots, the trawler that had attacked Dalton at the
warehouse in Sariyer, the акула. Levka, sound asleep in the guest

stateroom now, snoring audibly, had explained that the name was Ukrainian for "shark."

Dalton was maintaining a safe distance from the *Shark*, unwilling to come under the muzzle of that heavy machine gun again. Taking fire like that was sort of like being sealed inside an oil drum full of barbed wire and getting pushed down a fire escape.

He could still feel the sting of the concrete slivers that had peppered his right leg, and the back of his neck was stinging from the sheet of phosphorus fire that had billowed out from the warehouse as he made the leap for the *Subito*. He was reasonably sure the men on the *Shark* up ahead were not aware that they were being trailed by the *Subito*.

If they were, Dalton would find out as soon as they were a few miles offshore, when the trawler would wheel around and close in to rake them with machine-gun fire and send them to the bottom of the Black Sea.

If that looked as if it were about to happen, Dalton intended to turn tail and bolt, counting on the *Subito*'s superior speed to get them out of range. The radar array had a "tagging" option that allowed Dalton to enter the GPS coordinates of another ship and monitor their relative positions. The computer would sound an alarm if the GPS parameters changed in any way. He had marked the *Shark* and set the proximity alarm, and now all they could do was run silent and wait.

Mandy Pownall was standing at his left, her strong face uplit by the amber glow of an electronic navigation chart, tracing with her long white fingers a path across the sea to Kerch. She tapped the screen, sighing.

"God, Micah, it's almost five hundred miles to Kerch. What's our speed right now?"

"Fifteen knots."

"At that rate, it'll take us *thirty hours* to get to Kerch. Can't we go any faster?'

"We could. *Subito* will do thirty-five knots on a flat sea. But we'd overtake that trawler in thirty minutes. I don't want to tangle with her, but I'd like to see where she's going."

Mandy went back to the communications set, slipped on a pair of headphones. They were tuned to Channel 16, the universal frequency for marine radio distress calls, but she was also scanning other frequencies from time to time to see if she could pick up any chatter from the *Shark* up ahead.

She stood there in the dim glow of the pilothouse, moving gracefully with the lift of the sea, *Subito*'s long bow stretching out into the darkness in front, lit only by the faint glow from their cabin.

Dalton had the boat running with all of her bow lights off, although she was still showing stern and flank lights. Running completely dark would be suicidal in these busy waters.

Dalton hoped that this tactic, along with her low radar profile—she had no flying bridge and, from the side, looked a lot like a patrol boat—would keep her from being detected by the men on the *Shark*.

So far, it seemed to be working.

The downside to this tactic was the possibility of being rammed by a southbound freighter in the dark, but Dalton figured they'd see any freighter coming on the radar screen long before she posed a threat. *Subito* had a proximity alarm connected to the radar array that would recognize any incoming ship, compute her course, and sound a warning if a collision was likely. So running without bow lights was a risk worth taking.

That was his theory, anyway. He supposed there were other sailors, now sleeping their long sleep at the bottom of the seven seas, who had entertained similar delusions. But it was his call.

Mandy put the phones down, came back to stand beside him, holding a cup of hot black coffee in her hands.

"God, there are a lot of indecipherable languages loose on this planet. Why can't they all speak English?"

"Whose English? I seem to remember a bartender in London saying you had 'lorly garms and was very queenly-like.'"

"He also called me a 'bint.' There's nothing out there but chatter. I think there's a Ukrainian patrol boat out there over the horizon. I could hear some cross talk between somebody who sounded official and the captain of an Italian freighter. Other than that, a lot of buzz and crackle and foreigners babbling. Anything on the news?"

Dalton turned the dial on a shortwave radio tuned in to Istanbul, listened to some complicated tribal drumming, lowered it to a murmur.

"News isn't on again for an hour. All I got was, they found the chopper, and the Greeks are flying in to cooperate in an investigation of the crash."

"Have they put that together with a fire in a warehouse?"

Dalton shook his head.

"If they did, they're not telling the media about it. I'm surprised we don't have a Turkish Coast Guard vessel running us down right now. Or a chopper overhead. Hundreds of people watched that firefight. You'd think someone would have remembered the name of this boat."

Mandy sipped at her coffee, set it down on a gimbaled tray.

"Drugs, would be my answer. People run drugs all up and down the Bosphorus, Levka says. Maybe people have learned not to get involved when gunfire breaks out. I don't think the Turkish cops are all that popular either. A nasty reputation for random brutality, so I hear. Perhaps it's safer to keep a low profile. These aren't the Hamptons."

"No, they're not," said Dalton with a wry smile.

Mandy glanced down at the stairs that led to the main salon, thinking about Dobri Levka sound asleep behind the closed door of the guest stateroom, and looked back at Dalton, her expression somber.

"Now that we have a moment alone, you remember I said we'd found something on the boat?"

"Yes, something about Lujac?"

She reached into the pocket of her squall jacket and brought out a Sony memory chip.

"We found this taped to the back of a drawer in the master stateroom."

She slipped it into the reader slot of the boat's onboard computer, hit a function button. The MFD screen flicked from the radar input to a blank blue screen and then to an MPEG. Dalton braced himself for one of Lujac's horror shows, but instead he got a color image of a large, shapeless man wearing a striped shirt, unbuttoned, baggy gray slacks, the fly undone and some of his round hairy belly showing.

The fat man was sitting back into a couch—it looked like one of the leather ones down in the salon—at his ease, smiling at someone off camera. Music was playing in the background, and the setting had an end-of-the-evening feeling about it, two people sitting around relaxing after some larger group had said their good-byes and wandered off to their homes.

He was bald and bland, and had thick wet lips, disturbingly dark against his blue-white skin. His black eyes were small and sharp, like a gull's, and his hands, folded around a glass of beer, looked like fat pink flippers, his fingers thick tubes of pink sausage.

The man seemed to be unaware of the camera, and, from the angle, it was likely the camera was hidden. He leaned forward to refill his beer glass, spreading the fly of his overstressed pants, his belly pushing out through it like a fleshy balloon. Then he sat back in the creaking, overburdened couch again, his thick legs spreading wide. When he spoke, his accent was heavy and Slavic, but the language was English.

"So, we are done, and you are ready . . . ?"

A reply, offscreen, barely heard, a younger voice, clear, French. The man listened, his small eyes glittering, and then showed his cheap yellow dentures in a broad, wet smile, stretching his thick purple lips wide.

"Good . . . What?"

He seemed to be reacting to a question the mike did not pick up, leaning forward and putting his head to one side, looking puzzled. The question was repeated, and the fat man's smile went away, revealing the cold, calculating reptile that lived inside.

"None of us know the answer to that. And you should not ask. All you know—all *we* know—is that she must amend the transcript, and must do so without being in any way detected."

Another muffled interjection, and the fat man frowned.

"She *will* know . . . And she will also know what happens if she does it wrong or puts in any kind of trick." Here he sighed, and drained half his glass. "As for the old woman, she is to be an example. We have been over this. She is no longer an active member, but she is a *mentor* to them, a figure of reverence and affection. She is *cherished,* like a mother. What happens to her should be ambiguous, should be taken by the authorities as a natural death. That is *very* important, my friend, because—should you need it with your subject, to *complete* her motivation, you can then provide her with the visual proof that *you* in fact were the cause of her beloved mentor's death. The shock? The fear? These will be your bona fides, so to speak. What? Of course you will be *with* her. You read the personality analysis—the psychologists in Marksa Plaz confirmed this, you saw the films—her husband's betrayal hurt her deeply. She is a *physical* creature. Her husband said she was *insatiable.*"

The fat man stopped to run a wet white tongue, like the head of a blind cave snake, over his lips, his face creasing into an obscene leer.

"And look at *you!* How can she resist you? At any rate, one way or another, by charm or by force, you *will* be with her at the vital moment.

"Up until then, you must be *disciplined.* Your very generous remuneration will *depend* upon that, my friend, and you would not want to disappoint our employer. I mean that sincerely. Hear me. You do not want to draw their disapproving attention. But *afterward,* of course, indulge! A *bonfire* of indulgences, so long as she is dead at the end of them. Yes, at the end, a bonfire, a great cleansing fire, and then you can—"

The MPEG ended abruptly, the screen pulsing blue. Mandy pulled the chip out of the reader, her face solemn. The multifunction display flicked back to radar, and the screen came up again, the sweeping yellow bar, the tiny red blip of the *Shark* holding steady at two miles out, a few random returns at the outer limit of the arc, some high clouds far away in the west. Dalton stared at the screen, his face as solemn as Mandy's.

"Well," he said, "that's the proof you were looking for. My compliments, Mandy. You were right all along."

"We never actually see Lujac."

"We're not trying to prove this in a court of law. The film was taken on his boat. And we got a big reaction in Santorini when we threw his name around. And nobody knows where this Marcus Todorovich guy is. I'd say it was *his* body Sofouli pulled out of the Aegean. Levka seen this film yet?"

"Not yet. I'm not sure I want him—"

"I agree. Need to know. But we can take a slice, a still, of just the fat man, and show that to Levka. He has to be the Gray Man. Fits Levka's description down to the lips, the sausage fingers—"

"Yes, he does. But—"

"Look, with this film we could just break off, take this to Hank Brocius. Back it up with everything we know. He can't pass this off as more interagency bullshit. We could turn around now and go back to . . ."

He caught the look in Mandy's eye, the sardonic smile.

"Well, I guess I've kind of burned that particular bridge—"

"Along with half of that particular Istanbul—"

"There's an airfield at Yalta—"

"Micah, we don't need to *take* this to the NSA."

"Why the heck not?"

"God, and you a CIA agent. Because, you berk, I've already *sent* it."

"*Sent* it? What? Mailed it?"

She tapped the onboard computer.

"Welcome to the age of the Internet, Micah. The *Subito* has a satellite-linked wireless connection. I sent the MPEG to Hank Brocius's private e-mail address hours ago while you were on your way to blow up Sariyer—"

"Why not his office one?"

Mandy gave him a look.

"If we're looking for a mole, we have to assume that everything is compromised. Including the NSA's internal e-mail system. Brocius maintains a hardened and encrypted e-mail connection under his own code name—"

Dalton found himself staring up at her, a little slack-jawed.

"Which *you* have?"

"Pinky had it in his lockbox—"

He shook his head slowly.

"Along with half the state secrets of the Western powers, it seems. We're going to have to do something about Pinky's lockbox."

"You go right ahead. I'm sure Pinky would *love* to have you fiddle around with his lockbox. I also sent Brocius the details about Beyoglu Trading and the Russian Inter-whatever Board thingy and their address at Dizayn Tower in Istanbul. And what happened at the warehouse in Sariyer. And the phone number too. I told him to run everything through his databases and, basically, to hold up his end."

Dalton gave her back her own patented raised-eyebrow look.

"The Russian Inter-whatever *thingy?*"

"You know what I mean. Don't be such a wanker."

Dalton looked a little sheepish, and then his face hardened up.

"Did you tell him about Kerch?"

"No. I wasn't sure what we were going to do about that. And I didn't want him stepping all over our end of this investigation. He's got what he needs."

"Listen, Mandy, did you send all this to Cather too?"

Mandy's face lost its teasing glow.

"No . . . not yet."

"Because . . . you still have doubts?"

"Yes, I do. I mean, I *still* don't think Deacon Cather's a KGB mole, but until we can prove it I'd like to keep this between us. It looks as if the Russians are going all out to have an intercepted decryption altered, but we don't know *why*. We don't know who they're trying to protect."

"We *do* know that there's something in the cable they really don't want us to read. If Mariah Vale is right, it's something that might lead to a KGB mole somewhere inside the CIA—"

"Inside American intelligence, anyway," said Mandy. "What we don't know is—"

"Who's on Mariah Vale's short list. Other than Deacon Cather."

"Yes."

"Which is why you haven't sent anything to Cather. Just in case he actually *is* the mole. I have no problem with that. It was a good decision."

"But now what should we do? I mean, here, right now, on the boat. Do we keep going, go to Kerch, or wherever this takes us?"

They were both quiet for a time, feeling the rhythm of the sea, the soothing rumble of the ship's engines, the rush and ripple of the waves curling back from the cutwater, the heavy rise and fall of the ship.

"I think we push on, Mandy. You've given Brocius enough to stop this game on his end. All he has to do is take a good look at all his Glass Cutters and see which one has Kiki Lujac under her bed. But we can still take these Russians apart from our end. We broke up whatever Keraklis was doing. We took the *Subito*—you found that film—we torched their operation back in Istanbul, and now the survivors are on the run back to Kerch. We can follow that trawler, find the Gray Man, find out what that room in the warehouse in Sariyer was used for, maybe even blow the whole network out of the water. Hand the goddamned KGB their heads on a pike for a change. God knows, they've got it coming. We've taken it this far, Mandy. Let's finish it."

Mandy poured herself some more coffee from the thermos, offered Dalton a refill. Ursa Major, the Big Bear, was just visible above the northern horizon, and there was a violet glimmer along the curve of the earth that might have been the aurora borealis. Or perhaps the lights of Yalta bouncing off mist high in the stratosphere. Mandy put the cup down, stared out at the sea for a time, working it through.

"Yes," she said, finally, "let's finish it."

For a long time, they said nothing, since everything that could be said was already understood and what couldn't be said was better left that way.

After a while, Dalton switched the controls to Auto-Helm, an onboard computer linked to the navigation panel. Now the *Subito* would steer itself on the course he had already set. The GPS system was still monitoring the *Shark,* holding steady at two miles ahead, on a bearing directly for Kerch, the same course as theirs. He leaned back, stretching. His body felt as if it weighed three hundred pounds. His eyes were dry and burning.

"You should get some sleep," said Mandy. "There's a big, soft bed in the master stateroom. You've been up for almost thirty-six hours straight. Why don't you go have a shower, lie down for a while?"

Dalton rubbed his face with his hands, looked out at the sea. The night had come down, a black vault, and all the stars were out, a shimmering field of cold clear diamonds, behind them the pink haze of the Milky Way. The reflection of the stars scintillated on the calm water all around. On the northern horizon, the lights of a freighter floated in a void between sea and sky. Directly ahead, the running lights of the *Shark* seemed to hang motionless in the middle of their windshield. In the northeast, looming massively along the farther shore of the Black Sea, was the invisible threat—almost the magnetic pull—of Russia itself, a rising threat in the opening years of the new century, much too close for comfort and drawing nearer with every mile under the keel.

He turned away from it, now very aware of Mandy, standing quite close. She smelled of spice and coffee and cigarettes. She was standing so close, he could feel the warmth of her body, hear her steady breathing. Mandy was looking out at the sea, her face calm and still, an amber glow on her from the navigation screen. She was extraordinarily beautiful—poised, elegant, sensual—and much too close.

And where was Cora?

At her father's villa on Capri, a thousand miles away, a place as closed to him as the iron gates of a convent. Mandy felt his mood changing and turned to look at him, a surprised smile opening up, her gray eyes shining:

"Why, Micah, dear boy, I believe you're weakening."

part **three**

ISTANBUL

SARIYER

Nikki stayed well back from what was left of the warehouse, letting Sofouli deal with the Turkish cops. She had already gotten some sharp lessons in what the Turks expect from women. Her short skirt was offensive, she gathered, as was her blouse and her uncovered hair, and, as far as she could make out, her very presence here on the sacred soil of the homeland. Nikki, always sensitive to cultural nuance and Islamic male pride, had her BlackBerry out and was looking up the Turkish phrase for *"Go fuck yourself."*

Sofouli was standing in a circle of tan uniforms, speaking in a forceful rush of Turkish patois, with some Greek thrown in, to a tall, bent, dark-skinned man with a full white mustache and very sad brown eyes, the deep lines of his weather-beaten face seeming to melt around the cheekbones and run in channels down the side of his long, mournful countenance.

The cop's name, she gathered, was Melik Gul, and he was presented to her as the senior officer in charge of the Polis Merkezi, a team of experienced men who had jurisdiction over something the Turks were calling "Severe Crimes," which, she could see, included shooting the stuffing out of a warehouse by the side of the Bosphorus and then setting it on fire.

The firefighters were gathering up their gear now, rolling up reels of thick hose and sloshing through puddles of sooty water, some of the men staring at Nikki, their eyes white against the ash that covered the upper parts of their faces.

The warehouse smelled of hot steel and cracked earth, and something else: roasted flesh, a throat-catching reek that hung in the still air like a miasma. According to the fire chief, they had found three bodies in the ruins, all of them burned into twisted logs, hardly recognizable as human. They had been zipped into body bags and stacked in a coroner's wagon, taken away for a forensic examination in the morning. Nikki, watching the men loading up their trucks and wagons, tried to read Micah Dalton's mind in all of this.

Because she was reasonably sure that this had something to do with Dalton—leaving a trail of dead men and flaming wrecks seemed to be a Dalton trademark—and she'd listened in as a couple of young boys who had been fishing in a runabout just off the wharf described the Sarişin Şeytan—Melik Gul translated this for Nikki, with a mournful sigh, as "Blond Satan"—who had almost shot them dead as he fired a very big gun into the back of a fishing boat. No, they hadn't got the name. Nikki thought the kids had looked a little evasive when asked for particulars, but they were quite eloquent on the physical details of the Blond Satan. If it wasn't Micah Dalton, then it was his evil twin racing up the Bosphorus like Sherman through Atlanta, leaving fear, fire, and ruin in his wake.

Sofouli hadn't missed the similarities either, and had taken Nikki aside after the boys had gone off to make a written statement, speaking softly to her but with some force, not unkindly, yet unwilling to be "handled" by the NSA.

"This Blond Satan the boys speak of, this is your man, yes?"

Nikki could hardly be evasive here, even if she wanted to, and Sofouli was her only friend in the vicinity. She had admitted that it was. For a few minutes, Sofouli pushed her hard on the man's real identity, but she held firm on that point, saying only that, whoever he was, she and the NSA would dearly love to find him and have "a frank exchange of views," as she put it.

Sofouli had given her a wry smile and gone back to Melik Gul to work out some sort of investigative compromise. In the meantime, Nikki got on her BlackBerry, dialing up Hank Brocius in Crypto City. It was after midnight local time, which would make it around six in the afternoon in Maryland. The line buzzed a few times and then a woman's voice answered: Alice Chandler's, some tension in it, obvious even to Nikki.

"Nikki, is that you?"

"Yes, Alice. Is he there?"

"No, he's gone up to New York City. Took the shuttle to La Guardia. Is everything okay? Where are you?"

"In Istanbul, Alice—"

"Istanbul? I thought you were going to Greece?"

"Yes, and now I'm in Istanbul. Should I try his cell?"

"I already have, dear. There's a huge storm in central New York State now. All the way from the Adirondacks down to Philadelphia. We're starting to get some of it here. I think it's done something to the cell service. Is there anything I can do?"

Nikki thought it over.

"Yes, there is. Can you do a corporate search for me?"

"Of course. What do you need."

Nikki looked at the notes she had taken, what little she had been able to gather from the rapid cross talk among Sofouli, Melik Gul, and the fire marshal in charge of the site.

"Okay, I'm at a place in Istanbul called Sariyer. It's a fishing village on the Bosphorus, close to the Black Sea. There's been a fire here, at a warehouse. The warehouse is leased to a company called Beyoglu Trading Consortium." She spelled out Beyoglu, emphasizing the *g* since it was silent in Turkish. "The address is Suite 5500, Dizayn

Tower." She read out the rest of the address in military radio code. "In Istanbul. Got that?"

Alice repeated it, calm now, all business.

"I have. What do you need?"

"Anything you can get. As soon as you can get it. And while you're at it, do you have a way of seeing if any of our sister agencies made an inquiry about Beyoglu Trading?"

"Yes, we share the same databases. There'd be a 'Request Agency Source' number. They keep track of subscribers pretty well, partly for the budget. What sort of time frame?"

"Anytime in the past twenty-four hours."

"Okay, dear. I'll get right on it. Are you going to call the AD of RA?"

Nikki saw that the group was breaking up, Sofouli and Melik Gull now walking toward her talking softly.

"No. But when you get the information, can you text it to me?"

"I can. Look for it in a few minutes."

Nikki turned the BlackBerry to vibrate and put it back in her shoulder bag, straightening as the two men reached her, pulling her coat tight around her, partly because it was getting very cold and partly to cover her "infidel whore" wardrobe. She held the collar tight at her neck, the wind whipping her long auburn hair, her brown eyes wary in the light of the streetlamps. Mr. Gul, as he preferred to be called, spoke first, in fairly clear English.

"Some questions I have for you, Miss Turrin. What interest has your agency in this matter?"

"My interest falls under the protocols of international cooperation in criminal matters that your government agreed to in Alexandria last year."

Mr. Gul didn't like the answer, his face drooping even more.

"This is unresponsive. If you have information about what has

taken place here—there are three people dead—then, in any inter-
pretation of international law, I have a right to your information. I
wait on it now."

Sofouli gave her a warning look but said nothing.

Nikki knew she'd have to give him something if she didn't want
to be in a cop car and on her way to Atatürk Airport and the first
plane back to the USA in about five minutes.

"Captain Sofouli has told you about the two Americans who came
to Santorini asking about a Montenegrin national named Kirik
Lujac?"

Gul nodded, his face becoming a little less morose.

"He has," said Gul. "We have looked into what is known about
this man. He was reported dead a while back, according to Captain
Sofouli, but now there is some basis for believing that this is not so.
Am I correct?"

"Yes. Both Captain Sofouli and I think that he may be alive."

"And your interest, miss, in Kirik Lujac's health?"

"We have some reason to believe he may have killed a woman in
London."

"An American national?"

"Yes."

"Would this not then be a matter for your Federal Bureau of
Investigation? I do not recall the NSA as being a police agency?"

"The woman killed was a retired employee of our agency. I have
been asked by my superiors to assist in an internal investigation into
her death."

Melik Gul was following her fast enough to get to the end of her
thoughts before she did.

"An investigation the results of which you are not yet ready to
share with your brother agencies, am I right?"

Nikki kept her balance.

"Of course. Nor would you, Mr. Gul, until your work was complete. If my visit here can confirm that Kirik Lujac is dead, then I can go back to the States and leave you to your work."

Gul was silent for a time. Seabirds whirled above them, attracted by the reek of death, and the crowds gathered across the road, some of whom had brought their children out and were making a picnic out of the event.

"A boat was stolen this afternoon," said Gul, "out of a marina in the south. The Ataköy Marina. The boat was registered to the same firm that owns this warehouse. Beyoglu Trading. My people looked into the ownership and discovered that the boat had recently been bought from another entity. The entity was Kirik Lujac. The date of sale, according to information provided by Captain Sofouli, was a few days *after* Mr. Lujac's body was found in the Aegean. I think it is reasonable to conclude that a man interested in the fate of Kirik Lujac—I speak of our Blond Satan—known to Captain Sofouli as Mr. Pearson and to you as . . . as a man I suspect you will not name. Setting that aside, I think it is safe to . . . imply?"

"*Infer.*"

"Yes, thank you. It is safe to *infer* that the boat was stolen by the mysterious Blond Satan you will not name. I am so far okay with you?"

"You are constructing a theory. So far, that's all it is."

Gul bowed, an amused expression tugging briefly at his cheeks like someone behind a stage curtain pulling at the drapery. Nikki began to understand that she was running a real risk playing games with this man.

"You will be interested to hear that this evening one of our patrol boats found two men hiding on monument island down at the far end of the strait, an island we call 'Kiz Kulesi' but the Europeans call the 'Maiden's Tower.' The men had been stripped naked, all their belongings taken, and had been tortured as well. From their speech they were obviously Russians. We ran their photographs through our Intourist Visa program. They were identified as an Anatoly Viktor Bakunin, born in Krasnodar, Russia, and a Vassily Kishmayev, born in Smolensk. Each man had listed 'shipping facilitator' as his profession. Would you care to guess who their employer was? No? Well, I think it will not shock the observer if I tell you they were employed by Beyoglu Trading Consortium, the same firm that owns—used to own—this warehouse behind us."

"Did these two have any explanation for their situation?" asked Nikki genuinely puzzled. "Naked, tortured, and stranded on Maiden's Island?"

"They have said not one word to my people. Right now, they are in a military hospital being treated for hypothermia, burns to sensitive areas, and some dental injuries. When they are better, we will conduct a more vigorous interrogation. Now, as an *investigator,* I would like to ask you what you think should be our next line of inquiry?"

Gul put a stress on *investigator* that wrapped it in suspicion and gathering hostility. Sofouli, unwilling to see Nikki harassed—he felt an affection for her that was almost but not quite fatherly—sent Nikki a warning glance, and turned to Gul.

"Miss Turrin is here as an observer attached to my staff and as such falls under the protection of my service. She is, in effect, a Greek official here, with as much standing as I have. So I will answer your question for both of us. We should go immediately to the headquarters of this company and see what is to be—"

"I have already given these orders. My men are at the Dizayn Towers now securing the facility. They are holding a man for questioning. Do you wish to accompany us?"

They did.

GARRISON

NELSON'S CORNERS, ROUTE 9 SOUTHBOUND

Pushing forward now blindly, the visibility close to zero, crawling at less than ten miles an hour and expecting to smack into the rear of a stalled car at any moment, Brocius saw through a fleeting gap in the snowfall a road sign that said INDIAN BROOK ROAD, next to a narrow opening in a stand of trees. He slowed down enough to click the DRIVE selector into FOUR-WHEEL, made the right turn, and eased the big SUV around a gradual curve to the south again.

Scrub trees lined the slope, and the road began a descent into a thinly wooded valley. It was past six, and what pale winter light there had been was dying fast. Perhaps there was a sun high up above the granite-gray clouds, but the light from it was purely theoretical down on earth.

The whole landscape was falling into a deep-velvet blackness filled with falling snow, pierced only by the twin cones of the SUV's head-lights. The snowflakes spiraled inward, swept from the windshield by the wipers only to build back up again in a few seconds. He was still four miles from Briony's house, and the power bars on his cell phone were registering zero, the screen displaying a NO SIGNAL warning.

His chest had been getting tighter as the time stretched out, and driving in this kind of a snowstorm with only one good eye wasn't helping his stress level. Although he was a reasonably young man and in good condition, the pains in his chest and neck were worrying him more than a little.

There was nothing for it but to go on, get it done, and he went on, pushing the heavy machine hard as it ground through the piled-up snow, the bare branches of the trees hanging over his path so that he felt he was in a gray rock tunnel, burrowing his way deeper into the hillside.

The road rose above him, and he felt the truck shudder as the wheels dug in. The Escalade was huge and powerful, with deep-ridged snow tires, and with every mile he covered he thanked God and General Motors in no particular order.

He checked his odometer. It was about a quarter mile from the Indian Brook Road turnoff to a fork where Avery Road branched off and ran south another mile or so, until it ran into Philips Brook and Snake Hill Road. He looked up, saw the turnoff coming, gunned the engine to force the truck through a huge drift that had accumulated across the fork. The rear tires broke free, and the truck started to slide. He turned in to the slide, feeling control come back, keeping his foot off the brake. And then the rear end of the truck smacked into a wall of brush.

Brocius felt the rear end dropping. He straightened the wheel, dropped the selector to ALL-WHEEL LOW, and hit the accelerator as he felt the truck beginning to tip. The wall of brush marked a steep slope covered in thin trees, and although he was on the accelerator and plumes of snow were flying out behind the front wheels, the truck tipped up, and he felt the front wheels start to spin in midair. The truck was sliding backward now, out of control. He fumbled for the door handle as the Escalade suddenly dropped ten feet down a sheer slope. Brocius slammed into the roof-window brace, blood filling his eyes.

The truck stood on its tailgate for a moment before it began to tilt sideways, rolling onto the driver's side and then sliding down the slope, crashing though the slender pines and alders like a bear crashing through the undergrowth, leaving a hundred-yard-long swath of broken trees and plowed snow, finally coming to a smashing stop on its side up against a stand of hawthorn, all four wheels spinning slowly, the back buried in a deep drift of snow with only a thin red glow to mark the Escalade's taillights.

Its headlights had bored through the snowfall for a few feet and now played on a few bare pines, lighting them up like stick figures on a stage.

Although the Escalade was now tilted onto the driver's side, the engine—solid, bolted into a steel frame, and fueled by a very efficient closed-compression system—kept on running.

Inside the truck, Hank Brocius lay slumped up against the driver's-side window, semiconscious, stunned, his head bloody but otherwise unhurt. The tailpipe was jammed into a snowbank, not deep enough to choke the engine to a halt but deep enough to let some carbon monoxide seep back into the interior. Slightly heavier than air, it started to pool around the rear section, which was lower than the front, but after a time it began to seep forward, an invisible, scentless cloud working toward the driver's seat.

The air bags had automatically deployed, sending an alert to the truck's OnStar system. The internal radio attempted to send a digital DRIVER IN DISTRESS signal to the OnStar monitoring offices in Michigan. The system would continue sending this alert until it received a reply.

To do this, it relied on local cell phone tower systems, all of which were temporarily blanketed out by the huge snowstorm now covering most of New York State and the northern half of Pennsylvania. The screen on the cell phone Brocius had in his coat pocket showed a line of power bars. As the storm clouds moved slowly into the south, the bars ON started to change, and the screen went from NO SIGNAL to LOOKING FOR SERVICE.

The OnStar system was doing exactly the same thing, searching for a signal. In the rear of the truck, the carbon monoxide level slowly rose. Brocius began to breathe more deeply, and his color began to change from pale to pink. There was a break in the clouds, and OnStar found a signal and sent out a digital 911 alert. It was immediately answered by a young woman named Luwaana Brody, sitting at her console in Michigan like an air traffic controller at her screen, dealing with hundreds of calls that had been coming in from all over the Northeast since this huge storm had rolled down from Saskatchewan. Her voice, soft but authoritative, boomed through the truck's audio system:

"Sir, we are receiving an air-bag-deployment signal from your vehicle. Are you all right?"

Brocius reacted to the voice, but it was as if he were hearing it from the bottom of a cold lake. He opened his mouth, fighting through a terrible lethargy that was pulling him back toward the bottom.

"I'm . . . not . . . The air . . ."

"Sir, I cannot hear your reply. I'm sending help right now."

She looked at her screen, got the GPS coordinates—41 degrees 23 minutes 12.35 seconds north, 73 degrees 55 minutes 36.24 seconds west—New York State, at the intersection of Indian Brook and Avery. She hit the CALL button for the nearest New York State EMS station, got an answer, and read out the coordinates, describing the vehicle. The dispatcher was hopeful but not encouraging. ETA was thirty minutes to an hour. Luwaana Brody then got back on the radio to Hank Brocius.

"Sir, sir, can you hear me?"

Nothing.

No, she could hear *something*: a low, vibrating rumble, like wheels turning slowly. And, under that, a steady burbling sound.

She looked at the VEHICLE STATUS report.

The Escalade's engine was still running. The drive was engaged. But the truck was stopped—its GPS numbers hadn't shifted a yard—the air bags had deployed, but the wheels were still turning.

They were *freewheeling,* she realized. The truck had overturned, or at least had tilted onto one side.

"Sir, can you hear me? We've got an ambulance on the way. You hold on now. Can you hear me?"

The air . . .

She looked at the Escalade's exterior temperature. It was six below zero. She tried to rouse Brocius, heard a low moaning reply. Was he hurt? Was he having trouble breathing?

He's in a remote area, it's getting serious snowfall, the truck's on its side, the engine is running. Does he suffocate or freeze to death?

Luwaana Brody gave it another half second, reached out, shut the truck's engine off.

NIGHT HAD COME DOWN on the stone house in Garrison, but the snow kept falling, a steady, downward drift that reminded Anton Palenz of the way his mother would sift flour into a bowl when he was a child back in Riga. He followed Kiki's fluid shape as they went back up the stairs of the old house, one behind the other, coming up as silent as the shadows that filled the house, now that the last of the daylight, as thin and blue as skim milk, had finally died into darkness. Kiki did not move so much as he glided, moving up the stairs in a liquid flow that did not seem quite human, as if Kiki were more of a ghost or a nightwalker than a real person.

In Latvia, they lived close to the first forests of the world and the last to be walked by men. There were folktales about people like Kiki, and Anton wished with all his heart that he had found something else to do with himself after the old empire had collapsed.

But he had been a secret policeman in Latvia, what the people of Riga used to call "one of the heels of the Russian boot," and when Latvia had broken away and the Latvians had risen up, men like Anton Palenz had to run, and so did their families. His brother and father had been run down and beaten to death in the streets of Riga, and his younger sister Maya had been beaten and raped, and had her head shaved in the courtyard of Riga Cathedral by her own neighbors. Now Maya was in Kerch with Piotr, and Piotr would do exactly as he promised with Maya if Anton didn't keep Kiki under control.

He smiled a sick, sideways smile as he climbed the stairs behind Kiki. Keeping Kiki Lujac under control was like trying to herd a shark: you pointed it at something, kept your hands clear, and hoped it didn't see you out of the corner of its eye. They reached the landing, and Lujac put out his left hand, palm down, then raised it and pointed toward the open door of the master bedroom. Anton nodded, swallowing, looking down at the M14 rifle that Kiki had taken down from the weapon display in the great room.

It was loaded now: its box magazine held twenty rounds, powerful 7.62 NATOs, heavy in Anton's small pale hands as he followed Kiki down the long carpeted hallway to the door of the bedroom. Lujac pushed the door open slowly and stepped carefully into the evening glow of the bedside-table light. The room looked unchanged, the covers still rumpled and careless, the quilt in a heap at the foot of the bed.

The room smelled of Briony's scent, a rich, complicated aroma, and stale, less appealing cigarette smoke. Lujac looked at Anton, nodded for him to come forward. He had made a sketch, indicating what he thought to be the dimensions of the panic room set into the interior wall of the bedroom, a space that Lujac had estimated to be about fifteen feet by ten.

"It will have strong walls," he said, "but I doubt they will be bulletproof. Not against a few rounds from your Winchester. I think if we start to poke some holes in the box the voice of the rabbit will be heard in the land."

"What if we kill her?" Anton had asked, thinking more of Maya than of the American code breaker. If she died, the mission failed, and Maya went down that hallway to the other wing, which, after what the people of Riga had done to her, would very likely break her mind in pieces.

"One round, up high, should do it. She'll be flat on the floor. If she's not screaming for us to stop by three rounds, she's either suicidal or she's not in there. Stop carping. Let's go flush out our little grouse."

Now they were up in the bedroom, and the moment had come. Lujac nodded to Anton, held up a hand to stop him for a second.

"Briony, this is Jules. There's a man here with one of your grandfather's rifles. He is going to start shooting into your little room. The rifle has twenty rounds. Your room is about fifteen feet long. These are not good odds. Will you not come out now, and we can talk?"

Silence, and the bones of the old house ticking as the chill outside began to seep into its stones and timbers. Lujac made a sign to Anton, who raised the rifle, pulled the cocking handle back, and released it, scooping a round out of the magazine and locking it home in the firing chamber.

He raised it to his shoulder, grimacing in anticipation of the recoil. Lujac covered his ears as Anton began to squeeze the trigger, and faintly from the bowels of the old house came the muffled clang of iron on stone.

"The tunnel!" said Lujac, pulling Anton's hand away from the trigger guard. "There's a *tunnel* in the basement. It goes to the coach house!"

Anton stared at Lujac for a moment, uncomprehending. Lujac

turned and raced off down the hall, heading for the stairs, his bathrobe flying out behind him like wings of red silk, his bare feet whispering on the thick rug of the landing, turning to see that Anton was coming after him. His handsome, skull-like face was tight with a look Anton could not read, something like lust and joy and hunger combined, a look that was not at all human.

Lujac went pounding down the stairs, Anton right behind him, into the kitchen. Ripping open the basement door—the light was on—he ran down the rickety wooden stairs into the musty old space.

The walls were made of river rock and caulked with clay that was falling out in sections. Old, rough-cut beams, sagging a little in the middle, ran the length of the low, open space. The concrete floor looked new, and Lujac could see wispy traces in the dust on it—a woman's bare feet had crossed here. At the far end of the basement, half hidden in the shadow, stood the iron wall of the tunnel gate, made to look like an old steam boiler. It even had a brass label on it: PITTSBURGH IRON, 1854. Anton followed Lujac as he padded barefoot across the floor, silent as sleep. Lujac stopped before the door, indicated to Anton that he should cover it with the M14. Lujac fumbled a bit at the jamb of the door, where, he vaguely recalled, Briony had told him there was a spring-loaded latch.

He found it, braced himself on the floor, looked at Anton, and hauled the door back with a single muscular surge. The tunnel was lit. The floor, covered in ancient cobblestones, curved to the left about ten feet in. They stood for a moment listening, and in the silence they heard the distinctive sound of someone's breathing—rapid, short, sharp huffs, with an undertone of panic.

"Briony," said Lujac, "this is silly. We're just trying to help Morgan."

Silence then as even the breathing stopped.

Lujac hesitated at the entrance to the tunnel, unwilling to enter.

But the *idea* of that . . . fucking *cow* . . . reaching the coach house and somehow locking herself inside it until help came . . . it could not be *tolerated* . . . She owed him . . . *satisfaction*. Anton stood beside him, with the M14 at port arms, looking worried as hell but still ready to go forward.

Lujac took a breath, stepped into the tunnel, and padded down the cobblestoned pathway, the old stone walls closing in, around, and over him. He reached the curve, looked back at Anton, who had not followed him yet.

"Come on."

"Where does this go?"

"It comes out at the coach house, about sixty yards."

"What if she has a gun?"

"She *does* have a gun. But it won't fire. I jammed the muzzle."

Anton looked at the gate, half open, a massive black-painted iron wall looming in the half-light. "What if this closes?"

Lujac looked around, saw an iron bar leaning against the wall. He picked it up and tossed it to Anton, who caught it with one hand, fumbling a bit with the heavy rifle.

"Jam that into the hinge. Hard as you can."

Anton did, shoving the bar in deep, wrenching it sideways to fix it in place, huffing with the effort, skinning a knuckle as his hand slipped free.

"Okay," said Lujac. "Now, let's go."

Both men padded carefully down the tunnel, picking a path over the mossy rocks, avoiding the thin trickle of springwater that ran down the middle. The bulbs overhead were strung on ancient copper wire, one every ten feet, and they cast the stones in a dim glow.

Their shadows danced ahead of them as they went down the tunnel, shortened as they came up under the next lightbulb, and then stretched out behind them again as they made their way from pool of light to pool of light. Halfway along the tunnel, Anton noticed an old cast-iron pipe sticking out from the wall, with a brass mouthpiece attached to the end.

Anton looked at it as they passed, thinking that it looked a bit like the kind of communication tube they used to have on steamships, speaking tubes that ran from the bridge to the engine room. He thought he might have seen one in an old movie—*Wake of the Red Witch,* maybe.

He would have said something to Lujac, but Lujac had passed it by without comment, and he knew this old house pretty well, so Anton let it go.

They were almost at the far end when they heard the flutter of bare feet coming from somewhere behind them, carried down the shaft by an auditory trick of the stones, a whispery shuffle. Lujac turned then, his green eyes lit with a deep-yellow light. Cat's eyes, Anton realized. Lujac brushed past him, stumbled, falling forward onto the wet stones, then got up again. Now he was flying back up the tunnel, with Anton, his heart beating through his chest, racing after him. They came stumbling around the curve just in time to see Briony Keating, her hair matted with cobwebs, her face as pale as death, and barefoot, tugging at the iron bar. Lujac screamed in animal rage, and she looked straight at him, her eyes wide, her expression turning into contempt before she gave the bar one ferocious tug and stepped back, heaving hard at the door. It slammed shut, the lock catching just as Lujac collided with the other side, the force of his blow making the iron boom like a heavy brass bell and echoing around in the long shadows of the basement.

Briony stepped back from the iron door, her chest heaving, her heart hammering, and stared at it for a long time, listening to the sound of Lujac's fists thudding against the cold iron plating—*boom . . . bong . . . boom . . . bong . . . boom . . . bong*—as slow and steady as a heart of iron beating inside a man of cold, dead stone.

ISTANBUL

SUITE 5500, DIZAYN TOWERS

Melik Gul's men were holding a little brown teapot-shaped man in the reception area of the office, hemmed in by three large officers with the thick black mustaches that seemed to be part of the uniform for Turkish cops, even the women.

Nikki, entering the glass-walled and blond-wood-paneled space on the heels of Sofouli and Gul, saw over Sofouli's shoulder a tubby, sad-looking little man with bad skin and doughy cheeks. The pasty pallor of the "inside man" lay on him like the dusting on a sugar doughnut. And his dull-eyed, slack-jawed face carried the weight of long years of disappointed expectations on it, along with a kind of stoic acceptance of his current situation.

His soft-brown eyes flickered over the new arrivals, stopping for a moment to settle on Nikki, an expression of momentary confusion registering, and then he glazed over and went inward again, like a snapping turtle surrounded by sadistic schoolboys.

The office looked like any working space you'd find around the world, a few cubicles scattered about a large, open area, bland fluorescent lighting here and there in the acoustic-tiled ceiling, one large Dell PC with a huge flat-screen monitor, apparently turned off, on a long teak desk set off in a corner and littered with papers.

Several half-stuffed boxes sat around on the carpeted floor, and Nikki got the impression that the Teapot had been packing things up frantically when he got interrupted by Melik Gul's men. The place had that indefinable *aftermath* look, the decrepit, tumbled look of a complicated project gone horribly wrong. The senior men already flown, and no one left but the stiffs, saps, and gunsels to mop up the mess and take the heat.

Gul went over and stood before the man, staring down at him, and asked a question in Turkish, which was answered by one of Gul's Mustache Men. Nikki caught the name Ibrahim Sokak, and was about to make a note of it in her BlackBerry when it began to buzz in her hand.

Nikki stepped back out into the hall, closed the heavy glass doors with RUSSIAN INTER-ASIAN TRADE & COMMERCE BUREAU stenciled on it in gold, and looked at the text message from Alice Chandler:

Beyoglu Trading Consortium
Shell company wholly owned by BUG/Arkangel Industries,
Kiev, Moscow, Saint Petersburg. Sales rep for digital cameras,
electronics, trading internationally. Considered front for
Russian economic and Humint info gathering. No known KGB
affiliation. Re: prior queries other agencies, none on file.
More TK.
U OK?

Nikki sent a reply:

Query Russian Inter-Asian Trade & Commerce Bureau, also
Ibrahim Sokak, Anatoly Bakunin, Vassily Kishmayev, Melik
Gul. Also can you locate IP of computer here.

She got an answer back at once.

Is machine on? What kind of connection. I have phone
number 90 212 288 8515. Is this main line?

Nikki looked over at the men, who seemed to be busy arguing
about some procedural matter with the Teapot. She got the idea that
he was aggressively asserting the sovereign rights of Holy Mother
Russia and was being told where Holy Mother Russia could insert
her sovereign rights.
    She texted back:

Wait 1.

She walked quietly but with no particular air of furtiveness back
into the office and across to the computer, reached out, switched it
on, and got an ornate screenful of Cyrillic letters.

Российская
Интер-азиатской торговли и коммерции бюро

She texted a message:

Okay.
Plan B.
In Russian.
Can't read Russian. Looks like hard-wired phone line. No
wireless indicator. Try 90 212 288 8515.

A moment passed, then a message came back:

Leave machine on.
See what geeks can do.
More on BUG/Arkangel. They also run Internet site.

www.odessaflowers.com. Checked site. Internet dating site
for U.S. males seeking Russian, Ukrainian wives, girlfriends,
concubines. Disgusting! More TK. Keep machine on. Geeks
closing in on IP address. Anatoly Bakunin, Vassily Kishmayev:
KGB thugs from Moscow Center. Melik Gul: Turkish secret
police. Ibrahim Sokak: no file. no hit.
Word from AD RA 2 U at all?
Worried.

Nikki stared at the screen for a while, thinking about the feeling
she had gotten that Hank had been keeping something from her.
This had been during a discussion about Kiki Lujac. He had suddenly
taken a hard right and sent her off to find a picture of the man, a
search that had been unsuccessful at the time. Someone seemed to
have scrubbed the name Lujac from cyberspace.

Worried too.
Can you search recent files on AD of RA machine? Look for
name searches, background searches.

A pause.
Nikki could see Alice pursing her lips.

No. Confidential

Nikki typed back:

Vital.

Another long pause.

Will try. Wait.

Nikki waited.

Through the glass door, she could hear raised voices, and then the short, sharp sound of a slap across the face. The men were standing around the Teapot in a tight knot, and it looked like the left-behind sap was about to get what was coming to somebody much higher up.

No one was paying her any attention at all.

Nikki assumed this was because beating up suspects in Turkey was considered to be a man's job.

Fine by her.

After a few minutes, her BlackBerry buzzed her again.

Days ago he ran detailed background check on French national Jules Duhamel. No hits, no negatives. Did it himself, no file number. FedEx full paper report to B. Keating, Pershing Center, West Point Military Academy. This morning, he took shuttle to La Guardia, booked car, told me he was going to Garrison to look up B. Keating. Got 15000 Bear Mountain Beacon Hwy., phoned listed land line, no answer. Phoned his cell, rang rang rang, and then cut to message. Phoned west pt h.r. office, ID'd as NSA. Wpt hr says BK no show, no word.

Nikki read the long report, hit save message, and sent back:

Call NYS troopers urgent!

She got back:

OK.U come home. Geeks inside machine now copying hard drive files. Is anyone watching?

Nikki looked over, saw that the hard-drive indicator light was blipping on the face of the computer tower. No one but her was paying any attention.

No. But work fast.
Any image description etc. of Jules Duhamel?

She went back out into the hall, waited a moment, and got back:

Visa picture. Comparing with Lujac descrpt.

A long pause. Sofouli was heading back into the main room, his face closed and angry. He saw Nikki in the hall and headed for her. Her BlackBerry buzzed again.

Found MPEG in ad, private e-mail box.
Wait one . . .
Wait one . . .
Wait one . . .

Sofouli reached her, his expression softening as he got in closer, his professional cop getting a bit mixed up with his Greek lounge lizard.

"Look, Nikki, this is going to get complicated. Very quickly, Gul thinks you know more than you're saying. So do I. Am I right?"

She opened her mouth to say something oblique but her BlackBerry was buzzing again. She looked down at the screen.

MPEG taken on boat image of fat gray man talking to
someone off camera. Sent by M. Pownall, CIA London

Station, from vicinity Istanbul. Found on boat connected to
Kiki Lujac and to Beyoglu Trading. Pownall claims plot against
Glass Cutters. B. Keating is a Glass Cutter. Could be him,
Nikki, could be him.
Come home now!

Sofouli, leaning in, read the message on her screen, bared his teeth
in a grim smile, looked back over his massive shoulder at Melik Gul,
who was staring back out at them through the green-tinted glass, his
black eyes fixed and full of malice.

Sofouli turned back to her.

"I'm going now to pick up my chopper. I think you should come
with me. I think you should come now."

Nikki did not look at Melik Gul, but she could feel his glare.

"Do you think he'll let me go?"

"I have told him I am to arrest you. As a suspect in the stealing of
my helicopter. He'll have no choice. We have jurisdictional agreements. If he tries to stop me, he'll create an incident. Turks don't
want an incident with Greece right now. Turks are making too many
enemies in NATO, after buggering U.S. over Iraq War. Greeks are
in NATO, so Turks need Greeks."

"*Are* you arresting me?"

His look was stern, even grave, but there was humor in it, along
with a clear sexual appreciation for the woman he was looking at.

"Nikki," he said in a pleading whisper, "I will not leave you
with Melik Gul. He is with the Milli Istihbarat Teşkilati, their secret
police. No one knows what they do, only that people who go with
them do not come back. And he is no friend of America. Please, do
what I ask."

"Submit to being arrested?" she said with an edge.

"Yes. Please, submit. I ask you from the heart."

She looked up at him.

He gave her his best totally innocent smile, which made him look like a grizzly bear with a rose between its teeth. The man was a black-marketing rogue, and possibly a corrupt cop, and certainly a serial womanizer whom she wouldn't trust to keep his hands to himself anywhere other than in a chopper he would have to fly all by himself. He also smelled richly of tobacco and cognac and some kind of leathery citrus cologne, and, although old enough to be her father, he wasn't.

"Yes, all right, I submit."

His eyes widened and he grinned ferociously at her.

"Then you are under my protective arrest. Now we go, yes?"

Nikki looked back at Gul then, saw latent malice, and much worse.

"Now we go, yes."

"And while we go, Nikki, we talk, yes? About films, and the stealing of boats and helicopters?"

"I can't tell you everything."

"No," he said, turning her with a gentle hand on her shoulder, heading toward the elevator at a quick trot, "but you will tell me enough for me to keep my job, yes?"

The doors of the elevator were sliding shut, slicing off the black glare of Melik Gul. It was full of a soft light, and music was coming from a speaker overhead, something snaky and sinuous, with drums and cymbals under a melody carried by a silvery clarinet.

The floor quickly dropped away under her feet, as she stood looking across at Captain Sofouli, who was smiling at her with a certain possessive air. Nikki realized she was suddenly feeling quite unsteady.

KERCH

THE *SUBITO*

When it became light, Dalton backed the *Subito* off the *Shark*'s wake, slowing down, until the *Shark* was just a notch on the horizon. Although the day began clear, the sea remained blue-black, stretching out all around them, the surface almost mirrorlike, brushed here and there by the feather touch of light winds that ruffled the surface as they passed over it.

Dalton locked the ship's throttles when the red blip of the *Shark* steadied at six miles out, the limit of their radar unless they extended the retractable radar mast, which would likely draw the attention of the man driving the trawler.

There they stayed, as the miles slipped by the cutwater, and the day grew older and the light changed from clear to a sullen yellow haze, the stink of steel mills and coal plants drifting from the Russian coast, now coming in closer with every mile, a barren landscape of rock and bony bare hills matted with dirty scrub grass.

Sometime after midday, Levka had noticed a rainbow swirling in the black water as the light increased, pointing it out to Dalton as they cruised north. It seemed to be trailing out directly in the wake of the *Shark*.

"Look like gasoline, boss. Maybe you hit her fuel line?"

Dalton remembered punching a few large holes in the trawler's stern in that firefight back in Sariyer. Maybe Levka was right, although they were running just a little outside one of the busiest ship channels in Eastern Europe, and perhaps the filthiest. The debris on the surface did not bear close inspection and the hull of the *Subito* was streaked with oily slime.

As the light changed and the evening drew on, they saw that they were now part of a gathering flotilla of ships, all bearing down on the narrow funnel-like passage of Kerch—from an old Slav word for *throat*—a narrow, meandering strait that snaked up between low hills and rolling grasslands. To the west was the Ukraine, now independent, and, to the east, Russia, a growing threat.

Beyond the Kerch Strait lay the shallow, heavily polluted Sea of Azov, bordered on the west by the Ukrainian shoreline—low barrier islands and sand dunes, the largest being the Arrow of Arabat, and on the east by the long, jagged Russian shoreline with a shallow bay cutting inward to the city of Azov.

Unlike Istanbul and the Bosphorus, there was no trace of fable and romance in the Kerch Strait. The land was low and sullen and treeless, and over it hung the grimy miasma of coal smoke and industrial pollution. The water under the hull was filthy and black and streaked with yellow foam, studded with garbage from the tankers and freighters closing in all around them, and the dank sea air reeked of dumped bilgewater and raw sewage leaking from or deliberately pumped out of rusted-out keels.

The groan and rumble and mutter of heavy shipping was all around them now, as if they were traveling north with a herd of elephants—massive tankers rumbling into view, freighters with angular cranes sticking up like gibbets, stumpy containerships riding dangerously low in the dirty water—all coming in, closing up into a packed mass, heading for the mouth of the strait.

Dalton picked a careful way through the shipping lanes, keeping the black notch of the trawler fixed in the bowsprit of the *Subito* as if he were aiming a pistol at a target. To his right, on the starboard side, an oil tanker flying a Liberian flag, her sides streaked with rust and grime, boomed massively close, as a row of bored Muslim sailors stared down at the *Subito*, her clean lines and gleaming brass as out of place here as a stiletto in a toolbox.

In a while, they could see on the far western horizon a single black pillar, set out on a sloping headland. Levka, shading his eyes from the sideways slant of the pale match-head sun, pointed it out.

"That is Obelisk of Glory, on Mithridate Hill. Kerch is there."

Mandy was standing at the navigator's station, studying a chart of Kerch Harbor.

"There's a customs house, by this central mole here"—she touched the tip of a pencil to an image of a long rectangular dock reaching out into the sickle-shaped harbor. "We can dock there. Levka can show our papers—"

"We have *papers?*" said Levka.

"Yes. While I was at the Sumahan, I had the concierge fax our passports and the boat registry to Kerch—"

"The boat registry?" asked Dalton. She gave him a look.

"You can do a lot with Microsoft Office and a color printer," said Mandy. "What? Did you think I spent my whole morning rolling about in the bubbles with that—"

"No, I didn't," said Dalton, interrupting her. "Great work."

Levka looked dubious.

"You think will pass for customs at Kerch? Ukrainians very tricksy about Russians coming across the channel. Pricky—"

"*Prickly,* do you mean?" put in Mandy.

"Prickly, yes."

"What's the fee," asked Dalton, "for docking at Kerch?"

Levka considered this.

"One American dollar, about six hryvnia . . . Maybe two hundred hryvnia."

"What happens if we offer a thousand?"

"In American dollars or hryvnia?"

"U.S. dollars."

Levka's worried look went away.

"I think then all will be okeydokey, boss."

Mandy was looking at Dalton, who was staring out to sea, watching the shoreline of Kerch slowly filling up the western horizon.

"I've been thinking, Micah, about that film . . ."

Dalton glanced over at Levka, who blinked back, open and innocent, slightly confused. Mandy followed his look, shrugged.

"In for a penny. Levka, I want to show you something."

"Okeydokey, Miss Boss," he said, coming over to the multifunction screen to stand next to Mandy.

She noticed that since he had come into their service he was taking much better care of himself. She had bought him some clothes at the Sumahan: slacks, jeans, boat shoes, some sweaters, socks and underwear, a big yellow squall jacket, even a pair of Prada sunglasses.

He was also showered and shaved, and he smelled of soap and cigarettes. He looked years younger, and seemed to have filled out a bit as well, looking less vulpine and now more like a well-fed black Lab.

Mandy slipped the MPEG in, hit PLAY.

Levka watched for a moment, and then his face went a little pale.

"That's him. Peter. *Siva Čovjek*. The Gray Man."

"We thought it might be," said Mandy. "Listen to what he says in a moment . . . something about a clinic . . . Here it comes."

They reached the part where the fat man was speaking about the target, whoever she was. Levka was watching the screen, his face rapt.

"Of course you will be with *her. You read the personality analysis, the psychologists in Marksa Plaz confirmed this, you saw the films—her*

husband's betrayal hurt her deeply. She is a physical *creature. Her husband said she was* insatiable."

Mandy reached out, shut the MPEG off.

"Did any of that mean anything to you, Dobri?" she asked.

Levka said nothing for a time. She could see the agile mind working under the mop of black hair, behind the soft-brown eyes, the pale cheeks. He was a soldier of fortune, she knew, but it was a risk worth taking.

So far, he had been true and straight, tracking the *Shark* even while she had slept the night away . . . sadly, quite alone.

"Only this name," he said after a while, "Marksa Plaz."

"Marksa Plaz," she said, leaning in a little, "what does it mean?"

"There is street in Kerch, called Karla Marksa Plaz—Karl Marx Place—there is Психэатрична лэкарня . . . Big clinic, big hospital for teaching students to be doctors. Also is . . . crazy place? Like big hotel only with bars."

"A lunatic asylum?"

Levka nodded vigorously.

"Yes, lunatic asylum. One time, Uncle Gavel and me, we go to throw stones at bars, makes people all go crazy inside. Good fun."

Levka seemed to catch the shift in her mood, looked a little ashamed of himself for a fleeting second, then brightened.

"Oh, but we both big rolling drunk at time. Meaning no harm, eh?"

Dalton, at the helm, stiffened, checked the radar screen

"They've stopped," he said. "The *Shark*. It's dead in the water."

THEY WERE WITHIN a hundred yards of the *Shark* in thirty minutes.

It was wallowing in the swell, tossing in the wake of a huge tanker that had skimmed past her, a canyon wall of steel racing by at thirty knots, her props as big as windmills, the tormented sea at her towering stern a boiling cauldron.

Twilight was coming down fast, a cloak of indigo settling down on the brown slopes and the black water, lights winking on all along the Ukrainian shore, and the gathering glitter of thirty or forty ships closing in on the narrow strait. A single gull soared high overhead, calling and crying. The huge old trawler was bobbing in the wake and drifting rudderless, awash, pitching crazily over the swells. Two men in greasy knit sweaters and rubber overalls were visible, one standing on the bow with a checkered distress flag, the other—older, grizzled, with a white beard and small blue eyes narrowed in the sidelong light—in the stern, staring out at the *Subito,* as Mandy brought her within hailing distance.

Dalton stood just inside the pilothouse door, the oversized shotgun in his hands, his eyes fixed on the old man in the stern.

When they were within a hundred feet, Mandy backed the engines and brought the *Subito* to a standstill, her wake rolling outward, waves lapping at the mud-stained hull of the fishing trawler.

The name on the stern—акула—was almost completely obscured by a coating of fish scales and mold and fuel oil, but the holes Dalton had blown into the stern boards, four of them in a ragged line a few inches above the water, were clearly visible. Patched, badly, but visible.

Levka, standing next to Dalton with Dalton's Beretta behind his back, leaned out of the cabin, using a bullhorn to call across to the man in the stern.

"Вам потрэбна допомога? Are you in trouble?"

"Dah," said the man in the stern, then in English: "We are out of gas. Have you any to spare?"

Dalton whispered to Levka, "Ask him if he wants a tow."

"Do you want a tow?" asked Levka. "Kerch is only a few miles."

The man in the stern frowned and shook his head.

"No. No tow. Only gas."

Levka leaned back inside, spoke softly to Dalton.

"He thinks of the salvage law. We tow him, we own his boat."

In the meantime, the man standing on the bow had been staring hard at the *Subito*. Although a lot grubbier than she had been back at Ataköy Marina, she was still a slim, trim boat, and much too pretty for these waters. He called out to the man in the stern, a rapid flow of Russian. The man in the stern turned and said something back to him.

The other man—younger, with a dark face and a black beard—dropped down through a forward hatch in the trawler's bow and was gone. Dalton braced himself, setting a hip against the door: this shotgun kicked like a cart horse. Levka had the Beretta out and down by his right side now, his expression open and cheerful.

At the wheel, Mandy was listening to the marine channel.

"Dalton, I think somebody on that boat is calling Kerch."

"How can you tell?"

"Somebody just got on Channel 22. He's speaking in Russian, I think, but I just heard the name *Subito*."

Dalton moved up next to Levka.

"Ask him if he wants us to throw him a line."

Levka put the bullhorn up, and at the same time the older man in the stern ducked back into the wheelhouse.

"Boss, I don't—"

The old man popped out of the cabin again, something blunt and metallic in his hand, and leveled it at the pilothouse of the *Subito*. Dalton stepped quickly out of the door and fired three rapid rounds with the shotgun, three tremendous cracking booms, the muzzle flash lighting up the water between them. The bearded man disappeared behind the transom. There was a short, crackling fizz, and a fountain of red fire shot up from the stern boards.

"Flare," said Levka. "He fired a flare!"

Mandy hit reverse, pushed the throttles to high, and the *Subito* began to back up, waves crashing over her low stern. The trawler was on fire now. They could see the dark man running out onto the bow, carrying that big Russian .50. Levka leaned out of the window, put a couple of rounds into the man at a hundred feet, and he fell backward into the water. Mandy turned the ship, the *Subito* wallowing in the turbulent wake, as the trawler blew up in a flower of red oily smoke, chips of wood, chunks of meat and metal, rising up on a column of roiling fire into the twilit sky. The explosion lit up the black water all around and put a red glow on Mandy's face as she stared back at the wreckage, some of it still on fire as it hissed and spattered down a few yards short of the bow.

Levka pointed off to port, at a low black hull speeding toward them, a blue light flashing at the peak. Even at a half mile, they could hear the *whoop-whoop-whoop* of its siren.

"Are we in Russian water," put in Mandy, "or in Ukrainian?"

"Ukrainian, I hope," said Levka, a very worried look on his face.

"Micah," asked Mandy, "whose side are the Ukrainians on?"

"Ours, last time I looked. Levka, can you see a flag on that boat?"

Levka got the binoculars, trained them on the sleek gray arrowhead flying toward them across the water. They could hear its engines now, a deep, drumming vibration. Levka put the glasses down, sighing.

"Blue over yellow. Is Ukrainian."

"Well," said Dalton into the silence that followed, "I think this concludes the covert part of our journey. Levka, break us out a U.S. flag."

THE CLINIC at Karla Marksa Plaz, known as Керч Психэатрична лэкарня—Kerch Psychiatric Hospital—was a ghastly holdover from the Soviet occupation, a crumbling concrete box painted in garish sky blue and sulfurous yellow. The narrow street it sat in was lit by harsh blue globes that cast a pale light over the façade of the building.

Dalton and Mandy Pownall had come to finish this job. Levka was back at the customs house, seeing to the berthing of the *Subito,* keeping one eye on the seaside bar a few hundred yards south of the entrance to the Mithridate Staircase, the Double Eagle. Levka had expressed his intention to finish the day there, with a final double-vodka toast to poor Uncle Gavel, no offendings, and the capricious fortunes of war.

The young Ukrainian captain—his name was Bogdan Davit, and he seemed to consider the unexpected arrival of a shipload of CIA agents on the shores of this grubby little town to be a career-making opportunity to show his quality—stood next to Dalton, shaking his handsome young head as he pointed his swagger stick at the ragged iron awning drooping down over the entrance, lit by a sickly fluorescent glow that seemed to come from nowhere in particular like an emanation from a crypt.

"This is private, not open to public. Russians come over for the cure from vodka. Money comes from all private donation. Russian money, so I am told. I have not been inside, but I hear they have many sick-in-the-head types. But they have closed the place, it looks like, and when we called nobody answered. Come, we will go in and see what is to see."

Captain Davit nodded to a couple of officers waiting nearby, saying something in Ukrainian that neither Dalton nor Mandy could quite understand. They followed the little group as they crossed the deserted street, Davit reaching out when they stood before the fingerprint-covered greasy glass of the main doors to press the after-hours bell in its slot beside the entrance. They could hear the buzzing whine of the alarm echoing around the lobby. A bald head popped out from around a corner, wild-eyed, toothless. The body attached to it then tottered out from the corner and stood there in the hall, an elderly male, naked, grossly fouled, sucking his thumbs, both of them shoved together into his grinning mouth.

"Oh Jesus," said Captain Davit in Ukrainian, but Dalton and Mandy knew what he was saying because, under the circumstances, what else was there to say?

THE STAFF HAD FLOWN. Someone from the docks said a boat had come in from the Russian side of the strait and taken fifteen people, including a large fat man with purple lips, off the customs dock, heading out to sea at around three in the afternoon. Pursuit at this point was pointless. It was a matter for diplomatic negotiations with the Russians.

Whatever might happen later, the facts in front of them were that the entire staff of the clinic was gone, baby, gone, and the inmates had to be rounded up, chased down and collared or dragged blubbering from closets and toilet stalls on all five floors of the clinic; in the end almost fifty people, including about nine men from a locked-down section with a sign on it that read, in large red letters: Хронэ́чна Уорд.

"Chronic Ward," explained Captain Davit, watching with distaste and a trace of nausea as the ambulance people and a few unlucky junior cops went through the filthy ward, looking under tables and through unspeakable washrooms—looking, in the end, not so much for inmates as for survivors.

Mandy and Dalton trailed through, Mandy with a cloth held against her face, Dalton smoking a Balkan Sobranie, his expression cold and stony. A young medic came running up to Captain Davit, her broad, sweet face contorted in horror. Davit listened for a time, and then turned to look at Dalton and Mandy, his young face as hard as Dalton's now.

"In the basement. We must look. Please come."

In the basement—a medieval horror of crumbling concrete pillars, rubbish, rags, rusted-out medical gear, old moldering beds, huge laundry machines, a row of dryers large enough to tumble-dry a moose, dripping walls, and an appalling stench that seemed to stir up under the dragging foot like a pale green cloud—at the far end, under a low tangle of copper tubes, rags hanging from them like Spanish moss from a live oak, lay two bodies:

One male—a young man, with a military crew cut, a U.S. Navy tattoo on his left biceps, his hands tied behind him, his face a ruin. It had been beaten in with a lead pipe, which lay beside him, as if thrown down by the killer as he turned away. Droplets of blood, still red and still damp, sprayed out in every direction from the shattered remnants of the boy's skull.

And a woman, older, also naked, also bound, treated the same way. Both of them savagely beaten to death with the same three-foot section of lead pipe, both dead not five hours all told. It didn't take a forensic team to read it, it was all there in front of them, the pipe, the blood spatter not yet dry, even the white plastic suit the killer had worn, peeled off, and thrown in a corner like a condom after sex.

The three of them stood there, in a row, three good people—the English aristocrat, the Ukrainian policeman, and the gaunt, gray-faced Cleaner—all of them staring into the pit together.

"We failed," said Mandy after a long while, "didn't we?"

"Yes," said Dalton. "But what did we fail at? What was going on here? What did this all mean?"

"I don't know," said Mandy, "but I think I need to leave now."

"Yes," said the young captain, swallowing, "so do I."

CIA HQ

LANGLEY, VIRGINIA

THE ANNEX

They held the hearing in Room 19 of the Annex, a large wood-paneled conference room buried deep in the windowless interior of the building, shielded and armored, and lit from above by rippled glass that shed a diffuse violet light down on a huge oblong table of hammered oak surrounded by sixteen evenly spaced tan leather chairs. The room was filled with the kind of humming pressurized silence that comes from filtered compressors deep in the basement and the inaudible hypersonic whine of antisurveillance electronics. If you pulled out a pistol and shot yourself while sitting in one of these chairs, the sound of the shot would be like a puff of wind under a locked door. Not even God would hear your brains hit the wall behind you.

At the head of the table, flanked by two unsmiling aides—one female, one undecided—sat a whippet-thin, sharp-featured woman of indeterminate age with cool gray eyes and a bell of shining blue-black hair, wearing a charcoal gray pantsuit and a white blouse, open enough to remind the others that she was a woman, closed enough to remind the others that she was one of the "Virgins of Vigilance," part of a team sent over from the Counter-Intelligence Analysis

Group to do some long-overdue housecleaning here at the National Clandestine Service.

Her name, it will come as no surprise, was Mariah Vale, and before her lay a sheaf of papers that contained the essential details of one old man's history of deceit, betrayal, perfidy, and treason.

The old man in question—Deacon Cather, Deputy Director of the National Clandestine Service, who was currently suspended pending the results of this hearing—was apparently at ease. He was beautifully turned out in a satiny charcoal pin-striped suit tailor-made for his Lincolnesque body. Tall, angular, lean, almost cadaverous, with yellow skin and tobacco-stained teeth, dry, cold eyes, a leathery reptilian neck, and large hands with flat nails, he sat with them folded comfortably on the bare table in front of him: his calm, still gaze rested upon the pink-tinged forehead of Mariah Vale the way a hawk might look at a hen.

Next to him in the nearly empty room sat Micah Dalton, acting in a way as his aide in this matter. Dalton's left cheek still showed a livid scar where a bullet had scored a path across his face only a few weeks before.

In front of Dalton was a leather case, battered, tan, with gold fittings, unlatched but unopened. Dalton was wearing a navy blue pinstripe, a snow-white shirt, a gold-and-blue-striped tie held in place with a gold collar bar, and an expression of cold dislike in his pale blue eyes.

Somewhere off in the dark, a camera rolled and a recorder spun slowly. This was the third hour of the proceedings, and the matter had come down to the proof, as these things usually do, and Mariah Vale had "the proof" in her bony-fingered hands as she leaned forward to address the hidden watchers.

"We have here the decryption of Riga 157-alpha hotel, dated the twentieth of May, 1973, done by Miss Keating's staff and overseen by Miss Keating herself, which, considering the death of her son only a short time ago, calls for the highest commendation.

"We have all read the transcript, the decryption of which has been verified by an independent unit of the Glass Cutters, under the supervision of the DNI herself, but I will present it here in hard copy so you may refresh your memory if you need to. Is that satisfactory, Mr. Cather?"

"It is," said Cather in his Tidewater drawl, his Easter Island gravity undiminished, his humorless smile a thin curve on his bloodless lips.

Dalton reached out and took a copy from the pile, laid it out in front of Deacon Cather:

New York 20 MAY 1973 1425—WALDORF
PREACHER confirms to KEVIN that WG entry
Connects to RN. PREACHER confirms recordings exist of RN
discussing entry cover-up. PREACHER confirms
consequences.
Will be terminal to RN. Congress intends to force
RN resignation (six groups unrecovered), ADC in
Paris (nine groups unrecovered), confirmed by
Preacher.
In direct communication with (unrecovered sequence).
Recommend immediate communication with Giap to:
Secure treaty (nine groups unrecovered) document (eighteen
groups unrecovered).
By hand to Gordon by Preacher (four groups unrecovered).
Also Preacher insists on extended payment grade
citing:
Extreme risk of (six groups unrecovered) in reference.
To Hudson, Garza, others (eleven groups unrecovered).

Cable wire/Kevin to Gordon, copy Karla,
NY, 20 May 1973. End.

"You are aware," said Mariah Vale, "that Kevin has been confirmed by the man himself to be Oleg Kalugin, who from 1965 to
1970 was the so-called Press Officer of the Tass News Agency in New
York, and who admitted, after his defection to the United States, that
he recruited many agents from the diplomatic and military personnel,
who were at that time active in the States, including attachés to the
United Nations? You have heard of him?"

"Heard of him, Miss Vale? Goodness yes. I have gotten drunk with
him. A lovely man."

"And you're also aware that Gordon is Vladimir Kryuchkov, who
was Kalugin's immediate superior, based at Moscow Center, and that
Kryuchkov was the head of the KGB's counterintelligence division,
and that Kryuchkov reported directly to Yuri Andropov?"

"It is my job to be aware of these things. I was aware of such
things when you were still an attractive young woman, Miss Vale."

"It is our contention that you, Mr. Cather, are the agent known
as Preacher—"

"Come now," said Cather. "Deacon? Preacher? Would they be
that transparent?"

"They called Alger Hiss Ales. Winston Churchill was Boar. Their
cables are full of such clumsy pseudonyms. So, you have admitted,
for the record, that on this date—the date in question—you were in
fact the Aide de Camp—the ADC—in service to our representatives
at the Paris Peace Accords?"

"Yes, along with Colonel Garza, Colonel Hudson, Major Prescott,
and Colonel Dale, all of whom were attached as military advisers to
our envoys at the Paris Accords and all of whom made many trips
between New York and Washington and Paris during those very hectic weeks—"

"We are not concerned with all of these trips, Mr. Cather, but only with this one particular trip—a trip which you admit that only you made, a trip during which you conveyed critical information concerning the Watergate break-ins that convinced the Soviets that President Nixon was about to be investigated in connection with these break-ins, an investigation that would very likely render moot his prior guarantees to the government of South Vietnam to return to extensive Linebacker operations over Hanoi and Haiphong if the North were to violate the terms of the Accord. In a word, Mr. Cather, we are suggesting that your treason in this matter caused us to forfeit the Vietnam War."

"My dear Miss Vale, the Watergate affair began on the night of June seventeenth, in Washington, in 1972, and by the date in question here, the twentieth of May, 1973, a blind bat in a barn in Fargo could have told you that Nixon was in serious trouble."

Vale came back with heightened choler.

"Nixon was not under *serious* threat until the revelations concerning the taped evidence—the so-called Nixon Tapes—surfaced in the fall of 1973. There was, however, a lot of talk in D.C. and New York in the weeks before that he had, like many other Presidents before him, kept accurate records of everything that transpired in the Oval Office. We have shown that in March of 'seventy-three you yourself were made aware of this situation in a conversation, a taped conversation between yourself and Colonel Garza—"

"Who is dead, by the way. A suicide, you may recall?"

"The tapes are still with us, Mr. Cather. Do you deny that such a conversation took place?"

"I do not."

"So you admit that you were in possession of prior information concerning the Nixon Tapes—"

"I was in possession of professional speculation between two military intelligence officers concerning a matter that was of great interest to every American, Miss Vale. The fact that the FBI was taping Colonel Garza in connection with possible accounting fraud at Fort Campbell—"

"That does not negate the—"

Dalton leaned forward here, opening his case.

"Miss Vale, I think I can help clear this up for all of us."

"Captain Dalton, late of the Fifth Special Forces, for the record, and now one of Mr. Cather's more controversial assistants over at Clandestine Services. Yes, how could you clear this up, I wonder?"

Her tone was sarcasm laced with venom.

God help Clandestine, thought Dalton, *if she ever got her fangs in it.*

Dalton smiled back at her, reached into the case, and pulled out a pile of papers, passed one across to Miss Vale, who pulled it in close and peered down at it over her reading glasses.

"The first is a statement from a Mr. Dylan Keating—Briony Keating's ex-husband, now facing several charges under the Patriot Act—who states in this affidavit that eleven months ago he used a dating service known as 'Odessa Flowers dot.com'—I have enclosed a web shot—and that Odessa Flowers provides a forum for American men to contact Ukrainian and Russian women with a view to contracting marriage . . . of a sort . . . And Dylan Keating further states that he traveled in the fall of that year to visit a Marina Kelo, a nurse who was living in Odessa, in the Ukraine. We have shown you already, in a film clip, that a man known only to us as Piotr referred in this film clip to a man he called 'her husband,' stating that this man had provided, for reasons we don't have to get into, background information on Miss Briony Keating, his ex-wife. We have also shown that Odessa Flowers was run by an outfit called BUG/Arkangel and that it was a KGB front specifically designed to identify possible intelligence sources inside the United States. Dylan Keating admits telling this Marina Kelo that his wife was a top encryption analyst in the National Security Agency. Marina Kelo was a paid stringer for the KGB, and as soon as she heard this she took the information to the KGB, who encouraged her to go back to Odessa and to learn everything she could about Dylan Keating's wife—"

"None of this in any way mitigates—"

"So this scam began there, in Odessa—"

"'Scam'? This is not a scam—"

"Miss Vale, how many men were in a position to convey this information about the Nixon Tapes to the Soviet Union and how many of those men were also attached to the Paris Accords as military intelligence advisers?"

"You mean the short list?"

Dalton tapped the third sheet of paper.

"There are the names of five men, all of whom could have been the source for the information conveyed to the Soviets—"

"So you don't contend that the information was never conveyed—"

"No. The historical record is undeniable. Nixon's commitment to the Linebacker campaign forced the North Vietnamese to the table in Paris in January of 1973. On April twentieth, he and Thieu met at San Clemente, where Nixon confirmed his absolute determination to resume the Linebacker bombing campaign if the North Vietnamese broke *any* of the agreements under the Paris Accords. If the purpose of our intervention in Southeast Asia was to prevent a Soviet proxy from taking over South Vietnam, then the war was won—"

"There are conflicting views on that," said Mariah Vale.

"This isn't about *views*, Miss Vale, it's about an historical fact. It's also a fact that overflight surveillance missions show the Russians shipping arms and matériel to the North Vietnamese, beginning in

May of 1973. This is a few days after the Nixon Tapes rumor reached Andropov, delivered by Preacher through Kryuchkov. By August ninth, the Democrats, using Watergate as a lever, lowered the hammer on Nixon and the Republicans, forcing the passage of the Case-Church Amendment. The Case-Church Amendment effectively ended any possibility of further United States support for South Vietnam."

"A quagmire, as we all know now—"

"To people who dislike all military operations, there's always a quagmire around to jump into. By the summer, the Russians were going full speed ahead in their support of the North Vietnamese, something they would never have done if they hadn't known that Nixon was going to be in serious trouble. Nixon resigned on August ninth, 1974. Saigon fell in April of 'seventy-five. None of that would have happened if Congress had backed Nixon about the Linebacker campaigns. The Soviets would have let South Vietnam stand. Millions would still be alive."

"Thank you. Our case is made," said Vale, sitting back, smiling.

"Your case is made, but you've made it against the wrong man. You know what a 'Confusion Op' is, I'm sure."

Vale's face hardened.

"Thank you. I know what a Confusion Op is."

"You've been told about our observations in Santorini, in Istanbul, what we found in Kerch."

"Yes. You went through their network like a drill. Too bad you couldn't save Briony Keating's son, or Maya Palenz."

"What happened in Santorini and Istanbul was a dance, a waltz, a polka—the KGB set up a straw dog and we burned it down in ten days. Why was it so easy?"

"Easy? It didn't look *easy* from our perspective. They made a serious effort to kill you at the warehouse in Sariyer, and later in the approaches to Kerch Strait."

"Yes. But by then, their objectives had been achieved. You believe the whole idea of this Kerch network was to suppress that cable, right?"

"Yes. And it failed. Thanks to you, and to the singular courage displayed by Briony Keating."

"They failed to suppress a single cable, and in failing to suppress it they made damned sure the only thing we were going to pay real close attention to was that same damned cable—"

Mariah Vale's expression was slightly less confident.

"You're saying it was, what, a diversion?"

"Yes, I am."

"You're saying there is no mole, that this was all an attempt by the KGB to destabilize Clandestine Services?"

"No. There was a mole all right. But Deacon Cather isn't it. Look at your short list again—"

He passed over the third sheet:

Colonel Bevan Hudson
Major Luther Prescott
Colonel Emilio Garza
Colonel Colin Dale
Colonel Deacon Cather

"All of these men knew each other, all of them were in military intelligence, all of them saw service in the Vietnam War—"

"And only one of them fits the details of this cable—"

"Exactly my point. You were supposed to think the KGB was moving mountains to stop you from reading this cable. What you were *supposed* to do was look at nothing else but this cable."

"You're suggesting that the agent code-named Preacher was not Mr. Cather?"

"Yes, that's exactly right."

Vale sat back again, her face showing some uncertainty.

"And if Mr. Cather was not Preacher, whom do you suggest we look at next?"

"I have a candidate. It took us a while. We got some help from Nikki Turrin, at the NSA—"

"We're aware of her—"

"You should be. All these men had opportunity. None of them had any discernible motive. Or so we thought. We went through all of these men, through their backgrounds, looked at their service records, all of them were spotless. Each man was a hero of his nation. But only one man had this connection."

He slipped an envelope across the table.

Vale picked it up, held it in her hand.

"What is it?"

"It's a photograph. We found it in a yearbook. Take a look."

She slipped the photo out, an eight-by-ten glossy, a reproduction of a photograph taken back in the thirties, twenty-five young men, all wearing baggy football uniforms, all of them lean and strong, in the full flush of their youth. A boy in the middle was holding a trophy, and they were all smiling. There was handwriting in the lower-left-hand corner, in white ink, a scrawl but legible: "Loyola Bobcats, State Champions 1938."

"Okay, a football team. Buckle down, Winsocki, and all that."

"I've circled two boys. See them there?"

"Yes," she said, looking at two young men, one of them in the first row, tall and pale-eyed, with a stern expression, the other one, in the back row, smaller, softer-looking, a shy smile, large brown eyes.

"The boy in the back row, his name is Stephen Hopkins. He was born in a New York City hospital in 1925. His father was Harry Hopkins, one of Roosevelt's top advisers during the Second World War. Stephen joined the Marines, and was killed in action in the Marshall Islands in 1944."

Cather sighed, templed his long fingers.

"Harry Hopkins, as you will recall, was proposed as Unidentified Cover 19 in Venona 95, dated 8/7/1953. Micah, tell Miss Vale who the other lad is."

"The other boy is Colin Dale."

Mariah Vale shook her head in distaste.

"This is pure McCarthyism. You're suggesting that a glancing connection with the son of a man falsely accused of being a Soviet agent during the war is sufficient grounds for accusing Colin Dale of treason?"

"First of all, the guilt or innocence of Harry Hopkins has not been decided. Here is the original Venona memo that named him."

Dalton passed over two Xeroxed pages.

VENONA

USSR   Ref. No: ████████ (of 18/7/1958)

████████   Issued: ████ 10/9/74

                                        Copy No.: 3a

3RD REISSUE

"19" REPORTS ON DISCUSSIONS WITH "KAPITAN", "KABAN" AND
ZAMESTITEL' ON THE SECOND FRONT

(1943)

From: NEW YORK

To: MOSCOW

No: 812   29 May 1943

To VIKTOR[i].

"19"[ii] reports that "KAPITAN"[iii] and "KABAN"[iv], during conversations
in the "COUNTRY [STRANA][v]", invited "19" to join them and ZAMESTITEL'[vi]
openly told "KABAN"

[10 groups unrecovered]

second front against GERMANY this year. KABAN considers that, if a second
front should prove to be unsuccessful, then this [3 groups unrecovered]
harm to Russian interests and [6 groups unrecovered]. He considers it
more advantageous and effective to weaken GERMANY by bombing and to use this
time for "[4 groups unrecovered] political crisis so that there may be no
doubt that a second front next year will prove successful."

ZAMESTITEL' and

[14 groups unrecovered]

". 19 thinks that "KAPITAN" is not informing ZAMESTITEL' of important military
decisions and that therefore ZAMESTITEL' may not have exact knowledge of
[1 group unrecovered] with the opening of a second front against GERMANY and its
postponement from this year to next year. 19 says that ZAMESTITEL'
personally is an ardent supporter of a second front at this time and considers
postponement

[Continued overleaf]

VENONA

VENONA
~~TOP SECRET~~

2   (of 18/7/1958)

[15 groups unrecovered]

can shed blood

[13 groups unrecoverable]

recently shipping between the USA and

[40 groups unrecovered]

The "COUNTRY" hardly [9 groups unrecovered] "insufficient reason for delaying a second front."

No. 443   MER[vii]

Footnotes:/   [i]   VIKTOR   : Lt. Gen. P.M. FITIN.

              [ii]   19   : Unidentified cover designation.

              [iii]   KAPITAN   : i.e. "CAPTAIN"; Franklin D. ROOSEVELT.

              [iv]   KABAN   : i.e. "BOAR"; Winston CHURCHILL.

              [v]   COUNTRY   : U.S.A.

              [vi]   ZAMESTITEL' : i.e. Deputy - therefore possibly
                                     Henry Agard WALLACE, who was
                                     ROOSEVELT's Deputy (Vice-President)
                                     at this time: later he is referred to
                                     by the covername "LOTsMAN".

              [vii]   MER   : Probably Iskhak Abdulovich AKhMEROV.

VENONA

"You can see the handwritten reference to Harry Hopkins."

"That was put in by some historian, long after—"

"A military historian," said Dalton. "Eduard Mark, and only after doing better than a year of research into every Venona document."

"Still, gross speculation, sheer McCarthyism—"

Dalton did not rise to the taunt.

"Gordievsky reported that he attended a lecture given by Ichak Akhmerov, mentioned in this Venona transcript. He was the Soviet intelligence *Rezident* in D.C. all through the war, and Akhmerov identified Hopkins as his most important Soviet agent during those years—"

"The word of a . . . Look, this is quite beside the point. Nothing will persuade me that a glancing connection with the son of a man who might have been a Soviet agent is sufficient grounds for accusing Colin Dale of treason. Nothing."

"I agree. Although it turns out that Colin Dale and Stephen Hopkins were close friends, and that Dale spent a lot of time at the Hopkins's house, had a father-son relationship with Hopkins. But, you're right, it's not nearly enough."

"Good. Perhaps we can move on—"

"Will you read these documents for me?"

Dalton handed over a sheaf of legal-sized papers. Mariah Vale shuffled through them, looked up at Dalton.

"These are papers of incorporation, of a company called Conjurado Consulting. What am I supposed to make of them?"

"We've managed to pry the owner's name out of Delaware. It's on the last page."

She flipped through to the last sheet.

"Okay, Conjurado Consulting is owned by Colin Dale, so what?"

Dalton handed over another sheet.

"This is a printout taken from the hard drive of a computer belonging to a company called Beyoglu Trading Consortium."

"I know who they are. I know how you got that information too."

"One of the programs resident on the hard drive was related to the shipping of documents through Federal Express. Will you read this?"

One last sheet.

She took it with a wary expression, sighing heavily.

"It's a bill of lading for a package sent from Beyoglu Trading in Istanbul via Federal Express . . ." Her voice died away.

"Yes?" said Dalton, sitting back.

". . . to Conjurado Consulting, in Seaside, Florida."

SEASIDE

THE EMERALD COAST

Sundown at Seaside, in the turning of the year, and the heat was beginning to come back, along with the tourists. Down here, on the long white-sand beach, with the turquoise perfection of the Gulf laid out before him, the sharp clear line of the southern horizon setting off a twilight full of reds and golds and opal fire, Captain Jack was serenely content, at peace with his fellow man.

The first few stars pierced the perfect indigo sky like silver needles. He had a broad wooden Adirondack chair to sit on, his bare feet cooling in the sugary sand, a heavy tumbler of single malt in his hand, a cigar in the other. God was in His Heaven, and all was right with the world.

And then he heard the whispery squeak of footsteps coming down from the high barrier bluff behind him, turned around in the big chair, and saw a tall angular man in a navy blue suit carrying his black brogues in one long-fingered hand, a glass in the other, smiling broadly at Captain Jack, his thin blue lips stretching wide to show large yellow teeth like tombstones. The man came over to Captain Jack, looked down at the empty chair beside him.

"Colin, may I join you?"

Dale started to get up, his face wreathed in a smile, but Cather held out a hand, sat down heavily beside him, sighing as he twisted around to get his bony frame into some sort of truce with the chair.

"Deke," said Colin Dale—known locally as "Captain Jack Forrest"—"you look like hell. What have you got there?"

Cather looked down at his tumbler, swirled it around.

"Some of your Laphroaig. Hope you don't mind?"

"Not at all. You're welcome any time. Here's to merry meetings!"

The two old men clinked glasses, sipped at the scotch, and for a while nothing was said. They just sat there side by side, staring out to sea as the light slowly changed, breathing the sparkling air, puffing on their cigars. A strolling couple passed by, a young girl and her beau, holding hands, and they smiled and waved, dwindling into the long empty reaches of the gathering night.

"Well, Deke," said Colin Dale, after a puff, "I take it the jig is up?"

Cather showed his teeth, his leathery cheeks pulling back in a distorted rictus.

"Oh my yes. A heavy hand is being laid upon us all, Colin. This Vale creature . . . A new day is dawning."

"A red day, a sword day, and the world ending?"

"If she gets her way."

Another long silence, and now a slight chill was coming in off the water and the sand was a bit too cool.

But neither man stirred.

Finally, Dale stretched, reached down, picked up a bottle of Laphroaig, filled both glasses, and offered a last cigar to Cather.

After they had them fired up, the flare of the match lighting up their weathered faces as they leaned in toward the flame, Cather's eyes glinting in the dark as he watched Dale's hands, Dale began to talk.

"I guess it began when Stevie Hopkins died . . ."

"In forty-four, the Marshall Islands."

"Yes. You didn't know his father, but I did. A fine man, Deke."

"Smoked too much, I hear?"

"Oh yes," said Dale, turning the cigar in his long brown fingers. "Killed him in 'forty-six, but by then he was ready to go. Losing Stevie broke his heart, but it was Uncle Joe who broke his mind. You have to remember the times, Deke—the *times*—the Depression, then Roosevelt's New Deal. If you weren't a Communist then, you had no heart. Breadlines, and the bankers stealing everything . . . To Harry, to Lauchlin Currie and Alger Hiss and Dexter White, the Silvermaster set, it looked like Russia had all the answers. The West? Corrupt, greedy . . . doomed to fail. They were visionaries, Deke, and they looked to the East in those days, and my what a glorious vision they had . . . All lies, of course, all foolish Utopian illusions, with Uncle Joe in the middle of it all like a tarantula, spinning and plotting . . . But, in spite of his flaws, Harry Hopkins was a patriot, Deke, a true patriot. And more than a father to me than my own dad—"

"No offense, Colin, but your dad was a bully and a drunk."

"Yes, I guess he was. Anyway, one thing you never knew, I never told you, was how Harry Hopkins could talk . . . the sound of his voice . . . raspy but soft, never hectoring, always patient, a sweeping sense of history, a vision of what America *could* be . . . What a waste, Deke."

A silence.

"Colin," said Cather after a while, "we were together in the war—we saw what the North was doing, the Vietcong—how could you help bring those . . . *creatures* . . . down on the people of the South?"

Dale's face tightened as he looked back through the years.

"I guess by then they *had* me, didn't they? Owned me, the Soviets.

I'd already sent them whatever I could, and once you do that, well, there's no going back, is there? And I really did think that the North Vietnamese would make Vietnam a better place. I mean, there we were, working with Diem, those criminals, and look at some of our own people, in MAC-SOG and Phoenix, the things we did . . . the guns, the heroin, the women—"

"I don't regret the women," said Cather.

"The guns were great fun too," said Dale.

"Small-unit action," said Cather with a smile.

"Oh yes, that above all. Here's to humans, Deke. The best hunting there is," said Dale, lifting his glass.

Both men laughed out loud then, their harsh, crowing bray frightening a roost of sandpipers who had settled down for the evening on a dune a few yards away, taking off into the dark sounding like sheets fluttering in the wind, beeping thinly. The men watched them go. Cather pulled his coat around him, shivered a bit. Dale handed him a beach towel for his knees, and they fell into silence again.

Down along the coast, far to the east, they could see a solitary figure walking slowly toward them along the shoreline, a woman, tall, willowy, wearing a wide-brimmed sun hat, her shapely figure a flickering flame against the glowing sea, against the broad curve of lights, like the edge of a scimitar, that ran back along the shore behind her, stretching away southward into the night, a glittering necklace of light. Cather sighed heavily, set his glass down on the broad, flat arm of the Adirondack chair, leaned forward, looking out at the Gulf, his hands on his knees.

"Colin, why don't you take a walk? Do you some good."

Dale smiled grimly at that, pulled on his cigar, leaned down, and stubbed it out in the sand at his feet.

"You think so, Deke?"

"I do."

"Which way should I go?"

"You should go east," said Cather, rising to his feet with some difficulty. The cold was seeping into his bones, and he was suddenly very tired. They stood there for a moment, looking at each other across a great gulf. Cather took Dale's dry, bony hand in a tight grip, pulled him in, and gave him a hug, a couple of solid smacks on the back, as men do, and then Colin Dale turned away and walked off down the beach, his head up, shoulders straight, his stride long and easy.

A little way down the shore, Dale stopped and turned back to Cather.

"By the way, Deke, something you should think about . . . You know Yitzak Kirensky came in, don't you?"

"Yes. In Athens, I think. They put him on the *Orpheus*. Haven't gotten around to him yet, have they? What with all the excitement about the mole."

"Yes, I know. The mole. Well, a word in your ear, Deke, for old times' sake. Yitzak Kirensky never needed a pacemaker."

Dale stood there for a moment, his long hair fluttering in a wind off the sea, and then he turned away again. In a little while, he was a long black stick figure, standing out sharply against the coming night. Cather watched him go for a time, and then he turned away and walked slowly across the sugary sands, heading for the staircase that led up into the barrier dune.

His car was behind the dune, a military driver leaning against it smoking a cigarette. Cather reached the first stair, put a bony hand out for the railing, and heard a single sharp crack, muffled but with some weight in it, coming from down the shoreline in the east.

He looked back, waited there for a moment, thinking about Colin Dale, but he could no longer be seen, and there was only the slender black figure of the elegant woman in the broad-brimmed sun hat, a

woman who looked very much like Mandy Pownall, walking toward him along the shore, her shapely body a curved shadow inside a gauzy sundress.

She moved quietly by him, raised a slender, long-fingered hand in a parting gesture without looking at him, without speaking a word, passing by him now, and going softly away into the west with the dying light.

GARRISON

THE STONE HOUSE

Spring was coming to Garrison, with a softer warmth in the afternoon and the light in the trees showing a pale green tint, almost a mist, as the buds began to break out. There was snow still piled up in the deep crevices between the rocks and the roots, the stony ground was hard underfoot, and the evenings could still be biting, but the mountains across the river floated in a mist of light, and the air had new life in it, the earthy scent of growing things.

Hank Brocius sat near the open glass doors of the great room and looked out across the river valley, breathing it in, a glass of wine in his hand, Briony Keating in a lawn chair beside him, wrapped in a red fox fur, her pale face and drawn cheeks showing a tint of rose as the spring light lay on it. Sadness was deep inside her, Brocius knew, and she would never be the woman she was. Her fires had gone out or were burning very low.

But she was alive and safe, and here.

They sat for a time in silence, happy to be friends together, Briony aware of his concern but still wrapped inside her pain like a crystal glass wrapped in cotton. She sipped at the claret, shivered a bit.

"We never caught him," he said, his voice heavy with regret.

"I know," said Briony, her face still and her eyes empty.

"I still don't understand it," he said, shaking his head. "He had no resources, no papers. How the hell did he do it?"

"I don't know," said Briony, "and I don't care. I just want to let it go. Forget all about him."

Brocius was quiet for a while.

"You heard about the hospital ship, I guess?"

"You mean the *Orpheus*?"

"Yeah. I think everybody knows all about it by now."

"No secrets endure, Hank. How did the *Times* find out about it?"

"Looks like the Russians did them in. They got a guy onto the ship, supposed to be a defector—"

"Yitzak Kirensky?"

"Yes. Said he had a pacemaker. And he did. But inside the pacemaker, the KGB had hidden a GPS thing. Once they got a fix on it, somebody in Moscow called the *New York Times*—"

"I'm sure Moscow has the *New York Times* on speed dial—"

Brocius smiled at that.

"Anyway, huge scandal now. Floating CIA prison ship. The *Times* called it the USS *Guantánamo*. Heads will roll."

They both sipped some wine, and were quiet again.

"Your husband's going to prison," he said finally. "I guess you know?"

"I heard he was appealing it."

"Yes. It went to Appellate yesterday. He lost."

Briony shook her head, her long silver hair shining in the afternoon light, her skin pale as milk, her gray eyes hooded.

"Where will they send him?"

Brocius sighed.

"Leavenworth, is my bet."

"Poor Dylan. I hope he dies in there."

"Yes, so do I. And he probably will, one way or another."

He looked down at his glass.

Somehow or other, he had drained it.

"I'm putting this away like water. Would you like another?"

"I would," said Briony, handing him her glass with a pale smile.

He was gone for a while—she could hear him clattering around in the kitchen, opening cupboards and drawers—and then he was back with the bottle and two clean glasses. He poured some wine, settled back into the chair, his fingertips brushing over his scarred face as he always did when he was thinking about something in an absent-minded way.

"Briony, there's something wrong with your drains, I think."

"Really?"

"Yes. Have you checked them lately?"

"I always do, in the spring. It's early yet."

"I guess. Oddest thing, though. You know that old speaking tube you've got in the kitchen there?"

"Yes?"

"It's making . . . noises."

"Noises? What sort of noises?"

"I guess it's the wind, or something. Like a kind of moaning, sighing, crying sound. You ever hear that?"

"I used to," said Briony. "In February, I heard it a lot. But lately, not really anything. What do you think it could be?"

Brocius gave the matter some thought.

"I hate to say this, but you might have rats or mice down in that old tunnel. You ever check it out?"

Briony shuddered, pulled the wrap around her.

"God no, Hank. I don't do drains. Once the far end caved in back in 1997, I just let the thing go. Now it's too expensive to dig it all out again. The roof can fall in, for all I care. I hate the place."

"Do you want me to go down there? If you've got rats . . ."

"What if I do? Won't they just starve?"

Brocius looked at her with affection.

"No, they won't. There's water, I think, a little stream that runs along the middle. They can live a long time on just water."

"Don't they need food?"

"I hate to say this, Briony, but rats, if they get hungry enough, they'll eat anything. And I mean *anything*."

Briony looked over at him, her expression unreadable.

"What? You mean, like each other?"

"Yes, if they get hungry enough."

"Really?" said Briony, looking out across the river. "How terrible."